THE SPITFIRE GIRLS
FLY FOR VICTORY

Jenny Holmes

CORGI BOOKS

TRANSWORLD PUBLISHERS
61–63 Uxbridge Road, London W5 5SA
www.penguin.co.uk

Transworld is part of the Penguin Random House group of companies
whose addresses can be found at global.penguinrandomhouse.com

Penguin
Random House
UK

First published in Great Britain in 2020 by Corgi Books
an imprint of Transworld Publishers

A CIP catalogue record for this book
is available from the British Library.

ISBN
9780552175838

Typeset in 11.5/14 pt New Baskerville ITC by Jouve (UK), Milton Keynes
Printed and bound in Great Britain by Clays Ltd, Elcograf S.p.A.

Penguin Random House is committed to a sustainable
future for our business, our readers and our planet. This book is made
from Forest Stewardship Council® certified paper.

MIX
Paper from
responsible sources
FSC® C018179
www.fsc.org

1 3 5 7 9 10 8 6 4 2

For Gill
The dearest of dear friends

CHAPTER ONE

March 1944

'My my – two busy bees!' Bobbie Fraser stuck her head around the door of Angela Browne's recently vacated room at Burton Grange.

She found Mary Holland and Jean Thornton kneeling on the threadbare carpet, scissors in hand. Mary had laid out pieces of a dress pattern – bodice, sleeves, collar and skirt panels – on to a pretty, pale green rayon material, and now she and Jean prepared to snip. In the background the Andrews Sisters trilled the words to 'A Zoot Suit' on the record player that Angela had left behind.

'Would you like to lend a hand?' Mary glanced up at Bobbie.

'Me? I can't tell a sleeve piece from a collar interfacing.' Bobbie stepped carefully across the room then plonked herself and her pile of freshly ironed laundry down on the bed. She leaned back on her elbows and dangled her feet. 'Let me work out who intends to wear this wonderful creation when it's finished.'

On the gramophone the Sisters harmonized sweetly; according to them the whole world was playing samba.

'Mary, this is a new dress for you,' Bobbie surmised.

'How did you know?' Mary proceeded to cut.

'Pale green is your colour. Jean would have chosen a shade of blue. Now, the big question is: who are you intending to impress?' Above the crackle of static electricity, the drum-driven Latin-American rhythm filled the once elegant room of the Georgian manor house. In addition to a double bed with a faded green eiderdown there was a dressing table with a chipped glass top, two wickerwork chairs and an old mahogany wardrobe. Crimson damask curtains hung from a heavy wooden pole.

'Why should I be trying to impress anyone?' Mary's loose, mid-brown hair fell across her face and exposed the pale nape of her neck as she worked. She was dressed casually for her day off from ferry-pool duties in black slacks and a cream blouse.

'Pull the other one!' Bobbie laughed. 'We all know that Flight Lieutenant Cameron Ainslie is the lucky fellow, don't we, Jean?' The pair had declared their love shortly before Cameron had been posted to Aireby training camp, an hour's cycle ride away.

'What's a zoot suit when it's at home?' Knowing that Mary disliked being teased, Jean steered the subject towards the title of the song.

Bobbie took the bait eagerly. 'It's the latest fashion for men: a killer-diller coat with enormous shoulder pads and wide lapels. They're all the rage in Harlem, apparently.'

'But not here in Rixley,' Mary pointed out drily. Snip – she cut delicately into the material, careful to keep to the outline of the bodice piece. Snip-snip. Yes, she wanted to finish the dress in time for her longed-for meeting with Cameron, and what was wrong with that? Snip-snip. It wasn't anyone's business but hers. 'Yorkshire isn't New York – it's not even Chicago or Detroit.'

Bobbie yelped with laughter. 'No – imagine Cameron in a zoot suit!' She turned her head towards Jean. 'Or Douglas, for that matter. Good Lord above, the pair of them would be locked up for crimes against good taste.'

Trombones and trumpets, flutes and clarinets swung along to the honeyed American voices on the record.

'It's a pity Angela had to leave us.' Jean concentrated on cutting out a skirt panel. More snipping ensued. 'We'll all miss her now that she's been transferred to White Waltham, of course; but you more than most, Bobbie.'

Letting her head loll back against the wall, Bobbie stared up at the cracks in the ceiling and let out a long sigh. 'I did shed a tear when I waved dear Angie off at Rixley station,' she admitted in her strong Scots brogue. 'But the ATA needs her to train the new intake of recently signed-up ab initio recruits down there – two thousand applications last month alone, by all accounts.'

'All getting ready for the big push for victory.' Jean's steady hand finished cutting out the first skirt panel, which she placed over the arm of the nearby wicker chair. 'Whenever that may be.'

'Soon,' Mary insisted. 'That's what everyone's saying and I can't help thinking they're right.'

The whole country was in the grip of a fever, counting off the thrilling, nerve-tingling days on the

3

calendar, listening to the news on the wireless for the latest sign that Allied troops were ready to cross the Channel and gain a foothold in northern France. At a personal level, Bobbie, Jean and Mary, along with all the other ATA pilots at Rixley, shared the tension of the build-up, working at full tilt to fly fighter planes and bombers between ferry pools, maintenance units and RAF stations, in readiness for the all-out attack.

'The sooner the better.' Bobbie got up from the bed to gaze out through the long window at the sweeping lawns of the Grange – still out of bounds since an enemy bombing raid the previous autumn. Two large areas of the grounds were fenced off with barbed wire and the smooth green surface was pitted with bomb craters. That hadn't been the worst of it, though; an entire wing of the grand house that had served as a convalescent home for wounded servicemen had been destroyed, killing five of the patients as well as a young nurse and an elderly ward orderly from the village. Luckily the west wing of the building, which was used as billets for ATA pilots, had remained intact. 'Herr Hitler and his Jerry bombers won't know what's hit them when it does happen,' Bobbie predicted with unusual venom.

'And that'll be the end of us Atta girls.' Mary adjusted two or three pins on the pattern then began on a collar section. 'No more flying for me after Jerry admits defeat.' The Air Transport Auxiliary would be disbanded and there was every possibility that she would go back to working in a woollen mill, or perhaps as a shop assistant or an office worker if she was lucky. 'And I'm only just getting started.'

4

'Don't worry; you'll make first officer before we're through.' Jean couldn't see an early end to the war; not with the Japanese joining Hitler and going at it hammer and tongs against the Yanks in the Pacific.

'If you say so, Flight Captain Thornton.' Mary gave Jean a quick, ironic salute then fell back into seriousness. 'Is it wrong for me not to long for it all to end as soon as possible?'

'Wait – let me work that one out.' Bobbie continued to stare out of the window at the heather-covered hills rising out of the valley bottom and forming a jagged horizon marked by outcrops of dark rock. Patchy cloud drifted from west to east, driven by winds that brought squally showers interspersed with welcome patches of blue sky. 'Yes, what you said is as good as treason. But I do know what you mean – what will become of us women pilots once the war is over?'

'Right,' Mary said as she continued to snip.

'Try not to think about it.' Jean went to the record player, lifted the needle then chose another record. 'Let tomorrow look after itself; meanwhile, we Atta girls must take to the air in anything we're given.' Magister or Swordfish to White Waltham, Maidenhead or Chester. Hurricane or the glorious Spitfire to Lossiemouth or Lancaster. Anything to anywhere – that's what their outfit was famous for. ' "Paper Doll" by the Mills Brothers, anyone?' Jean suggested. 'Or how about Glenn Miller and a touch of "That Old Black Magic"?'

'I've finished sewing the bodice and the sleeves,' Mary reported to Bobbie that evening over a glass of Dubonnet and lemonade in the Fox and Hounds in nearby Rixley village. 'Now all I have to do is attach the top to the skirt and sew the hem. I'll do that tomorrow evening.'

'That was quick work.' Bobbie had spent her free afternoon writing letters and reading magazines.

'I've arranged to see Cameron next weekend,' Mary admitted. 'You were right – I do want to look my best for him.' And why not? Mary put great store by these meetings, which were rare and therefore precious.

'You see!' Bobbie winked then raised her glass to Jean, who sat across the room with her husband, Douglas Thornton. The newly married pair looked blissfully happy despite the naysayers – those like fellow pilots Agnes Wright and Horace Jackson, who had been quick to judge when the engagement was announced: surely the hard-of-hearing ex-RAF man with the gammy leg was far too old and crabby for cool-as-a-cucumber, ultra-elegant, ace-pilot Jean? 'Anyway, it's nothing to be ashamed of: wanting to look your best for the man you love. As a matter of fact, I envy you.'

Startled, Mary took a quick drink and felt the sweet heat of the Dubonnet hit the back of her throat. 'You mean . . . ?'

'No, silly!' Bobbie leaned across the table to pat Mary's free hand. 'I don't mean that I'm jealous of you and Cameron. He's a good friend but I never thought of him in that way. I'm only wishing there was someone special in my life, too.'

'There will be,' Mary promised. She was glad that Bobbie was looking to the future. It meant she was slowly emerging from the horrors of last autumn's dreadful episode with Teddy Simpson, about which the less said the better. 'I mean it, Bobbie. One look at you in that get-up . . .'

Bobbie's dress for their evening in the local pub was a delicate shade of lavender, with a scalloped neckline and long, tight-fitting sleeves. She wore her sandy-coloured hair pinned back from her face and rolled under at the back, with small pearl earrings and a matching necklace as the finishing touches. *Real pearls*, Mary observed, *lucky thing*.

'If you say so.' Bobbie didn't quite believe Mary. She thought of herself as too short and somewhat lacking in the curves department. In fact, in all her twenty-two years, despite a life of privilege as a laird's daughter in the Scottish Highlands, she'd only really felt at home either on horseback, riding the heather moorlands or, more recently, behind the controls of a Spit or a Hurricane. Men remained a mystery and, since Teddy Simpson, a definite threat. Bobbie wished it weren't so, but it was. 'Now, as for Angela—' she began as a fresh influx of customers entered the small snug and went to order drinks at the bar.

'None of us is on a par with Angela,' Mary interrupted. 'She's a one-off.' If you'd mentioned men to the much missed society girl, Angela would have reeled off the names of those who had escorted her to the 400 Club in London's West End – Group Captain this and Squadron Leader that. The words Bentley and Bugatti tripped from her lips, along with Schiaparelli and Chanel.

'That's not what I meant.' Bobbie spoke above the raucous voices of the squaddies at the bar. 'I was about to say that Angela gave me a valuable piece of advice on that front. Be yourself – that was her motto.

If men are attracted to the natural you, then all well and good; if not, they're not worth bothering with.'

'Quite right, too. Look at Jean over there.' Mary nodded towards their fellow pilot, settled in her seat, her long blonde hair swept up to show off a swan-like neck, hands resting in her lap. 'She's got bags of confidence in herself – quieter but just as strong as Angela. That's what I'd like to aim for.'

Bobbie glanced at Jean, who talked and smiled with Douglas and ignored the disruptions around her – the blast of cold air as the door opened and yet more young soldiers from the training camp just out-side Northgate barged in, then the shifting of tables and setting up of a game of darts in a corner of the room. 'I can see you and Cameron tying the knot in the not too distant future,' she confided. 'A small ceremony, without fuss – just like Jean and Douglas.'

'I wouldn't bank on it.' Mary shook her head. 'It's harder now that Cameron's moved away from Rix-ley. I scarcely see him.' She felt a painful pressure around her heart as she spoke the words.

'But you have letters and telephone calls to tide you over. And it's obvious that he'd fallen head over heels in love with you before he was posted to Aireby.'

'How do you know that?'

'I just do.' Bobbie recalled the looks that had passed between the two of them as Mary had rushed on to the runway each morning with parachute pack, flying helmet and chit for the day, the worried preoccupa-tion in Cameron's eyes until she had returned safely to base at night.

'Let's hope you're right,' Mary said. 'I'm not very

good at waiting for letters to drop on the mat or for the phone to ring. In between I persuade myself that Cameron has changed his mind about me and I have nightmares about it too.'

'Good Lord above!' Bobbie's favourite expression of surprise rolled off her tongue. 'We're a pair of silly geese – me with my tongue-tied awkwardness around men, you with your doubts and dark thoughts.'

'Yes, it's not easy.' A sudden smile lit up Mary's features. 'It makes flying a plane a doddle, though.'

Bobbie spluttered then grinned as she drank from her glass. 'You can say that again.'

'Now then, girls.' A soldier with corporal's stripes and the worst haircut in the world – scalped at the back and sides, with tufts sticking up from the crown – approached their table. He was accompanied by an equally unprepossessing private, whose chin sported a small sticking plaster and whose khaki jacket hung open to reveal a shirt missing two of its buttons. 'We can't have you sitting all on your ownios – not two stunners like you.'

The soldiers drew up stools and made themselves at home. 'I'm Colin. This is Leftie,' the unbuttoned one said. 'What do you two girls do for a living? Let me guess: you're hoofers on tour with ENSA, entertaining the troops with your high kicks and your twirls – am I right?'

'Two more pints of Tetley's!' a voice at the bar yelled. Elbows jostled, drink was spilled, recriminations followed. 'Watch out!' 'Watch out yourself, you bloody idiot!' Landlady Florrie Loxley threatened to ban any troublemakers on the spot.

'We don't hoof, as you call it,' Mary replied

frostily. Her younger brother, Tom, was an army private so she knew what she was dealing with.

'We fly Spitfires,' Bobbie informed them.

'Bloody hell!' Leftie's jaw dropped. 'You've got to be kidding.'

'You're Atta girls?' Colin croaked in disbelief. 'You can't be!'

'We are,' Bobbie and Mary said in unison.

'Lads, lads; come over here.' Leftie beckoned to his rowdy mates. 'You're never going to believe this . . .'

Mary glanced at Bobbie and raised one finely shaped eyebrow. Without saying a word they stood up simultaneously then swept through the door out into the clear, cold night with never a backwards glance.

'Chips?' Mary spotted a van parked outside the railway station – a ramshackle, converted ambulance with a serving hatch, emblazoned down the side with the words 'Maltby Cod – The Best in Yorkshire'.

'You bet.' Taking out her purse, Bobbie ran ahead. She stood on tiptoe to lean on the counter and place her order with a winning smile. 'Two portions of chips, please, and don't be stingy with the salt and vinegar.'

'It's awfully small.' Douglas cast a wary eye around the farm labourer's cottage on the boundary of the Burton Grange grounds. The land, and indeed the whole of Rixley village, was owned by the Parseval family, who continued to run the estate along feudal lines. Douglas had acquired the key from Florrie Loxley the previous evening and come here with Jean first thing on Sunday morning.

'Florrie did warn us not to expect too much.' Jean

took in the tiny kitchen dominated by an old-fashioned, black cooking range and a plain deal table. There was an uneven flagged floor, a stone sink and a small mullioned window looking out on to Burton Wood.

'It won't get much sunlight, not with those trees in the way.' Douglas wanted better for his new wife – a modern place with a gas cooker and fitted cupboards. But in wartime beggars couldn't be choosers. The expression on his square, clean-cut face was dejected as he limped towards the door leading into the chilly, cramped living room.

Jean followed him. 'Look on the bright side – we're within a stone's throw of the ferry pool, ten minutes' walk at the most. Think how easy it'll be to get to work.'

He nodded then gave a fleeting smile as Jean slipped her arm through his. The living room had a sooty inglenook fireplace, a tattered dark blue rug and faded curtains. He noticed that the lumpy horsehair sofa was missing a leg and the only lighting seemed to be from two oil lamps hanging from a ceiling beam. 'When was it last lived in, I wonder?'

'Florrie didn't say.' Jean recalled that the only information the pub landlady had provided along with the key was that the last tenant – a doddery old chap called William Varley – had been a worker on the Parseval family's estate. Taking in the pipe rack on the stone windowsill with two pipes in it and a pair of worn slippers under the sofa, she failed to suppress a shudder.

'Shall we look upstairs?' Once more Douglas led the way, his mood worsening as he surveyed

patches of damp on the bedroom ceiling and cobwebs festooning every niche and crevice. 'We can't
possibly . . .'

'Yes, we can.' What choice did they have? The
Grange didn't provide married quarters – male and
female pilots were billeted on separate floors. If she
and Douglas wanted to set up a life together, they
would have to move out. 'I can ask Bobbie and Mary
to help me sort this place out. We girls will work
wonders with our buckets and mops; you'll see.'

'It'll take more than that.' Pots of paint, brushes,
hammers, nails – not to mention a roofer to replace
some slates, a plumber to mend the leaking U-bend
under the kitchen sink, and a plasterer to cover the
worst of the cracks throughout the house. 'Where's
the toilet?' Douglas wondered.

Jean led him to the window and pointed to a stone
lean-to in the backyard. 'In there, I expect. There's
no bathroom, of course.'

He shook his head. 'We can't accept this,' he
decided. 'We'll have to return the key to Florrie and
carry on looking.'

With her back to him, Jean stared down into the
yard. 'It's not as bad as you make out. We can carry
on taking our baths back at the Grange and I'm sure
we can make something of this place if we try.'

Douglas came up behind her and slipped his arms
around her waist. Her skin smelt of Palmolive soap
as he kissed her cheek. 'I'd hoped for one or two little luxuries, a place we could call home.'

Jean turned to him and put her arms around his
neck. 'We can do that here,' she assured him, stroking the back of his head then smoothing away his

frown with her fingertips. 'We can do that anywhere we like, just so long as we're together.'

Her voice was sure, her eyes more blue than grey in this bright morning light. God, she was beautiful. Douglas wanted to sweep her off her feet, take her to the bed behind them and lie with her, let nothing else matter except their closeness and their love.

But the iron bedstead had no mattress and there was grime and decay everywhere – dust on the floor, a fall of soot in the ancient grate, mouse droppings under the bed.

'If you say so,' he murmured.

'I do say so.' Jean pictured a vase full of sunny daffodils on the scrubbed kitchen table, a fire in the living-room hearth, freshly washed net curtains at the bedroom window. Every morning blackbirds would waken them with a dawn chorus from the branches of the elm trees outside their door.

'Then we'll take it and make it our own.' Douglas kissed her and held her close. He laid his cheek against her silky fair hair and breathed in the blessing of having found Jean Dobson and made her his wife.

'Heigh-ho, heigh-ho!' Bobbie and Mary sang with gusto as they slung spades and forks over their shoulders and marched towards the kitchen garden at Burton Grange. Off to work they went, Disney-fashion, down the steps at the side of the grand building into a courtyard flanked by rows of stables, then under the clock tower and out into an expanse of walled garden where they intended to dig for victory until it was time for dinner.

Bobbie was dressed in a pair of brown dungarees borrowed from one of the ground crew at the aerodrome. The bottoms were rolled up to reveal black wellington boots. Her thick hair was hidden beneath a green woollen headscarf tied firmly under her chin. A bare-headed Mary had made do with old slacks and a Fair Isle jumper stretched out of shape by years of wear. A morning frost nipped at their fingers as they set down their tools.

Ernest Poulter, the Grange handyman, eyed the girls from the door of the greenhouse that ran the length of the south-facing wall.

'Good morning, Ernest.' Mary was the first to spot the grizzled veteran of the Great War. Though barely fifty, his shoulders were stooped and his walk stiff and lopsided as he limped across. Rumour had it that the handyman had suffered from bad shell shock after his time in the trenches and had been unable to work for many years, until the Parsevals had stepped in and offered him his present job and a tied cottage to go with it.

'Someone's keen,' Ernest commented as he took out his pocket watch. 'I make it just short of half past eight.'

'You know what they say about the early bird.' Bobbie thrust her spade into a weed-strewn bed.

'Aye, but it's Sunday. Didn't either of you fancy a nice lie-in?' Taking his pipe and tobacco pouch from the top pocket of his overalls, the handyman had to control the tremble in his fingers before stuffing sweet-smelling shreds into the bowl. He tamped them down with his thumb then struck a match.

'No rest for the wicked,' Mary replied. The smell

of tobacco smoke reminded her instantly of home and the scowl etched deep into her father's face as he sat smoking in his fireside chair. There was no love lost there – in fact, Mary had been glad to escape both her pa's tyrannical presence and the confines of the terraced house overlooking the canal, within sight of the tall mill chimney where she'd worked as a carder. 'Bobbie and I are keen to dig this rough patch ready to plant early potatoes.'

'Any road, it's a good job someone's showing willing,' Ernest commented in his broad Yorkshire accent. 'Sir Thomas is due a visit this coming week. Nowt escapes his beady eye.'

'The man himself.' Mary dug enthusiastically while Bobbie heaved out clumps of couch grass and tossed them into a nearby wheelbarrow. 'I haven't met the lord and master. What's he like, Ernest; is he a decent sort?'

'He's right enough.'

'But . . . ?' Mary prompted.

'But Sir Thomas is a stickler for discipline. You've met him, Bobbie?'

'Just once; he came to a service at St Wilfred's with his wife.'

'I'm right, aren't I? Oh, don't get me wrong – he's better than most. After all, he's given over Burton Grange to the military; just don't argue with him, that's all.' Ernest sucked on his pipe and stretched out the conversation as long as possible. It pleased him to watch these Air Transport Auxiliary girls getting stuck in, thrusting their spades into the soil, really putting their backs into it.

'We probably won't be here when he visits anyway,'

Mary pointed out. 'We'll be busy checking hydraulics and petrol gauges, tail-wheel locks and what have you, preparing for take-off.'

'Rather you than me.' Ernest popped out small bursts of smoke through his thin lips. 'You wouldn't get me anywhere near one of those contraptions.'

'No?' Bobbie raised her head in surprise.

'No. If God had meant us to fly he'd have given us wings.'

Bobbie laughed as she stopped to take off her headscarf. 'Blimey, this is warm work. Seriously, Ernest, haven't you ever been up in a plane?'

'Not on your nelly.'

'You should try it. Come up with me in a nice Wellington or a Manchester some time – they're safe as houses.'

'Aye, until Jerry decides to take a potshot at you,' the handyman pointed out. Then the sound of a car tearing up the drive drew his attention. There was a flash of red and silver beyond the garden gate. 'What the . . . ?'

The car's tyres spat up gravel, then its brakes squealed to a halt in the stable yard and the engine cut out.

Bobbie and Mary stopped digging. Who that they knew drove a red sports car in that reckless fashion?

'Are we expecting anyone?' Bobbie asked.

'Not as far as I know.' Mary was mystified.

Curiosity drew all three towards the yard where they found the car abandoned with the driver's door open but no sign of the driver.

'It's an SS Jaguar 100!' Recognizing the make and model, Bobbie ran forward eagerly. 'These were all the rage when I was growing up.' She leaned inside to examine the walnut dashboard.

Mary could see the attraction of the low, gleaming machine. The chrome headlights sat either side of the silver grille like bright frogs' eyes and the tan leather interior gave it extra sophistication. 'So who's the lucky devil?' She glanced up at the house in an attempt to solve the mystery.

Hilary Stevens appeared in his squadron leader's uniform at the top of the steps leading up to the terrace. 'Bobbie, Mary; a word, if you please.'

'What now?' Bobbie muttered as she prepared herself for a dressing-down. That was the thing about Hilary: he always made one feel as if one had done something wrong. There he stood, ramrod-straight, calling out in his clipped, authoritative voice.

'Let's see what he wants.' Mary resented being called away from their gardening task but gave Ernest a resigned shrug. Perhaps a P.1.W. – a Priority One Wait – had come in unexpectedly, despite it being a Sunday. She led the way up the steps. 'Yes, sir?' she asked smartly as they joined their commanding officer on the terrace.

But it wasn't an emergency sortie, where the pilot must do whatever was necessary to deliver the aircraft, that Hilary wanted to talk to Mary and Bobbie about. 'Ernest, park that Jaguar properly, there's a good chap,' he called over the stone balustrade. 'You two, follow me.'

He strode ahead of them into the house, skirting the old servants' quarters and coming out into the main hallway with its high ceiling and black-and-white tiled floor. He seemed surprised then irritated to find no one there. 'I gave specific instructions for her to wait here,' he muttered to himself.

'Who's "her"?' Bobbie supposed that he meant the driver of the Jaguar. She glanced up the once-impressive staircase, damaged during the bombing raid, past the torn portrait of a long-gone Parseval in crinoline and white wig, and along the landing that led to the women pilots' quarters.

Hilary didn't answer. 'Specific instructions,' he repeated with a tap of his toe. 'I'm sorry. I'd hoped to introduce you to our new third officer. She'll be moving into Angela's old room once we've tracked her down.'

'Angela's room?' Bobbie echoed. It was the one next to hers, overlooking the front lawns.

'A new third officer?' Mary said. A replacement for Angela was to be expected, but even so things seemed to be happening with indecent haste.

'Yes; Third Officer Vivienne Robertson, to be precise.'

'That's me, but you can call me Viv.' A slight, dark-haired figure breezed out of the library and across the hallway towards them. 'Hey, what a place! These guys, the Parsevals, they must be filthy rich. Have you seen the size of the chandeliers?'

Bobbie and Mary stared. The new third officer was around five feet four inches tall. She bounced along in flat, two-tone brogues and dark red high-waisted trousers, with matching jacket and a nifty pork-pie hat complete with contrasting cream flowers attached to the brim. From what they could see of her pinned-back hair, it was almost jet black against a skin that sported a healthy tan.

She looks Italian, Bobbie thought. *But she sounds American.*

What the heck is someone like her doing here in Rixley? was Mary's first reaction. The phrase 'fish out of water' came to mind.

'Is that your car?' Bobbie asked before Hilary could make the introductions. 'I mean the Jaguar 100?'

'Borrowed, worse luck. From a sweet guy I met during the crossing. Piers lives in Kensington, within spitting distance of the palace. His family is also rolling in it. I only mix with the best people, don't you know. Say, what does a girl have to do to get a cup of coffee around here?'

'Third Officer Robertson, this is First Officer Roberta Fraser and Third Officer Mary Holland.' Hilary overdid the formality in an attempt to stem the newcomer's exuberant flow.

'Hi; pleased to meet you,' Viv bounced back. 'That sea crossing was something! And I'm not talking about the storms and me not finding my sea legs until we were three days out, though that was bad enough. No, I'm talking Fockes and Messerschmitts turning the whole Atlantic Ocean into a crazy shooting gallery. Only five of our convoy made it – we lost two vessels to U-boats, had to watch them get blown out of the water and there was not a thing we could do to stop it.'

'Mary and Bobbie, please show Vivienne to her room.' With a no-nonsense nod Hilary backed away. 'Third Officer Robertson, please be ready to report for flying duty tomorrow morning, eight o'clock sharp.'

'Yes, sir!' Viv shot back. 'Oh boy!' she whispered to

Mary and Bobbie, scarcely pausing for breath as Hilary left by the main door. 'Someone got out of the wrong side of the bed this morning. Or is Squadron Leader Stevens always that way?'

'Always,' they said in unison.

Viv took off her hat with a grin. '"Please be ready to report for flying duty tomorrow morning, eight o'clock sharp,"' she mimicked in a stuffed-shirt voice before turning to take the stairs two at a time. 'Come on, girls; what are we waiting for? Show me my billet, then we can get to know each other over a cup of coffee.'

'It'll have to be tea,' Mary warned with an uncertain sideways glance at Bobbie.

'Hot and strong without sugar,' Bobbie added. 'That much we can do.'

CHAPTER TWO

'So you're sure you don't mind?' Jean had been reluctant to ask for Bobbie's help to clean up Fern Cottage but she realized that it was impossible to undertake the job single-handed.

'Of course not.' Late on Sunday evening Bobbie had knocked on Jean's door to tell her all about the unexpected new arrival and her Jaguar 100. But before she could share the news, Jean had delivered her own bombshell: she and Douglas were busy making plans to move out of the Grange into married quarters close by. 'But the place won't be the same without you,' Bobbie sighed. 'I'm still trying to get used to Angela not being here, and now this.'

'Oh, you won't get rid of me that easily.' Jean cleared a space for Bobbie to sit beside her on the bed. 'We'll still run into each other at the ferry pool every day. Anyway, it won't happen straight away – there's a lot to do in the cottage before Douglas and I will be able to move in. That's why I thought that perhaps you and Mary could lend a hand?'

'Count me in. Stay here while I go and ask Mary.'

Bobbie jumped up from the bed and dashed off. In less than a minute she was back, dragging their friend by the wrist and leaving the door ajar. 'She was in her room, busy hemming her new dress. And her answer is yes.'

'You don't even have to ask,' Mary assured Jean. 'Just point me to the nearest bucket and mop.' She was in her pyjamas, barefoot and with her hair brushed back from her freshly scrubbed face, looking younger than her nineteen years.

'Thank you – I really mean it.' Jean's face glowed with gratitude. 'I should warn you, though: the place is in quite a state. Douglas was convinced it wasn't up to scratch when we first saw it but in the end I managed to persuade him to take it.'

'Of course you did; you've got that man wrapped around your little finger.' Bobbie remembered a time not so long ago, before Jean's arrival at the ferry pool, when Douglas had kept his head down in his office from dawn till dusk, examining weather reports and assigning chits to the Rixley pilots. You rarely got a smile out of him back then; just work, work, work and a strong sense of nostalgia for his RAF glory days. Enter Jean stage left to light up his life and lo – he was a man transformed!

'You'll need to leave a door key where Bobbie and I can find it.' Mary worked out the practicalities. 'That way any one of us can get cracking whenever we have a spare couple of hours.'

'Where is this cottage exactly?' Bobbie still sat on the news about Viv Robertson, the original reason behind this late-night visit. 'Is it the one we pass on our walk to work?'

'Yes, at the edge of the woods. You almost don't notice it, it's so overgrown. It belongs to the Parseval estate.'

'Doesn't everything in this village?' Mary chipped in.

'Knock knock,' a voice called, followed by a light tap on the door. 'It's me!' Viv stuck her head into the room then her whole bubbly self, complete with clinging cream negligee and a mass of black curls surrounding her heart-shaped face.

A startled Jean forgot her manners and turned in bemusement to Bobbie and Mary.

'I was about to tell you—' Bobbie began, her face flustered.

'I'm your new recruit,' Viv interrupted. 'All the way from Vancouver.'

'Isn't that in Canada?' Mary was confused. 'We thought you were American.'

'Puh-lease!' Viv swanned into the centre of the room. 'Sure, I've recently spent time in California, but I'm Canadian born and bred, part of the far-flung British Empire on which the sun never sets. I'm Viv Robertson.' She approached Jean with a flashing white smile. 'I just got here, ready and willing to support the mother country.'

'Pleased to meet you. I'm Jean Thornton.' The two women sized each other up as they shook hands – one tall and elegant, the other small in stature but irrepressibly bright and breezy.

'But wow, is it chilly in these old Yorkshire houses!' Viv showed everyone her goose bumps. 'Why don't they light a few fires, heat the place up?'

'Coal is rationed, I'm afraid.' Jean, like Bobbie and Mary, thought it would be advisable for Viv to don a few extra layers. 'So are a lot of other things – coffee, butter, sugar, bacon . . .'

'Sure; I keep forgetting.' Viv had the common sense to hold back from sharing her first impressions of England when she'd disembarked in Liverpool then travelled by train to the ATA training centre at White Waltham – the soot and the greyness; the dirt and poverty; the men dressed in shabby raincoats with puny moustaches; the clattering, cluttered mess of the training-school canteen. Not to mention the snobbery of the British officer class that she'd encountered there.

The disdain of those toffee-nosed women had fired Viv up, made her more determined to show the stuck-up so-and-sos what she could do, and she'd passed her course with ease. Naturally – for she was a fearless flyer with over 200 hours under her belt, starting with an Arrow Sport biplane at home on Vancouver Island and graduating from there to whatever the stunt directors in Hollywood had wanted her to fly. That part of Viv's story was for later, she decided as she took in the somewhat frosty stares of her fellow ATA fliers.

'You must come for a spin in the Jag some time,' she said to Bobbie. 'Piers says I can keep it for a month then it has to go back, boo-hoo.'

'I'd like that,' Bobbie replied cautiously. What to make of this lively newcomer; that was the question.

'Meanwhile, I can't wait to get my hands on a brand-spanking-new Spit. They say she's the best; a real thoroughbred.'

'She's a joy.' Bobbie offered Viv a blanket from Jean's bed to wrap around her shoulders. 'I saw two

Mark Nines on the runway earlier today. Douglas might give you one tomorrow if you're lucky.'

'She means First Officer Thornton,' Mary explained. 'He signs off all the chits.'

'He's my husband,' Jean rushed to add as she saw Viv trying to work out the link. 'We got married in January.'

'Congratulations.' Seeing an opportunity, Viv wasn't slow to grab it. 'Say, about that Spit – maybe you could have a word . . .'

But Jean gave a quick shake of her head. 'Sorry, no can do.'

'Fair enough; I guess I'll just have to wait my turn.'

The conversation tailed off and Mary couldn't suppress a yawn. 'Time for bye-byes,' she said as she drifted from the room.

'Yeah, and it's my big day tomorrow.' Handing back the blanket, Viv too headed for the door.

'If you do get one of the new Spits, make sure you read up about it in your Pilots' Notes before take-off.' Bobbie supplied the friendly advice to Viv's back view. 'And remember, you'll find the airspeed indicator to the extreme left – not where you might expect it. The boost gauge is to the extreme right; rpm indicator higher up on the right.'

Viv paused to look over her shoulder. 'Yeah, thanks for that.'

'You're welcome.' Did Viv mean it? It was difficult to know. 'Tell me to mind my own business – I won't take offence.'

'No, seriously – thanks.' Viv smiled briefly. Her vivacious manner concealed the inevitable home-sickness that came with her decision to cross the

Atlantic and fight for the Allied cause. 'And now, girls, it's goodnight from me and sleep well.'

'You too,' Bobbie and Jean chorused.

A deafening silence followed Viv's departure, broken by a low whistle from Bobbie and a 'Well I never!' from Jean.

'So that's where she got that tan,' Bobbie concluded. 'California, no less.'

'I wonder what Piers's second name happens to be?' Jean murmured.

'Cholmondley-Smythe?' Bobbie suggested with a mischievous grin.

'How is Viv going to cope without the Californian sunshine?' Jean wondered.

Bobbie shrugged. 'I have no idea, but have you seen the forecast for tomorrow? The last I heard, it said heavy rain and winds up to fifty miles per hour.'

'Where's Third Officer Robertson?' It was ten past eight the next morning and Squadron Leader Stevens was on the warpath. Hilary surveyed the crowded canteen. He took in more than a dozen pilots drinking tea and waiting for the control tower's announcement over the Tannoy. There was a jumble of chairs and tables, a jug of pussy willows and catkins on a shelf by the noticeboard, and two girls doing PE exercises in a space that they'd cleared. They kept up the provocative chant of '"I must, I must improve my bust!"', much to the amusement of several ground-crew engineers playing cards by the window.

'Third Officer who?' Gordon Mason asked above the hubbub. The rangy West Indian master mechanic looked up from his cards.

'Vivienne Robertson,' Mary informed him. She sat at the next table with her parachute pack, helmet and goggles, ready for the call. This was a day for the full Sidcot suit and fur-lined boots – the thermometer by the side door at the Grange had told her that the temperature was just above freezing and the poor daffodils had shivered in the wind during her walk through the woods. 'She's Angela's replacement. There was no sign of her when we knocked on her door earlier.'

'And?' Stan Green, Gordon's fellow mechanic, demanded additional information. He invited confidences with his straightforward, easy-going manner and twinkly smile. 'Come on, Mary; I know you. You've got that look.'

'And – nothing.' Bearing in mind that Mary herself had only recently been through a conversion course to become a pilot, she didn't think it fair to pass comment. So she sipped her tea and watched apprehensively as the ferry-pool commander sought out Viv.

'Have either of you seen her?' Hilary asked Bobbie and Jean, who sat close to the canteen door.

They shook their heads. 'She definitely wasn't in her room when we knocked on her door,' Bobbie told him. 'And the Jag wasn't in the yard.'

'Douglas has just finished the rota. He put Third Officer Robertson first on the list. He's keen to get her off the ground before the bad weather sets in.' Lack of punctuality was the limit as far as Hilary was concerned. It was bad at any time, but on a first day in a new ferry pool it was inexcusable.

As if on cue, the public announcement system

27

crackled and a female voice made the familiar call. 'Will all pilots report to the operations room for their chits! Repeat: all pilots—'

In a flash everyone was on their feet and scrambling for the door. They jogged in a close huddle across the small square of neatly clipped lawn towards the two-storey brick building attached to the control tower, then jostled for position at the bottom of the concrete stairs leading up to the ops room where Douglas's secretary, Gillian Wharton, would hand over their chits.

Bobbie and Jean were ahead of the main rush – up the stairs to the small hatch where they found Viv already waiting, cool as a cucumber.

'There you all are!' Viv stood with her chit in hand. 'I'm bound for Aireby in a light twin – an Anson, apparently.'

'How did you get here so fast?' Bobbie demanded. She noticed that Viv was wearing only her gold-trimmed, navy blue ATA jacket and skirt, with immaculate seams in her nylon stockings and neat black court shoes. 'Hilary's tearing his hair out looking for you.'

Viv shrugged. 'I got here early so I parked the Jag inside one of the hangars then took a look around. There's an old, beat-up Mitchell inside there. I pity anyone who has to fly that old crate.'

'Where's your Sidcot suit?' Bobbie asked. How anyone managed to look so glamorous in uniform was a mystery – perhaps it was due to Viv's thick dark curls, the long, curled lashes and the tan.

'In my locker. Will I need it for a thirty-minute hop?'

From inside the office Gillian tapped on her hatch window. 'Step aside,' she called to Viv. 'Next!'

Jean received her chit – a long haul to Bristol in a Class 5 Albemarle – not the easiest thing to fly because of its heavy tricycle undercarriage. It would entail a late-night train back to Rixley and so there would be no chance of starting work on the cottage today. 'Thanks,' she said to Gillian with a nod and a tight smile.

'You'll need your sheepskin jacket at the very least,' Bobbie told Viv meanwhile. 'Those Ansons are draughty blighters.' Then she called to Mary further down the queue. 'Did you hear that? Viv is flying to Aireby. Should she say hello to Cameron for you?'

Mary didn't enjoy the jest. As other pilots nudged and commented under their breaths, she shook her head and shrank into herself.

'Oh, that's right – you're seeing him on Saturday in any case.'

'Cameron?' Viv pricked up her ears.

'RAF. Flight lieutenant.' Bobbie gave a shorthand explanation as she stepped forward for her chit. 'A real catch.'

'Then I'll say hi anyway,' Viv decided with a wink. 'OK, I'm out of here. Only kidding. I won't go near your flight lieutenant – not if he's already taken,' she flung back over her shoulder at Mary as she ran down the stairs.

Out on the runways, Stan, Gordon and the rest of the ground crew carried out final checks on the air-craft. Planes glinted in weak sunshine as the team of mechanics crawled over them, checking cowlings, propellers and oil levels before take-off.

'What are you dicing with today?' Mary asked Bobbie as they sheltered from the wind under the wing of a Hurricane and cautiously assessed serious black clouds massing in the east.

'Lucky me; I got one of the new Spits. The bad news is: it's Cardiff.' Bobbie was all too aware of the Welsh aerodrome's reputation as a tricky landing spot due to its notoriously short runway and the snowstorm of seagulls that typically greeted your arrival. On one occasion two of the damned birds had flown straight into her windscreen and shattered it to smithereens, resulting in a ferocious blast of cold air that had almost ripped Bobbie out of her harness, and there'd been feathers everywhere. 'It could be worse, though; it could be the dreaded Dumfries Valley en route to Prestwick. How about you?'

Mary tucked her chit into her top pocket. 'To Bristol in the old Mitchell, worse luck. It comes with a One Landing Only warning and a snag sheet as long as your arm.' She pointed to where the geriatric aircraft was being slowly towed out of Hangar 2. Her destination was the maintenance unit on the Bristol Channel; there engineers would cannibalize the Mitchell for useable parts then send the rest to the scrap heap.

'I'd take it easy if I were you,' Bobbie advised with a final apprehensive glance at the gathering storm. 'If they even recommend take-off, that is.' She calculated that visibility would be well under 200 yards once the clouds blew in.

'I expect I'll risk it anyway,' Mary said firmly. 'Watch out; here comes Vivienne.'

The new pilot sprinted from the locker room wearing her helmet and her fleece jacket with her parachute pack slung over her shoulder.

'She's in a skirt!' an astonished Mary muttered. 'What is she thinking?'

'I did warn her.' Viv's choice of clothing was no longer Bobbie's concern. 'You've got your map?' she called out as Viv ran on towards the Anson.

'You bet!' Viv stopped to introduce herself to Stan before she climbed on board. 'What happens if I hit that lump of cloud?' she asked.

'Officially, you watch for the red flare from the control tower and if you see it you turn back.' He wiped oil from his hands on to a rag, which he then stuffed into the pocket of his overalls.

'And unofficially?'

Stan spoke out of the side of his mouth. 'You open up the throttle and climb over it; but don't tell anyone I said so.'

'OK, I'll bear that in mind.' Viv knew that climbing through cloud meant losing sight of the ground, and without a radio and only basic training in reading the instruments on the control panel a pilot was flying blind, relying on a simple compass plus gut instinct to work out directions and distances.

'If in doubt, bail out,' Stan chanted the motto drilled into all ATA recruits.

'Got it.' Lowering her goggles, Viv hitched up her skirt then stepped up on to the wing of the Anson. She slid neatly into the cockpit and strapped on her parachute before buckling herself in. *Give me flying over the Mojave Desert any day*, she thought as the first spots of rain darkened the runway. *Sun, blue skies, no wind.*

She waited nervously as the ground crew removed the chocks, methodically checking hydraulics and trimmers, petrol mixture and pitch. Almost time to unlock the controls and by God did those clouds look nasty. But if Mary and the others were determined to fly in these conditions then darn it Viv would too, her competitive instinct kicking in. *Don't open up too fast*, she reminded herself as she began to taxi down the runway. *Turn into the wind, wheels off the ground, ease back on the stick, increase revs and up we go!*

'Good for Viv,' Jean commented as she joined Bobbie and Mary on the runway. The three Rixley old hands had stood and watched the Anson's smooth, textbook-perfect take-off.

Now Viv's plane rose steadily, carrying out a circuit of the airfield at 600 feet before heading west, with the wind and rain behind her.

'I wonder if she's flown without a radio before.' Mary was next off Runway 3 so she fastened her helmet then donned her sheepskin gauntlets. 'Except during training, of course.'

The absence of a radio in the planes they ferried was a hot topic among ATA pilots. Some reckoned it was a decision made purely on the grounds of cost – two-way radio equipment was an expensive loss in the event of one of the planes going down.

But Jean didn't buy that argument. The value of the radio was a drop in the ocean compared with the £9,000 outlay on each new Spit that rolled off the assembly line.

Another theory was that the RAF hogged all the available radio channels and that the need of fighter pilots was considered greater than the ATAs'.

'That's more likely,' Bobbie would say whenever the subject came up. 'In any case, they don't want Jerry picking up our transmissions when we fly the newest batch of Spits from A to B.'

Mary still regarded the arguments as weak. 'The head honchos made a hash of that decision,' she would insist. 'They won't admit that lives are lost because we don't carry radios.'

'Luckily Douglas is easing Viv in with a short hop to Aireby,' Jean observed from the runway as a sudden gust of wind brought heavier rain. 'Right; I'd better crack on.'

She strode on towards the Class 5 Albemarle. It was a cumbersome aircraft with twin fins and rudders, used mainly for reconnaissance and the transport of paratroopers into enemy territory. It had a top speed of 320 mph – not a patch on the lighter Class 1s and 2s. Still, the workhorse Albemarle was as important to the RAF as any other plane, so Jean set her mind to the job in hand. She rechecked her chit then quickly referred to her Notes for any quirks that the particular type might have.

'Ignore the portside fuel gauge,' Gordon told her as she approached her crate. 'It'll show empty, but if you switch to the second tank then back again it'll give you the right reading.'

'Right you are. It's a good job I can trust you, Gordon.' Jean climbed into the cockpit and began procedures, casting a glance towards the control tower to check for a potential red flare but determined to press ahead anyway.

Gordon climbed up after her to tinker yet again with the dicky fuel gauge. 'What do you make of our new third officer?' he asked casually.

'You mean Viv? What makes you ask, as if I didn't know?'

Gordon gave a conspiratorial wink. 'I take it she's unattached?'

'As far as I know. I haven't had chance to find out.' *Check the gills, superchargers and gauges – run through the whole list.*

'No ring on her finger.' Gordon tapped the fuel gauge. 'That's a good sign. I hear she lived in California before she came here. I wonder what she did out there.'

Jean smiled and wagged her finger. 'Why not ask her yourself?'

'I will, don't you worry.' With a final tap of the control panel, Gordon clambered out of the cockpit. 'It wouldn't surprise me if Vivienne Robertson was a film star in Hollywood,' was his parting shot.

'You think so?' Gordon's unabashed enthusiasm amused Jean.

'I certainly do.' Back down on the runway, Gordon called for chocks away. 'With looks like hers, a girl can be anything she wants.'

CHAPTER THREE

Jean's Albemarle was safely off the ground and Mary was next in line for take-off. She approached the old Mitchell on Runway 2 with her usual gritty determination.

'Treat her gently,' Stan advised as he completed his checks.

'Thanks – I've studied the snag sheet.' Taking the weather into consideration, the sooner she was off the ground, the better.

'She's heavy to fly at the best of times.' Stan's soft spot for Mary was evident in the care he took over the preparations for take-off. 'You'll need two hands on the stick most of the time. And don't try more than one landing – she probably won't stand a second attempt.'

'Don't worry; it's all written down in big red letters.' Mary patted the pocket where she kept her chit.

'Rightio.' Reluctantly Stan instructed Bob Cross, his young Air Training Corps cadet, to begin removing the Mitchell's chocks.

The wind whipped under Bob's oilskin cape and made it balloon upwards as he sprang into action. Soon Stan had joined him and given the thumbs-up to Mary to begin her taxi run down the runway.

With dark clouds behind and wispy white ones ahead, Mary mastered the nerves that tightened her chest by taking a deep breath before she opened the throttle. There were a thousand things that could go wrong on any flight even if your aircraft was sound, but the odds of hitting a problem in an old crate like this and in these weather conditions were considerably higher. If ever her defiant spirit was needed, it was now.

There was a clunk from her undercarriage as she taxied forward and the wheels hit a puddle, threatening to put her into a ground spin, which she avoided by stamping on her rudder pedal. Then she increased her speed and the nose tilted upwards. With split-second timing she was clear of the ground, skimming over Burton Wood, gaining height and breathing a sigh of relief.

'Bloody hell,' Stan muttered to Bob as the Mitchell flew off and he stood miserably in the wind and rain. 'What a washout of a bloody day!'

'Here we go.' Bobbie sat in the cockpit of one of the newest Spits, surrounded by aluminium, steel and Perspex. The plane was a little beauty, every inch the modern fighting machine, with her slim belly and leaf-shaped wings. Her speed and manoeuvrability gave you confidence – you could jink your way out of trouble or roll quicker than any potential pursuer by flicking into a half-roll, diving then speedily pulling away. The one thing you had to watch was the G-force created by those wing-tip turns; pilots had been known to black out on occasion so Bobbie must bear that in mind. The other thing was the tendency of the new Spit to kettle-boil if you stayed too long on the ground, so before she closed the canopy she leaned out of the cockpit and yelled at Gordon to get a move on.

'Hold your horses – I can't go any faster.' Rush, rush, rush – that was Bobbie Fraser to a T; a small bundle of unstoppable energy. Gordon ran his final checks then, with a glance up at the blue-black clouds to the east, gave the thumbs-up.

At last! Bobbie taxied off, slipping effortlessly over the runway as if she were on skates. Without overdoing the revs, she felt the kick of the Merlin engine and the upward tilt of the nose. And she was off, rising like a bird of prey, soaring through the air, banking to port and skimming the edge of the cloud bank, feeling the shudder of her wings as squalls of wind caught hold. *With luck I'll manage to stay ahead of this lot,* she thought as she headed north.

Fifty miles from her destination in the south-west of England, Mary ran into serious trouble that had nothing to do with the weather and everything to do with the parlous state of her machine.

To call the Mitchell a dog's dinner was an understatement. Mary could see from her cockpit that her starboard wing was patched up with thick black insulating tape. What's more, her wheels, which had retracted after take-off at the press of a button, had jolted down again without warning. Worse still, as she followed the landmark railway line towards Bristol, nursing her aircraft along as best she could, her port engine coughed, vibrated then failed. The propeller stuttered to a halt and fumes filled the cockpit.

Thankfully Mary was wearing her oxygen mask and managed to keep a clear head as she limped on.

She had one engine and only one stab at bringing the Mitchell in to land. With her heart in her mouth Mary began a slow descent – Bristol Channel directly ahead, the city protected by lines of barrage balloons that it was vital to avoid. Airstrip in view. Circle three times at 600 feet to alert ground crew. Dry mouth, heart pumping hard. Two hands on the stick for the final descent. A terrific bump as she hit the ground and slammed on the brakes.

For a few seconds Mary closed her eyes. When she opened them again, the Mitchell had slewed sideways off the runway and ground to a halt. Black smoke billowed from the port engine and a crash wagon was on its way with fire hoses.

'Get out of there pronto!' a firefighter yelled up at her as he and his crew jumped from the wagon.

So Mary detached her oxygen mask and harness, and with trembling fingers she opened the smoke-filled cockpit and climbed out. White foam hissed from the hoses that snaked across the ground to smother the fire.

'Need a hand?' The head of the fire crew offered to help Mary climb down from the wing.

'No, ta.' Despite a desperate weakness in her legs she was determined to do it herself.

'What went wrong?' The stocky firefighter walked her away to a safe distance while his men worked on.

'What didn't go wrong?' she retorted. 'Hydraulics failure, petrol leak, oil leak, engine failure – you name it.'

'But you're all in one piece?' he checked. It was a

miracle, really, when you stopped to consider. As Mary removed her helmet and let her hair fall to her shoulders, he saw how young she was. Pretty too.

'I'm right as rain,' she assured him. 'Just point me in the direction of the canteen. What I need right now is a good strong cup of tea.'

'We don't have many daffodils in Canada.' At the end of her first week of flying, Viv strolled through Burton Wood with Gordon Mason. It was four o'clock on Friday afternoon and both had clocked off for the weekend. Viv was still in uniform, wearing trousers for once, with her forage cap perched at a jaunty angle on top of her glossy black curls.

'We didn't have them in Jamaica either.' Gordon explained that his parents had come to England when Gordon was eight. They had set up a successful fruit and veg stall in Digbeth market, close to Birmingham city centre, and the family had not been back to the West Indies since. Gordon was a confident, athletic type, worldly in his outlook and making the most of the free and easy ways that the war had brought with it.

'We have mountains,' Viv went on rather wistfully. 'Plenty of them, it has to be said.'

'Palm trees?'

'Nope.'

'Bananas?'

'Nope.'

'I miss bananas,' Gordon admitted. 'And oranges.'

'There are zillions of orange trees in California.' Overcoming a sharp pang of homesickness, Viv let the conversation drift on without it catching alight, and when they stopped in a small clearing and her companion slid an arm around her waist, she quickly un-slid it again. 'No offence,' she said with a bright smile as they walked on towards the edge of the wood.

'None taken.' Gordon wasn't put off his perch – though Viv was spectacularly good-looking and she could knock a chap out with one bat of her thick lashes, as far as he was concerned there were plenty more fish in the sea. 'What are you doing for the rest of the evening?'

'Buzzing around in the Jag, I expect. I promised to take Bobbie for a spin.' Of all the ATA officers at Rixley, Viv had found that the Scottish girl was closest to her own wavelength, with the same fizz of energy about her and a willingness to live in the moment instead of looking ahead and considering consequences.

Gordon stopped at the edge of the wood and thrust his hands into his pockets. 'Don't get up to any mischief,' he said wryly.

'We will,' Viv contradicted with a glint in her deep blue eyes.

'Fair enough.' Gordon grinned from ear to ear. Yorkshire had better watch out for Viv and anyone she drew into her orbit.

'I need to choose something decent to wear.' Leaving her would-be beau standing and staring, she swayed her hips as she sashayed through the long grass towards the Grange. *Good-looking guy*, she thought as she passed a small house partly hidden by trees. *But not really my type.*

Viv would have walked straight by the house

except that two figures emerged round the side of the building wielding brooms and mops. She recognized Mary and Jean in dungarees and galoshes. 'Hey, what's with the Mrs Mopp outfits?' she called.

Jean handed over her brush to Mary then came to the gate. 'This is where Douglas and I plan to live once we've smartened it up.'

'Here?' Surely not – the place was practically falling down. 'You'd leave the Grange to live here?' Swap chandeliers for lamplight, rooms the size of tennis courts for this cramped, dingy bolt-hole?

Jean laughed. 'It's not where you live but who you live in it with.' She liked what she'd seen of Viv so far, but she didn't think they had much in common. Jean's studiousness and preference for quiet nights in didn't sit well alongside Viv's easy gregariousness.

'And what you do in it, I guess.' The risqué remark came with a wink. 'Can I take a quick look inside?'

'Feel free.' Jean opened the gate then stood to one side. 'Mind your head on that low branch; watch you don't trip over on the broken flag.'

Viv bounded ahead and was through the door into the kitchen before Jean had finished her sentence. She was greeted by the smell of carbolic soap and the sight of Bobbie on her hands and knees, hard at work with a scrubbing brush. The sound of hammering came from upstairs, and through the small window she caught glimpses of ATA driver Olive Parsons and young Bob Cross cutting back undergrowth with scythes.

'It's a team effort,' Jean explained.

'In that case . . .' Viv took off her jacket and rolled

41

up her sleeves. 'Point me in the right direction and tell me what to do.'

Dusk fell before Douglas came downstairs and called it a day. 'I've fixed the hinges on the bedroom door,' he reported, 'and knocked most of the loose plaster off the walls.'

'So I see.' Jean brushed dust from his shoulders and thick brown hair then gave his arm a squeeze. 'Bad light stops play,' she announced to Bobbie, Viv and Mary, who promptly packed away their brushes and tipped buckets of dirty water down the drain. Then Mary popped outside to pass on the message to Olive and Bob.

Olive came in carrying a flask of tea. 'Do we have any cups?' she asked Jean.

'In the cupboard above the sink.' William Varley's motley assortment of china cups were chipped and cracked but it was decided they would do.

'Any oil in these lamps?' Bobbie stood on a stool to find out. 'Yes, we're in luck. Douglas, do you have a light?'

'One, two, three, four, five, six, seven.' While Bobbie lit the two lamps, Viv counted heads then helped Olive to set out the cups.

'Not for me, thanks,' Douglas said quickly. 'I have to see a man about a dog.'

'Me neither.' Bob was anxious not to be left alone with a gaggle of women so he departed soon after Douglas.

'Which leaves the superior sex.' Viv watched Olive pour the tea in the flickering lamplight. 'Say, I'm glad you thought ahead about refreshments, Olive.'

42

'Never go anywhere without a flask of tea,' the ATA driver said solemnly.

'That's the best advice anyone's given me since I reached these shores,' Viv agreed with a laugh.

'And it gives me chance to say thank you.' Jean took a full cup and raised it over the middle of the table. The others clinked their cups together then they all drank a toast.

'To Jean and Douglas; may they live here in married bliss!'

'How are you finding old Blighty?' Olive asked Viv as each tired girl found a perch. 'Cold, I expect?'

'It's pretty much the same temperature as Vancouver, so I'm used to it. It rains plenty there, too.'

'But Yorkshire is colder than California?'

'You bet. It was eighty degrees when I left Los Angeles.'

To Bobbie Los Angeles meant only one thing: Hollywood. 'What took you there?' she wanted to know.

'Work.' Viv's answer was matter of fact. 'I flew stunt planes for MGM.'

'You don't say! And now you're sitting in the dark in the wilds of Yorkshire, drinking tea from a chipped cup,' Olive observed as the others gasped. 'Are you mad?'

'The job's not as glamorous as you think.' Viv set the record straight. 'I preferred working for the flying circus back home. That's where I learned lines and loops, spins, hammerheads and all the rest.'

'Tell us more!' Bobbie dug a sceptical Olive in the ribs before she could put a dampener on things.

'Well, you can do dives and lazy eights in a Piper

Cub. The Stearman is a better biplane, though, with a 220 hp radial engine and seven cylinders. You can do great wing walks in a Stearman.'

Even Olive's eyes widened at this.

'No, I didn't mean the technical guff,' Bobbie cut in. 'We want to know what it was like working for a film studio. Did you meet the stars?'

'Some,' Viv admitted with a hint of discomfort. She remembered the advice given to her by her friend Piers Wentworth on board ship. 'They'll think you're a Yank when you get there,' he'd warned her. 'And we Brits come out in a nasty rash when a Yank shoots his mouth off and tells us how great he is and how he'll win the war for us. So remember: play it right down.'

'Who exactly did you meet?' Bobbie shot back, while Jean, Mary and Olive kept their eyes fixed on Viv. 'Greta Garbo? Douglas Fairbanks?'

Viv shook her head. 'I did once sit in a trailer with Clark Gable, though.'

'Good Lord above, the King of Hollywood!' Bobbie's eyes were out on stalks. ' "Frankly, my dear, I don't give a damn"!'

'What's he like?' Mary leaned forward and gave free rein to her curiosity.

'Yeah, he's a decent guy – pretty quiet.'

'He was here in England last year,' Jean recalled, 'making a documentary film at an RAF base.'

'Sure – I met him soon after MGM persuaded the Air Corps to bring him back home for noncombat duty. Gable is way too valuable an asset for the studio to lose.'

Olive drained her cup then rapped it down on the

table. 'I don't see what all the fuss is about,' she muttered. 'Clark Gable's ears stick out and he mumbles his words.'

'Olive!' Bobbie, Jean and Mary turned on her. 'Wash your mouth out! How can you say such a thing?'

'I'm just giving you my opinion.' Olive stood her ground. She preferred her men less suave, more down to earth. Jack Hawkins and Kenneth More were more her type and they were both British born and bred.

'But Clark Gable!' Bobbie was practically speechless. She stared at Viv as if her new Canadian friend were covered in stardust. Viv drove a red Jaguar and had mixed with Hollywood royalty, for heaven's sake. This put her a definite rung up the ladder even from Angela, the most glamorous person Bobbie had met in her admittedly sheltered life.

'When they're not acting they're pretty ordinary people.' Viv tried in vain to convince her. 'You wouldn't look twice if you passed them in the street.'

Mary's pale green dress had turned out well, especially after she'd added the mother-of-pearl buttons and belt buckle. She'd teamed the dress with white shoes, white gloves and a dainty straw boater – all borrowed from Bobbie.

'Wow, someone looks a million dollars.' Viv whistled when she met her on the stairs at the Grange. 'Who's the lucky guy?'

'Cameron Ainslie,' Bobbie reminded her. 'You remember; I told you about him. He and Mary are love's young dream. Every day they're apart is torture for them.'

45

'It's not too summery?' Mary asked. Her lift into Northgate was waiting for her in the stable yard so it was too late to change her mind about the outfit whatever the verdict.

'It's perfect,' Bobbie insisted, giving her a shove from behind. 'Go!' she ordered.

It was Olive who had volunteered to drive Mary into town and their talk was mostly of recent world events – the bombing of the Vatican, the build-up to another battle at Monte Cassino.

'God knows what the Japs are up to in India,' Olive said with a heavy sigh. 'I can't keep track.'

'They don't tell us everything on the news,' Mary pointed out as they approached the outskirts of Northgate, 'only what they want us to know.'

Closer to town, their car was held up at a level crossing. This gave her still more time to sit and fret in her customary way – would she and Cameron still share the same deep feelings for one another that they had before his departure from Rixley or might things have shifted in some fashion? Might he be more distant – in which case how should she react?

'Don't worry; he'll wait,' Olive commented drily as Mary fidgeted in the passenger seat. The thirty-year-old driver was the type who never flapped or fussed; she was always methodical in her ways and solidly built with her dark hair cut short.

At last the goods train rattled by, the signalman raised the barrier, and Olive and Mary completed the journey.

'There he is: the man himself.' Olive was the first to spot Cameron standing directly under the railway station clock. She pulled into the kerb then applied the handbrake.

So the moment had arrived. Mary paid no attention to the swarm of Saturday shoppers emerging from the station; she took in no details about the shops and restaurants, the grand municipal buildings or the Odeon cinema lining Station Square. She saw only Cameron standing in his flight lieutenant's uniform, hands clasped in front of him, staring up into the far distance. Her heart beat fast, her mouth felt dry and she didn't move.

'What are you waiting for?' Olive leaned across to open the passenger door.

Mary drew a deep breath. 'Ta for the lift,' she said faintly as she stepped out of the car into a brisk breeze and dappled sunshine.

She approached Cameron with a confusing mixture of strangeness and familiarity. In the five weeks since she'd last seen him, he seemed to have grown paler and more gaunt. His features hadn't altered – still the same clean-shaven, square chin, high forehead, pale-rimmed glasses and grey eyes set wide apart under straight brows – but the upward tilt of his head was defensive and the clasped hands seemed to separate him from what went on around him. Mary was within two yards of him before he noticed her.

He gave a start. 'There you are!'

'I'm sorry I'm late.' Her hand flitted towards his arm.

'You're not.' He caught hold of the hand and held it to his chest. A smile transformed his features. 'I was early.'

Mary's earlier worries melted away. 'How are you?'

'All the better for seeing you.' He kissed her gently on the lips. 'Come on, let's go somewhere quieter.'

Tucking her arm through his, Cameron steered them across the busy square, past the statue of a plump Queen Victoria, empress's orb and sceptre in hand, towards a tea shop famous before the war for its dainty continental cakes and pastries. Bright purple and yellow crocuses grew on the small lawn surrounding the grimy statue; hopeful symbols of spring.

'Will this do?' Cameron asked Mary when they reached the door of the café.

She hesitated. The place seemed too genteel for her but she overcame her doubts and nodded.

They went in and a waitress dressed all in black with a white, lace-trimmed cap and apron showed them to a table set out with delicate china, starched napkins and polished silver cutlery.

'Who would think there was a war on?' Cameron asked as he removed his cap and they sat down. He studied Mary carefully. She looked wonderfully young and fresh but nervous, like a colt setting foot in an unfamiliar pasture, ears pricked for any sign of danger.

'Let's skip the cakes and just have tea,' she suggested as she glanced at the complicated menu and the mysterious array of knives and forks.

He agreed. 'After this we can go for a spin up the dale.' Perhaps they should have done that first, he thought. 'But in the meantime, what have you been up to?'

'The usual,' she replied. 'It's been a busy week. We all feel something big is in the offing. How about you?'

'Likewise. All the roads down south are jammed with army vehicles. I've sent ten new pilots to join squadrons on the Kent and Hampshire coasts in the last two weeks alone.'

'And I'm ferrying up to three planes a day.' Mary chose not to tell Cameron about the close shave she'd had in the old Mitchell. She'd already succeeded in putting the incident out of her mind so what would be the point in worrying him? Anyway, she would much rather hear his news.

'When I say I've sent ten new pilots down south, that would be me and Don Bullen between us. He's new to training command, like me – from America originally, Texas. He used to fly as a mercenary for the RAF and had fifteen kills to his name before he came to Aireby, so the man is a force to be reckoned with.'

'But you don't like him?' Mary guessed.

The waitress approached with pad and pencil in hand.

'Just a pot of tea for two, please,' Cameron told her. 'How did you know I'm not keen on Bullen?'

'From your tone of voice.'

'Well, you're right.' Cameron hitched his chair forward and spoke more quietly. 'I've always reckoned that there are three types of pilot in this or any war – first off, the ones whose sole objective is to stay alive, and they're about as useful in combat as . . . well, you get my drift.'

Mary nodded to show that she understood.

'Second, you have my type, if I say so myself. I get the job done but I make sure I don't take unnecessary risks.'

49

'I'm glad to hear it.' Mary reached out to close her hand over his. She knew this must be true because in thirty combat missions over the North Sea and Belgium, Cameron had lost only one aircraft. He'd bailed out of his stricken Hurricane and been picked up by a fishing vessel in the English Channel, none the worse for wear.

'Third, there's the Don Bullen type with only one thing in mind – kill, kill, kill. He doesn't take any account of the risks, just goes at it like a maniac. His squadron leader loves him for that, of course. But even he saw it was high time to take the brainless so-and-so out of Bomber Command for a while.'

'Was there a particular reason?' The tea came and Mary poured.

'Yes. Bullen took off in his Lancaster without enough preparation. Clipped the wing of a Miles Magister coming in to land. Mid-air collision. His propeller cut through the Magister's open cockpit and killed the pilot outright. Claimed it wasn't his fault – the Magister is a training aircraft – it should've used a different runway, apparently. Bullen got away with it but that's how come he's cooling his heels at Aireby with me. Anyway, enough about him. How's Hilary? How are Douglas and the rest of the Rixley crowd?'

'Everyone's fine. Oh, did I mention that we have a new pilot to fill Angela's shoes?'

'No. Tell me more.' Cameron wished he hadn't gone on about Don Bullen; it was considered bad form to criticize a fellow officer and, besides, he'd intended to stay positive during this precious meeting with the girl he loved.

'What can I say? She's from Canada.' Amid the tinkle of teaspoons and the chatter of mostly well-dressed, middle-aged lavender ladies seated at nearby tables, Mary described the new arrival. 'She's a natural in the cockpit. She has nerves of steel and she can fly anything Douglas asks her to.'

'Hmm.' Cameron's nod of approval was accompanied by a glance at his watch. He didn't know how much longer he could sit here exchanging small talk with Mary when all he wanted to do was to take her in his arms. 'Are you ready to bail out of here?' he said with a swivel of his eyes towards the door.

No sooner said than – at an answering nod from Mary – Cameron had paid the waitress and they were out on the wide pavement.

'Phew!' Mary said with something like her old spirit. 'What shall we do now?'

'Come this way.' He whisked her up a side street to where his car was parked. 'I know a spot in the countryside not far from here,' he promised.

Once more they acted on the spur of the moment. Hang petrol rationing, hang everything; Mary and Cameron must make the most of every moment.

'This is it.' Cameron drove for half an hour, then turned off the road that wove along the bottom of the dale to follow a narrow lane over a packhorse bridge. The back road then took them to a hamlet with half a dozen cottages, a plain Wesleyan chapel, and at the end of the lane a large farmhouse looking out over the valley. 'Let's walk,' he suggested after he'd parked the car beside a stile with a public footpath sign pointing across sloping fields.

Mary looked down dubiously at her white shoes. 'They're not mine,' she explained.

'Which is why I chucked these in the boot, just in case.' Cameron strode to the back of the car and produced two pairs of wellingtons.

Mary grinned as she kicked off her shoes and put on the smaller pair of boots. 'I bet you were in the Boy Scouts.'

'I was,' he admitted. '"Be prepared" is still my motto. Come on; I'll race you down to the river.'

Mary ran as best she could in the ill-fitting rubber boots, enjoying the wind in her hair and a sudden, wild sense of abandonment. She and Cameron were like two children, climbing stiles and jumping into the mud, letting out squeals and yells as they slipped and slithered down the rough grass slope towards the riverbank, where a high current ran in swift brown eddies. Then they stood hand in hand and with hearts beating rapidly, listening to the water lapping against low willow branches and slapping against black rocks.

For a while they said nothing. Mary enjoyed watching new lambs at play across the far side of the river – they seemed to spring up into the air out of pure joy, then run across the hillside in rapid starts and stops until their mothers' warning bleats brought them skipping back.

'Are you cold?' Cameron put his arm around her shoulder and drew her in. 'Let's get out of the wind.'

They found a fisherman's hut with a bench outside where they sat and watched the river.

'I was jittery about today,' Cameron admitted. 'I wasn't sure we'd be able to slip straight back into the way we used to be.'

Mary looked at him in surprise. '*You* had the jitters?'

'Yes – it's hard to write down what I'm feeling in letters, and our phone calls are always rushed.' He spoke quietly, leaning forward and staring at his hands, knowing from experience that he would have to be the one to open up the subject of what they each felt. Mary had been known for her shyness and reserve during her time as an ATA driver and even now he sometimes found it hard to work her out. He felt her lean her head against his shoulder and slide her arm around his waist. 'Do you care about me?' he ventured.

'You know I do.'

'How much?'

Mary didn't answer at once. She thought back to the time when Cameron had been Rixley's second in command, when she had been a lowly, tongue-tied member of the ground crew. She'd observed him in the canteen or in the ops room dishing out brisk orders and seen nothing beyond the studious reading glasses and uniform. True, he was fair-haired and dashing and the girls had all talked about him behind his back – 'Would you walk out with him if he asked you to?' 'Are you kidding; of course I would!' And naturally Cameron knew every last thing there was to know about the ferry pool and the aircraft that flew in and out of Rixley. But his professional manner and his rank had kept admirers at bay.

What a surprise then, when on the night of Jerry's attack on Burton Grange, Cameron had suddenly, out of the blue, broken down the barriers. Mary and he had driven badly wounded patients from the

Grange's convalescent wing to hospital in Highcliff and afterwards he'd praised her, then let her stretch out and sleep in the truck's cab overnight while he'd slept in the back.

'How much do you love me?' he repeated softly as they sat at the river's edge.

'Do you need to ask?' she whispered back, her face in the shadow of an overhanging branch.

'Yes.' He was desperate to know. 'Because you mean everything to me, Mary.'

Her breath caught in her throat and she lifted her face towards him. 'Do I?'

'Yes. I lie awake thinking about you – what I would say if you were there beside me, what we would do. I never think of anyone else.'

His words made Mary's head spin. She leaned away so that his blurred features grew clearer. 'Neither do I – I only think of you.'

Cameron's face softened as Mary's words dissolved his fears.

'I made this dress especially for today,' she murmured.

'It's lovely. You're lovely.' He slipped his hand under her warm woollen jacket and stroked the smooth green fabric.

'I wish we could see each other more often.' His touch melted her, changed her into someone more self-assured.

'Hold me,' she murmured.

He held her then and kissed her in the places he dreamed of kissing her – her white neck, her cheek, her lips. Her skin was warm. The sound of the river rushing by filled his head.

Her words formed under his fingertip touch, his lips and the intensity of his gaze. 'I care about you an awful lot,' she murmured between kisses.

'Do you love me?' Cameron asked.

'Yes,' Mary sighed. By the river, under the soaring clouds. 'I do love you and I never want to let you go.'

CHAPTER FOUR

'You call that parking?' Ernest Poulter criticized Viv's careless treatment of the borrowed Jag as she pulled up in the stable yard. It was exactly a week since her arrival and Viv had that morning taken Bobbie for a spin in her friend Piers Wentworth's sporty little number.

Viv slid out from behind the steering wheel and whipped a bright red beret from her head. She ran a hand through her tousled black curls. 'Why, Ernest – what would you call it?'

He frowned back at her. 'It won't do your tyres much good, slamming the brakes on like that.'

'They're not my tyres to wreck.' Viv winked at Bobbie.

The handyman shook his head in a this-won't-do manner. 'We're expecting a visit from Sir Thomas. You've taken up three whole parking spaces by leaving it there.'

Viv chucked the car keys to him. 'Good catch. See if you can do any better.' Then she went on with Bobbie up the steps and along the terrace, through the main door of the house. 'Well?' she asked as they stood in the hallway. 'How was that?'

'Marks out of ten for the Jag? I'd give it the full ten.' Bobbie had thrilled to the throaty roar of the car's engine and the cold spray hitting the wind-screen as its tyres had ploughed through puddles at the side of the narrow, winding roads. 'I've always loved the look of it and I wasn't disappointed by the ride it gives. Even so, it's not a patch on flying a Spit.'

'I'll take your word for it. I've yet to get my hands on one of those little demons.' Viv unzipped her pilot's jacket and straightened out the creases in her dark green skirt. 'What now?' she said, looking round aimlessly.

Bobbie unwound the scarf from around her neck. She wore trousers and a thick jumper to ward off the cold. 'How about popping over to Fern Cottage for an hour or two?'

'You can if you like.' Viv made it clear that she wasn't in the mood for spring cleaning. She ran her forefinger along a shelf close to the entrance to the library then inspected the finger for dust. The result made her wrinkle her pretty snub nose. 'I thought you might like to show me around the rest of this place.'

'Most of it is out of bounds.' Bobbie suspected that this wouldn't matter to Viv. 'All the ceilings came crashing down in the old convalescent wing and the whole thing is a mess.'

'How about in here?' Viv tested a panelled door to the right of the main staircase. It opened on to a large lounge with tall bay windows. She spotted a bar at the far end and an array of stools and easy chairs scattered around the room. Colourful Turk-ish rugs added a touch of cheer to the otherwise drab decor.

'The officers' mess,' Bobbie informed her. 'We can go in there for a drink in the evening.'

'That's good to know.' Viv closed this door then tried another, which seemed to be locked. 'What else have you been hiding from me?'

'I didn't mean to keep you in the dark.' It had been a strenuous week of long flights and overnight stays in B and Bs, so Bobbie had scarcely clapped eyes on Viv.

'Only joking, kiddo.' A third door resisted at first but then the latch gave way and the door creaked open to reveal an almost empty room with walls painted in faded Wedgwood blue, with elaborately carved plaster cornices and a central ceiling rose. The blackout blinds were half raised, allowing Viv to make out bare floorboards, a stack of large boxes and trunks in one corner, and several portraits hanging crookedly on the walls.

Viv's heels clicked over the floorboards as she ran to examine the pictures. 'Say, would you take a look at these,' she breathed.

Bobbie followed slowly. The old school phrase 'out of bounds' had popped out of her mouth and that was how this felt; as if she and Viv were naughty twelve-year-olds breaking the rules. 'Perhaps we ought not to . . .'

'But some of these aren't bad.' Viv pointed out one in particular – a fairly recent painting, to judge by the style of the subject's hair and clothing. The woman was elegant, with a long face and neck and serious, rather intellectual features. Her fair hair was crimped into regimented waves, the emerald gown low-cut and sleeveless. Her pearl-white skin seemed to glow in the semi-darkness. 'I wonder what she was sad about,' Viv remarked before going over to examine the stack of cardboard boxes. She opened the top flaps of the nearest one and lifted out a toy train and a child's ballet tutu. 'Hey, look over here – this is full of kids' stuff.'

Rummaging through the contents, Viv found illustrated books and dolls, a pair of almost pristine pink ballet shoes to match the tutu, a toy yacht with a torn sail and sections of track for the train.

Bobbie had only just ventured across the room when a quiet but authoritative voice interrupted them.

'If you don't mind, those things are private.'

Bobbie and Viv swung round to see a tall figure in silhouette. The light was behind him and they could make out none of his features.

He came into the room and turned on the electric light. 'Good morning. I'm Giles Parseval. My father was otherwise engaged so I'm standing in for him. Who might you be?'

Bobbie's stomach churned as she snatched the toy train and ballet dress from Viv and stuffed them back in the box. 'I'm awfully sorry. I . . . we . . .'

Sir Thomas Parseval's son would have made a striking impression in any situation. He was six feet tall and lean, with springy light brown hair that refused to lie down neatly to either side of a failed parting. His eyes were grey and his unlined face was clean-shaven. Bobbie and Viv could see at a glance that his dark blue suit was expensive; here was a man used to getting his own way.

'We didn't mean any harm.' Fighting a momentary dip in confidence, Viv met his gaze and stepped boldly

59

forward to offer her hand. 'Vivienne Robertson – but everyone calls me Viv. Pleased to meet you.'

Giles picked up on the accent straight away – Canadian; this dazzling, suntanned, glossy-haired sight for sore eyes was a long way from home. He shook Viv's hand without smiling.

'I'm First Officer Bobbie Fraser of the Air Transport Auxiliary.' Embarrassment had flushed Bobbie's fair features as she stepped forward. 'We're truly sorry; I really can't apologize enough.'

Scottish, well-bred, easy on the eye. Giles gave Bobbie the once-over then nodded briefly. 'The door should have been kept locked. I'll have a word with Ernest when I see him.'

'This is all family stuff, right?' Viv gestured around the room. 'Who's in the picture: the beautiful woman in the green dress?'

'My mother.' Giles's lips scarcely moved as he spoke and his voice came from far back in his throat, giving a nasal effect to some of his words.

Viv thought he sounded and looked rather like Edward, the popular playboy king who had abdicated a few years back. 'And you're the boy with the cute dog in the picture on the left?' She hazarded a guess without waiting for an answer. 'You're cute, too – in the picture, I mean.' Angelic, even; with his hair a few shades lighter and the eyes bluer than they were now. Viv thought he looked adorable. 'Who's the girl on the right?'

Giles glanced at the portrait of a girl whose dark hair had been cropped into a short bob. She wore a pale blue dress and sat with her head to one side, with a wistful expression and her hands resting palms upwards in her lap. 'My sister, Veronica. Now, if you don't mind . . .' He strode purposefully to the door and held it open.

'So sorry,' Bobbie mumbled again as she followed Viv into the hallway.

'It's a swell place you have here,' Viv said cheerily. 'Handing it over to the war effort must have been mighty hard.'

'We have other, more up-to-date houses,' Giles said with a dismissive shrug. He decided to keep up the stern act to see how long it took to dent the Canadian girl's breezy self-assurance. She really was quite something, he thought – like a breath of fresh air blowing through these musty, dusty corridors. 'I can't say I was unhappy to see the Grange put to better use.'

'What about the rest of your family – how did they react?'

No visible dents, Giles observed. Quite the opposite: Viv exuded bulletproof confidence, in contrast to the bashful Scottish girl. 'My father is a personal friend of Lord Mountbatten. He was one of the first in the country to volunteer in this way, saying to the War Office: take the house and put it to good use.'

Giles reminded Viv of a hard, shiny nut – glossy and attractive but tough to crack. Why the heck didn't the guy open his mouth and pronounce his words more clearly?

'We'll let you get on,' Bobbie said hastily, before Viv could ask more impertinent questions. 'We've taken too much of your time as it is.'

'Ah, there you are!' The main door swung open and their conversation was brought to an abrupt end.

Giles, Bobbie and Viv turned towards a smiling man

61

casually dressed in sports jacket and open-necked shirt. He had neat dark hair, long, symmetrical features and walked with a spring in his step as he crossed the hall towards them.

'I've been searching everywhere for you, Giles old man. I might have known there'd be two pretty girls in the picture.'

Without a flicker of embarrassment Giles cleared his throat and began the introductions. 'Ray, this is Vivienne Robertson.'

'Viv,' she corrected him, quick as a flash.

'Viv, this is my friend, Ray Moore.'

'Pleased to meet you, I'm sure.'

'And Bobbie . . . ?' Giles searched his memory in vain.

'Fraser,' she said quietly. She found that Ray's handshake was as firm as his smile was broad.

'Giles caught us red-handed exploring forbidden rooms in the old ancestral home,' Viv explained, rapping her own knuckles with her fingertips. 'It's like Bluebeard's Castle around here.'

'No corpses behind locked doors, I hope?' Ray's smile quickly developed into a laugh. 'Did Giles play the Lord Snooty card?'

'You bet he did. He made poor Bobbie feel two inches tall.'

Ray tutted. 'I apologize on his behalf. Did he also tell you that the Parsevals are living off past glories? These days the family scarcely has two halfpennies to rub together.'

'It's perfectly true,' Giles admitted, straight-faced, to Bobbie and Viv's surprise. He waited a few seconds to enjoy their astonishment. 'Actually, quite untrue,' he contradicted with a grin that softened his features and made him appear boyish. 'That was Ray's idea of a joke.'

'Now I don't know who to believe.' Bobbie was relieved to find that the early tension had lifted; nevertheless, she stared cautiously from one man to the other.

'The Savile Row suit gives it away.' After a couple of seconds of consideration, Viv brushed an imaginary speck from Giles's lapel. 'Tailoring like this doesn't come cheap. My bet is the Parsevals are still rolling in it.'

'Ten out of ten for observation.' Ray applauded briefly. 'It's a rather fine piece of tailoring, isn't it?

'Very fine,' Viv agreed as she circled the wearer. 'It fits its owner perfectly.'

Ray seemed to enjoy talking about Giles as if his friend weren't present. 'Flattery will always appeal to his vain streak. That's just a small tip from me to you.'

Giles Parseval had plenty to be vain about, bystander Bobbie admitted to herself. He was remarkably good-looking – well groomed except for the wayward light-brown locks and with a charming smile now that he'd dropped the grand seigneur act. Still, she wasn't quite sure of him – perhaps because she glimpsed an unhappy reminder of Teddy Simpson in Giles's newly playful glances.

Viv, meanwhile, was getting on like a house on fire with Ray. 'So what brings you to Burton Grange?'

'An MG TC; why do you ask?'

Viv brushed aside his over-literal reply. 'Ha ha. Is the MG yours or Lord Snooty's here?'

'Mine. My father's, actually. He runs a yard in

Thresham, about fifteen miles from here. A racing yard,' Ray explained in response to Viv's puzzled expression. 'We train thoroughbreds.'

'You don't say. Not that I'd go within half a mile of a racehorse myself. You can never tell what's going on inside his pea-brain.'

'Says the girl who thinks nothing of flying a Tomahawk or a Wellington from A to B without so much as a radio on board,' Giles pointed out. 'Listen, everyone, I've had a bright idea for once. Let's all meet up in an hour after I've gone through the books with Squadron Leader Stevens.'

'Meet up to do what?' Viv demanded. Their day off was looking up, if she and Bobbie played their cards right.

'To drive out for a spot of lunch. What do you say?'

'We say yes!' Viv decided on the spot.

'Drive out for lunch in what?' Ray pointed to what he saw as a flaw in Giles's plan. 'My MG only holds two people.'

'Then it's a good job I have the Jag,' Viv countered. 'Two in that and two in Ray's car. We girls will see you in the stable yard in exactly an hour and don't dare be late.'

Bright sun shone through the newly cleaned windows of Fern Cottage. Floors were scrubbed, walls whitewashed, and curtains hung in the bedroom and living room. Outside in the small garden, Douglas, Stan and Gordon were hard at work cutting back brambles and clearing weeds from the patch where vegetables would be grown.

At the stone sink in the kitchen Mary was up to her

elbows in soap suds, washing crockery. 'It was grand to see Cameron yesterday,' she confessed to Jean with a happy sigh, leaving off to stare dreamily out of the window. 'I didn't realize how much I'd missed him.'

'Yes; how *was* the love of your life?' Jean stood on a tall stool to refill the oil lamps. 'I'm sorry; I should've asked earlier.' In truth, she'd been too caught up in putting the finishing touches to the house where she and Douglas were to live to give her usual consideration to others.

'He's well,' Mary replied hesitantly. The warm cocoon of love that had spun itself round her heart as she'd sat with her lover on the bench overlooking the river was starting to unspool. Already the worries had begun to creep back in. 'Looking a bit peaky, but apart from that . . .'

Jean stepped down from the stool. 'Is he working too hard? That's a silly question – of course he is. Aren't we all?' She often worried about Douglas's own workload. At thirty-five and with some complications relating to his old leg injury plus his recently diagnosed deafness, the strain of liaising each day with Central Control, the weather boys and the ops room was taking its toll. 'Douglas and I are lucky if we get fifteen minutes together at the end of the day.'

'So the sooner you two move in here the better.' Mary stopped daydreaming and got back to work. 'Cameron sends his best wishes, by the way.'

The rhythm of steady work soon took over. Mary dried saucers and plates then cups, handing each item to Jean for her to arrange in the cupboard above the sink. Through the open window they heard the sharp snip of secateurs and the heavier chop of loppers followed by the sound of branches being dragged towards a bonfire that smoked quietly in a corner of the backyard.

'Another five minutes and we'll call it a day.' Outside in the garden Douglas stood in shirtsleeves at the edge of a freshly dug patch of earth. His strong forearms rested on his spade handle as he watched Stan and Gordon build up the fire. A glance over his shoulder told him that both Jean and Mary were watching them through the window so he waved and smiled.

'It's funny how we allow ourselves to worry about the small things instead of the big ones,' Jean reflected as she returned the wave. 'I manage to block out the fact that any one of us could be blown to smithereens if Jerry decides on another attack and yet I lie awake and fret over whether or not the hand-me-down curtains will fit the windows.'

'Yes, and we fly those planes without a second thought, breaking every rule in the book if we think it'll get us where we need to be in one piece.' Mary recalled her recent experience in the Mitchell. She emptied the enamel bowl of dirty water down the sink then dried her hands, noticing that Gordon had already put on his jacket and set off for home while Stan still chatted with Douglas. Saying a fond goodbye to Jean, she went outside.

'You don't mind if I walk with you?' Stan asked Mary as she set off towards the Grange.

'Isn't it out of your way?' Stan's billet was in a Nissen hut at the edge of the airfield.

Stan retrieved his bike from the outhouse and pushed it through the gate. 'No; I promised Ernest

I'd take a quick look at his wireless. It's on the blink, apparently.'

'Blimey, is there anything you can't fix?' Mary and Stan fell into easy conversation as they walked through the woods. Stan was a wizard when it came to maintaining aircraft – that went without saying – but now it seemed he knew about wireless valves, fuses and electrical circuits as well.

'Yes; I can't fix my love life,' he joked. For long enough he'd worshipped Jean Dobson – as she was then – from afar then, after Jean had got together with Douglas, he'd gone out for a while with Gillian Wharton from the ops room but the affair had soon petered out. His own fault, he'd reflected afterwards – a bright, attractive girl like Gillian deserved more than an occasional night out in the Fox followed by fish and chips from the van.

Mary thought for a while. 'You're a good catch,' she reassured him. 'Handy around the house and you're not bad looking either.'

Stan barked out a short laugh.

'I mean it.' Stan's sturdy build was attractive to many girls. He was broad-shouldered and deep-chested, with a wide face and dark brown eyes. But his main asset was his cheeky-chappie nature, which carried him through emergencies and made him the type you could rely on come rain or shine. 'A girl could do a lot worse, believe you me.'

'Ta, Mary – I think.' As Stan wheeled his bike over bumps in the woodland path, his tone became more confiding. 'So what am I doing wrong?' he asked.

'Let me see.' Mary always loved the quiet peace of Burton Wood – their footfall was silent on the leaf-strewn path and she could sense the rustling, bustling activity of birds, squirrels and field mice all around. On top of which, the first green spears of bluebells had already appeared. 'A girl likes to be given a present of chocolates every now and then. You could save your coupons to show her how special she is.'

'Chocolates.' Stan made a mental note. 'Ta; I'll remember that.'

'And nylon stockings.'

'Stockings.' He added them to the list.

Mary smiled at his serious expression. 'I hope that helps.'

'Oh, it definitely will.' They'd reached the edge of the wood and the Grange came into view at the bottom of a gradual downhill slope. 'Hop on; I'll give you a lift.' Stan stabilized the bike and gave Mary space to mount.

Without even thinking, she perched side-saddle on the crossbar while Stan sat astride and steered the bike down the hill. It gathered speed and Mary's scarf blew back across Stan's face. He raised one hand from the handlebars to grab it then wrap it back around her neck, his fingers brushing her face.

'Brake!' she squealed as they approached the gate.

Laughing, he squeezed the brakes hard and came to a sudden stop, just in time. Mary fell back against him and had to be set upright again.

'Stan Green, you did that on purpose!' As soon as her feet touched the ground she gave him a hard push off-balance before running to open the gate.

'Yep,' he acknowledged, swinging his leg over the crossbar to dismount. If all girls were like Mary – good sports when you got to know them and game for a laugh – Stan would know where he was with them. Come to think of it, if all girls were as pretty as Mary that would be a bonus too.

This thought stayed with him as he wheeled his bike into the stable yard.

'Bye-bye and thanks for the company,' Mary called as she ran up the steps towards the house.

He watched her disappear around the corner on to the terrace. *A pity she's spoken for*, he thought. *Or is she?* Stan could be patient when he needed to be, and with Flight Lieutenant Ainslie busy training pilots in Aireby these days, fingers crossed things on that front could always change.

'You say you grew up with horses?' Ray honed in on Bobbie as he sat across the table from her at the White Hart restaurant in Highcliff. Their table gave them a clear view of the harbour and the sparkling, open sea beyond.

'Yes, we're all riders in my family. My father put me in the saddle when I was three and I never looked back.' Happy days, out in the glen in all weathers on Charlie, her Shetland pony, then later on North Star, her grey thoroughbred gelding.

'A real outdoors girl.' Ray had already learned that Bobbie preferred rambles in the countryside to sitting quietly with a book or going to the cinema. 'It's good to know that a chap could take you out without even dipping his hand in his pocket.'

'Hey, would you listen to yourself.' Viv vied for Ray's attention while Giles visited the Gents. The smart seaside watering hole wasn't busy and her voice carried across the room, to the evident amusement of two middle-aged waiters standing by the serving hatch. 'You need to know who you're dealing with here,' she went on. 'Bobbie is a stylish girl, in case you hadn't noticed. That sporty look of hers costs plenty to maintain so it's a good job her father owns half of Scotland.'

'He does not,' Bobbie protested.

'OK, then; twenty-five per cent of the Highlands and Islands. How's your knowledge of single malt whisky, Ray – Laphroaig, and such like?'

'Not good, but I can always bone up on single malts.' Ray met Viv's challenge head-on. He was enjoying himself more than he'd expected with these two Atta girls, though Viv was perhaps too forward for his taste. He was glad when Giles returned to the table and he was able to focus on Bobbie once more.

'Has Ray been boring the pants off you while I've been away?' Giles beckoned the waiter to ask for the bill.

'No – pants still firmly in place.' Over lunch Viv had learned from Giles that he helped his father to run their two farming estates, Newpark in Derbyshire and Abbot's Gate near Gloucester, which entailed a lot of running about between places and kept him exempt from active service for the duration of the war. 'Much to my mother's relief,' he'd told Viv. She'd tried to find out more about the family set-up but Giles had clammed up. So then she'd told him about her time in Hollywood and entertained the whole restaurant with tales about Lana Turner on the set of her latest movie. 'No one thinks she can act for toffee, but she gets by on her looks.'

70

'I'll say,' Ray and Giles had cheerfully and enthusiastically agreed.

'And they say times are changing.' Bobbie had quietly pointed out that after years of struggle women had finally got the vote, yet still they were valued for their appearance over and above their ability or brain power.

Ray had let out a low whistle of surprise. 'Great Scott, where did that come from?'

'I didn't have you down as a latter-day suffragette,' Giles had added with obvious amusement.

'We can be both, can't we?' Viv had tossed in her opinion. 'I mean, beauty and brains can go together.'

'There's no arguing with that in present company.' Ray had brought the conversation to a gallant end.

And now, with the bill paid, the convivial group got up and left the White Hart then strolled down to the harbour to take in the sea air.

'We've had a terrific time.' Viv linked arms with Ray and promenaded with him along the stone jetty. Trawlers and smaller fishing boats were anchored close to the shore, while far out on the horizon, a small convoy of Royal Navy battleships and merchantmen sailed slowly by. 'It's far and away the most fun I've had since I set foot in ye olde England.'

'You must come to Thresham and visit the yard some time. Oh no, I forgot – you're not keen on horses.' In fact, Ray had a clear recollection that Bobbie was the horsewoman, not Viv. He glanced over his shoulder and extended the invitation to her.

'I'd love to when I get the chance,' Bobbie told him as she walked with Giles. Boats bobbed in the water and waves slapped against the rough stone

71

jetty. The air smelt strongly of salt and fish. A breeze swept Bobbie's hair from her face and she took a deep breath. 'We pilots are run off our feet at the moment; we never know from one day to the next whether we'll be in Lossiemouth or Lancaster.'

'She'll make the time to visit,' Viv promised Ray as they reached the end of the jetty and stayed to watch the convoy sail on. 'In fact, we both will, won't we, Bobbie?'

'Now, now, ladies – one at a time,' Giles teased. It was the usual thing: girls swooning over Ray the minute they clapped eyes on him. 'We don't want any squabbling.'

'We're not,' said Viv.

'We wouldn't,' Bobbie added, quick as a flash.

'How do you do it?' Giles asked Ray after they'd parted from the girls and were making their way back to Rixley in Ray's MG.

'What? I don't do anything.'

'Come off it; I saw you making eyes at the little Scottish one. Not that I blame you.' On they sped along moorland roads, discussing the various merits of Bobbie and Viv.

'Well?' Viv asked from behind the wheel of the Jag. Ray's cream MG was ahead of them, taking the bends at speed.

'Well what?' Bobbie didn't really want to talk; she would rather sit quietly and run through the day's events, to work them out in her own mind. But that wasn't Viv's way.

'Giles or Ray?'

'I don't know – they both seem nice.'

'What's nice got to do with it?' Viv took a bend

with a squeal of tyres. 'Anyway, it's Ray every time for me. He definitely has what it takes.'

'Whatever that is.' Bobbie couldn't disagree. Ray Moore had made quite an impression with his dark good looks and quick wit.

'I wouldn't write Giles off, though; not completely.' Viv breezed along, red beret pulled firmly down, hands at ten to two on the wheel. 'He's probably more your type, in actual fact.'

'Do you think so?'

'Yes – similar family backgrounds, part of the smart set.'

'A deb's delight.' Bobbie swayed in the passenger seat as the car rounded another bend.

'Whatever that is,' Viv commented but wasn't interested enough to ask. Giles Parseval or Ray Moore? Not a bad choice when it came to it. 'Hold tight,' she warned Bobbie as she read the road sign. 'S-bends for two miles. Sit back and enjoy the ride.'

CHAPTER FIVE

'Swell!' Viv turned away from the hatch and waved her chit in the air. 'At last Douglas gave me a Spit – the latest model, with all the bells and whistles.'

At eight o'clock on the Monday morning – a fine day with no weather warnings – she stood to one side to allow the queue of eager pilots to shuffle forward.

'Lucky you,' Mary commented. She'd had her own eye on the Spit waiting on Runway 2 but it had gone to Viv, which was fair enough. Everyone should get their turn.

'For as long as I've been in the business I've wanted to fly one of these.' Delight lit up Viv's features as she shouldered her way past Mary and Agnes, then bumped slap-bang into Fred Richards from the met room as she made her way downstairs. 'It's my dream machine – the best of all the Spits.'

'Good luck with her.' Bobbie ran into Viv at the bottom of the stairs. She'd been to her locker to pick up her parachute pack, helmet and goggles before collecting her chit, so as yet had no idea where she was bound or what in. A flicker of disappointment flitted across her face when she realized that Viv, who was still a newcomer, had bagged the type they all wanted to fly. 'You'll love her, you'll see.'

Viv sprinted on across the lawn towards the runway. This was a big deal for her – a chance to prove that she was as good as, if not better than, the other Rixley pilots. And just look at that little beauty gleaming in the sun by the side of the runway – instantly recognizable with her simple, clean lines and wing shape like no other. Aerodynamically perfect. Viv just couldn't wait to get in that cockpit.

'Hold your horses.' Gordon looked up from working on the engine and saw the newest Atta girl advancing rapidly towards the Spit. He put up both hands to slow her down. 'We haven't checked the hydraulics or the fuel tanks yet.'

'Oh please, let me get my hands on her!' Viv hopped from one foot to the other as the mechanics completed their tasks.

Jean stood nearby, zipped up in her Sidcot suit, waiting to climb into the cockpit of an Oxford: a reliable light twin that had none of the glamour or the speed of the Spit. 'Where is Douglas sending you?' she asked Viv.

'To Bristol. How about you?'

'The same.' This meant that in all probability Jean and Viv would travel back to Rixley together later in the day. 'I'll see you down there.' Jean noticed the impatience building up in Viv – the hopping about, the fidgety checking of her chit and then her Pilots' Notes. 'You've brought your map?' she reminded her.

'In here.' Viv tapped her top pocket.

'Go easy on the brakes as you taxi, don't let her overheat.' Jean's reminder received only a small grunt of acknowledgement from Viv but she continued anyway. 'I'm probably teaching my grandmother to suck eggs, but remember the Mark Nine's undercarriage is pretty narrow and she has nine extra inches added to her tail section. You have to take that into consideration before take-off.'

'Gotcha.' Viv was, in fact, grateful for the advice. But, God; the ground crew guys were taking for ever!

'See you in Bristol,' Jean added. Stan had signalled that her Oxford was ready so she said goodbye to Viv then set off at a run towards her aircraft. She stepped nimbly on to the wing then climbed into the cockpit where she went through the routine checks – hydraulics, trimmers, throttle friction, et cetera, until she came to the point where it was safe to unlock the controls, boost the superchargers and release the tail-wheel lock. She looked out of her window to see Stan give her the thumbs-up for chocks away. *Here we go!* Jean returned the signal, opened the throttle and rolled on to the runway.

Meanwhile, Viv scarcely noticed Jean's perfectly smooth take-off or any of the bustle of activity going on around her. Her mind was fixated on the beautiful Spit and how it would feel to be up there in the clear blue yonder.

'All set?' Gordon ducked under the plane's wing and beckoned Viv across.

'You bet!'

'Just one thing,' the mechanic advised as she leapt lightly aboard. 'The reason she overheats on the ground if you're not careful is that there's a poor airflow through the radiator duct on the starboard side – it's the way she's designed. So keep an eye on your temperature gauge. Once you're airborne you won't have a problem.'

'Gotcha.' Viv eased herself into position, closed the cockpit and revelled in the amazing sensation. It was as if she'd been born to fly this machine; she was instantly part of it, sitting in a seat that fitted snugly around her slim frame. At Gordon's signal, she rolled slowly on to the runway and heard the rumble of the Merlin engine as she gradually upped the revs. *Remember: not too much brake and keep an eye on the temperature dial.*

Viv was aware of her quickening heartbeat and put it down to a mixture of excitement and a sudden, unexpected attack of nerves. She felt her stomach tighten and clench – all eyes were bound to be on her as she gathered speed. *Cut out the jitters, concentrate on getting off the ground,* she told herself. *Just grit your teeth and do it.*

But in her desire to prove herself, Viv overlooked Jean's advice about the Spit's narrow undercarriage. There it went: the long back end lurching suddenly to the left. Viv stamped on the rudder pedal and quickly corrected the swing. Push the stick forward; ask for more power, more speed – like a kick in the pants. Whoosh! The nose tilted and she was airborne.

Soaring over the hills and valleys of the Peak District at 6,000 feet only minutes after take-off, Viv experienced complete freedom. She was queen of the skies; invincible.

Below her was a miniature world of snaking mountain roads and tree-covered hillsides, of vast reservoirs glinting in the sunlight. Railway tunnels burrowed deep underground then emerged with a bright flash of steel. Ahead and above there was nothing but blue.

The superb thrill of flying at 400 mph made Viv light-headed. She tried banking steeply to port and saw the brown and green land slip away. Then she righted the Spit and manipulated the ailerons to perform a complete roll to starboard. For a split second Viv hung upside down and felt the pressure of the harness straps that anchored her to her seat. From the roll she came out into a horizontal line, fast and true and then into a clean vertical up to 10,000 feet – all tricks she'd learned as a stunt pilot on Vancouver Island. From there into a dive and a lazy eight, fighting the G-force, laughing like crazy as she tried another loop, this time to port – effortless at full throttle and quite the most exciting thing she'd done in her life. *Oh boy, oh boy!*

Then back to reality – it was map-time. Viv steadied the Spit and put her mind to the task at hand as she cleared the hills of the Peak District and headed south-west. The map was bulky and it took her a minute or two to extract it from her pocket and open it up, then another two or three minutes to get her bearings. Sobering up after the delight of executing the stunts, she held a straight course. Soon she picked out several conurbations sitting under palls of grey industrial smoke – Manchester to the north, then Liverpool with its busy docks overlooking the River Mersey, then mile after mile of green fields and gentle hills, bordered by the grim, grey mountains of the Snowdon range. All was new and unfamiliar – mountains that were scarcely more than pimples compared with the Canadian Rockies, fields so small that the ground from above looked like a patchwork quilt. A glance at the map told Viv that she should soon expect to see the Bristol Channel straight ahead. Sure enough, the gleaming estuary was in sight, and – surprise, surprise – so was Jean's Airspeed AS10 Oxford, 2,000 feet below, heading for the same RAF station as Viv and her Spit.

Time to have more fun. Putting the fighter plane into a steep descent, Viv soon came up alongside the lumbering Oxford, whose main roles were as a training aircraft and air ambulance. It was a pretty simple, low-wing monoplane with a wooden frame and heavy engine cowlings that formed blind spots which made it vulnerable to enemy attack. Viv took advantage of this design flaw by approaching the Ox-box from behind and appearing as if out of nowhere.

Jean descended steadily towards the estuary, then, out of the corner of her eye, she saw a flash of bright blue, vivid as a kingfisher. *Spit Mark 9. Viv playing silly devils.* Determined not to react, Jean didn't alter her speed as she watched her fellow pilot overtake in a flash then turn on a sixpence so that Viv was flying directly towards the Oxford, only banking to port at the very last second and missing Jean's wing tip by a matter of a few nerve-tingling feet.

It's me! Viv mouthed through her Perspex canopy as she flashed past.

'I know it's you,' Jean muttered crossly. Deciding to carry on ignoring Viv, she descended over the Avon Gorge exactly as planned.

Viv approached again from behind. The song of the Merlin engine filled her ears as she overtook the

Ox-box a second time. *Watch this*, she mouthed. Ahead of Jean she went into a steep descent, overshooting the land mass and following the line of the widening estuary before banking again and returning low and straight towards the Avon Gorge.

Jean swallowed hard. By now it was clear what Viv planned to do.

A glance at the map as she approached the narrow, rocky gorge showed Viv the town of Clifton on the northern side and the county of Somerset to the south. Clifton Suspension Bridge spanned the gap between the two.

'She's going underneath!' Jean gasped from her bird's-eye view. Flying below Brunel's famous bridge was a notorious trick attempted by only the most foolhardy of pilots.

The gorge narrowed. Viv had an overhead clearance of 250 feet at most so she swept down to 150, whizzed through the gap at 200 mph and out the other side. *Nothing to it! A total breeze.*

Idiot! Jean was furious. Viv had unnecessarily risked a bad accident in a valuable RAF aircraft, not to mention her own life. And such antics were strictly against the ATA rules. Jean approached the airfield north of Clifton with mounting anger. Hilary would throw the book at Viv if he ever found out what she'd done.

Jean pulled sharply on the overhead knob to lower her undercarriage and made a final turn towards the aerodrome. She skimmed low over houses and then fields, cleared the last hedge and felt her wheels kiss the tarmac. She drew to a dignified halt without a swing or a bounce.

Viv was still up there, playing silly tricks. But when

she finally did decide to land, Jean would be waiting for her. And boy, from her superior rank of Flight Captain she would have a few choice words to say to daredevil Third Officer Robertson!

You could cut the atmosphere with a knife. Olive glanced in the overhead mirror at Jean and Viv sitting on the back seat of her Ford. Scarcely a word had been exchanged since she'd picked them up from the RAF canteen at Clifton, which was going on for an hour ago. There Jean sat, at her most frosty, her forage cap square on her head, her tie tightly knotted, fair hair swept up out of sight. And there was Viv, tie loosened and top shirt button undone, staring fixedly out of the window at the dreaming spires and hallowed courtyards of the Oxford colleges.

'Who wants to stop here for a quick cuppa?' Olive volunteered.

'No thanks.'

'No, I'm OK.'

'Are you sure? We've still got a fair way to go.'

'Quite sure.'

'I'd rather keep motoring on.'

Blimey! Olive negotiated the narrow streets. She knew Jean could be distant and distracted at times, but this was something else; this was haughty with knobs on. What on earth had Viv done to upset her?

Viv redirected her gaze to the back of Olive's head. Boy, had she had a hard time keeping her lip buttoned when Jean had laid into her back at the Clifton base – irresponsible this, reckless that. What had Viv thought she was doing, risking the Spit with a stunt like that?

'Honey, it's what I did for a living,' Viv had wanted to retort. 'And what's wrong with having a bit of fun once in a while? You should try it.'

Luckily she'd managed to keep her mouth shut.

'Well, Jean – how are you and Douglas getting on at Fern Cottage?' Olive broke the tense silence by venturing into what she hoped was safe territory.

'We're almost ready to move in,' Jean replied without elaborating. She couldn't easily forget the look of sulky defiance on Viv's face back there in the canteen – jaw clenched, eyes narrowed, refusing to meet Jean's gaze.

'And what about you, Viv? How are you finding life at the Grange?' Olive continued, though it was like wading through treacle, getting a civil word out of either of these two.

'Cold,' Viv replied. This summed up her experience in more ways than one – cold rooms and icy water went along with frosty glances of disapproval if she so much as stepped an inch out of line.

That went splendidly, Olive thought. *I'm doing my best here, girls, if you did but know it.* She drove on in silence, up into the smoke and steam, grit and grime of England's industrial heartland.

Lord, oh Lordy! It was Viv whose nerve gave way first. She turned to Jean and attempted to break the ice. 'Look; I'm sorry, OK?'

Jean stared straight ahead and replied stiffly: 'High spirits are one thing; we all know the thrill of going up in a Spit for the first time. But we don't all act the fool with one of the RAF's top fighter planes.'

Aha! So this is what it's all about. Olive was all ears.

'I am sorry. I won't do it again.'

'You realize you could've killed yourself?' Jean glanced quickly at Viv and saw that her apology was sincere. 'We take enough risks as it is. Wait until Jerry's taken a potshot at you and you have fire licking at your boots or an engine fails at ten thousand feet – then you won't be so keen to take unnecessary risks.'

'Point taken.'

Go easy on the poor girl. Olive pulled into a lay-by to check her map. *She's only just got here. Give her time to find her feet.*

'It's not a game,' Jean insisted.

'Listen, I know I was out of line.' Viv bit her bottom lip and hot tears came into her eyes as, for the first time, she considered the consequences of what she'd done. 'Will you tell the squadron leader?'

'I'm not sure. I haven't decided.'

For heaven's sake, cut her some slack. Olive had taken to Viv from the start. She liked the way the Canadian pilot had exploded into Rixley like a firework on Guy Fawkes Night: a Catherine wheel whizzing round and giving off golden sparks. Of course, by the sound of things, Jean was technically in the right and Olive knew that Flight Captain Thornton was the type to go by the rule book . . .

'What will happen to me if you do?' Viv asked.

'Hilary will have to write a report and send it to White Waltham. Then it'll be out of his hands.'

Viv groaned and covered her face. She'd worked so hard to qualify and fulfil her dream of flying with the ATA; she'd travelled halfway across the world, for God's sake. 'I'm a fool,' she whispered faintly.

'I couldn't believe my eyes when I saw what was happening.' Jean relived the heart-stopping moment when Viv had flown under the bridge – straight as a die, without a moment's hesitation.

'I didn't stop to think. For me it wasn't a big deal.'

Jean took a deep breath. 'You have some nerve; I'll give you that.'

Olive set off again and drove the car along a cobbled street with tall factories to either side. A ginger cat shot out from an alleyway, with a black-and-white mongrel dog snapping at its heels. Olive slammed on the brakes just in time then glanced over her shoulder. 'Well?' she asked Jean without looking round.

'Well what?'

'Are you going to give her a second chance, or not?'

Bobbie was back early from four short hops between local ferry pools and RAF bases. She'd put in a couple of hours in the garden at Fern Cottage before dark then returned to the Grange, got changed, eaten dinner then gravitated towards the mess, where she hoped to find company for the evening. She had some news that she wanted to share.

She found Viv sitting alone at the bar, nursing a whisky on the rocks. George the barman chatted with Ernest while Agnes sat with Fred Richards by the fire; otherwise the room was empty.

'Sir Thomas has a lot on his mind,' Ernest told George, a Rixley villager and long-term tenant on the Parseval estate. 'That's why he sent young Giles at the weekend instead of coming himself.'

Some weeks earlier George had asked his landlord to make repairs to his leaking roof and he had not yet received a reply. 'The roof won't mend itself,' he grumbled as he served Viv another drink.

'Mind if I join you?' Bobbie sat on the stool next to Viv's. She saw that the recent arrival was still in her uniform, looking lost and lonely. 'What's up?' she asked as she ordered her Dubonnet.

'Nothing; why?' Viv rattled the ice around her refilled glass.

'Come off it.' Bobbie had never seen Viv look so glum. 'Have you got a touch of the homesick blues? I wouldn't blame you if you had.'

'OK, then – what if I were to say that my career as an Atta girl is over before it's taken off, no pun intended?'

'You're kidding!'

'No, I'm serious. I did something stupid today and Jean saw me do it.'

'Why? What did you do?' Bobbie ran through various options – flying into the wrong aerodrome, kettle-boiling the Spit, upsetting a member of the ground crew.

'I flew under the Clifton Suspension Bridge.' Viv admitted the bald fact with a frown and a shrug.

'Good Lord above!'

'Exactly.' Viv had come straight to the bar to drown her sorrows after Olive had dropped her and Jean off. 'I'm in deep trouble if Jean tells Squadron Leader Stevens and he files a report.'

'Yes, I see.' What to say? Bobbie took a sip from her glass while she thought it through.

'Will she or won't she tell on me? That's the question.'

'What on earth made you . . . ? No, OK; I won't

ask.' Bobbie realized that Viv's thrill-seeking nature had kicked in and her heart had led her head. 'Would you like me to have a word with Jean for you?'

'No thanks.' Viv shook her head. 'Talk of the devil,' she mumbled as Jean and Douglas came into the room. Her stomach churned as Douglas sat down and Jean approached the bar.

'Are you the kind soul who's been hard at work at the cottage today?' Jean addressed Bobbie without saying hello to Viv. 'Douglas tells me the veg plot is ready for planting.'

'Yes; that would be me.' Bobbie looked uneasily from Jean to Viv. 'I had a couple of hours to spare.'

Jean thanked her then acknowledged Viv with a slight nod before continuing in an undertone. 'I'd like a quick word, if you don't mind. Somewhere private.'

Viv grimaced then slid from her stool before following Jean out into the entrance hall. Her heart hammered against her ribs and her fingers were tightly crossed behind her back.

Jean cut to the chase. 'I've decided not to say anything to Hilary.'

'Oh God; thank you!' Viv felt dizzy with relief. She barely resisted the urge to seize Jean's hands and dance her out on to the terrace.

'Against my better judgement,' Jean warned. 'But I've thought about it and I see that it was a spur-of-the-moment thing.'

'Yes, yes; it won't happen again.' A reprieve, a chance to prove that she could do this job as well as Bobbie, Mary and Jean herself. 'I promise, I totally swear! And I'll do my best to stick to the rule book in future.'

'Life is tough enough; we girls have to stick together.' Jean knew that there were always critics – mostly men – standing on the sidelines, ready to dismiss the very idea of female pilots. 'The hand that rocks the cradle wrecks the crate', and so on. Jean didn't want to add fuel to this asinine argument. And she did genuinely believe in Viv's exceptional flying ability. 'Does anyone else know?' she continued.

'Only Bobbie. Oh, and Olive, of course.'

'Well, I'll make sure we all keep schtum.'

'Thank you – I won't let you down.' Viv was ecstatic. Damn it, she was going to give the girl a hug whether she liked it or not. 'You're the best, Jean; I really mean it.'

Blushing to the roots of her hair, Jean extricated herself. 'As far as I'm concerned, it never happened,' she promised awkwardly. 'We'll begin afresh – starting first thing tomorrow.'

Bobbie waited in the bar watching people come and go – Ernest downed his pint then left while Jean came back and sat with Douglas in their favourite corner. As yet there was no sign of Viv returning.

Bobbie was longing to share her news about a short phone call from Ray Moore. Quite out of the blue he had telephoned to ask her to visit the yard in Thresham on Saturday. 'Just me?' she'd asked. 'Or are you including Viv, too?'

'Would Viv be interested in the horses?' Ray had asked in a doubtful tone.

'Probably not.' Strictly speaking that hadn't been a

lie, Bobbie told herself. Still, she recalled Viv's initial enthusiasm about visiting the yard and felt mean to have answered the way she had.

'Then come alone,' he'd said. 'I can pick you up from the Grange – half past ten; how does that suit you?'

'It suits me very well,' Bobbie had replied, without giving herself time to think.

But now she felt guilty. In fact, she was altogether mixed up about having said yes at all. Setting aside Viv's hurt feelings, Bobbie wondered what she'd let herself in for. Yes, of course she would love to see the horses on the training yard and talk with Ray about her own beloved North Star, whom she missed dreadfully. But she was apprehensive too, because of the aftermath of the Teddy Simpson affair. *Let's face it*, she thought as she sat at the bar with her rapidly emptying glass, *that sort of attack is not something a girl easily gets over, even with the help and support of the best friends in the world.*

There had been no rape trial; shockingly, Teddy had died in a catastrophic crash involving his motorbike and a German plane that had run out of fuel and had been attempting to crash-land on the Maltby road. Her cruel attacker's life had ended in a ball of flame and no one at Rixley had been sorry, least of all Bobbie. But her distrust of men was slow to dissolve; it still lurked deep inside her, like a sharp blade capable of inflicting terrible hurt if twisted.

I'll invite Viv to come on Saturday after all. Deciding that there was safety in numbers, Bobbie went in search of her new friend, glancing questioningly at Jean as she left the room.

Jean nodded reassuringly. 'If you're looking for Viv, she's with a visitor. Ernest passed on a message for her to go down to meet said visitor in the stable yard.'

'Thanks.' Bobbie hurried on, out along the dark terrace then down the steps into the yard.

'Bring me the key this minute,' a woman's imperious voice ordered. 'I won't move a step from this spot until you do.'

'Why should I? You have no right,' Viv argued back.

Bobbie came down into the yard to find Viv confronting a tall, thin woman dressed in a dark two-piece suit, matching trilby-style hat and fur stole. As her eyes got used to the gloom, she made out a black Bentley parked under the clock tower with a chauffeur at the wheel.

'I have every right,' the woman insisted. 'I know your type; you took advantage of my brother. Piers was an idiot, as usual. I'm here to see that he gets his car back in one piece.'

'He gave me the loan of that Jaguar until the end of the month, fair and square, no arm twisting involved.' Viv's voice rose to an indignant pitch. She waved her arms in the direction of the car in question.

'What man in his right mind lends an expensive car to a woman he doesn't even know?' The sister's voice dripped with scorn.

'Piers does know me. I sailed the Atlantic with him. His cabin was next to mine. I stayed at his house in Kensington.'

The silence that followed was deafening. A supercilious raised eyebrow said all that there was to say.

'Listen here,' Bobbie thought it was time to step

in, 'couldn't we settle this with a telephone call? Surely Piers himself is the person to talk to?'

The sister didn't bother with explanations. 'This is none of your business,' she informed Bobbie icily. 'Please don't interfere.'

'Bobbie's right: call Piers to check out my version of events.' Viv's resolution wavered when she saw the uniformed chauffeur get out of the Bentley and join them in the yard. 'Go ahead; call him,' she said shakily.

'Is everything all right, Mrs Deerlove?' the chauffeur asked, glancing from Viv to Bobbie then back again.

'Quite all right, thank you, Thompson. The Jaguar is here as Piers said it would be. I'm simply waiting for the key to be brought.'

'You'll wait a mighty long time,' Viv muttered under her breath. Jesus Christ, what a day this was turning out to be.

The chauffeur took a step towards her. He was six feet tall and barrel-chested, and he clasped his hands behind his back as he fixed Viv with his imposing stare.

'The key,' Piers's sister insisted. 'Or would you rather I spoke with your commanding officer?'

Bobbie quickly drew Viv to one side. 'Is it worth it? It's only a couple of weeks before you were due to hand the car back anyway.'

'It's the principle.' Viv seethed inwardly. 'I'm no gold digger. Piers is a good friend of mine. He's out of the country until the start of April – that's why he loaned me the Jag.'

'Thompson, go and find the person in charge,' the woman ordered in her haughtiest tone.

Her chauffeur strode across the yard and up the steps.

'OK. OK.' Hang the principle – Bobbie was right; this was an argument that couldn't be won. 'Mr Thompson, stop right there – I'll bring her the damned key.' Viv overtook him on the steps and disappeared into the house.

Bobbie waited in the yard. She had nothing to say to this Mrs Deerlove, a woman she would have disliked even without the unwarranted attack on Viv's character. Did she ever come down off her high horse? she wondered.

'Here!' Viv returned, out of breath from having run up the stairs to her room. She tossed the car keys to the chauffeur who caught them and silently returned them to his employer. 'And good riddance,' she added before turning on her heel. 'Come on, Bobbie; what say we have another drink?'

CHAPTER SIX

For Bobbie, Viv, Mary and Jean the rest of the week that had begun so badly for Viv was filled with fast and furious flying. By Wednesday, Jean had put Viv's foolhardy stunt behind her and felt increasing admiration for the way the Canadian girl handled any crate that came her way – from nimble Spit to stately Miles Magister. With scarcely more than a glance at her Pilots' Notes, Viv would jump cheerfully aboard. Her handling of aircraft on the runway, her smooth take-offs and her confident ascents were wonders to behold.

'She's a natural,' was Douglas's quiet observation from the control tower. He sang Viv's praises to Hilary, who was slow to alter his first impression of the recent recruit as brash and ill-disciplined. 'Some people are born to fly and Third Officer Viv Robertson is one of them.'

Jean herself never tired of the thrill or the privilege of flying. She loved to see the ground crew crawling all over her aircraft in the build-up to chocks away and the inevitable jolt of nervous energy that ran through her whole body whenever she received the thumbs-up. Then the beat of the propeller blades would calm her and the roar of defiance from the engine as she took off would boost her courage – she only had to open up the throttle for an extra kick and she was off.

'By Jove, she's a dab hand at that,' Gordon remarked to Bob as the two mechanics stood by a hangar door watching Jean's ascent in a Hudson bomber, bound for the Wirral. 'Look and learn, boy – look and learn.'

It was well known that the Atta girls had banded together in the early days of the service, in 1940 and '41. At first they'd been dubbed the Always Terrified Airwomen by their male counterparts, who were sceptical of women's ability to handle the deadly flying machines. But the men had watched those girls – high-society debutantes in the first instance – fly out in the face of bad weather that they themselves would have baulked at.

'She'll crack through and fly over anything,' they said of world-famous Amy Johnson after she'd joined the youngsters flying Spits between ferry pools, until her fatal crash in January 1941 when she became a martyr to the cause. And, wonder of wonders, girls from all ranks of society had flocked to follow her, managing to get their heads around the intricacies of map reading and meteorology, navigation and mechanics. In the end the men had been forced to admire the casual bravery of the Lettice Curtises and Margaret Fairweathers of the flying world and reluctantly admitted them to the clan.

'I don't know about you, but when I'm up there at six thousand feet, all my worries disappear,' Bobbie waxed lyrical to Mary on the Thursday over tea and sandwiches. 'I sit in my cockpit behind my instrument panel with nothing but the blue sky all around me and it's bliss – it's a kind of poetry.' She'd just landed at Hamble and met her fellow pilot in the canteen, having brought in a Spit for repair at the Vickers works there. Dodging the avenue of barrage balloons as she'd come in to land had been that particular day's biggest challenge.

'It's not always sweetness and light, though.' Mary had just heard the tale of two girls at Hamble who were engaged in a bitter feud. They were the sort who competed furiously for types and were disgruntled if they didn't get the aircraft they wanted. Only that morning, one of the pair had barged in front of the other while taxiing for take-off then cut in front again when landing. According to the ground crew, their squadron leader had come down hard on the offender and demanded an apology.

'Did she say sorry?' Mary had asked.

'Yes, but afterwards, in private, she threatened to knock the other woman's teeth out,' was the completely serious reply.

'Sometimes it's dog eat dog,' Mary acknowledged. 'But not amongst the Rixley girls, thank heavens.'

As soon as Bobbie was airborne again – flying a Fairey Swordfish back north – her spirits soared once more. She thought only of what it took to reach her destination: of how to battle the wind driving in from the west and buffeting her crate this way and that, of remembering to keep a keen eye on her stalling speed, of climbing above a sudden lump of cloud, hoping for a break in a few minutes' time that would reveal vital landmarks below. Bobbie would live each moment on the edge until she had cleared the cloud bank: misty white cloud to port, blazing sun to starboard, a rainbow in the offing and on top of the world once more.

Then, as the week ended, it was back to earth with a bump. After an hour with washboard and wringer down in the servants' quarters, Mary ticked laundry off her weekend list. Bobbie telephoned her mother to learn that Rufus, one of the gun dogs on the estate, had had pups and they had employed a new gamekeeper to help Murdo look after the grouse moor. Meanwhile, Jean packed the last of the boxes of books and clothes that she and Douglas were to take to Fern Cottage later that evening, while Viv wrestled with a reply she was writing to Piers in response to a letter of apology she'd received from him the day before.

Dear Piers,

It really doesn't matter about the car – it was your sister's notion that I'd taken an unfair advantage that bugged me. Please tell Mrs Deerlove that she got me all wrong. Thank you anyway for being kind to a wet-behind-the-ears kid from Vancouver. You ask if I had fun in the Jag – you betcha, I did! Look me up if you're ever in Yorkshire.

Chin-chin,
Vivienne

Afterwards, as dusk fell, the girls met in the stable yard. They piled Douglas's car boot and roof rack high with his and Jean's belongings then set off on foot through Burton Wood to meet him at the far end.

'You'll sleep well tonight,' Bobbie told Jean, who looked weary after her Herculean efforts to get the cottage ready.

They were wrapped up in coats, hats and scarves, having to find their way carefully in semi-darkness. The girls had enjoyed every moment of working together and walked arm in arm, deliberately avoiding any flying-related topics. When all was said and done, this was leisure time, and all work and no play made Jackie a dull girl.

'What do you say we all adjourn to the Fox later on?' Bobbie suggested as they entered a clearing in the wood. The sky was cloudless and the north star clearly visible.

'Except for you and Douglas, perhaps?' Mary said to Jean.

'Sure; you'll be busy doing other things,' Viv said with an exaggerated wink. 'What?' She spread her hands and professed ignorance while the others, including Jean, exchanged embarrassed smiles.

A drink at the Fox and Hounds was agreed upon as a just reward for their house-moving efforts. 'So, Viv, how many broken hearts have you left behind in Hollywood?' Mary wanted to know as they walked on. 'Dozens, I expect.'

'A few,' Viv admitted.

'Do tell!' Bobbie demanded. 'Does it include anyone famous?'

'You're kidding. The studios make sure that extras and members of the stunt crews don't get within an arm's length of their precious stars. They're high above us in the firmament.'

'So Clark Gable was the exception?' Mary asked.

'Yeah, he's different – more like one of us.' What Viv didn't mention was that the great man shared her love of all things aeronautical and had spent many hours talking to her between takes.

'Whose hearts did you break, then?' Bobbie wanted to know.

'Let me think.' Viv couldn't resist the chance to kid along. She held up her fingers and began to count. 'There was Marty, Glen and Dirk . . . Richie Senior, Richie Junior.'

'Good Lord!' Bobbie gasped. 'You went out with the father and the son?'

'Both at the same time,' Viv assured her with a straight face, followed by a splutter of uncontrollable laughter.

'You're joking, thank heavens.' Mary was the first to cotton on. 'Seriously, though?'

'Seriously, there was a boy once, back home in Vancouver. His name was Luke. He got engaged to someone else: a girl from Whistler. According to him she was a better skier than me. Plus, she was better looking.'

'Impossible,' Jean commented.

'Agreed,' Bobbie and Mary added.

'You haven't seen me ski,' Viv pointed out, as a gleam of light from the Fern Cottage windows became visible.

'No, but "better looking" – I mean, honestly!'

Viv felt it was time to get serious. 'You girls are good for me, I want you to know. To tell the truth, I've been feeling a little homesick lately, but five min-utes' walk through the wood with you three is a real pick-me-up.'

Bobbie caught up with her. 'You're not still bothered by Mrs What's-'er-name – Piers's sister?'

Viv shook her head. 'No, it's just so . . . I don't know . . . different over here. Believe it or not, I'd never seen bombed buildings before and everything is rationed: food, clothes, gas, nylons.'

'Chocolate?' Jean suggested.

'I guess it'll take a while to get used to.' *If ever,* Viv thought. Homesickness hit her hardest in the evening when she'd be sitting on a train or in a car on her way back to Rixley or else alone in her room, getting ready for bed. It squatted heavily on her shoulders as she stared at her own increasingly pale reflection in various rain-spattered windows – alone and finding it hard to connect.

'That's why you need cheering up after we've finished here,' Mary decided. They reached the cottage to find Douglas already unloading the car. 'Take hold of the other end,' he told Bobbie as he balanced a box on the rim of the boot. As Bobbie received her share of the weight, he greeted Jean with a smile reserved only for her. 'I've wedged the door open. Everyone else, grab whatever you can carry and bring it inside.'

Saturday dawned grey and misty. Clouds had gathered overnight and hung low over Burton Wood when Douglas woke to the song of a territorial blackbird in the elm tree overhanging the garden wall.

He slid from the bed and stole to the window, where he twitched at a corner of the curtain to check the weather – an early morning habit that he didn't break, even on a rare day off. The outside world was damp and cold, while inside the warm, white room Jean slept on, her hair spread out across the pillow, cheeks suffused with a pink glow. He stood and watched her, not wanting to break the peace and perfection of this, his first morning of waking beside his wife in their own home.

The pugnacious blackbird sang on in the mist. Jean woke slowly to see Douglas standing by the window. 'Come back to bed,' she murmured.

He returned willingly to the silky warmth of her body. She lay on her side facing him, sleepy-eyed and smiling, snuggling against him.

'Is this really happening?' he asked, his lips against her cheek, breathing her in. He spoke slowly, in a tone of disbelief, thinking of the night before, after the team of helpers had departed and he and Jean had been alone in their house, wrapped in silence, holding hands as they wandered from kitchen to living room then up the stairs to bed. Someone had left a pot of primroses on the windowsill, a splash of pale yellow against light blue curtains.

'Who did that, I wonder?' Jean had been more pleased than she could say. Tears had come to her eyes.

Douglas had held her tight. Loving her, waiting for her, knowing there was no rush. Then the swooning sensation when she'd kissed him and held him and led him to the bed where she lay now; the certainty that all was right.

'Yes, it's real,' Jean murmured back. Her soft breath was on his chest as she intertwined her fingers with his then raised their hands to her cheek and held them there. 'Listen to that bird.'

Outside on a branch, full-throated and sure.

'Perfect,' Douglas breathed. He meant life in that morning moment, with Jean at his side.

'Stand by your beds!' Bobbie rushed into Mary's room, drew back her curtains then raised the black-out blind. 'Come on; rise and shine.'

'What time is it?' Mary fumbled for the alarm clock by her bed.

'It's eight o'clock.' Bobbie was already dressed in a red-and-green striped sweater and brown slacks. 'We're needed downstairs, Hilary's orders.'

'On our day off?' Mary grumbled as she swung her legs over the side of the bed.

'You're as bad as Viv,' Bobbie complained. 'I had to practically drag her out from under the covers, even when I told her that Giles was beating a path to our door as we spoke.'

'Giles who?' Mary's brain was slow this morning. She could almost feel the cogs grinding away inside her head. That's what came of one too many sweet martinis at the Fox the night before.

'Giles Parseval, of course. Viv's finished in the bathroom, now she's in her room making herself presentable. You've got five minutes to do the same.'

Mary stretched and yawned. 'What does Hilary want us for?'

'Lord only knows.' Bobbie hoped that whatever it was, it would be over and done with before Ray came to pick her up at the prearranged time. Making sure that Mary was fully awake and struggling into her dressing-gown, she ran from the room.

Out in the corridor she found Viv standing in her doorway, hairbrush in hand.

'Is Giles here yet?' Viv ran to the head of the stairs, looking wonderful as ever in a blue silk shirt and dark trousers, a combination that gave her an elegant, sporty air. 'Why do I care?' she wondered aloud. 'We both know he's not even my type.'

Bobbie smiled awkwardly. Her well-intentioned conversation with Viv about coming with her to Thresham had hit the skids when Viv had reminded her that Ray's car was a two-seater. 'So it's a no-go unless you want me to sit on your lap,' she'd said with a shrug. 'Honey, relax; you go and have fun. I'll stay home and dig for victory with Ernest, plant some potatoes, whatever . . .'

'You're sure?' Bobbie had asked.

'Sure I'm sure.' *Play it cool,* Viv had told herself. *There are plenty more eligible bachelors in Yorkshire besides Ray horse-trainer Moore. Take Giles Parseval, for example . . .*

'Bobbie, Vivienne!' Hilary's voice summoned them from below. Giles's arrival was imminent; there was scarcely time to brief the girls before his car pulled into the yard.

'Coming!' Bobbie led the way while Viv tossed her hairbrush on to her bed then rushed after her. 'Mary's on her way,' Bobbie reported as she reached the entrance hall.

Hilary was off-duty, dressed in his sports jacket and twill trousers. But his face was officious as usual. His straight, dark hair was immaculately combed back from his forehead in a severe style that emphasized his aquiline features. His shoulders were back, his chin pulled in towards his prominent Adam's apple as if separating himself from any trivial conversation that might occur. 'I want you to prepare a room,' he began. 'Make up a bed and so forth.'

'Who for?' Bobbie was curious. Jean's room on the first floor was now empty, likewise Douglas's on the men's landing.

'Giles didn't give me a name.' Hilary walked briskly on to the terrace to listen for the sound of a car arriving. 'All I know is that a room has to be got ready below stairs.'

Viv frowned. 'What does "below stairs" mean?' she whispered to Bobbie as Mary joined them. She'd never come across the term before.

'He means in the servants' quarters,' Bobbie whispered back.

'The person concerned is to take up duties as housekeeper here.' Hilary paced the terrace. 'Giles's idea, not mine. In my opinion a permanent civilian presence at the Grange isn't altogether desirable. But mine is not to reason why.'

Mary caught only the tail end of Hilary's explanation, so remained in the dark as he led the way down the side steps into the stable yard to coincide with the arrival of a sleek grey Austin 12, agleam with chrome headlights and radiator grille. Giles parked then stepped out with a brief wave in their direction. He moved casually round the back of the car, pausing to raise the boot lid and take out a small brown suitcase before walking round to the passenger side where he opened the door.

'Giles Parseval,' Bobbie verified in response to Mary's questioning nudge. She was more interested in the passenger than the driver.

Hilary felt in his pocket for a key, which he handed

102

to Mary. 'For the room next to the old butler's pantry. You and Vivienne run ahead and open the window, let in some fresh air, make up the bed. Bobbie, stay here with me.'

So Viv and Mary were sent off without catching sight of the new arrival. They made their way into the house via a side door, along a dark corridor lined with rows of servants' bells, down some stone steps and along a shorter corridor with a glazed door that Mary recognized as opening on to a room where George the barman stored beer and spirits – the butler's pantry. Next to it was the door they were looking for. Mary put the key in the lock and turned it.

'You've got to be kidding!' Viv gasped as Mary fumbled with the light switch.

A dim bulb illuminated a dingy room with one small, high window coated in grime. There was a fireplace with a grate that was choked with grey ash, a wooden rocking chair, a narrow bed with a horsehair mattress and a set of dusty bookshelves. 'Someone has to live here?' she said in astonishment.

'Hilary can't know what a state it's in.' Mary could only assume that their first in command was following Parseval orders.

'It's not right.' No way could they make this fit for human habitation without hours of work. 'Why can't they give her Jean's room?'

'This is for the housekeeper. That's the way they do things.' Mary agreed it wasn't ideal, but who was she to overturn centuries of privilege? 'Come on, let's find some dustpans and brushes and make a start.'

*

Giles held the car door open in gentlemanly fashion and a tall, extremely thin woman stepped out. She wore a grey mackintosh over a dark brown dress and her hair was covered by a black headscarf printed with small red rosebuds.

'Follow me,' Giles told her as he handed her the suitcase.

The woman kept her head lowered as she crossed the yard. Her face was pale and gaunt, but delicate, and with traces of the beauty that good health would have bestowed. She was perhaps twenty-five or thirty years old; it was difficult to judge.

Giles strode ahead and greeted Bobbie enthusiastically. 'We must have lunch again some time. Let me know when you're free.'

'This is her?' Hilary looked doubtfully at the woman trailing up the steps behind Giles. 'Are you sure she's up to carrying out household duties?'

'She's stronger than she looks,' Giles assured him. 'We've had her at Newpark for two years and she's been very little trouble. Come along, Anna; come and meet Squadron Leader Stevens.'

The woman joined them on the terrace with her eyes still cast down and clutching the suitcase in front of her. She reminded Bobbie of a bird with dowdy plumage: a sparrow or a wren.

'Anna Janicki, this is Bobbie Fraser.' Giles began the introductions.

At least he remembered my name this time. Bobbie offered her hand. 'Pleased to meet you, Anna.'

The hand was taken shyly and there was no responding pressure in the handshake.

'I hope you'll be happy here.' Bobbie kicked herself

for sounding too much like her lady-of-the-manse mother. She attempted a more friendly approach: 'Really, we're a jolly crowd once you get to know us. I've been here for almost a year now.'

'Yes, Bobbie will be happy to show you the ropes.' Hilary invited Giles and Anna inside. 'Have a cup of tea while we're waiting for your room to be made ready.'

'I can't stop, I'm afraid.' Giles was in a hurry to be off. 'Anna has brought her Newpark uniform with her – dress, cap and apron – so there'll be no need to provide her with a new one. Her surname is spelt J-a-n-i-c-k-i – Polish, as you can probably guess. Her English is decent.'

He was halfway out of the door before Bobbie ran after him. 'Is Anna expected to keep the whole house clean,' she wanted to know, 'or will she have help from the village?'

'She can manage by herself; she's a good worker.' Linking arms with Bobbie, Giles walked her along the terrace. 'She's had to be. My father is a hard taskmaster.'

'She doesn't look sturdy enough.'

'Appearances can be deceptive. And Anna is eager to please. She left Poland in a hurry before Hitler invaded and can't go back under any circumstances.'

'She's Jewish?' Bobbie realized.

'Quite. She came here via France. Father came to hear of her from a friend at his club and she's been with us ever since.'

Bobbie nodded then withdrew her arm. 'Thanks; I'd better be getting back.'

'Goodbye, then. Oh, and enjoy your visit to

Thresham later on today,' Giles said, taking the steps two at a time.

Bobbie leaned over the stone balustrade and called after him, 'Ray told you?'

'Naturally.' Giles reached his car then turned to look up at her. 'He meant to make me jealous and by Jove he succeeded.'

She blushed then retreated, listening to the Austin's engine cough then start up. Her chest tightened with apprehension about the impending visit as she went inside to take over from Hilary, who glanced impatiently at his watch.

'It seems Anna's room won't be ready immediately,' he reported. 'Show her around the house and grounds, would you, Bobbie? There's a scullery downstairs where you can make her a cup of tea.'

'This is first rate.' Top notch, the bee's knees. No description did justice to the training yard at Thresham. Bobbie had never seen such immaculate stables – hardly a straw out of place, with deep, clean beds, a constant supply of fresh water for the horses, each door clearly numbered and wheelbarrows, brooms, shovels and forks propped with regimental precision against a wall in what must once have been a cart shed. Two grooms in jodhpurs and green polo-necked sweaters trailed rubber hoses from tap to water trough while a third forked hay into a barrow, ignoring Bobbie and Ray as they went about the daily business of looking after some of the most expensive horse flesh in the country.

Ray's family house stood behind the yard. Bobbie had glimpsed it from the drive – a solid, square and symmetrical building with an impressive central portico, built during the reign of King George III, according to Ray. He lived there with his father, his mother having died a few years before.

'How long has your family been running the yard?' Bobbie peered into the first stable they came to and spied a chestnut gelding rustling through the straw towards them. The horse stretched his noble head over the door and she reached up to stroke the white flash on his nose. 'Yes, you're very handsome,' she murmured as he shook his magnificent mane.

'Dad is the third generation. We started when horse racing really was the sport of kings – or princes, at the very least.' Ray sauntered ahead to the next stable, hands in pockets, with his cap tilted back and his wavy brown hair just curling over his collar. 'Not so much these days; the war has hit us pretty hard, worse luck.'

He didn't sound upset; in fact, Ray's mood had been buoyant since the moment he'd picked Bobbie up at the Grange. So she pressed ahead with the questions that interested her. 'The government tried to ban horse racing, didn't they?'

'They had a go, back in nineteen forty. But the Jockey Club fought it and we're left with some local meetings, so long as we don't have to travel far – petrol rationing, and so forth. We can go to Ripon and Thirsk, but not York or Redcar. They'd turned that course into an army camp, the last I heard.'

'So I expect that owners put more pressure on you to win?' With fewer meetings and less prize money, Bobbie saw that times must indeed be hard. A groom led out a skittish grey mare from the third stable in the row then tethered her close by.

'I don't feel too much pressure,' Ray assured her. 'I leave liaising with the owners to Dad. I'm more involved in the vet side of things and keeping the horses in good nick. I ride out on the gallops with them most days.'

'Lucky you!' The grey reminded Bobbie of her own North Star. She went up, intending to pet her until the groom growled a timely warning.

'Watch her; she bites.'

So Bobbie and Ray walked on, discussing running costs and owners with tight purse strings and unrealistic expectations.

'We can ride out today if you like.' Ray's sudden offer took Bobbie by surprise as they came to the last stable.

'Now?' She looked down uncertainly at her corduroy trousers.

'If you want. I can lend you a pair of boots and a hard hat.'

'If I want!' Bobbie repeated.

'I take it that's a yes.' Ray grinned at her eager face, shiny and scrubbed as a schoolgirl's. And the RAF relied on this young slip of a thing to fly Spitfires and Hurricanes to wherever they were needed. He smiled in disbelief as he strode to the tack room to fetch the riding equipment they would need, bringing back two saddles and bridles, which he handed to the groom mucking out the grey mare's stable. 'I'll take Tudor Queen,' he instructed. 'We'll give the young lady Glasgow Girl.'

'I like the sound of that.' Bobbie was positively

gleeful at the prospect of riding one of these thoroughbreds. She offered her forearm. 'Go on, pinch
me – show me I'm not dreaming.'

Ray duly pinched her arm then went back for
boots and hats. 'It'll be grand up there on the gallops,' he assured her. 'The clouds are lifting. There's
plenty of blue sky ahead.'

CHAPTER SEVEN

'I'm afraid this will have to do.' Mary stood back to survey the new housekeeper's meagre living quarters. She and Viv had swept away cobwebs and dusted surfaces, put clean sheets on the bed and climbed a stepladder to wash the high window. 'She can add a few homely touches as she goes along.'

'Who in their right mind would want to call this home?' Viv wasn't happy – there was hardly any daylight in the drab room and certainly no view through the window.

'It depends what her previous living quarters were like.' Mary had an inkling that the newcomer might be used to conditions even worse than this. 'You'd be surprised what servants had to put up with in the bad old days and still do, as a matter of fact – tiny spaces up in attics, damp cellars with no heating, always at their mistress's beck and call.'

'She can have one of the rugs from my room.' Viv decided that this would cheer the place up. 'Do we have anything else to lend her?'

'I have a spare mirror. And I don't really need one of the wicker chairs by my window.'

'Did Jean and Douglas leave anything useful

behind?' Viv wondered as Mary led the way past the butler's pantry, back towards the main part of the house.

'We can ask them when we next see them,' Mary replied. 'Right now, we have to let Hilary know that the room is ready.' He would no doubt be champing at the bit to get on with more important things.

But Viv and Mary found no sign of their first in command. Instead, they found a scribbled note from Bobbie saying sorry, Ray had arrived and she'd had to dash off, and that they would find the house-keeper waiting for them in the library. 'Her name is Anna,' she'd added in a quick PS. 'I gave her tea and biscuits. Good luck with settling her in.'

'I don't agree with this,' Viv muttered crossly. 'It's like posting a package without a proper address, handing her from one person to another.'

'It's all right – you go off,' Mary offered.

With a grateful nod Viv hurried away and Mary went on alone into the library. 'Hello?' she called when at first she failed to spot anyone in the stuffy, book-lined room, heavy with the smell of dust and old leather. 'Hello – Anna?'

There was an airless silence. The blinds were down and only the outlines of chairs and tables were visible until Mary's eyes grew used to the dim light. There was no one in the window seat and the leather chair by the fireplace was unoccupied. It was only a small movement in an alcove to one side of the near-est floor-to-ceiling bookcase that gave away the new housekeeper's presence.

Anna emerged from the alcove without speaking. She had put down her suitcase and taken off her coat and headscarf, laying them over the back of a chair, so she stood awaiting Mary's inspection in a long-sleeved brown dress that came high up her neck and midway down her thin calves. Prim white cuffs and collar relieved the plainness but only added to the nun-like impression.

'There you are.' Mary was relieved. 'I thought for a moment that we'd lost you.'

'I am sorry.' Anna's dark, unblinking eyes met Mary's but gave nothing away. Her black hair was drawn back severely from a long face with high cheekbones and smooth, pale skin. 'They told me I must wait here.'

'That's right.' Was she scared, Mary wondered, or just shy? For who wouldn't be in the situation that Anna had been thrown into? 'I'm Mary Holland; one of the ATA pilots. Your room is ready now if you'd like to come this way.'

So Anna picked up her things and obediently followed Mary below stairs, looking to neither right nor left as they went down the steps and along the dark corridor. Glancing over her shoulder, Mary noticed that the housekeeper seemed to show no interest in her new surroundings.

'It's not much,' she apologized when she opened the door to Anna's room, 'but it's all yours – you can arrange it how you like.'

'Thank you. I am happy.'

Oddly, happiness was the last thing that showed in Anna's gaunt face. 'Would you like me to show you where the cleaning things are – the polish and the dusters, and so on?' Mary offered. 'Or would you rather wait until later?'

'I wait,' Anna decided.

'Yes; you must be tired.'

'Yes.'

'There's a sink next door in the butler's pantry and a gas ring for you to boil a kettle.'

'Yes, I have seen through window.'

'Bobbie left you with tea and milk?'

Anna nodded. 'Thank you.'

'Then I'll leave you to it.' Giving up the attempt to draw Anna out of herself, Mary backed out of the room. 'If you need anything, you'll find me on the first floor, third door on the right.'

Anna gave a single nod and the smallest exhalation. There was a strong sense that the new arrival was desperate to be left alone.

She waited for the click of the closing door, then, as if giving herself long-awaited permission, she sat down heavily on the edge of the bed, buried her face in her hands and wept.

'Shy doesn't cover it.' Mary went straight up to Viv's room to share her first impressions of Anna. 'I could hardly get a word out of her. To be honest, I felt for her – all alone in a foreign country.'

'Foreign, you say?' Viv's interest was piqued – it seemed that she and the newcomer had something in common. 'Where's she from?'

'I don't know exactly – Hungary or Poland by the sound of it. Maybe Bobbie will have found out more; we'll ask her when she gets back from Thresham.' Mary perched on Viv's window seat, gazing out at white, wispy clouds. 'I wonder why the Parsevals sent her here.'

'No idea.' Viv sorted through photographs that she'd taken on her nine-day voyage across the Atlantic – pictures of other passengers and of Piers Wentworth in particular. 'Shall I give Giles a call and do a little sleuthing?'

'Yes, if you have his number.' Mary was both intrigued by and sorry for Anna, whose face had a haunted, sorrowful look.

Viv looked up from the snaps spread across her bed. 'Are you worried about her?'

'Yes, and so will you be when you see her. There's not an ounce of spare flesh on her bones and she looks as if any loud noise would make her jump out of her skin.' Mary lowered her gaze to see two men walking and talking on the terrace below. She blinked and looked a second time before leaping to her feet. 'It's Cameron!'

'Where?'

'Here, on the terrace with Hilary.' Mary was out of the room before she'd finished her sentence.

Viv cocked her head to listen to the clatter of Mary's footsteps on the stairs. *Someone's in a hurry*, she thought as she gathered together the pictures of Piers. The photographs didn't do him justice; his smile for the camera had been stiffly self-conscious. In any case, his sister had put paid to any chance Viv might have had to take things further with him. Like her first sweetheart, Luke, generous and fun-loving Piers belonged firmly in the past. 'Another one bites the dust,' Viv murmured as, with regret, she tore the photographs into small pieces and threw the scraps into the waste-paper basket.

*

'I needed Hilary's advice.' Cameron explained to Mary the reason behind his spur-of-the-moment visit. He looked harassed, with dark circles under his eyes that his glasses couldn't conceal, and his voice sounded tense. 'I could have asked him on the phone but there's nothing like a face-to-face chat.'

'You came all this way?' The situation must be serious then.

'Yes; I've known Hilary for a long time. He'll tell me straight if I'm looking at things cock-eyed.' Cameron and Mary had taken refuge in a quiet corner of the empty bar. Slowly he felt the tension drain away as they sat on a sofa together, his arm around her shoulder, Mary with the sun on her face, her grey eyes still wide with surprise.

'And are you?' she asked in her usual forthright way.

'I might have got things out of proportion,' he admitted. 'That's Hilary's opinion, at any rate. It's this Don Bullen chap I mentioned before. He and I don't get on and that's putting it mildly.'

Mary had the sense to realize that Cameron would tell her more in his own good time. Meanwhile, she basked in his unexpected presence.

'Don's family is a big name in the Texan oil business and boy, does he let you know it. But that's not the point.'

'No?'

'No. You remember that he had a major prang and one of our own bought it good and proper?'

She nodded.

'Well, Bullen got away with that but it seems he didn't learn his lesson. Something else cropped up yesterday and that's where Hilary comes in. I know

115

he's had similar cases of misconduct to deal with in the past.' Cameron paused, frowned and squeezed Mary's hand. 'Listen to me going on. I'm sorry to be such a wet blanket.'

'No, carry on – why does Hilary think you've got things out of proportion?'

Cameron sighed, then leaned forward with his elbows on his knees so that Mary could see only his profile. 'I caught the blasted idiot playing silly devils in a Hurricane. He kept her taxiing on the ground until he'd built up enough revs to pull her up into a half-loop, so he was hanging upside down at the end of the runway and heading in completely the wrong direction.'

Mary gave a low gasp. 'Did anyone else see?'

'Yes; half the bloody batch of new recruits. I didn't know where to put myself – Bullen is meant to set a good example, for Christ's sake.'

'Did you report him?'

'Not yet.'

'And will you?' She could guess at the struggle that was going on in Cameron's mind: his deep-seated dislike of the American pilot versus a desire to make a judgement based solely on professional criteria.

'Hilary says not to if I want to avoid an out-and-out feud between senior officers, which is obviously bad for morale. He doesn't classify the offence as serious.'

'I'm shocked; Hilary is usually such a stickler.'

'Yes, but he reckons there's a bigger picture to take into consideration here. Strictly off the record, Hilary says to hang fire; a man like Bullen is sure to come a cropper sooner rather than later and then it won't be my responsibility to hold him to account.'

Mary thought of another way around the problem. 'What about tackling this Bullen chap face to face?'

'Maybe.' Cameron didn't hold out much hope that this would have the right outcome. 'Bullen is a hot-tempered so-and-so – he could easily lash out.'

'Then don't,' she said quickly.

'The thing is, Mary – now I can hardly stand being in the same room with him. I feel as if I'm going to explode every time he comes near me.'

Slipping her hand under Cameron's chin, she tilted his head towards her. 'This isn't like you,' she whispered. 'You've sailed through much worse; you held your nerve every time you flew out on a bombing raid – how many times?'

'Thirty,' was the quiet reply. 'Do you know what Hilary suggested if I really can't bring myself to work with Bullen any longer?'

Mary said nothing and listened with mounting dread. She knew in her bones what Cameron was about to say.

'That I should apply for a new posting.'

Her heart lurched. 'Where to?'

'Anywhere so long as Bullen is out of my hair – the ATA are crying out for trainers at White Waltham. Or else I could apply to go back into active service with the RAF; that's the other option.'

'All because of one bad penny?' Mary's voice was strangled and she clutched Cameron's hand. The man she loved was making a plan to go far away, possibly into fresh dangers.

'Perhaps it's the right thing.' He gave her a desperate, searching look. 'I can't go on like this, Mary; I really can't.'

Glasgow Girl approached the gallops with a spring in her step. Head held high and ears pricked, the chestnut mare forged ahead of Ray's horse, up the lane towards a flat, grassy stretch where the grooms regularly exercised the thoroughbreds.

'Tighten your reins a tad,' Ray advised from behind. 'She'll take charge if you let her.'

So Bobbie checked her horse's stride and fell in beside her companion. 'It's good of you to trust me with her; I appreciate it.'

'She's a good-natured sort; she'll look after you.' Ray rode Tudor Queen, the grey mare with the tendency to bite. Her ears were flat against her head and she rolled her eyes at Glasgow Girl: *Don't crowd me, give me space.* 'Not like this one,' Ray conceded as his horse tried to barge ahead.

Bobbie checked Glasgow Girl again. 'Good girl,' she murmured, then smiled to see her horse flick her ears and turn them responsively at the sound of her rider's voice. Her pace at a walk was smooth as silk and there was a beautiful arch to her slender neck.

'With you on board we should change her name to Highland Lassie.' Ray's attempt to humour Bobbie elicited a broader smile. 'Ready to trot?' he asked as they came to the end of the lane.

Bobbie nodded then squeezed her legs against her horse's flanks. She made a smooth transition into trot and her eyes were directed straight ahead as they approached the start of the gallops. Bobbie beamed at the prospect of going flat-out.

'All set?' Ray glanced over his shoulder.

She nodded again.

'Tudor Queen doesn't have any brakes to speak of,' Ray warned. 'Don't worry if she gets ahead of you – I'll wait for you at the far end.'

Will you indeed? Ray underestimated Bobbie if he thought she would let him get away with that. 'You hear?' she murmured to Glasgow Girl. 'He thinks he can beat us.'

Her horse pranced on the spot as her rival jostled and barged to stay ahead. The two riders crested the ridge at a trot and felt the breeze stiffen. Bobbie saw the land ahead flatten out: the long, straight, grassy run had heather and scrub to either side, with a small copse to mark its end.

'Here we go,' she whispered. Perched on the ridiculously small saddle, with her stirrups much shorter than she was used to, she squeezed again – into a gallop with a thrilling burst of speed, keeping pace with Tudor Queen, kicking up sods of soft earth, feeling the horse's power explode beneath her.

Ray glanced sideways. Bobbie stuck in the saddle with unexpected tenacity. Her balance was perfect and she let her horse gallop on, neck to neck with Tudor Queen. He gave her a look of surprised admiration. 'Right; you're on!'

Such speed and strength; the wind tugged at Bobbie's sweater as she raised herself up out of the saddle, jockey style, and let Glasgow Girl run. They pulled ahead of Tudor Queen by half a length before

Ray urged his mount to greater efforts. The grey overtook, her hooves thundering over the turf, horses and riders going at full stretch.

Oh no you don't! Bobbie and Glasgow Girl fought back. The ash tree copse drew nearer. Rooks rose from their bare branches and wheeled away into banks of pale grey cloud as the galloping horses approached. Neck and neck again, furiously fast – mounts beginning to blow and heave air into their lungs, at the limit of their stamina.

'Whoa!' They reached the end and Ray pulled Tudor Queen back with all his might. Breathing hard, she slowed to a trot then to a walk.

'Whoa!' Bobbie and Glasgow Girl wheeled off to the left. 'A dead heat!' she cried as they trotted to rejoin Ray and Tudor Queen.

'Nice work,' Ray told her. 'I wasn't expecting that.'

Bobbie grinned. 'Never judge a book ...' Her cheeks were flushed, her heart pounding, as they headed for home at a leisurely trot. 'I was put in the saddle almost as soon as I could walk.'

'Is that so?' Ray readily appreciated the finer points of her horsemanship – the firmness of her seat, her light touch on the reins.

'Yes and I've had my thoroughbred, North Star, for the last seven years – he came to me as a two-year-old from a top breeder in Ireland.'

'And do you miss him?'

'Yes; more than anything.'

'Well, feel free to come and ride here any time you like,' Ray offered. He'd taken to Bobbie from the off; the girl was shiny bright and neat, easy to get along with. But now he'd seen another, more competitive side and he liked her even more. 'I mean it; come any time.'

'Thank you, I will,' she agreed.

They came down from the gallops into the lane leading to the yard, exchanging riding tales and so caught up in their conversation that they didn't notice the approach of a green Riley until it was almost too late.

The car rounded a bend at full throttle, tilting on to two wheels before the driver slammed on the brakes.

Bobbie's horse reared. She held her seat and attempted to calm her while Tudor Queen barged sideways across the lane and into the ditch. Ray was thrown forward but managed to scramble back into the saddle then reverse his mount back on to level ground.

A small, grey-haired man in riding breeches, long boots, flat cap and tweed jacket got out of the car and slammed the door. 'What the hell do you think you're playing at?' he yelled at Ray then gestured towards Bobbie. 'Who said she could take Glasgow Girl out without my permission?'

'It's all right, Dad; calm down,' Ray began.

A startled Bobbie held her horse back and waited for the man's temper to cool. His face was lean and lined, with an outdoors, weather-beaten look. His bow-legged stance was that of a man who had been around horses all his life.

'It's not all right, damn it.' The older man scowled as he walked up to Glasgow Girl and roughly snatched her reins. He left his car where it was and led the chestnut mare down the lane without looking up at Bobbie. 'Typical; trying to impress the women, as usual,' he muttered. 'That's Ray all over.'

Bobbie said nothing. Her soaring spirits went into quick reverse.

'You're lucky you didn't break your neck,' Ray's father continued. 'My son is a damn silly fool.'

They came to the yard. Scarcely waiting for Bobbie to dismount, he handed the horse over to a nervous-looking groom, who led her into her stable. Ray too dismounted and handed over his mare. His face was pale with anger. 'Dad, this is Bobbie Fraser,' he said through clenched teeth. 'Bobbie, meet my dad, Derek Moore.'

'And you can cut that out too,' Derek retorted, turning on his heel then striding across the yard towards the house. 'I don't care who she is; just get rid of her.'

Mary had wandered off aimlessly after Cameron's departure from the Grange.

'Please think before you act,' she'd begged as they'd stood in the stable yard. 'Promise me you won't do anything rash.'

'You know me,' he'd replied with a distracted air. 'I'm not the rash type.'

Not usually, she thought now as she meandered through Burton Wood. In fact, quite the opposite: Cameron had been well known at Rixley for always taking the time to consider the facts and make fair judgements. Despite his strict and rather detached manner, Mary had discovered the gentle, generous side to his nature and an intensity that she hadn't expected. Nothing would ever come between them, he'd vowed; he would always love her and cherish her, come what may.

How sweet that had sounded. Whispered words and close embraces. His touch, the light of love in his eyes.

But war could come between all people of any race, class or creed. She and Cameron courted death on a daily basis, along with every other serving sailor, soldier or airman as well as those in civilian life – just ask the Londoners who had taken refuge in underground stations during the Blitz or the current residents of Frankfurt, Dresden and Berlin. War had snatched Cameron away from her to RAF Aireby and now to who knew where? *But please, not back to Bomber Command!* In the quiet stillness of the wood, Mary tilted her head back and closed her eyes, breathing in the green smell of the earth in spring.

'Now then, Mary; what's up?' Stan found her standing motionless beneath the trees. He'd dropped off some gardening tools – a fork and a pair of shears – at Fern Cottage and was on his way back to the ferry pool to carry out some checks on the PR Spitfire 4 that Jean was due to fly to Walsall later that afternoon. The reconnaissance Spit had a Priority One attached to it and Stan knew it had to be blacked up and made ready for clandestine ops before take-off. 'What are you doing out here all on your own?'

Stan's voice made Mary jump. She drew a sharp breath as she opened her eyes and saw him. 'Why? There's no law against it,' she answered defensively.

'Steady on there.' She was in one of her prickly moods. 'No need to bite my head off.'

'Sorry.'

Stan had been about to walk on but then changed his mind. 'What's wrong? Did I catch you at a bad time?'

Mary nodded. Her body quivered and she found she was unable to speak. *I can't cope if you're nice to me*, she thought.

'I saw Cameron's car at the Grange earlier.'

She nodded again. Stan took another step forward; his broad face was close to hers and looking serious for once.

'Did you two have a row?'

'No.'

'What, then?'

'Cameron might have to move further away to a new posting,' she said plaintively.

'Ah.' He could see her fighting back tears. Her hand trembled as she swept her hair from her face. She had no idea how beautiful she was. That was one of the things Stan liked about Mary: that she wasn't vain. 'Come here.' He opened his arms and waited.

'Oh,' she sobbed. With a sudden loss of control she collapsed against him, and felt his arms close around her as she leaned her head on his shoulder. Her cheek was against the rough tweed of his jacket. His hand stroked the back of her head.

'There,' he soothed. 'There, there.'

Mary's head reeled. She knew this ought not to be happening but seemed helpless to stop it. A pair of strong arms held her tight and she succumbed to Stan's softly whispered words.

From the window of the cottage Jean watched Mary and Stan embrace. She glimpsed them through the trees but said nothing to Douglas as he sat by the second-hand wireless trying in vain to tune into the station that would give them the latest news. He twiddled the knob to produce a hiss of static and a series of short, chirruping sounds.

Jean saw Stan hold Mary tight and stroke her hair. Mary raised her head. Stan kissed her on the cheek then on the lips. Jean stared in disbelief. She couldn't believe this of Mary, whose devotion to Cameron had never previously been in doubt. What was behind this secret embrace? How was it possible?

In the cottage kitchen Douglas gave up on the wireless. He switched it off with a sigh and a click. 'Shall I make us a cup of tea?' he asked.

Viv had never seen a woman try so hard to make herself invisible as Anna Janicki did during her first few days at Burton Grange.

She would be seen kneeling in the entrance hall, head bent, scrubbing the black-and-white tiles, or on the stairs with dustpan and brush. The smell of beeswax signalled Anna's presence in the officers' mess or the library and there she would be, polishing away, dressed all in black, refusing to look up from her work. She ate alone in her room and stayed there in the evenings, never emerging to exchange pleasantries in the bar.

Once or twice Viv had tried to engage her in conversation – 'Hi, Anna; how are you today?' or 'Great weather for a change' – as she set out for the ferry pool.

She had received not so much as a heavily accented 'I am well' or even a 'Yes' by way of response, so Viv had shaken her head, shrugged and gone about her day. But her curiosity was piqued – Anna Janicki must have a life beyond the Grange – family back in Poland, perhaps, and connections with the Parsevals, for sure. Viv must remember to call Giles and ask a few questions about how and why Anna had landed in this neck of the woods.

'There's one thing I know for sure about our new housekeeper,' she said out of the blue to Hilary when she ran into him outside Hangar 2 on the Wednesday following Anna's arrival. Viv was between hops, ferrying Class 2s from Rixley to Lancaster. 'No one should have to work as hard as she does: sweeping and dusting that enormous place from top to bottom. Why can't you get her some help?'

Hilary was taken aback. He hadn't thought Viv was the type to pay much attention to the ins and outs of Anna's domestic duties. 'She doesn't complain,' he pointed out. A glance inside the hangar told him that an Amazon truck was about to tow Viv's next aircraft on to the runway: a Mustang P-51 bound once more for Lancaster. So he drew Viv away from the door and spoke above the chug and whine of the truck's engine. 'Not to me, at least,' he added.

Viv lowered her parachute pack to the ground then eased her shoulder by rotating it forward and back. 'I get the impression that Anna wouldn't complain even if she were at death's door.'

'So what exactly is the problem?'

Viv's attention was taken by the Mustang at close quarters. She liked its frameless, rounded windscreen – an ultra-modern touch from the American team of designers – but wasn't so keen on its reputation for poor high-altitude performance. And, thanks to the large-capacity fuel tanks in its belly, it lacked the sleek elegance of its sister Class 2, the matchless Spit. 'Huh?' she said when Hilary asked the same question a second time. 'The problem is that the house is too big for one person to manage,' she insisted. 'Surely the Parsevals can afford to pay for extra help.'

'They're not in charge of the purse strings.' Hilary looked more closely at Viv – beneath the Sidcot suit and leather helmet was a woman who was not afraid to voice her opinion on any subject whatsoever.

'Who is then?' The ground crew unhitched the Amazon from the Mustang then began final checks.

'Me,' Hilary informed her. 'I oversee expenses here on the base and at the Grange.'

'Then problem solved!' With a clap of her hands, Viv magicked up a solution. 'Employ another cleaner, the sooner the better. I can find someone for you if you like.'

'Where?'

'From the village. Let me talk to the landlady at the Fox; she'll definitely be in a position to hand over a few names.'

'Not so fast.' Hilary needed time to do the arithmetic and to think this through. 'I should point out that, from what I've seen, Anna might not appreciate what you propose.'

Oh, for heaven's sakes! The man was such a stuffed shirt; why couldn't he loosen up once in a while? 'Still, I'll ask Florrie tonight,' she proposed quickly.

'No, not tonight.' Hilary's face showed signs of irritation. 'Though Sir Thomas doesn't bear the expense of hiring an additional housemaid, it's a matter of common courtesy to keep him and Lady Jane informed.'

Lady Jane Parseval: Giles's mother and the sad woman in the emerald-green dress in the painting in Bluebeard's room. No blood on the floor, but definitely out of bounds – Giles had made that absolutely clear. Lady Jane above all people must know how many servants it had taken to keep the Grange ticking over. 'She'll say yes, won't she?'

'I can't possibly tell.' Hilary's face gave nothing away. In fact, he'd only ever had two brief conversations with Sir Thomas's wife and was aware of her reputation as something of a recluse. He noticed that Gordon had climbed down from the Mustang's cockpit and was beckoning to Viv. 'Leave the matter with me,' he instructed as she picked up her parachute pack then set off towards the runway. 'And remember: don't mention it to Anna until I've come to a definite decision.'

Yeah, right, Viv thought, climbing into the cockpit and settling into the pilot's seat to begin her pre-take-off checks. *I'll wait till Domesday for that to happen.* So she hatched another plan: she would get on the blower to Giles as soon as she got this crate off her hands and found a phone booth where she could make the necessary call. *Lancaster and all points west, here I come!*

CHAPTER EIGHT

The met boys warned of heavy rain later in the day but still the ATA pilots gathered in the ferry-pool canteen on the morning of Friday 24 March, determined to fly at all costs.

'Frankfurt bought it good and proper again last night.' Horace Jackson shared the latest news with his fellow junior officer, Agnes Wright, over a breakfast of bacon and eggs. He spoke against the background hum of conversation in the crowded Nissen-hut canteen, uncertain whether to celebrate the British offensive or to feel sorry for the poor bastards who'd been bombed to smithereens in their own homes.

'It's them or us,' Agnes pointed out. She was a Londoner with little sympathy to spare for the citizens of Frankfurt. 'We took our fair share at the start of the war. "Kill without pity or mercy"; those were Hitler's orders.'

A slight young man with an already receding hairline, Horace was the cautious, risk-averse type who invited a certain amount of scorn among fellow pilots. He lacked initiative and was the opposite of the dashing, archetypal Douglas Bader airman held so dear by the British public. 'Still,' he said between mouthfuls, 'you have to wonder if two wrongs ever make a right.'

'You might but I don't.' Agnes scraped back her chair and left Horace to what she considered to be his nigh-treasonous reflections. She marched across the room to sit with Olive and Dotty Kirk from the met room, passing a corner table occupied by Jean, Mary, Bobbie and Viv.

'Cheer up, Agnes,' Bobbie called after her. 'It might never happen.'

'It already has – according to Horace.' Agnes sat down with her back to him, awaiting the Tannoy announcement for pilots to report to the ops room to collect their chits.

'"You are my sunshine, my only sunshine . . ."' Viv burst into ironic, lilting song at the sight of Horace's glum face.

'Leave the poor bloke alone,' Mary said. She winced when she spotted Stan at the table in the far corner then pretended that she hadn't seen him, a tactic she'd been employing all week. *That kiss was a big mistake!* She'd known it the moment it had happened. Regret had kept her awake most of the night – and each night since – and now guilt squatted heavily on her shoulders. She decided to go against Agnes and Viv by sticking up for Horace. 'He's entitled to get out of the wrong side of the bed once in a while.'

'By the way, Douglas and I had a four-legged visitor first thing this morning.' Jean changed tack with a tale that she hoped would cheer everyone up.

'Let me guess – a squirrel,' Bobbie suggested.

'Rabbit?' Mary added.

'Fox?' Viv asked.

130

'Wrong!' Jean was glad to have claimed their attention. Nerves seemed frayed this morning – Mary (no doubt with a guilty conscience) was studying her bowl of porridge without eating it, and Bobbie too seemed listless; only Viv had risen above the general gloom with her short, satirical burst of song. 'It was a dog.'

'Whose dog?'

'What kind of dog?'

'Was it lost?'

'A sheep dog; you know, a Border collie – without a collar. Douglas heard him whining and scratching at the door when he went down to make a cup of tea. He said he would drop him off with Florrie on his way to work.'

'Why Florrie?' Bobbie asked.

'Because if anyone in the village knows who it belongs to, she will.' Jean had come downstairs and given the stray dog a drink of water and some scraps of food left over from the night before. 'It didn't look lost exactly.' In fact, the collie had made himself at home on the kitchen rug until Douglas had encouraged him into his car with half a digestive biscuit.

The Tannoy system crackled and Gillian Wharton's voice made the announcement they'd been expecting. 'Will all pilots . . .'

On your marks, get set . . . Everyone sprang up and shot towards the door, leaving tea half-drunk and toast half-eaten. There was a scramble across the lawn towards the two-storey, concrete control tower and the first-floor ops room.

'What did you get?' Jean was immediately behind Bobbie in the queue that formed outside Gillian's hatch. She reported for duty, took her own slip and followed Bobbie down the concrete stairs.

'A Hudson, worse luck.' After five years of reconnaissance work, the light bomber was getting long in the tooth. If Bobbie remembered rightly, this Mark 4, without its ventral gun, was a rare type.

'Where to?' Jean read her own slip and saw that she'd got a Spit Mark 3 to Bristol.

'Coastal Command north of Bristol. It seems we're losing planes over the Atlantic hand over fist.'

'Bingo; me too.' She and Bobbie would fly over the Avon Gorge together, this time without the acrobatic display that Viv had put on for her benefit. Jean knew that her five-feet-three-inch, newly promoted first-officer friend was an excellent pilot but she had her head screwed on when it came to antics in the air. Bobbie had experienced too many near misses for it to be otherwise.

The two women walked purposefully towards Runway 1. They paused when Douglas hailed them from inside Hangar 2 then limped towards them.

'Florrie says the dog belonged to William Varley.' Douglas hastily passed on the information to Jean. 'That's the old man who lived in Fern Cottage until Christmas. After he died, the dog was taken to live with his sister near York.'

'How did it find its way back here?' Jean didn't have time to give it much thought. Instead, she walked on with Bobbie, who seemed to have something else on her mind. 'I'll see you in a couple of hours,' she assured her before she went to claim her Spit from Stan.

Bobbie nodded. Since the disturbing incident in the lane at Thresham the previous weekend, she'd heard nothing from Ray – no message, no apology on his father's behalf – nothing. His silence preyed on her mind and she longed to discuss it all with Jean, but it would have to wait. For now she must concentrate on the task in hand so she took out her Pilots' Notes and flipped through the pages. *Forget about Ray Moore,* she told herself briskly. *Forget about men in general; who needs them when there's flying to be done?*

'It's not looking too clever up there.' Stan glanced up at the bank of blue-grey clouds forming on the horizon.

Jean nodded but didn't comment. Instead, she watched Bob Cross screw down the Spit's port-side engine cowling. These days the young ATC mechanic looked the part in his oil-smeared overalls, with spanners and wrenches tucked into his back pockets – very different from when he'd first arrived at Rixley, innocence and inexperience personified.

'Get a move on,' Stan grumbled at his apprentice as he wiped his hands and wondered about Jean's offhand manner, which was most unlike her usual gracious self.

'She's all yours,' Bob told her as he jumped down to the ground.

'Good, then I'll be off.' Refusing Stan's offer of a leg-up on to the wing, she was soon ensconced in her pilot's seat and about to close the hood when she realized that Stan wanted to have a quick word.

'She's had her thirty-hour inspection check,' he called up. 'New oil filter, fuel pipes and prop spinners all checked and good to go.'

Still not trusting herself to be civil, Jean gave him

the thumbs-up then turned on the engine. She couldn't rid herself of the image of Stan and Mary in the wood, locked in an embrace – what had they been thinking, for goodness' sake!

'Run her to high revs, would you?' he yelled over the throaty sound of the Merlin. 'We need to check the prop constant speed unit and the magnetos before you go.'

So Jean sat tight and opened up the throttle while Stan and Bob lay down on the tail fins as human ballast. She watched the pair of mechanics in her overhead mirror, lying flat on their stomachs with their heads bent down against the force of the slip-stream as she increased the revs, until Stan raised his thumb and she was able to ease off the throttle.

But still he wasn't satisfied. As Jean idled the engine to avoid kettle-boiling, she saw him leap up on to the wing once more to give a final polish to the Spit's canopy. Every last speck of dirt must be removed.

He leaned in to purse his lips and blow on the Perspex then rub furiously with his soft cloth. His face was level with Jean's, with only the clear windscreen dividing them. *Close enough to kiss*, Jean thought, then she frowned. *Damn it; I ought to have said something either to him or to Mary about what I saw. Then again, I don't suppose it's any of my business.*

Affairs of the heart were complicated and who was she, Jean Thornton, to judge others? Meanwhile, she must tackle that lump of weather: climb up over the top then hope for a break in the clouds.

Viv found to her delight that her type for the day was the very latest Spit, all the way to Southampton and then back on an overnight train. Sure, there was a spot of bad weather in the offing, but this little beauty would be up and over it before she knew it. Viv practically sprinted on to Runway 1 in her eagerness to be in that brand-new cockpit and off the ground.

'Hold your horses,' Gordon warned as he saw her about to leap up on to the wing. She was a keen one, was Third Officer Robertson. 'You're at the back of the queue – Third Officer Wright and Second Officer Jackson are ahead of you.'

Viv dropped her parachute to the ground with a frustrated shrug.

'Why not go back to the canteen and have a cigarette?' Gordon suggested.

'No, I'll wait here and watch the experts.' As novice pilots with fewer than 200 hours under their belts, Agnes and Horace were hardly in Viv's league – hence the sarcasm.

Keen and a bit too big for her boots, Gordon thought as he checked the Spit's hydraulics. At this rate he doubted that Viv would win any prizes in the popularity stakes. All the blokes agreed she was a bloody knockout, though.

Viv folded her arms and leaned against her crate's bright blue fuselage, recalling how she'd put in the phone call to Giles from a booth outside the canteen at the Lancaster ferry pool the day before.

'I'm sorry, Mr Giles is not here,' she'd been told.

'OK, when will he be back?'

'I'm afraid I couldn't say.' She was obviously speaking to some type of manservant on the other end, most likely following orders.

'Can you pass on a message? Tell him Viv Robertson called and will call again?'

'Mr Giles may be away from home for some time.'

Oh, please – don't give me that!

There'd been a pause then a different, more superior female voice. 'Who is this speaking, please?'

Viv had given her name again, heard the long pause, and repeated it one more time. Then, 'Is that Giles's mother?' Not too wild a guess, as it had turned out.

But Viv had made the mistake of blurting out her mission to Lady Jane – 'Anna Janicki [*remember her?*] needs someone to help her at Burton Grange. That's OK with you, isn't it?'

No answer. There had been no outright refusal but there had been a click and then the line had gone dead. Honestly, these stuck-up Brits! The only saving grace had been that Viv had managed to strike up a short conversation with Anna herself first thing that morning. Having checked beforehand in a foreign-language dictionary in the library, Viv had made an admittedly lousy attempt at good morning in Polish. '*Dzień dobry*,' she'd said.

Anna had looked up from her cleaning on the staircase with the ghost of a smile.

'Hi, I'm Viv, all the way from Vancouver.'

'Anna, from Torzeniec in Poland.' Her voice had been deeper than expected, her eyes when they were directed straight at you dark and suspicious.

Nevertheless Viv had been encouraged. 'I sailed here in January on HMS *Kestrel*. How about you?'

'Through France then to England on boat.' Steady, cautious, eyeing Viv guardedly.

'By yourself?'

'Yes; alone.'

'I'm twenty-five. How old are you?'

'Twenty-five also.'

Viv hadn't noticed Hilary hovering at the top of the stairs. 'You worked for the Parseval family before you came here. How come?'

But Anna had spotted Hilary and her face had changed, as if a door had slammed shut. 'I must make clean,' she'd muttered, head down, polishing the brass stair rods. Shop closed.

What was the betting Hilary hadn't yet made a move towards hiring a girl from the village? But Viv had had the very clear impression that now was not the time to remind her squadron leader or to confess that she'd gone against his order not to interfere. After all, the short conversation with Lady Jane had not gone well. *Maybe later*, she'd thought as he'd rushed past.

If there was a complicated, slow way to do things, you could bet your bottom dollar that the Brits would find it, Viv reflected now as she stood by the runway.

'How long now?' She looked at her watch, itching to be out there judging the Merlin engine's roar, feeling the nose lift and the powerful kick as she eased the stick forward with the lightest of touches.

'Five minutes,' Gordon informed her.

Then, joy of joys, Viv would be free to fly.

'"From Hull, Hell and Halifax; may the Lord preserve us,"' Stan quipped as he handed over his third Spit of the day to Mary.

She'd divulged her destination north of Hull in an unadorned monosyllable, reluctant to meet his eye. Her nights of little sleep were taking their toll

137

and her legs had felt shaky as she'd walked across the grass towards her plane.

Stan, on the other hand, was delighted when he saw Mary approaching with her parachute pack. *Crikey,* he'd said to himself after the kiss in the wood, *I wasn't expecting that!* How long had he known her? Since May of the previous year – ten whole months without a single sign that she thought of him in that way. Mind you, Mary wasn't the flirting sort so a chap would always have to make the first move. To give Cameron his due, he'd been sharp enough to spot that. But now Stan was convinced that Mary and Cameron's cosy, lovey-dovey situation was changing – Mary said that the flight lieutenant might be on the move again and naturally she was upset about it. But out of sight was out of mind in Stan's simple book. With luck there would soon be a Cameron-shaped hole in Mary's life and he might just be the bloke to fill it.

'I said, "From Hull, Hell and—"'

Mary cut him off. 'I heard you the first time.' *Look him in the eye. Tell him you made a terrible mistake.* Oh, how she regretted the moment when she'd weakened and found herself sobbing into Stan's tweed jacket – madness, pure and simple. *Say you're sorry if you led him on; you didn't mean to.*

'Are you all right? You're looking a bit peaky.' Stan reckoned that she was feeling guilty. It was under-standable; indeed, it would have been worrying if Mary went around kissing all and sundry without developing a bit of a bad conscience. Anyway, he would tread carefully for a little while; pick up from where he and Mary had left off before The Kiss.

'I'm all right, ta.' She was anything but. Her head

was spinning, and when she hadn't been hating herself during the wee-small hours for kissing Stan she'd been frightening herself over Cameron choosing to go back into Bomber Command. Mary had imagined him spearheading sorties over Cassino or Frankfurt, Rome or Nuremberg in one of the Spits or Tomahawks that she and other Atta girls delivered to ferry ports along the south coast. As yet she hadn't heard a word from him and so everything was still up in the air.

'I do love you,' she'd vowed by the riverside. 'And I never want to let you go.'

'Bob and I have run through everything.' Stan guided Mary's attention towards the practical. 'We found a blockage in one of the vent pipes. It had been doped over by mistake. By rights the fitter in West Bromwich should've picked it up.'

Mary nodded her thanks. It was an important factory oversight; engine failure could have been the disastrous result.

'She's good to go and with luck you'll be back in time for tea.' Slapping the side of the fuselage as if the Spit were a horse, Stan helped her up into the cockpit.

Luck has nothing to do with it. Mary glanced at the clouds gathering over the runway. *Skill and judgement are what it's all about.* She would take off and straight away bank to port where the cloud looked less dense. She would prepare to climb and fly blind through cold, grey mist, fight any cross-currents, keep up the revs and keep on climbing until she emerged into clear blue sky.

I love you, Mary. Cameron's whispering voice came back into her head. He said these words every time they parted. It was how he signed off his letters – *I love you and I miss you with all my heart*.

'Maybe we'll have a drink at the Fox later on?' Stan looked up hopefully from the runway.

'Sorry, I'm busy tonight.' *Tell him!* Mary opened up the throttle. But somehow she couldn't make herself do it. Instead, she closed the hood without looking down.

She ran through her list as she taxied down the runway: *hydraulics, trimmers, throttle friction . . . flaps, gills, gauges*. She didn't turn to give Stan the final thumbs-up before take-off. *Check everything, prepare to fly through those clouds*. The first raindrops fell as Mary cleared the hedges then reached 200 feet. The windscreen blurred and visibility was quickly reduced. Still she continued her ascent without a backwards glance, with only her compass and altimeter to guide her on her way.

When Ray pulled up in the yard behind the Fox and Hounds in his MG that evening, he was surprised to see Giles standing by the back door with an elderly woman dressed in a flowered cross-over apron and stout lace-up shoes. They were talking earnestly and appeared not to notice his arrival.

'So everything is satisfactory?' Giles asked Florrie, who nodded. He towered over her but took care not to be abrupt and authoritative, as he might usually have been with women of her class.

Ray got out of the car and slammed the door. 'Giles, old boy – what brings you all the way up here?' He strode across the yard, pleased to see a familiar face.

'Remember: mum's the word,' Giles muttered sotto voce to the landlady. It was a hackneyed phrase that nonetheless ought to appeal to the old woman's sense of drama. He pictured with some amusement stacks of Agatha Christie and Daphne du Maurier novels on her bedside table. 'Ray!' Giles stretched out his hand with a nod and a smile. 'I might ask you the same thing.'

Ray shook the hand enthusiastically. 'You never mentioned you'd be in this neck of the woods this evening. Is something up?'

'Not a thing.' Giles felt in his jacket pocket for his car keys. 'There were one or two outstanding problems needing my attention, but they were easily sorted out; at the Grange, you know.' Enough said. He found the keys and dangled them ostentatiously in front of Ray's face. 'Sorry I can't stop.'

'Not even for a quick one?'

'No – much as I would like . . .' Giles made it clear that he was in a tearing hurry, stepping out of the narrow doorway and rattling his keys. 'Other commitments this evening; awfully sorry and all that.'

Ray watched Giles as he strode across the yard – tall, lithe and strong, like a middle-distance runner or a professional footballer, with his wayward lock of hair falling over his forehead. What could possibly be so urgent? Ray shrugged off the chance encounter and entered the building.

Jean and Bobbie had landed in Bristol without major incident. True, the Hudson had been a handful for Bobbie on landing – she'd approached at 290 mph and pulled the stick back as the ground rushed up

141

to meet her. Her crate's response had been more sluggish than she'd expected and the nose had jerked upwards to obscure her vision. She'd felt the Hudson bounce then settle as she'd hit the tarmac and there'd been a violent swing to starboard as she'd jammed on the brakes. A stamp on the rudder pedal had corrected the swing and Bobbie had emerged from the cockpit unscathed.

Jean had experienced no such difficulty in the easy-to-handle Spit, and she'd landed smoothly then met Bobbie in the canteen as arranged. They'd had just enough time for refreshments before collecting new chits to fly a Defiant apiece back to Rixley where they'd landed in time for tea.

'Would you believe it: the dog's come back.' Douglas emerged from his office to speak to Jean as she and Bobbie signed off at Gillian's hatch. He carried an untidy pile of typewritten pages and seemed preoccupied. 'I called in at home on my way back from Foxborough where I'd had a meeting and there he was, sitting on the doorstep large as life.'

'What did you do with him?' Jean asked.

'I was in a hurry so I left him there.' In truth, Douglas hadn't been sure quite what to do. Without wanting to admit it, he was developing a soft spot for the poor creature.

'I can take him back to Florrie's for you,' Bobbie suggested brightly. 'And have a drink while I'm at it.' Two birds with one stone – and a pleasant end to the week.

So it was agreed: Bobbie and Jean would walk through the wood together. Bobbie would pick up

142

the stray dog, leaving Jean at Fern Cottage to cook the evening meal.

Ray sat in the snug at the Fox nursing a pint of best bitter. He sipped it slowly, uncertain whether it had been a good idea to come in the first place. He was on a mission to apologize. Almost a week had gone by since the row with his father over Glasgow Girl. Ray had waited for the dust to settle at home before deciding what to do next. On the Sunday there'd been more yelling and shouting from his dad then the old man had suddenly dropped the matter. Everything was back to normal – there was a yard to run, races to be entered, feed to be ordered, the bank in Northgate to be visited so that wages could be paid. Derek had had all on to negotiate new terms with a dissatisfied owner and this had taken up much of his and Ray's week. Was it then too late for Ray to say sorry to Bobbie for his dad's behaviour? Shouldn't he simply call it a day?

But no, in his spare moments Ray had found himself thinking about the Scottish livewire more than was good for him. That girl could certainly ride. And there was something about her that fascinated him – a bright look, a quick movement of her head, a lovely, pale-skinned innocence. So, in the end, here he was in Rixley on a Friday night, supposing that he might run into her here in the pub where ATA officers were wont to congregate.

'Same again?' From behind the bar Florrie's eagle eye spotted Ray's empty glass.

He nodded then watched the landlady pull a fresh pint. To save her the bother of bringing it across to him, he went up to the bar and squeezed in between a bunch of rowdy mechanics still in their overalls.

At the same moment Bobbie tied up the black-and-white Border collie outside the entrance to the Fox and stood on the pavement watching the sky darken. There was a pale flush of pink in the west and she heard a train hiss and rattle along the track at the back of the pub. It must have been an express because it didn't stop at the village station but sped on in a cloud of white steam.

The startled dog gave a sharp bark. It strained at the rope tied around its neck as a temporary lead.

'Sit.' Bobbie spoke firmly and the dog obeyed. A hum of noise from inside told her that the pub was busy tonight. *Just a quick one*, she told herself as she straightened her jacket, fluffed up her hair then went inside.

'Look who it isn't.'

'Bobbie; come and join us.'

'Let me buy you a drink.'

Voices called to her from various corners of the crowded snug. There was a log fire blazing in the grate, oil lamps hanging from the beams, and the glint and chink of glasses and bottles at the bar.

'No thanks; I'll get my own.' Bobbie pushed through the crush at the bar. 'I'm returning one stray Border collie,' she reported to Florrie. 'And I'll have a Dubonnet and lemonade when you're ready.'

'Blasted dog,' the landlady grumbled. 'I turned my back for a second and there it was gone.'

'Well, I brought him back for you. He's tied up outside.'

Florrie took Bobbie's money and poured her drink.

144

'I tried to track down William Varley's sister in York, but no luck.'

'So what'll happen to the dog?'

'Maybe one of the farmers round here will want him.' Florrie was too busy to give the problem much attention. 'You sit down and have your Dew-bonnet.' She said the word to rhyme with 'sonnet' as she came out from behind the bar. 'I'll tie him up in the shed round the back and see what I can do tomorrow.'

Bobbie leaned forward to reach her glass.

'Here – let me.' Ray had seen her come in, still dressed in her pilot's tunic and trousers, her wavy, light brown hair ruffled by the wind. He was sure she hadn't noticed him so he'd had time to prepare himself. *Play it cool, smile nicely and hope that she doesn't storm off.*

Bobbie's heart skipped a beat. 'Ray – hello,' she murmured, instantly wishing that the ground would swallow her up. She must look a mess after her long day in the air.

'Sorry; did I make you jump?' She looked a little startled.

'Yes. What are you doing here?' He had every right, of course. 'Sorry . . .'

'I wanted to see you.' Ignoring the buzz of activity at the bar, Ray focused solely on Bobbie's confused blushes.

'You did? Yes, sorry; I—'

'No, it's me who should apologize.'

Bobbie's hand trembled as she raised her glass to her lips.

'Come outside where it's quiet?' Ray asked.

She nodded. 'I'll follow you.'

'Excuse us,' Ray said as he led the way. 'Thanks. Excuse us . . .'

They made their way on to the pavement and stood under the pub sign. It was almost dark. There was no sign of Florrie or the dog.

'That's better; a bit of peace and quiet.' Ray drew a deep breath. 'I meant to get in touch earlier in the week,' he began.

A car with blackout headlamps went past, two dim, horizontal slits lighting its way. There was the hoot of an owl and a fluttering swoop of its wings. It took Bobbie's eyes a while to grow accustomed to the darkness, but when they did she became aware of Ray gazing directly at her. The look made her more uncomfortable still.

'I wanted to say sorry about Dad. He was out of order.'

'Thank you. Let's forget it, shall we?'

'He's got a lot on his mind.' Damn it, this was going nowhere. It was obvious that Ray had embarrassed Bobbie all over again. 'Two of our owners left the yard this month. We're not sure how much longer we can make ends meet.'

She resisted saying that she was sorry to hear it; there had been quite enough apologies already. If only she'd made time to talk to Jean or Mary about the incident at the yard last Saturday, to straighten out her thoughts.

Forget about the father; do you like the son? Mary would surely have had a way of getting straight to the point.

Yes, but I like his horses better. Bobbie might have made a flippant reply to cover her confusion. Did

146

she – *could* she – like any man after Teddy Simpson? More to the point, would she ever trust them?

'It's no excuse for being rude to you, though,' Ray continued. 'I told Dad straight out. In the end I got him to back down and agree to your visiting Thresham and riding Glasgow Girl any time you like.'

'Honestly?' Bobbie wondered if this turnabout could possibly be true. In any case, did she want to run the risk of a second encounter with the appallingly rude Derek Moore?

Ray nodded unconvincingly. His father was an unpredictable, ignorant old so-and-so who drank a bottle of whisky a day. No need to tell Bobbie that, though. 'Hand on heart.' Ray led Bobbie down the street, away from the creaking pub sign towards St Wilfred's church. 'Or if you'd rather not come to the yard, we could go for a drive together; to the seaside, perhaps?' He held his breath for an answer.

Out of the blue another invitation landed at Bobbie's feet. Her heartbeat quickened again. 'I'm not sure, Ray.'

'About the seaside or about me?'

Either. Both. Which was the truth? She stopped by the church gate and stared across the graveyard to the square tower outlined against a jet-black sky.

Do you like the son? Mary's imaginary voice played on inside Bobbie's head. Ray continued to stare at her with quiet intensity. His eyes were a rich dark brown and his mouth had a natural upwards curve. *Yes*, she decided; *I do like him.* 'The seaside would be very nice,' she said quietly.

Ray smiled triumphantly and they walked on. Bobbie's acceptance had loosened his tongue and, unexpectedly, he began to tell her about his brief war service with the RAF, which had been brought to a sudden halt after a direct hit by a Messerschmitt – cockpit filled with smoke, fires in both engines, ending up in the chilly waters of the English Channel with pneumonia and three broken ribs. Ray ran through the events quickly with casual shrugs and smiles.

'I had no idea!' Bobbie was amazed. If she'd thought about it at all, she'd imagined that he had always been at Thresham helping his father to run the yard.

As they strolled on towards the grounds of the Grange, Ray decided to get the whole lot off his chest. 'I took the Messerschmitt pilot down with me – he was close enough for me to see the whites of his eyes before his plane blew up in mid-air. I'll never know why I made it and Jerry didn't.'

Coastal Patrol had picked Ray up but it turned out that he'd completely lost his nerve. 'Jitters, hallucinations – a hopeless case,' he confessed to Bobbie in the same light-hearted manner. 'The medical officer examined me and took me off front-line ops. Eventually I got "LMF" stamped on the front of my file – "Lacking Moral Fibre" – that's what the doc had me down as.'

Bobbie shook her head. 'You don't say,' she whispered again, grasping Ray's hand and drawing him to a halt.

'A write-off at twenty-five; how about that?' he asked almost jokingly, with no hint of self-pity. He'd told her the truth – let her do with it what she would.

Bobbie was puzzled. She couldn't understand why

Ray would want to make light of his situation or why he seemed to have landed back in civilian life without regret. Was it a front to hide what he really felt? 'You're not a write-off,' she told him. 'There's still a lot you can do.'

'Fire Warden or Home Guard?' he said with a laugh. 'Oh yes, I can see me volunteering for the Dad's Army.'

'I'm serious.'

'And so am I – as serious as I'll ever be.' Ray kissed her suddenly and briefly, then took her by the hand and they walked on together into the shadow of the wood.

CHAPTER NINE

'What do they say over here: that March comes in like a lion and goes out like a lamb?' Viv made small talk from the top of a stepladder that she and Anna had carried out on to the terrace at the Grange. The task this sunny Sunday morning was to wash the front windows of the ATA wing of the house – eight windows in all, each one ten feet high and divided into fifty small panes. Viv had counted them and done the arithmetic: that made a total of 400 fiddly panes of dirt-encrusted glass to clean.

It was far too much for one person so she had offered to help, and to Viv's surprise Anna had accepted.

'What I mean is, I like the British version of spring,' Viv went on as she took a damp chamois leather from Anna. '"Oh to be in England!"'

'"Now that April's there,"' Anna added. Then in response to Viv's questioning look, she told her, 'I was student of English Literature in Warsaw before war.'

'You're kidding!' Viv said above the squeak of the wet leather against the panes.

'No – serious.' Anna's face didn't change. 'My father was musician, my mother teacher. They wish me to read Shakespeare, Wordsworth, Charles Dickens.'

All this came as the biggest surprise to Viv; she couldn't wait to pass it on to Mary, Bobbie and Jean and watch the looks on their faces. 'Gee whiz!' she exclaimed. 'I'm impressed. So what do you think about the real thing?' Viv waved her free hands towards the sloping grounds where hosts of golden daffodils sunned themselves.

'Beautiful,' Anna said solemnly.

Viv threw down the chamois leather for Anna to catch then rinse in her bucket. 'Back in Vancouver my dad drives a truck, my mom stays home to take care of the kids. I have three younger brothers,' she said wistfully. 'That's why I ran away to join the circus – the flying variety; those three boys were driving me nuts.'

'Nuts?' Anna echoed. She handed back the leather then retied the flowered headscarf she'd worn when she'd first arrived. It was a sunny morning but the breeze was chilly.

'It means crazy,' Viv explained. 'I was heavily out-numbered in my house – one girl against three boys. How about you?'

'I have one sister – older.'

'Where is she now?' Viv climbed higher to reach the top panes. 'Did she get out of Poland in time?'

Anna turned away then flapped her arms and stamped her feet to ward off the cold. 'No,' she said softly. 'Mother, father, sister – all dead in Treblinka.'

Viv felt her heart thud against her ribs. The actual events behind Anna's flight from Poland hadn't hit home until this very moment; that's how thoughtless she was capable of being. So she came down from the top of the ladder and spoke quickly and ear-nestly. 'Forgive me, Anna – I shouldn't have pried.'

Anna acknowledged the heartfelt apology with a gentle nod. 'My father send me on train to continue studies in Paris before invasion – I am lucky.'

Viv didn't think it could be considered lucky to lose your whole family to the Führer's insane Final Solution policy. 'Oh my God!' she breathed, grasping Anna's hands. 'I am so sorry.'

Anna stared back without blinking. She didn't try to withdraw her hands. 'You are good person,' she said as softly as before. 'You help me.'

It was several seconds before Viv realized that Anna had gently closed the door on her tragic past and was referring to the window cleaning. 'Of course I do!' she blustered. 'I've already told Hilary that you can't do this all by yourself.'

'Thank you, but please, I go on alone. It is better.'

There was a force behind Anna's halting words that made Viv rethink her future tactics. Giving her thin hands one last squeeze, she climbed back up the ladder. 'You know something,' she began from the top step, 'as soon as we've finished here, you and I are going down into that butler's pantry and we'll do what the Brits all do.'

'What is that?' Anna picked up the heavy bucket and emptied dirty water down the nearest drain.

'We're going to boil that kettle and make ourselves a strong, sweet cup of tea.'

Jean picked daffodils from the bank sloping down to a stream that ran through the wood close to the cottage – she thought them such brave, bold blooms to fight through the previous autumn's decay to announce the arrival of spring. Carrying the flowers home, she put them into a green jug. They would take pride of place in the centre of the kitchen table. Glancing up from the sink, she saw Douglas stooped over and measuring out rows ready for planting onion sets. His white shirt was stretched taut across his broad back, his dark head was bowed. There he was; her husband, intent on what he was doing, not knowing that he was observed.

May this moment last. May we be free from harm.

The unspoken Sunday words wove themselves around Jean's heart.

There was a rustle in the bushes beyond the garden and Douglas glanced up. He heard a whimper and then saw a black-and-white shape appear at the gate. 'Jean, come and look,' he called through the open door.

She went out to see him stroking the stray dog's head. The creature looked up at him and wagged its tail hopefully.

'Not again.' Jean stood with her hands on her hips.

'He still thinks it's his home.' Douglas's injured leg made it difficult for him to crouch, so instead he sat on the brick path then put his arm around the dog's neck. 'I had one just like this when I was a boy – the same cock-eyed ears, one up, one down. He came everywhere with me.'

'But we can't keep him.' Jean could guess where this was going.

'Why not? No one else seems to want him.' The dog licked Douglas's hand. 'I haven't got anything for you,' he said with a smile.

In fact, Jean was stuck for a good reason to object.

'What if William Varley's sister shows up?' she offered doubtfully.

'She won't.' Douglas looked up at his wife with the hopeful eyes of a ten-year-old.

'How do you know she won't?'

'I just do. Anyway, this is where he belongs; don't you, boy?'

The dog wagged its tail furiously.

'See?'

Jean let out a sudden peal of laughter. 'Go on, then – have it your way!'

'Yes?' Douglas struggled to his feet, causing the dog to spin round in circles like a whirling dervish. 'You mean it?'

'Yes,' she laughed. 'Yes, yes, yes!'

He threw both arms around her and kissed her. The dog jumped up in a flurry of joyous yelps.

'Anything to keep you happy,' she whispered. A husband and now a dog. Planes to deliver. A war to be won.

Hilary was not a man you said no to, which is why Stan found himself at the Grange on his first day off in a fortnight, lying flat on his back under the squadron leader's car.

'Check the exhaust pipe for me; there's a good chap.' Hilary had collared Stan outside Hangar 1 and made him promise to bring his bag of tools to the stable yard on the Sunday morning. 'It's making a damned funny noise – could be the manifold, by the sound of it.'

Yes, sir! So here Stan was in his overalls, spanners at the ready, wishing he was anywhere else but there.

'Uh oh, and who do those legs belong to?' Mary spotted a pair of feet sticking out from under Hilary's car and spoke before she had time to think. Dressed in V-neck jumpers, woollen headscarves and corduroy trousers, she and Bobbie wheeled their bikes under the clock tower. They were fresh from an exhilarating ride around Rixley reservoir that had whetted their appetites and lifted their spirits at the end of another hectic week.

Stan slid out from under the car. 'As it happens, they're attached to me, Corporal Mechanic Stanley Green – at your service. Hello, Bobbie. Hello, Mary.'

'Hello, Stan – no rest for the wicked, eh?' Bobbie exchanged cheerful greetings and went to store her bike in the nearest disused stable.

Mary's face was already flushed from the fresh air and exercise but now its colour deepened. She mumbled hello and would have walked straight on but Stan deliberately blocked her path.

'What's up, Mary? Have you got the hump with me?'

'No, I . . .' she murmured with downcast eyes.

'Because I get the impression that you've been avoiding me lately – ever since—'

'Hush!' she begged with a nervous glance towards the stable that Bobbie had just entered.

'I'm sorry if I upset you,' he said quietly.

'It wasn't your fault. I don't know what came over me.' Mary's heart pounded and her head whirled. Now was the time to face what she'd been avoiding; to explain to Stan that the kiss had happened during a moment of weakness – that it had been a dreadful mistake. He was an important part of her life at Rixley: sensible and kind, steady as a rock.

Now she hardly knew where to put herself when he spoke to her.

'It won't happen again,' he promised. 'Not if you don't want it to.'

'I don't,' she told him quietly. 'No offence, but can we forget it ever happened?'

'If that's what you want,' he said with a frown.

'Yes; it's for the best. And please, you must promise to keep it to yourself. Will you do that for me?'

'What's it worth?' Stan's truculent question hung in the air.

Just then Bobbie reappeared at the stable doorway. 'Here, give me your bike,' she told Mary. 'I'll put it away for you.'

'No, I'll do it.' Mary wheeled her bike past Stan who stood with his feet wide apart and head to one side, as if waiting for a response.

'What was that all about?' Bobbie wanted to know after Mary had hurriedly stored away her bike then dashed up the steps to join her on the terrace. 'Have you and Stan argued?'

Mary stopped short of the main entrance. Her heart still raced after her conversation with Stan and the confession spilled unfiltered from her lips. 'If I let you in on a secret, you'll keep it to yourself?'

'I promise,' Bobbie assured her.

So Mary leaned against the stone balustrade and took a deep breath. 'I made a mistake – Stan and I kissed.'

'When – just then?' Bobbie's grey eyes widened. It was as if Mary had told her that the Martians had landed.

'No – last weekend.'

Bobbie took Mary's hand and led her to the wide steps that looked down over the front lawn. Then she spoke to her in a firm voice. 'Let's sit here and you can tell me how it happened.'

Mary sat down heavily. 'There's nothing to explain – we kissed in the wood near Fern Cottage. I was worried about Cameron.'

Bobbie said nothing but pulled her Good-Lord-above face.

'Don't ask me why I did it.'

'Who made the first move – you or him?'

'Both.' Mary spoke with a hoarse whisper. 'It wasn't Stan's fault. I was crying over Cameron's news that he might rejoin his old squadron.'

Bobbie thought for a while. 'Only a kiss?' she checked.

'Yes, but that's bad enough.'

'No, wait. A kiss is just a kiss. Perhaps you're reading too much into it.'

'Am I?' In the eight days since it had happened, guilt had dug deep under Mary's skin; eight silent days with no letter from Cameron. Mary had written twice to him but unusually had received no reply. There'd been no signing off with 'I love you and miss you with all my heart' – not a single word. Eight days of wishing she could wind back the clock and erase The Kiss.

'Yes – take me and Ray, for instance.' Staring out across the lawn which was pitted with bomb craters and sectioned off with barbed-wire barricades, Bobbie came out with a confession of her own. 'The same thing – we kissed but I have no idea how much it meant to either of us. No idea at all.'

The news dragged Mary out of her own dilemma.

She demanded to know the ins and outs – when did it happen, why and where?

'Ray came to Rixley on Friday – he's invited me to visit him at Thresham again.' Bobbie supplied the details. 'But you know me, Mary – I'm hopeless as far as men are concerned. I never know which ones to trust.'

Mary listened carefully. 'This Ray chap – do you like him?'

Bobbie flashed her a quick, bright smile. 'I knew you'd ask me that.'

'But do you?'

'I like certain things about him, yes.'

'Such as?'

'He smiles a lot. He's not too serious.'

'And?'

'He knows about horses.'

'But?' Mary sensed a hesitation.

'I can't work him out. On Friday he came all the way to Rixley to explain about his father's behaviour and to say sorry for the old man's rudeness. He told me a lot of private stuff about himself, which I won't go into.' Bobbie put up a hand to ward off further questions. 'Then out of the blue he kissed me and we went for a walk and he joked and teased again. That was after he'd invited me to go to the seaside with him. Then he left.'

'Without making a firm arrangement?'

'Not as such – just a cheery ta-ta for now. So you see: Stan and you, me and Ray – what do we make of it?'

'A little or a lot?' *Nothing or everything, or something in between.* 'If I were you, I wouldn't rush – I'd take my time.' Mary gave the best advice she could, based on the knowledge that Bobbie had yet to fully recover from Teddy Simpson. 'Work out what you like and don't like about Ray then see where it goes.'

'Thanks – I will.'

'And be yourself.'

Bobbie gave a grateful smile. 'Yes; that's what Angela always said. "Be yourself – a girl shouldn't change who she is for any man."'

'And she was right,' Mary agreed.

Bobbie and Mary sat on the step in companionable silence, their troubles lessened and their hearts eased after their talk.

'Shall we go inside?' Mary asked, after a few minutes of appreciating the golden fanfare of daffodils on the lawn and two sparrows scuffling and squabbling in a dusty corner of the terrace.

'Yes,' Bobbie agreed. They stood up then entered the house.

'Someone did a good job of cleaning these windows,' Mary remarked as they went inside.

The windows along the length of the terrace glinted in the sun. There was a smell of furniture polish on the stairs and not a speck of dust to be seen.

'Hello, Anna,' Bobbie said as she and Mary passed the housekeeper on the landing.

Anna dipped a small curtsey. 'Hello,' she replied with almost a smile.

'Still no letter from Cameron, I assume?' Bobbie had seen Mary checking the post before she'd set off on foot for the ferry pool. It was a cold Wednesday morning and Bobbie encountered her for a second time that morning as she zipped up her heavy-duty

Sidcot suit in the locker room by the control tower at Rixley. There was a buzz of conversation, a slamming of metal doors, and the usual sense of anticipation at the start of another working day.

'No, nothing.' Mary's fingers were all thumbs this morning. Her suit felt stiff and heavy as she walked out into the cold air with Bobbie. 'Brrr; frost at this time of year,' she complained with a shudder.

'And how are things with Stan?'

'The same.' *Awkward and embarrassing, to say the least.* 'You and Ray?' she asked Bobbie as Viv rushed by with her chit. 'Any word on your jaunt to the seaside?'

'Another new Spit,' Viv crowed. 'Boy, this is my lucky day!'

'No, I've not heard a thing,' Bobbie reported. 'I've decided to forget about him.'

'Easier said than done.' Mary was bound for Prestwick in a Class 3 light twin Blenheim. She said goodbye to Bobbie and had just taken out her Pilots' Notes for a quick recap when Hilary poked his head out of his office.

'A word,' he said to her in his offhand way.

What now? Had Mary done something wrong: filled out a snag sheet badly, for instance? If so, Hilary would be down on her like a ton of bricks.

'Sit down,' he told Mary when she went in. 'Now, I don't want you to go off the deep end when you hear what I have to say.'

'No, sir.' She sat warily on the edge of her seat, facing him across his desk. The coarse, stiff fabric of her flying-suit squeaked against the shiny metal chair.

'I want you to take this news in your stride.'

'Yes, sir.'

160

Hilary cleared his throat. 'Better to find out from me rather than hear it on the grapevine. It's about Cameron.'

He's leaving. He's gone already. He couldn't face telling me. Mary gripped the front edge of her seat and leaned forward.

'He's facing a court martial.' Hilary made no bones about it then waited for her reaction.

'That can't be right,' she said sharply. 'There's been a mistake.'

'No mistake. Cameron is being held in military prison at his training camp at Aireby. He's accused of misconduct. I'm afraid it's serious.' Hilary himself had scarcely been able to believe it when he'd received the phone call from Hubert Norris, head of the training programme there. Cameron of all people! 'He's charged with striking a fellow officer and knocking him unconscious.'

'It's not true.' It couldn't be. It didn't make sense. Mary gripped the seat more tightly.

'A chap called Don Bullen,' Hilary informed her. 'He's the one who brought the charge – American, apparently.'

Mary sat back suddenly to absorb what she'd been told. 'Yes, Cameron's talked about him. He doesn't like him.'

'Why, what has he said?' Hilary's tone grew more terse. 'No, never mind – don't tell me. And I'd keep that fact under my hat if I were you.'

'Yes, sir,' she murmured.

'I can see this has hit you hard. Do you feel able to fly or would you like me to remove you from today's rota?'

161

'No.' Mary stood up. 'No, sir; I'm quite all right.'

'You're sure?' Pilots continued to fly after receiving much worse news than this. Hilary remembered a flight lieutenant in his old squadron who had been told that his wife and new baby had both been killed during a raid on Coventry. The chap, who was called Jennings, had fallen down in a dead faint on hearing the news; then when he came round he'd insisted on carrying on as normal that day, piloting an Anson with seven top-brass passengers from Liverpool to Southampton. He'd chalked up eight kills after that before eventually being brought down by a damned Heinkel. The hood of his Wellington had jammed and Jennings had gone into free fall without a chance of getting out alive. That particular disaster certainly put Mary's present situation into perspective.

'Yes, sir, I'm sure.'

'I checked with Douglas; it's Prestwick in a Blenheim?'

'Yes, sir.' *Speak up, don't tremble; show him you can do this.*

'Olive will pick you up at your destination. She had to stay overnight in Edinburgh so she can drive you back via the training camp if you wish.'

'Yes please, sir.' *To Aireby to see Cameron, to find out the truth.* 'Thank you for that.'

'You're welcome, Third Officer Holland.' Mary had plenty of pluck; Hilary took her word for it that she could carry out her duties as planned. 'Now, by my watch you're five minutes behind schedule so please make your way to Runway Three double-quick.'

*

Instinct took over as Mary prepared to fly north in her Blenheim. She paid scant attention to the ground crew who readied her crate for take-off, simply climbing into the cockpit and strapping herself in without a word. She responded to Gordon's thumbs-up signal with a brief nod then ran automatically through her thirteen checks. Still dazed, she taxied down the runway then took off with scarcely a glance at her instrument panel. A quick look at her hand-held compass told her she was heading in the right direction.

'What's up with Mary this morning?' Gordon asked Stan during their tea break.

The two mechanics stood by the canteen door smoking Woodbines and staring up into a cloud-less sky.

'Why? Was she in one of her moods?' Stan had only seen Mary from a distance, staring fixedly ahead as she'd approached her aircraft. He'd noticed that her take-off hadn't been as crisp as usual.

'You can say that again.' Gordon threw down his cigarette then ground it underfoot. 'Women, eh?' he said as he made his way to Hangar 2.

Once airborne, Mary was forced out of her daze. The ground below was divided by neat hedges into brown, ploughed squares, with the curves and indents of the coastline visible to the east. The blue sea reflected the colour of the sky and was fringed by white waves breaking on the shore.

I'm sure it's a mistake. Her hand was steady on the stick as she dabbed the rudder pedal to steer north. Before she knew it, she'd be past Carlisle and well on the way to her destination. *After the dust has settled, everyone will realize that it can't possibly be true. Cameron would never get into a fight without good cause.* This conviction shored Mary up as she spotted the Ribblehead Viaduct and from there followed the railway line north. It occurred to her that the ferry pool she was heading for was often referred to as the Naughty Boys' Pool, because it was a tricky place to fly into and out of so only the toughest, most experienced pilots did it with ease.

Luckily today the weather was decent, with good visibility as Mary approached the narrow Dumfries Valley, so she decided not to skirt around the western side (a safer but longer option) but to fly up the valley itself. The entrance was wide at the start but grew narrower until there was no room to turn around if you suddenly hit a lump of cloud. *Fingers crossed*, Mary thought as the mountains to either side crowded in.

Luckily for her, the weather held and she was able to immerse herself in the bleak beauty of her surroundings. She flew past dark, rocky tors and white, tumbling streams, through the dramatic neck of the valley and out the far side where she breathed a sigh of relief. ATA pilots had occasionally been caught out by cloud and crashed into those mountainsides. In fact, an accident report had been posted on the Rixley ferry-pool noticeboard since Mary's conversion from driver to pilot – '12 November 1943. Hurricane JS346. Flight Captain Gerald McArthur. Near Langholm, 9.30 hours, aircraft flew into hill, the pilot having persisted too far into hilly country in bad weather contrary to orders.'

Not today, thank goodness. Mary pressed on towards her destination where she found Olive waiting with a tank full of petrol for the drive south.

'I'll park here by the sentry box,' Olive told Mary when, after a long, mostly silent drive, she dropped off her passenger at the Aireby training camp. Something was obviously eating away at Mary, though Olive didn't know what. Anyway, she didn't have the energy to try to find out; she had driven 400 miles in two days so she was completely done in and not in the mood to talk any more than Mary was. It had reached six o'clock in the evening and bed was what Olive wanted, not small talk.

'I won't be long,' Mary promised as she closed the car door and approached the younger of the two sentries manning the entrance. She didn't have time to state her business and show her identity card before he lifted the barrier and ushered her through.

'It's all right, I know who you are,' he explained, quickly examining her card for form's sake. 'We were expecting you. Group Captain Norris gave orders to escort you to the prison wing.'

Mary assumed that Hilary had been on the phone to his fellow officer and was grateful for this. She walked with the sentry away from the tall wire boundary fence towards a large gravelled quadrangle surrounded by green wooden huts, and from there towards a flat-roofed, two-storey concrete building with small, barred windows – the military prison where Cameron was held. The prison block backed on to a stand of tall, dark pine trees with glimpses of open moorland beyond.

'Wait here, please.' The young sentry left Mary at the door.

'Third Officer Holland from Rixley ferry pool, here to see the prisoner,' Mary's escort reported to the guard in a half-broken, squeaky voice.

There was muttering then some shifting of chairs and the sound of a key turning in a metal lock. Mary clenched her fists in an effort to control her nerves.

The sentry reappeared. 'You can go in,' he told her.

She stepped back into the nightmare she'd experienced when Hilary first gave her the news that morning, crossing the threshold to find Cameron sitting behind a bare trestle table, his hands resting on its rough surface, his head bent forward. The room was no more than six feet square. Its walls were painted dun and dark brown; the floor was bare concrete. A burly guard stood to attention by the metal door that led into the cell where Cameron was held. The guard's eyes swivelled towards Mary as she went in, then back towards the rear view of the prisoner's head.

For a split second she hesitated, then she edged forward and sat on the chair facing Cameron. 'How are you?' she gasped.

He looked up at her without fully raising his head. 'I'm all right. It's good to see you.'

She reached across the table to touch his hands but he quickly withdrew them on to his lap.

'Hands on the table,' the guard ordered with one eye on the clock on the wall behind Mary.

She winced. Cameron looked dreadful – his creased uniform had obviously been slept in and he was unshaven. He was without his glasses and the

166

shadows under his eyes seemed darker. They were reluctant to hold her gaze. 'Don't worry, you'll soon be out of here,' she whispered.

'Speak up.' The guard again, like a dog barking.

'You will,' she insisted. 'Once they know the truth of what went on, they'll let you go.'

'It's good to see you,' Cameron repeated with a warning glance over his shoulder.

Mary realized that, with the guard listening to every word that passed between them, she must avoid talking about the charge. She nodded slowly then grasped his hand. 'Olive drove me all the way down from Prestwick. I was permitted to visit, thanks to Hilary.'

'You must be tired.' He clasped her hand and breathed deeply.

'Yes, a bit.'

'Did you fly up the valley?'

'I did,' she admitted.

Cameron gave a faint smile. 'I knew you would have.'

'There was no cloud.'

'Even so.' His grasp grew tighter and for the first time he looked straight into her eyes. 'It's a risk.'

'But it saves on petrol.' The presence of the guard in the claustrophobic space was almost overwhelming. His expressionless eyes kept on turning in Mary's direction as she struggled for safe, inconsequential things to say. 'Jean and Douglas have adopted a stray dog. Oh, and Bobbie has struck up a friendship with a chap whose father trains racehorses.'

'Good for her.'

'And good news – it turns out that Viv Robertson

is one of the best pilots around. I told you about her – you remember? She's Canadian. She's stepped into Angela's shoes as the ATA glamour girl.'

'You're *my* glamour girl.' Cameron glanced over his shoulder again as if challenging the guard to contradict him. Thank heavens Mary had come and reminded him there was a world out there beyond his cell walls. He drank in every detail – her chestnut brown hair, tucked up under her forage cap; her warm hands holding his; her clear grey eyes that held so much meaning.

'You must meet Viv.' Mary was still convinced that the court martial was a mix-up and that Cameron would soon be released. 'But be prepared: she's not everyone's cup of tea.'

He nodded. 'I look forward to making up my own mind once I get out of here.'

'Soon,' she assured him. Even if it did get as far as the courtroom, Cameron would defend himself cleverly and calmly. He would be believed and that would be the end of it.

All too soon the clock's minute hand reached the hour. 'Time's up.' The guard stepped forward.

Mary pursed her lips and grasped Cameron's hands more tightly.

'I have to go,' he murmured.

'Is there anything at all I can do – anyone I can talk to?'

'No.'

'Hilary – can he help us?'

Cameron felt the guard's meaty hand on his shoulder. 'No; I got myself into this mess so it's up to me to get myself out again.'

'Time.' The guard's steely gaze rested on Mary, who slowly got to her feet.

'Try not to worry too much.' In a misjudged attempt to keep the mood positive, Cameron missed his opportunity to lean across the table and kiss Mary goodbye. The guard's hand slid from his shoulder to the small of his back and he felt himself being propelled from the room.

'I'll try.' With a sinking heart Mary watched him go. *I do love you – you know I do!* She hadn't said the words, here in this soulless, airless room, but she would write them in a letter and post it first thing tomorrow morning. And she would talk to Hilary anyway; her commanding officer would be able to uncover more details about the case and help her understand how the court martial would work.

So Mary left the prison block and set off across the quadrangle towards the gate. A class in one of the green huts had just finished and a bunch of cooped-up RAF cadets poured out into the courtyard. A dozen or more young men and their instructor followed Mary's progress across the open space. There were wolf whistles and a few calls of 'Hello, what's a pretty girl like you . . . ?', much jostling for position and some cruder comments about the visitor's vital statistics.

'OK, you guys.' The instructor stepped forward to take control. He was tall and trim and there was no mistaking his American drawl. 'Cut that out. I said, cut it out!'

One of the recruits had been elbowed sideways and he staggered across Mary's path; a gawky lad with a large nose and narrow-set eyes. 'Sorry, miss,' he croaked as his instructor yanked him upright and thrust him back against the wall.

Mary ignored him. She stared at the American who was over six feet tall with short dark hair and light blue eyes. There was no doubting it: this was Cameron's accuser, Don Bullen.

'Ma'am, I apologize.' Bullen's deep, slow voice silenced the recruits, who shuffled off sheepishly in different directions. He looked closely at Mary's flushed face then glanced in the direction of the prison block, pushing out his bottom lip as he realized the probable reason for her visit. 'They were just fooling around,' he said by way of explanation for the trainees' raucous behaviour. 'I truly am sorry if they bothered you.'

Perhaps naively, Mary had expected someone different from this mannerly, strikingly handsome airman. In her mind's eye the oil magnate's son ought to have swaggered and pushed his weight around, not offered an elaborate apology on behalf of his recruits. 'They didn't bother me,' she said stiffly.

'Good, I'm mighty glad to hear that, ma'am.'

Bullen plainly wasn't stupid – he'd seen her come out of the prison block and must have guessed who she was, so why carry on with this display of good manners? Mary decided to cut to the chase. 'You're the man who brought the charge against Cameron.'

'And you're his lady friend.' The blue eyes held steady and the response, apart from a hesitation as he sought for the right word to describe her, gave little away. Oddly, his features scarcely moved as he talked, giving his face a somewhat mask-like appearance.

'I'm Mary Holland,' she acknowledged.

'Don Bullen, at your service, ma'am.' He was completely at ease as he indicated that he would escort her to the gate. They walked slowly, hands clasped behind their backs, looking straight ahead. 'There was no build-up to the fight, by the way; whatever Flight Lieutenant Ainslie says in his defence. The guy hates me pure and simple; he came at me out of nowhere and socked me on the jaw – end of story.'

'He wouldn't do that.' Mary flashed Bullen a defiant sideways look.

'Believe me, he did.'

They reached the gate where one of the sentries prepared to raise the barrier and Olive sat waiting in the car. 'Believe you?' Mary stopped and turned towards the Texan. 'That's just it; for me to believe you I'd have to admit that Cameron was lying. That's why I'm sure that it was something you said or did that brought this on.'

Bullen unclasped his hands then thrust them deep into his trouser pockets. He rocked back on his heels. 'That's not how the witnesses see it,' he informed Mary in his long, lazy drawl. 'Yeah, that's right – luckily there are half a dozen wannabe wireless operators and air observers ready to testify that I never laid a finger on Flight Lieutenant Ainslie; swear to God and hope to die.'

CHAPTER TEN

Four weeks into her time with the ATA, Viv was no longer sure why she'd chosen this topsy-turvy existence in the Yorkshire outback: one moment soaring through the air at 400 mph in a gleaming killing machine, the next planting potatoes to feed the Rixley troops. Call it loyalty to King and country and leave it at that.

'You do get stuck in – I'll say that for you.' Ernest voiced his approval as he stood in the greenhouse entrance. He'd been pricking out tomato seedlings and replanting them in rows of terracotta pots before watering them in. But as soon as he'd seen Viv arrive with her spade, he'd downed tools for a chat with one of his favourite Atta girls.

Viv went on digging a deep, straight furrow. 'I might as well make myself useful,' she said cheerily. Dig for victory, fly a Spit into the face of the enemy – it all came down to the same thing.

'It's Friday night. Why aren't you getting dolled up for a night out?'

She paused to lean on her spade. 'Why, Ernest; is that an invitation?'

The veteran of the Great War laughed. 'I'd ask

you out like a shot if I was twenty years younger, but I'm not – more's the pity.'

'Oh, come on – I bet you have a couple of pretty girls hidden away in the village.' As always Viv enjoyed playing along. 'A good-looking guy like you.'

'Aye, back in the day . . .' Before the first war, when he'd been young and fit. The trenches had put paid to that. 'You're a fine one to talk, Third Officer Robertson. I've seen the way the fellows look at you. I'd bet a week's wages that it won't be long before one of them has snapped you up.'

'Let them try.' She laughed back at him before thrusting her spade into the clean earth.

'There's Horace Jackson for a start. And if he's not exciting enough for you, Gordon Mason might be more your cup of tea. He's a man of the world, right enough.'

'Not my type,' Viv assured him. She hadn't changed her opinion of Gordon as the sort to wine and dine a girl and then move on. No thank you – she'd come across plenty of men like him while working on the Hollywood lots. Anyway, wine was in short supply in the north of England and any dining was likely to be done on sausage and mash.

Ernest watched a while longer. If he'd had a daughter he would have liked her to turn out like Viv – lively, game for a laugh and bloody lovely. 'I was talking about you earlier,' he informed her. 'I expect your ears were burning.'

'Talking, who to?' Viv's spade hit a large stone and she stooped to unearth it.

'To Florrie Loxley, as it happens. She said you called in at the Fox last night.'

173

'That's right, I did.' She'd downed a couple of pale ales – she was acquiring quite a taste for it – and pestered the landlady again to see if she knew of any female who might help out at the Grange. In doing do she'd ignored Hilary's warning, Lady Jane's sharp words over the telephone and Anna's plea for her not to interfere – quite a battery of disapproval, all told.

'Poking your nose in, according to Florrie.'

Viv stopped digging. 'Only because Hilary hasn't done a darned thing about it and Anna doesn't have the confidence to stand up for herself. I don't think it's right that she doesn't have any help.'

Ernest nodded. 'Maybe you have a point. Then again, maybe you should leave well alone.' He looked directly at her to drive home his point.

'Honestly, I don't get it.' Viv felt increasingly as if she were hitting her head against a brick wall. 'First Hilary, then Florrie and now you. You'd think somebody would stand up for Anna after all she's been through.'

Ernest frowned and took a step backwards. 'Nay, I know nowt about that.'

'She's a refugee, for Christ's sake. The rest of her family didn't get out of Poland in time; that's what. And Florrie has a nerve, telling me to keep my nose out.' Viv let her mouth run ahead of her more considered thoughts as per usual.

'Florrie's not to blame.' Ernest retreated to his row of seedlings inside the greenhouse and Viv followed. 'She was only pointing out the truth, which is that Anna Janicki should count her blessings.'

Now Viv was seriously mad with the pub landlady, the hub of all Rixley gossip. She was still on the warpath as she followed Ernest down the central aisle of the long glasshouse. 'So now it's a blessing to work your fingers to the bone?'

'At least Anna has a job, thanks to the Parsevals.'

Viv gave a grunt of disgust. 'But have you seen her room? It's more like a dungeon. A person should be able to see fields and trees out of her window, not just blank walls. And have you ever watched Anna eat a good, square meal? No, neither have I. It's my belief she lives on thin air.'

'I don't hear her complaining, do you?' Ernest lined up more pots then filled them with compost. Then, dibber poised above the first pot, he gave Viv another of his direct, no-nonsense stares. 'Like I said, leave well alone. That was Florrie's advice to me and that's what I'm passing on to you – for your own good as much as anything.'

Viv balled her hands into fists. 'What's Hilary going to do – line me up against the wall and shoot me along with anybody else who disobeys his orders?'

'That's not funny,' Ernest muttered. 'And it's beside the point.'

'Sorry – yes. But it drives me nuts, the way everyone overlooks Anna's point of view.' Disregarding the fact that this might be exactly what she herself was continuing to do, Viv stomped back outside to resume her labours: heaving soil, finishing her trench.

Ernest remained in his greenhouse and adjusted his opinion of the Canadian beauty. Lively was fair enough, but this Anna Janicki business smacked of stubbornness. Someone else should have a quiet word in Viv's ear – Bobbie or Mary, or better still, Jean. Popping a seedling into the hole he'd made, he resolved to mention it to Flight Captain Thornton the very next time he saw her. Jean, if anyone, would be the one to make Viv see sense.

'Surprise!' Giles strolled into the hallway of the Grange as Viv came down the stairs, still disgruntled after her earlier disagreement with Ernest. He was impeccably dressed in his Savile Row suit with gold cufflinks and a pale blue silk tie.

Boy, oh boy; he's the finished article! Viv surveyed him from a distance. Neat and polished to the tips of his fingernails, with that understated elegance unique to the English upper class. 'Giles, what are you doing here?'

'You mean, "Giles, how very nice to see you. My day has suddenly improved immensely."'

'You flatter yourself,' she remarked with a pronounced pout of her full lips. Nevertheless, she paused at the bottom of the stairs to see where this conversation might lead.

'Tell me, Vivienne, how has your social life been since we lunched together at the White Hart?' Giles seemed in no hurry to resume whatever it was he'd been doing. He stood by the door leading into the room that had been declared out of bounds, appreciating the outdoor, gypsy look that Viv seemed to have adopted – a white blouse with gathers at the neck and a row of red embroidery around the hem, plus navy blue trousers and a pale blue scarf from which wisps of black hair escaped at the nape of her neck and temples.

'Lousy,' Viv declared. 'I've been too busy learning the ins and outs of the Mark Nine, making sure she doesn't stall at low altitude, which she has a tendency to do, believe me. You know she has the highest value of all the fighter planes – that's why we have to keep moving the Nines about from base to base, to keep Jerry guessing.'

'Fascinating,' Giles said, implying the opposite.

She smiled mischievously as she continued to blind him with science. 'The great thing is, I feel part of that Spit, settling in the pilot's seat snug as a bug, taking her up and turning her and feeling that G-force. You know that her Merlin Sixty-one engine has twenty per cent more power than the previous model? Take her up to fifteen thousand feet and you feel that automatic boost from her engine like a kick in the seat of the pants. And you know what: a Nine can sneak up behind a Focke-Wulf 190 or an Me109G and let them have it without them even knowing that she's there.'

Putting up his hands in a gesture of surrender, Giles backed into the room from which he'd emerged. But as he did so he stepped on the toes of an older man coming to find out where he'd got to.

'Mind where you're going,' the grey-haired man snapped. He was an older version of Giles – tall and erect, impeccably dressed in country tweeds, effortlessly imposing his presence – and so there was no doubting the father–son relationship. 'Come and give me a hand with these boxes.' Glancing across the hall, Sir Thomas noticed Viv and was about to dismiss her as a gardener's assistant or perhaps a stray Land Girl who had somehow wandered on to the estate.

'Father, I'd like you to meet Vivienne Robertson, a pilot with the ATA.' Giles stepped in smartly with the introductions.

'Aha, my Sunday name again!' she said brightly. 'My hands are filthy from digging so I won't offer to shake.'

'Quite.' Sir Thomas arched an eyebrow and his own hands remained firmly at his side. 'Do I detect an American accent?'

'Canadian,' Viv and Giles corrected him simultaneously.

'Ah, I have a cousin who emigrated to Canada shortly after the Great War.' Sir Thomas warmed a little to the untamed beauty standing before him in stockinged feet. He could see why Giles had been distracted from the task in hand. 'I understand that Lionel has set up a successful logging company in Quebec.'

Viv nodded affably. 'We have plenty of trees where I'm from, that's for sure.'

'And how are you finding England?'

Managing to swallow the heavy condescension that accompanied the question, Viv shot off a flippant reply. 'A, it's cold; B, it rains a lot; C, the food isn't up to much; D, the natives are friendly on the whole . . .'

'Quite.' Sir Thomas's thin lips stretched into an unconvincing smile. 'Come along, Giles – these boxes won't lift themselves.'

'Here, let me help.' Viv hurried after them into the Wedgwood room to find that all the pictures had been taken down from the walls, leaving oblong patches of darker, original blue. The boxes of toys had been shifted closer to the door.

'There's no need,' Sir Thomas insisted. 'Giles and I can do this between us.'

'Or I could run and fetch Ernest?' she suggested. The boxes looked heavy – an extra pair of hands would definitely be an advantage. 'He's working in the greenhouse.'

'Good idea.' Giles reacted quickly. 'But you stay where you are – I'll go.' He left before objections could be raised.

'Where are you taking all this stuff?' Viv's curiosity carried her forward. She lifted the lid of the nearest box to reveal the flimsy tutu. 'I'm guessing that whoever wore this is through with learning ballet. I bet she's more into jitterbugging these days.'

Without replying, Sir Thomas pointedly closed the box.

Viv felt that the intervention had been more forceful than necessary but she put it down to the old man's impatience to get on with the job. Her gaze fell on the portrait of the dark-haired girl in the blue dress, which was propped against a wall in front of the picture of the sad-looking woman in green. 'Giles and his sister were lucky kids, having these things to play with and living in a house like this. It's a pity the bombs did so much damage; it'll cost you a fortune after the war to rebuild that wing.'

'Oh, we won't ever return here.' Sir Thomas restacked the pictures so that the faces of his wife and daughter were turned towards the wall. 'The family will remain in Newpark. This house will be sold in its present condition, along with the estate.'

'Wow!' Viv envisaged the changes that would follow and wondered if tenants in the tied cottages were aware. 'The end of an era, eh?'

'As you say.' Sir Thomas wouldn't elaborate. Instead, he went out into the hall to wait impatiently for Giles and Ernest.

Viv stayed behind to carry on examining the family possessions, coming across several silver-framed photographs of Giles and his sister as children, complete with ponies. There was also one of Burton Grange in all its former glory, where the terrace was draped in wisteria and there was a party of guests on the front lawn dressed in the fashions of twenty years earlier. It must be sad to leave all that behind, she reflected, but times changed and perhaps it was the case after all that the Parsevals had fallen on relatively hard times – hence the need to pack up and sell Burton Grange.

She went out to join Sir Thomas in the hall. 'While we're waiting . . .' she began.

He turned with an air of surprise, as if he'd forgotten all about her.

'I've been angling for Hilary to hire an extra housekeeper. I expect either he or your wife mentioned it to you?'

'They did not,' Sir Thomas replied before striding out on to the terrace.

'Look at these windows,' she insisted, following him and sweeping her arm down the length of the terrace. 'One person can't possibly clean all these; Anna needs help.'

Sir Thomas's back was stubbornly turned and Giles was on his way back with the handyman. Jeez, this was like getting blood out of a stone! 'Giles, you're my last resort – will you please give Hilary the go-ahead to get Anna an assistant?'

The question stopped Ernest in his tracks and he looked uncertainly at his employers: first at Giles, whose face had turned to stone, and then at the old man, leaning forward and supporting himself on the stone balustrade. Crikey O'Reilly, hadn't Ernest just warned Viv not to meddle? And now look!

Seconds passed before Giles clicked back into action. 'Leave it with me,' he muttered at Viv before sweeping on along the terrace and into the house. 'Come along, Ernest; the sooner we shift these boxes the better.'

Meanwhile, Sir Thomas levelled his gaze at Viv. 'It's been a pleasure to meet you, Vivienne. Please don't let us hold you up a moment longer.'

Dismissed – given the old heave-ho in no uncertain terms! For once Viv was speechless.

She retreated with her tail between her legs, into the house and up the main stairway to her room, reaching the first landing before Giles called her name.

'Viv; wait a second.' Taking the stairs two at a time, he joined her on the landing. 'I say, I'm sorry if it was rather awkward back there.'

'You could say that,' she agreed. Giles's apology seemed sincere; his fair complexion had coloured up and a frown creased his forehead. 'But it's probably me – I'm the proverbial bull in a china shop.'

'You caught Dad at a bad time; dealing with things he'd much rather not. I won't go into details, if you don't mind.'

'No, I get it. Packing up the old family home can't be easy.'

'Quite.'

181

The echo of the old man's thin-lipped response made Viv smile. Like father, like son.

'I can make it up to you.' Giles looked hurriedly over his shoulder. 'Come to the races at Slingsby with me.'

'When?'

'Tomorrow. I'm staying in Rixley overnight. I can pick you up at noon.'

'You forget; I don't like horses.'

'You'll like these,' he assured her. 'They're the crème de la crème. I'll take you to the cinema afterwards if you like.'

Now he was talking. 'Horse racing and then David Niven at the Northgate Odeon?'

'Done!' Giles held out his hand, waiting for Viv to wipe hers on her trousers then shake. 'Midday tomorrow,' he confirmed. 'We'll have a terrific time, I promise.'

Quelle coincidence!' Viv flopped down on Bobbie's bed. Both were in their dressing-gowns and Viv had called in late that evening to bring Bobbie up to speed with recent events. 'You're telling me that Ray has invited you to Slingsby races tomorrow?'

'Yes, and Giles has asked you.' Bobbie unwound a towel from around her head and began to rub her hair dry. 'As you say, quite the coincidence.'

'Did you say yes?' they chimed.

'You give me your answer first,' Viv suggested.

'I said I would go.' Bobbie had waited all of five seconds when Ray had called her on the telephone and proposed a visit to Slingsby races instead of the seaside. Endless days of being left high and dry after

182

their intimate chat in the Fox followed by the romantic (or not?) walk in Burton Wood melted away and she'd agreed enthusiastically. 'Did you say yes to Giles?'

'Yeah, why not? And don't look so surprised – underneath that suit Giles is quite a hunk.'

'So he's in favour now?' With a knowing smile Bobbie took up her brush and ran it through her damp hair.

Leaning over to take a bottle of pearly pink nail polish from Bobbie's dressing table, Viv unscrewed the top. 'May I?'

'Yes – feel free.'

'What's a girl to do?' Viv said with a sigh. 'A certain someone has already bagged dreamboat *numero uno*.'

'You mean Ray?' Bobbie put down the brush. 'I wouldn't say bagged exactly.' She was on the point of sharing some of Ray's troubled RAF history with Viv but thought better of it. 'I've only agreed to go to the races with him; that's a long way from till death do us part.'

Viv applied the polish with a practised hand. 'Anyway, I've decided to take Giles on as a project – let's see if I can get him to drop the la-di-da, stiff-upper-lip act and introduce him to more modern ways of thinking.'

Bobbie looked doubtful. 'That's quite a challenge. But if anyone can do it . . .'

'Honey, watch this space.' Viv blew on the nails of her left hand then began work on the right. 'Do you by any chance have a cream shirt I can borrow to go with my blue two-piece?'

Bobbie went to her wardrobe and picked out a rayon blouse with pintucks down the front and fastened at the neck with a soft bow.

'Are you sure you don't mind?' Viv asked.

'Take it,' Bobbie insisted as she laid the blouse flat on the bed. She planned to wear her dark green dress with padded shoulders, with a cream three-quarter-length jacket over it. 'Now hats,' she went on briskly, opening another section of the wardrobe. 'I like this bright green one with the narrow brim and the half-veil. Or perhaps this cream felt one with no brim at all.'

'The bright green.' Viv chose for her. 'Then I can borrow the cream one to match my shirt.'

Douglas decided that the dog was to be called Patch because of its colouring. 'Not very original,' he admitted to Jean, 'but it's a good, workmanlike name for a Border collie.'

'It suits him,' she agreed. The dog had the look of a pirate, with a black splodge over one eye on his mainly white face. Oddly, the left eye was brown while the one on the white side was pale blue. 'Patch it is.'

'I'll take him for a good long walk today.' Douglas had already handed over Saturday's ops to Gillian, who was a bright girl and perfectly capable of handing out the chits that he'd organized the previous evening. 'I'm only sorry you lost your free time at the last minute.'

Another P.1.W. had cropped up – a case of utmost urgency, according to the chaps on the Isle of Wight. Without a moment's hesitation Jean had volunteered to fly the photo-reconnaissance Spit to Ventnor, where she would see for herself the much talked-about build-up to the invasion of occupied Europe. She fully expected to see military vehicles backed up in all the lanes and landing craft strung out around the island and all along the south coast – sure signs of the push to come. 'I'll be back before you know it,' she insisted as she drained the dregs of her morning cuppa and left the cottage.

'You're forgetting something.' Douglas detained her with a soft, lingering kiss. 'Another,' he murmured as Jean drew back. They kissed again.

'Now, I really must . . .' She smiled and zipped up her sheepskin jacket, ready for the swift walk through the wood.

At the airfield, after she'd received her chit from Gillian and collected her parachute pack from her locker, she found Stan and Gordon on Runway 1 carrying out the checks on her aircraft. Its underside was painted with black-and-white zebra stripes, she noticed.

'To identify her as friendly from the ground,' Gordon reminded her as he gave the windscreen a final polish. He'd already worked on the fuselage, insisting that this gave the Spit an extra few miles per hour. 'Which, I don't need to tell you, could mean the difference between life and death,' he commented as Jean climbed aboard. 'She's bound for Sixteen Squadron,' he added. 'No weapons as yet; just four cameras. Look after her, won't you?'

Jean nodded then prepared for take-off. She'd made it her business first thing that morning to read up about the cameras – each one could take

500 photographs, snapping at a scale of 1:12,000 from a height of 30,000 feet, giving valuable, almost real-time intelligence of what the enemy was up to. So this particular Spit would have crucial strategic importance in the weeks ahead.

At the thumbs-up from Stan, Jean waited for chocks away. Though she'd sat at the controls of a fighter plane hundreds of times before, this morning felt special. Priority One Wait made it different for a start; it meant you must reach your destination come hell or high water. She took a deep breath as she built up her revs and taxied down the runway. Weather: good and set fair all the way south – nothing to cause her much trouble in that department. Soon she was airborne and climbing fast, oxygen mask at the ready. She rose to 5,000 and then 10,000 feet; over Derbyshire before she knew it, keeping her eyes peeled, in front, behind, above and below.

Over Snake Pass her attention was caught by the sight of double contrails disappearing under her Spit's nose 2,000 feet below. Messerschmitt 262; Jean recognized its long nose and twin jets instantly. She shuddered and gritted her teeth. The damned thing could reach 560 mph, a good 100 mph faster than her Spit, and it had four nose-mounted cannons to her none.

Had the lone pilot spotted her? Perhaps not, but then he began to turn and home in on her. Yes, he'd seen her and she must act fast. A quick glance through the clear dome above her head told her that there was a thin covering of cloud some 2,000 feet up. She must climb as quickly as possible and hope to lose herself in the clouds. But Jerry was on her tail, causing her stomach to churn as she opened the throttle wider still.

She kept the Messerschmitt in her sights through the overhead mirror, saw him swing this way and that as he sat on her tail, almost as if he was playing with her before opening fire.

If this is it, I'm going out in a blaze of glory, Jean decided almost coolly. She and her Spit would not come cheap.

They were five seemingly endless minutes into the deadly game of cat-and-mouse, at 15,000 feet and in the midst of swirling cloud, when – disaster – her propeller slowed and the wing fuel tanks cut out. Within a split second (still cool, still in control) Jean had switched to the main petrol tanks and kicked the engine back into life. But now the Messerschmitt was closer than ever, forcing her to climb to 18,000, still desperately hoping that the cloud would thicken and he wouldn't be able to follow.

But before that could happen, out of the blue, the German pilot levelled off then turned to port. His nose was down and he was rapidly losing height. Jean groaned with relief, realizing that the enemy crate must have run out of fuel. The 262 was a notorious petrol guzzler compared with her Spit. Its maximum flight-time was ninety minutes. Jerry might or might not make it back to northern France; meanwhile, Jean's fuel gauge told her that she had fifteen minutes' flight-time of her own left and a choice of two RAF bases in Kent at which to touch down for refuelling. *Breathe, take in oxygen, make a slow, steady descent. Live to fight another day.*

*

187

'My dearest Cameron,' Mary had written, sitting at her dressing table and struggling to come to terms with recent events. The days had sped by and there he still was, incarcerated in the prison block at Aireby while procedures for the court martial inched forward.

'It's more complicated than we first thought,' Hilary had informed Mary, after taking her to one side in the bar at the Grange the previous night. 'There's no doubt that the incident on the charge sheet did take place; Bullen was found lying unconscious in the pinewood that backs on to the training base and Cameron was the one who'd administered the blow. There are several witnesses willing to testify as much.'

At first Mary had tried to underplay the event as merely a spat between Cameron and Bullen that had spun out of control, but Hilary had shaken his head and stopped her.

'Cameron's version is that Bullen experienced a sudden and complete loss of nerve on the runway. Without warning, Bullen refused to go ahead with a demonstration that had been planned for that morning. Cameron tried to remonstrate with him, only for events to spiral out of control. Bullen promptly took out a knife and threatened him.'

'Wait!' Cameron had described none of this to Mary when she'd visited him and she'd been shocked by Hilary's account. 'These witnesses – can they confirm the part about the knife?'

'Apparently not, because at this point Cameron says they were out of sight, in amongst the pine trees. But if Bullen had run amok as Cameron claims, then a punch to the jaw is one of the few ways out of the jam – I've seen it happen on more than one occasion.

The punch is delivered solely to bring a gibbering wreck to his senses.'

Mary had understood the logic of this and had taken heart. 'I'll write Cameron another letter telling him that I understand why he did it,' she'd told Hilary. 'And I'll visit him again as soon as I can.'

'One more thing.' Hilary had felt it best to put Mary fully in the picture. 'Bullen's counterclaim is that Cameron had been drinking heavily and lashed out at him without cause.'

'Drinking?' Mary had echoed. 'While he was on duty? That can't be true.'

'But difficult to prove one way or the other,' Hilary had pointed out. 'I'm sorry to be the bearer of bad news, Mary, but to be frank I have been concerned lately about Cameron's frame of mind. He's seemed a bit het-up over this Bullen chap.'

'I met him and I didn't take to him either,' Mary had admitted quietly.

'Keep that to yourself,' Hilary had reminded her. 'And don't write anything in your letter that could be misconstrued.'

Mary had promised to be careful.

'My dearest Cameron,' she wrote on the Saturday morning. 'It's hard to know what to say to you under present circumstances except that I love you with all my heart and I believe in you. It upsets me to think of you in your current predicament. I hope they allow you to have books and that they feed you well. Keep your spirits up, my dear.'

Mary's fountain pen hovered over the paper. She'd been about to write 'The truth will out' but then dismissed the hackneyed phrase.

'We must rely on the court to get to the bottom of this,' she continued instead. 'Meanwhile, be patient if you can. Easy for me to say, I know. I have plenty to occupy my time – every day we fly more and more planes between ferry pools and time speeds by without me having a moment to stop and think.'

She paused again. Was it permitted to write such a thing? If the letter were to fall into the wrong hands, the 'more and more planes' phrase might prove useful to the enemy. Mary turned her head at the sound of a knock on the door and the handle being turned.

Anna opened the door to see Mary seated at her dressing table, pen in hand. 'I am sorry,' she murmured, about to close it again.

'No, no, come in.' In fact, Mary welcomed the interruption.

Anna entered reluctantly with brush and dusters. 'I am cleaning all pilots' rooms on first floor but I come back later.'

'No, there's no need.' Somehow the sight of Anna entering with her head bowed and offering her halting explanation made Mary sad. The young housekeeper struck her as terribly lonely, living as she did without family, no doubt on a very poor wage and with little realistic prospect of improvement. *That could have been me*, she thought with a sharp twinge of guilty recognition. *For that matter, it could be me again in the near future, once the war ends and I'm back to square one, hobbled by my lack of schooling.* 'Come in,' she repeated, standing up to greet Anna properly.

Anna had already noticed that Mary spoke differently to the other women officers. It was a subtle thing: a softer, more considerate tone, perhaps. Not that Agnes, Bobbie or in particular Viv were unkind, but Anna felt instinctively more at ease with Mary so she didn't feel awkward cleaning the room in her presence.

'I'm sorry I'm so untidy.' Mary whisked her pyjamas from the bed, folded them and slipped them under her pillow. Then she picked up her slippers and stowed them in the wardrobe.

Anna began by sweeping the lino surrounding the threadbare rug. 'It is good day,' she said conversationally.

'Is it?' Mary had been so wrapped up in writing her letter to Cameron that she hadn't noticed the sunshine streaming into the room. She went to the window and looked out to see Ray Moore and Giles Parseval standing on the terrace, smoking cigarettes. Craning her neck, she glimpsed their cars parked in the stable yard and remembered that the pair were here to pick up Bobbie and Viv for a day at the races. 'It's all right for some,' she observed as she drew Anna to the window to point out the two lucky race-goers emerging on to the terrace, one in green, one in blue – both dressed in the latest fashions.

Anna saw Ray and Giles greet the girls and immediately shrank back. Her pale face blushed scarlet. 'I must work,' she insisted but she had to steady herself on Mary's dressing table, brushing the half-written letter to the floor as she did so. She crouched to pick it up. 'I am sorry.'

'Don't be.' Mary had to help her up. 'Are you feeling dizzy? Come and sit. Let me fetch you some water.'

Anna allowed herself to be led to Mary's bed. 'Do not tell,' she pleaded.

'Tell what?' Poor thing, from flushed she'd turned deathly pale. Her cheeks were hollow, her eyes dark and haunted.

'I am not strong. But I do my work.'

'You do; I know you do,' Mary comforted as she poured water from the jug on her bedside table.

'I do not sleep.'

'I see.'

'You will not tell?' Anna looked up anxiously. She took the glass and sipped.

Mary wondered what exactly had rattled her about seeing Bobbie and Viv together with Ray and Giles. Had the Parsevals been too strict with her at their Newpark home and did she live in fear of being disciplined or dismissed? 'I won't say a word,' she promised. 'And give me that duster. You sit there and have a rest while I finish the tidying up.'

'I cannot stop; I think about Poland. I cannot sleep.' The confession spilled out without Anna intending it. 'They burn my town, they shoot our men. We are *untermenschen* so they kill us like dogs.'

Mary sat down beside her. 'We will beat them,' she promised quietly. Neither named the Nazi opposition, as if speaking the word conceded power to the enemy.

Anna shook her head.

'Yes; we will.'

'I hope; then my mother, my father, my sister – they do not die for nothing.'

What was there to say in the face of such misery? Mary put her arm around Anna's thin shoulder and watched the tears fall. Before long both their cheeks were wet so Mary took two handkerchiefs from the drawer in her bedside table.

'*Dziękuję*. Thank you.'

'You're welcome. You can talk to me any time – don't think you can't.' Mary wanted to do more but didn't know how. She vowed to herself that she would look out for Anna in future and draw her into conversation whenever possible. She would try to be her friend.

'*Dziękuję*. You are kind person.' Drying her eyes before handing back the handkerchief, Anna drew a deep breath then stood up. She ought not to have weakened, she told herself. In future she must not lower her defences and let people in – even kind Mary. 'But I do my work now, please.'

Mary nodded. There was a jolt in the conversation and then a stiffening in Anna's demeanour as she picked up from where she had left off – methodically sweeping the lino with her soft broom, gathering the dust into her dustpan while millions of tiny motes rose and danced in the sunlight, and two car engines started up then drove out of the stable yard on to the Slingsby road.

CHAPTER ELEVEN

'Imagine – the Secretary to the Minister of War Transport wanted to turn this track into a camp for POWs.' Ray stood in the owners' enclosure at Slingsby race course with Bobbie, Viv and Giles. They watched the parade of beautifully turned-out runners in the first race: two grey and four chestnut fillies and three dark bay geldings led by expressionless grooms in flat caps, tweed jackets and cream breeches, their black riding boots polished to perfection. 'A chap called Noel-Baker; I expect you've heard of him? It was either that or a landing strip for the RAF; or, worse still, they could have ploughed the whole thing up for food production.'

'What changed Noel-Baker's mind?' As the horses paraded, Bobbie took an interest in her fellow racegoers: bluff mill-owning types and their florid, overdone wives, with a smattering of what she would call more sophisticated, old-money landowners who felt less need to show off their wealth. There was one couple in particular who scarcely gave the horses a second glance, preferring to set themselves apart under a shaded awning. The woman wore a peach-coloured dress and a silvery fur stole with a wide-brimmed black hat trimmed with a filmy veil that covered half of her face. Her complexion beneath the veil was pale and flawless. When the small, pompous-looking husband caught Bobbie pointing them out to Viv he quickly turned his back.

'The Jockey Club soon put paid Mr Secretary's plans,' Ray explained. He was on the lookout for his father who had entered Tudor Queen into the second race of the day. So far there'd been no sign of him. 'They got up a successful petition to save Slingsby and here we are: still going strong.'

A chestnut filly reared up then skittered towards the white railing as it passed within inches of where Viv and Giles stood. The groom quickly got her back under control and walked her on.

'Not for all the tea in China . . .' Viv muttered through gritted teeth. Sure, there was an impressive spectacle connected with horse racing – the jockeys in their multicoloured silks, the lawns mown nearly as smooth as the jockeys' shirts, the hoity-toity women and the men with their fat cigars – but she held to the view that anyone prepared to jump fences on those nervy thoroughbreds had to be crazy.

'Unlike Aintree.' Giles was apparently in his element, touching the brim of his trilby hat by way of greeting every second person in the owners' enclosure. 'The Grand National was abandoned three years ago and they've yet to reinstate it; Lord knows why.'

'You see that grey?' Bobbie pointed to number seven at the far side of the paddock. 'It says here in the programme that she's called April Fool; pretty appropriate, considering the date.'

'My money's on her,' Viv declared without a

second thought. 'How about you, Giles – who will you throw your money away on?'

'The dark bay,' he decided. 'Black Knight; I like the look of him.'

'I'll go along with you, Giles.' Ray knew the horse's pedigree and recent history. 'He was second to Dante at Newmarket last season. You can't go wrong with him.'

Black Knight's coat shone in the sun. He wore blinkers and carried his head high. His mane was beautifully plaited; his long tail swished as he glided along.

So the group left the paddock and went to place their bets while the jockeys mounted. At the last minute Bobbie saved her money to put everything on Tudor Queen in the next race, then they went up into the stand and waited for the thrills and spills to begin.

'Here they come.' Giles was the first to spot the runners emerge from the paddock on to the course. The horses cantered easily towards the first brushwood fence then back again to the start line where they assembled under starter's orders. 'Aren't you glad you came?' He gave Viv a nudge with his elbow.

'As a matter of fact, I am.' There was something so peculiarly English about the lush green grass and the strands of fluffy white clouds in a mostly blue sky, the general restraint of the crowd and the narrow sounds of their voices as they gathered by the rails to watch the race begin.

'Mind you, they could have got a fair wheat yield out of this.' Giles gestured towards the track. 'Nice and flat, on a fertile plain. I wish the land we farm at Newpark and Abbot's Gate were half as good.'

Viv was looking out for April Fool and her jockey's purple-and-white striped colours. But April Fool played up at the start line, prancing and spinning round, barging her rear end against the horses to either side. *Trust me to pick the most badly behaved mount in the whole bunch*, Viv thought.

'And they're off!' Ray declared and suddenly all attention was on the track.

First over the first fence was April Fool, followed by a couple of chestnuts then by Black Knight. One of the geldings fell, dislodging his rider before scrambling up then racing around the side of the hurdle, stirrups flapping, to chase after the other horses. Three fences on, April Fool held on to the lead while Black Knight had moved up into third. By now, Viv was on the edge of her seat.

'She went too early,' Ray murmured to Bobbie. He saw Viv's horse already beginning to tire as she approached the fifth.

Sure enough, April Fool missed her stride and took the fence awkwardly. She was overtaken by a chestnut then by Black Knight.

'She's fading fast, damn it.' Viv sat back in her seat with a frown. 'A swell effort, though.'

The rest of the field charged on, hooves clattering against the tops of the hurdles then thundering towards the last. By this time the crowd by the rails had flung reserve to the winds and yelled raucously for their favourites. They jumped up and down, threw their hats in the air and urged their horses towards the finish line.

'Come on, Black Knight!' Giles and Ray were

on their feet. 'Come on!' Their magnificent favourite took the lead by one, two and then by three lengths, whipped on by his rider. He was clear over the last and eventually crossed the line six lengths ahead.

'Most satisfactory.' Smiling broadly, Giles sat down again. He leaned across Viv and Bobbie to shake hands with Ray while a disappointed Viv watched April Fool trail in second to last.

'Come on; back to the paddock.' Ray stood up and led the way in time to see Tudor Queen enter for the second race with his groom, Ronnie Evans. The grey mare was wearing a number one, which Viv and Bobbie took to be a good sign. And she walked calmly, looking straight ahead on a short lead rope and seemingly enjoying the attention.

Spotting Ray in the crowd, Ronnie touched his cap in acknowledgement.

'There's your father.' Bobbie pointed to the centre of the paddock where Derek Moore stood with a jockey in white silk with a black star on its back and front, together with a tall, stout man who was presumably Tudor Queen's owner.

'Dad has high hopes,' Ray told her quietly.

'So I can safely put my money on Tudor Queen?' Bobbie was eager to place her bet and by now Viv was getting the hang of things, so the two girls went ahead to join the queue at the bookies' stalls, leaving Ray and Giles to study the form.

The long, snaking queue edged slowly forward, giving Bobbie and Viv plenty of time to chat.

'What do you think; did the boys plan the day together?' Bobbie asked. It mattered to her more than it ought – the idea that she was part of a four-some, rather than it being simply her and Ray.

'Probably.' Viv didn't much care. 'Those two are thick as thieves, if you ask me.' She looked more closely at Bobbie's crestfallen expression. 'Don't worry; Ray has eyes only for you.'

'Do you think so?'

'I know so,' Viv declared as she reached the front of the queue. 'Half a crown on number one to win,' she told the bookie.

'Five shillings on number one,' Bobbie said when her turn came.

'Both ways or to win?' The man who took her bet was as round as he was tall, his checked waistcoat stretched to bursting point over his bulging belly. He wore a pork-pie hat and a yellow tie.

'To win,' Bobbie said firmly. Why hedge her bets? Tudor Queen was firm favourite and bound to come in first; she felt convinced.

'Second.' The race was over in a flash. Tudor Queen had lost by half a length to a horse called Glendower. 'That's five bob down the drain,' Bobbie said glumly.

'Some you win . . .' Ray had the urge to hug her and make things better. Instead, he suggested going back to the paddock to watch the unsaddling and awarding of prizes. 'We'll see you two later,' he told Giles and Viv, who were heading for the bar.

'I was sure she'd win.' Bobbie hardly ever gambled and she took her loss badly.

Ray squeezed her hand. 'The owner will be happy with second,' he predicted as he ducked under the rail to enter the paddock.

They sidestepped horses with steam rising from their overheated bodies and grooms throwing buckets of cold water over them, threading between trainers and owners until they reached Ronnie Evans and an exhausted Tudor Queen, who was still blowing hard.

'Where's Dad?' Ray asked the groom.

Ronnie jerked his head towards Derek and the bald, broad-faced man with the look of a civic official about him. At any rate, Bobbie could imagine him wearing a chain of office. The mayoral man was smiling and shaking hands with Derek and slapping him on the back. Derek's back was towards them but at Ray's tap on the shoulder, he turned. He too was grinning.

'Congratulations, Mr Addyman,' Ray said to Tudor Queen's owner above the hubbub. 'Dad, you remember Bobbie Fraser?'

'Of course I do.' Derek seemed to have forgotten the awkward circumstances attached to their first meeting. He was all bonhomie and wrinkly smiles. 'Are you enjoying the races?' he asked her.

'Yes, I'm having a grand time, thank you.' Perhaps he didn't really remember her and was just pretending.

'I haven't seen you at Thresham lately,' Derek said with a pointed glance at his son. 'Ray, why don't you fix up another visit with Bobbie here?'

'I will, Dad – I will.'

That was it; the trainer turned back towards his gratified owner. Bobbie looked quizzically at Ray, who grinned and took her by the arm to lead her back towards Tudor Queen. 'Dad has a better way with horses than he does with people,' he said. 'That's right, isn't it, Ronnie?'

'Right enough,' the groom said without hesitation. 'Mr Derek would admit as much.'

Bobbie stood back warily from Tudor Queen, who seemed to be eyeing her with the intention of taking a quick bite. But she smiled to herself. 'Well?' she prompted.

'Well what?' Bobbie looked stunning in that outfit – Ray reminded himself to tell her so in private. Green went well against the slight red tint in her hair. But as always it was the ever-changing light and shadow of her expressions that fascinated him.

'When shall I come back to Thresham to ride Glasgow Girl?'

'Oh, that.' Ray swept her away and ducked her under the railing so that he had her all to himself as they wandered back towards the stand. 'How does tomorrow sound?'

'Hello there, Giles – long time, no see.'

'How's the family? Give my regards to Sir Thomas.'

'Good to see you, Giles old chap. You're looking well.'

Viv stood impatiently at the bar, waiting for Giles to order their drinks. It seemed he knew everyone and their aunt.

'We haven't been introduced.' One of the friends offered to shake her hand. 'I'm Neville Stott.'

'Viv Robertson,' she replied, blushing under the man's top-to-toe scrutiny.

'Very good,' he said when he'd finished looking her up and down. Then he old-chapped Giles again: how was Lady Jane, was Sir Thomas still trekking all the way up to Yorkshire on a regular basis, and so on.

Somebody give me a good strong drink, Viv said to herself, blowing out her cheeks and trying in vain to attract the barman's attention. Elbows jostled her while Giles talked on. Eventually, still without a drink, she gave up. 'I'm going to powder my nose,' she mentioned to Giles, who assured her that a dry martini would be waiting for her when she returned.

Off she went to find the ladies' cloakroom and was mid-powder in front of the mirror above the sinks when she noticed the woman in the peach dress and silver-fox stole approach her, obviously with the intention of speaking to her – and not in a friendly way.

'You two ought to know better than to go about in public,' Peaches said without preliminaries.

Viv snapped the lid of her powder compact shut. 'Excuse me?'

'You heard me.'

'And you are?' Viv was ready for a fight. She squared up to Peaches, preparing to give as good as she got.

The woman batted away the question. 'You and Giles; have you no shame? Obviously not. Still, for propriety's sake, I thought even Giles Parseval would have been more circumspect.'

'Listen, lady, I don't have the faintest idea what you're talking about.' Viv's heart beat fast as she turned her back on Peaches to concentrate on her own reflection. She took a lipstick from her purse.

Ignoring the frequent comings and goings in the

cloakroom, the woman continued her attack. 'Don't play the innocent with me. You know perfectly well that parading your affair in public is bound to cause a scandal.'

Affair? Scandal? OK, enough! 'What business is it of yours who I choose to be seen with? Why should it even matter?'

Without the slightest pause, Peaches delivered the killer blow. 'Because Giles has a wife in Gloucestershire, as if you didn't know.'

Viv stared at the woman's reflection – venomous, unblinking behind the gauzy veil. Her heart thudded and she lowered the lipstick without applying it to her lips.

'Don't pretend to be shocked.'

'Giles is married?' The news threw Viv and yet somehow it came as no surprise. How could both reactions occur simultaneously? She tried to catch her breath.

A scornful smile appeared on the woman's face. 'Oh dear me, it seems that I've done you a favour. You really didn't know?'

Married! Giles had tricked her and treated her like a fool. And yes, come to think of it, he was too smooth by half. He flattered too easily and took nothing seriously.

'His wife is called Nora. Fortunately there are no children.' The informant's superior smile didn't fade as she opened up her own handbag and took out a gold powder compact.

And Ray: how come he hadn't warned her? Viv's fighting spirit returned full force. *Thick as thieves, indeed; the two of them*. Well, she wouldn't take this lying down. 'Interesting,' she said with as much dignity as she could muster. 'Thank you.'

'My pleasure,' Peaches said between dabs, her good deed for the day accomplished.

Viv nodded and altered the angle of her cream beret. '*C'est la vie*, eh?'

'Indeed.'

Viv tucked her purse under her arm then swept from the cloakroom, down the steps and out on to the area where the bookies called the odds and chalked on their boards – on towards the exit gate without a backwards glance.

'I saw the artificial harbour they've built at Hamble.' At Fern Cottage Jean kicked off her shoes and sank into the only armchair. 'It was quite a sight.'

Douglas was on hand with a cup of tea. 'Is the build-up as big as they say?' He knew for a fact that over 2,500 new aircraft had rolled off the productions lines in March alone. But he had seen none of the south coast preparations for himself.

'Bigger,' Jean replied. 'Ashton Down and White Waltham are due to be designated as invasion pools any day now. And the War Office is sending back soldiers from the desert war in readiness.'

'Who told you that?'

'One of the ground crew at Ventnor.' After her skirmish with the Messerschmitt and her enforced stop for refuelling, Jean had finally reached her destination only to learn that she must fly straight back to Rixley in a Mitchell bomber. It had been a heavy crate to handle, needing the usual two hands on the stick for take-off and landing. She'd been accompanied by a young flight engineer who had operated the fuel cocks and undercarriage levers, yet in spite of his help she'd arrived home exhausted.

The dog, Patch, came up and nuzzled her hand.

'I envy you; you know that?' Douglas perched on a stool by the warm hearth. 'I wish it was me up there in a Mitchell or a Stirling, ready to give Jerry what-for.'

'I know you do.' She rested her head back against a cushion and closed her eyes.

'I'd give anything to be involved.'

'You are involved.'

'Not like I used to be.' Douglas still regarded his time in the RAF as his glory days. Flight Lieutenant Thornton, with DW43792 inscribed on the Bakelite dog tags he'd worn around his neck, one red, one green. 74 Tiger Squadron with four kills and seven hits to his name. 'What I do now doesn't come close.'

Jean turned her head to look at him with a heart full to bursting. 'I wish I'd known you back then.'

'In my prime.' He smiled fondly at her as she rested her tired head and turned her attention back to the insistent dog. 'But I don't think you'd have liked me much.'

'Oh, and why not?'

'I was a proper so-and-so, according to the erks on the ground – do this, do that and don't argue. Nothing mattered except chalking up another kill.'

'I'd have seen beyond that,' she assured him. 'I'd have known how kind and true you were beneath the surface.'

'I believe you would.' Anyway, injury had put paid

to his active service and now tinnitus had to be dealt with on top of the gammy leg. He got up from the stool and took her cup and saucer from her. 'But do you ever regret ending up with an old crock like me when you could have had your pick of any of the Kens, Joes and Terrys wearing flight lieutenant bands on their cuffs?'

'Not for a second.' Giving the dog a final pat, she stood up and joined Douglas at the sink. The sun was low in the west, casting long, dark shadows across their patch of garden. The noisy blackbird was busy building its nest in the branches of the elm tree just beyond the gate. 'I only think how lucky I am.'

Douglas considered Jean's voice to be one of the most beautiful things about her. It was low and soft, never rushed, always sincere, and it went with the rest of her; the gleam of her blue-grey eyes, the elegant curve of her neck, the grace of her every movement. 'Me too.' He turned to kiss her.

She nestled against him, her head on his shoulder and one arm around his waist as he rinsed the cup.

The bird outside trilled its evening song. Patch stood up and wagged his tail.

'Stay.' Jean raised her finger and the dog sat obediently on the rug. He gave a low whimper as she led Douglas to the bottom of the stairs. 'Stay,' she said again.

Upstairs the room still held the day's warmth. The bed sheets were already turned back.

Jean took off her jacket then eased the pins out of her hair. She let Douglas unbutton her shirt. And when they were both undressed, they pulled back the sheets entirely and lay down without covers, warm skin against skin, touching and stroking and soaking up every sensation, pushing away the world and its woes, sinking into the luxury of love.

Mary's latest letter hadn't turned out well and had ended up in the wastepaper basket along with several earlier versions. However she phrased it, her feelings for Cameron refused to shine through the dross of everyday gossip. Besides, since her talk with Hilary she couldn't overcome her worries about putting things in writing that might later be used in the court martial.

What's stopping me from going to see him instead? She woke up early on Sunday morning with this fresh thought in her head.

No one except Anna was up when, minutes later, Mary hurried downstairs in trousers, checked blouse and flying jacket in search of a quick breakfast of toast and jam.

'Good morning, Anna.' Mary paused by the door to the Parsevals' private room that had recently been emptied.

'*Dzień dobry.*' Anna immediately ducked back into the room and closed the door behind her.

Below stairs Mary found bread but no jam in the main pantry. Dry toast washed down with tea would have to do. It was quickly done and within ten minutes Mary was wheeling a bike out of the stable yard on to the lane at the back of the Grange. By eight o'clock she was well on her way to Aireby.

This is a much better idea than writing, she decided. The chill in the air invigorated her and the exercise would do her good. She took in details by the way-side: the hawthorn hedges sprouting green and even the first hopeful shoots of bluebells growing on the grass verges. In the fields to either side she was pleased to see lambs leaping and cavorting in dizzy fashion and a pair of hares boxing on a low ridge, outlined against a pale grey sky.

In just over an hour Mary was within sight of the training base where Cameron was held. The approach lane was long and straight, said to be part of an old Roman road. It was pitted with potholes so she steered carefully around them until she came to the gate where the same armed sentries as before were posted.

'Aye aye,' the younger and friendlier of the pair warned the other with a raised eyebrow when Mary turned off the lane and got off her bike.

The two men watched her carefully as she approached the barrier.

'Yes?' the second sentry barked. He was fiercer than the first, with sharp features and small, beady eyes.

'I'm Mary Holland. I'd like to see Flight Lieutenant Ainslie, if that can be arranged.'

The second man's face seemed to be etched in stone. 'Come again?'

Mary stopped dead. It hadn't struck her until this instant how ridiculous it would be to turn up at Aireby unannounced and expect to be allowed straight through the gate. 'I'd like to visit Flight Lieutenant—'

'Yes, I heard you the first time.' The man's face didn't alter. 'It's not on, though.'

'I'm his—'

'I don't care if you're the Queen of Sheba; you still can't come in.'

Mary swallowed hard. 'Couldn't you ask permission from whoever's in charge?'

The younger, squeaky-voiced sentry joined the first. His tone was more sympathetic – after all, the girl looked harmless enough. 'Listen, love, I doubt if Group Captain Norris is even up and dressed at this hour on a Sunday morning.'

Mary stood on tiptoe to peer over the men's shoulders at the row of green Nissen huts visible from the lane. 'Isn't there someone else you could ask?'

'The answer would still be a big, fat no,' the stroppy sentry assured her. He stood with feet wide apart, one arm across his chest and the hand resting on the barrel of his rifle. 'Wouldn't it, Spud?'

'Hold on – let me go and find out.' The errand would at least break the tedium of the early morning shift so the young sentry set off at a run towards the nearest building.

'Your flight lieutenant isn't doing himself any favours,' the other informed Mary, his sharp voice grating on her already frayed nerves. 'He swears blind that our Texan friend went berserk and pulled out a knife. That hasn't gone down well with the group captain or with any of the lads who saw what happened, for that matter.'

'What do you mean?' Mary's heart sank rapidly and she had to steel herself to meet the sentry's gaze.

'Flight Lieutenant Bullen can do no wrong around here. Maybe it's the chewing gum and the American cigarettes he shells out that does it.' He stared directly at Mary to judge her startled-rabbit reaction.

'On the other hand, the trainees aren't too keen on your chap.'

She shook her head in speechless protest. This wasn't fair!

'There's no point shaking your head at me, love. A go-by-the-book chap like Ainslie is never popular. They prefer someone who's willing to bend the rules a bit.'

'Like Don Bullen?'

'Yep.' The man clammed up as Spud returned.

'No can do,' was the breathless report.

Mary's frustration brought tears to her eyes. 'Who did you ask?' she demanded. 'No, don't tell me – it was Flight Lieutenant Bullen.'

'Bingo!' was the reply. 'No can do' was a toned-down translation of what Bullen had actually said. Talk about turning the air blue.

Just then the man himself appeared in a doorway, watching intently. Mary recognized the confident thrust of the Texan's jaw and his over-relaxed stance, hands in pockets, leaning one shoulder against the door jamb. 'I see,' she said quietly.

'I could try to get a message to your chap later.' Spud tapped the side of his nose – *Between you, me and the gatepost.*

Mary nodded and thanked him. 'Ask him to write me a letter. Tell him I came.'

'Rightio.' Spud prepared to return to his post with his sullen companion. 'I'm sorry you had a wasted journey,' he said as he departed.

She breathed in deeply. *Not wasted*, she thought. She'd learned that the odds were unfairly stacked against Cameron and that Bullen was enjoying having the upper hand. She felt him still staring at her from his position in the doorway, watching her with a mocking smile as she got back on her bike and rode away.

CHAPTER TWELVE

Early Sunday morning was an ideal time for Stan and Bob Cross to go rabbiting on the Warrens, an area of open grassland close to Rixley reservoir that rose steadily towards moorland stretching all the way to Maltby and the coast. The two mechanics had set off when a low mist still clung to the hillside and the earth was soft and damp underfoot. They soon left the reservoir behind and passed through a gate leading to the Warrens; still on Parseval land and hoping to bag three or four rabbits for the cook back at the barracks. And sure enough, the misty hillside was alive with the little beggars, some poking their heads out of burrows, others nibbling and hopping around in full view. Stan put a restraining hand on Bob's arm, a signal for them to stay put.

Bob nodded then slowly and smoothly raised his gun and set his sights.

Stan scanned the hillside. He could practically see the sun's rays burning off the mist, leaving their quarry fully exposed. So far the rabbits had taken no notice of the men's stealthy approach.

Rabbit stew would make a nice change! Chuck in

a few onions, potatoes and carrots with meat tender enough to melt in your mouth. Stan too raised his gun.

Bob waited for the next signal. You only got one go at this; miss and there'd be no second chance. The cunning blighters would vanish down their holes and stay there until the hunters went away.

Stan aimed then nodded.

Bang! Bang!

Mary started when she heard the shots echo down the valley – five altogether. They pierced the silence as she cycled along. A pair of pheasants rose from the hedgerow, their wings clattering as they flew clumsily out of range of the guns.

'Gotcha!' Stan had bagged two rabbits while Bob had got just one. The two hunters strode across rough grassland to stuff the corpses into the canvas satchel slung over Stan's shoulder.

Mary stopped to watch the two men go about their bloody business. It was a distraction from what had been going round and round in her head since she'd left Aireby, and when Stan looked up and noticed her on the lane, she waved then waited for him to send Bob off with the morning's kill before striding up the hill towards her.

'Now then, Mary; where've you been at this hour?' Stan wanted to know. He climbed the nearest stile and joined her at the roadside.

'I've been to Aireby to see Cameron,' she confessed.

'They didn't let you through the gate, did they?' He could tell by her woebegone expression what must have happened.

'No.' And damn it, the tears came without warning,

welling up and trickling down her cold cheeks – a repeat of the previous situation in the wood.

Stan didn't go in for a second kiss, however – not after his disappointing heart-to-heart with Mary in the stable yard at Burton Grange – instead, he pulled out a clean handkerchief and handed it to her. 'I could've told you that.'

'I know; I'm a fool.' Stan really was the bigger person, she decided; a thoroughly decent sort.

'Yes,' he said evenly, accepting back the damp hankie and shoving it in his pocket.

Mary trusted him with a further confession. 'It doesn't look good for Cameron.' Her lip trembled but she kept control. 'They're ganging up against him.'

'Says who?'

'A sentry on duty at the training camp. According to him, everyone is on Bullen's side.'

'Come on, let's walk back together.' They were a mile or so from the Grange; enough time for Mary to get things off her chest. As they skirted the reservoir Stan decided to listen and bide his time.

'The sentry says Cameron is too strict. They like Bullen better because he bends the rules.' Feeling that she was about to break down again, Mary took a deep breath then walked more quickly. 'There's something else,' she admitted. 'Hilary told me last week that Bullen has accused Cameron of drinking too much – that's the reason he lost control.'

'Did he now?' This cast fresh light on the matter.

'But it's not true,' Mary insisted. 'It can't be.'

Stan thought back to when Cameron had worked at Rixley. The stickler for the rules part was true but besides that, everyone had been aware that Cameron had liked the odd dram of an evening. This meant that alcohol might well have played its part in the unseemly fracas between the two instructors.

'Bullen is lying.'

Stan shrugged. What was that saying about the lady protesting too much?

'I'm hopeless at letter writing.' Mary shot off in a new direction. 'I can't put down what I mean. And Cameron hasn't written to me since this all blew up. I don't know what to think.'

'He's got a lot on his mind,' Stan said quietly. 'He probably doesn't want to worry you.'

'But I am worried!' Following a public footpath sign, Mary flung the remark over her shoulder as she wheeled her bike by the water's edge. 'I can't concentrate on what I'm supposed to be doing, even when I'm flying.'

'That doesn't sound good,' Stan commented.

'It's not.' She stopped and looked at him. 'Stan, I trust you to give me a straight answer. What would you do if you were me?'

He waited a long time before speaking. 'I'd write to Cameron and let him know that I'd stand by him whatever happens.' Boy, did it hurt to offer that little gem, considering what it did to Stan's own chances. But Mary had asked him point-blank and honesty was always the best policy. 'I'd do it today if I were you.'

She accepted the advice with a nod. 'You're right, I will.'

Damn, damn, damn! Stan cursed silently as he walked by her side. The morning mist still lingered over the surface of the reservoir. *Damn and blast, buggeration!*

'I'll make time this afternoon,' Mary decided.

Stan hung back and walked half a pace behind his newly determined companion, convincing himself that he'd played it badly. On second thoughts, if the court martial did go against Cameron and Mary subsequently fell to pieces, as was likely, then he, Stanley Green, steady as a rock, would be the man she'd turn to. He would be there to set her back on her feet. After that, who knew?

'I came home by train.' Miracle of miracles, the weather was warm enough to sit out on the terrace on this early April morning, so Viv had dragged a deckchair from one of the stables used as a storeroom. She'd dusted it down and was relaxing when Bobbie accosted her and demanded to know how and why she'd left the previous day's race meeting so suddenly. 'There's a direct line from Slingsby to Rixley. I simply hopped on the two-thirty *et voila!*'

'But why?' Bobbie was still in her dressing-gown, recalling events of the previous day. 'Where on earth is Viv?' she'd asked Giles as the afternoon had worn on. Giles had had absolutely no idea. 'The lady vanishes,' he'd quipped, seemingly unperturbed, before turning his attention back to the runners in the final race of the day.

'Because!' Viv raised her sunglasses and rested them on top of her head. She'd put on a white halterneck top and navy blue shorts in the hope of topping up her fading tan.

'That tells me nothing.' As a matter of fact, Bobbie considered Viv's sudden disappearance to have been

216

bad form and she was upset with her. 'I want to know what's going on.'

'No, you don't.'

'I do.'

'OK then, here it is.' The smile playing on Viv's lips didn't quite convince. 'It turns out that Giles Parseval is married. How about that?'

The news stunned Bobbie and she leaned back against the balustrade. 'How do you know?' she whispered.

'Let's say a little bird told me.' Viv preferred not to go into the humiliating details. On the train journey home from the racetrack she'd given herself a firm talking-to and decided that she would play this out not as a tragedy but as a farce worthy of the silent melodramas of 1920s cinema – husband plays the field behind wife's back, finds himself a good-time girl until wife storms in and exacts revenge. Viv would hide any hurt she felt, just as she had when Piers's sister had arrived at Rixley and thrown unfounded accusations at her. Concealing her true feelings was what Viv did best.

'Did Giles admit to it?' Bobbie was still aghast.

'I didn't wait to find out. Once I'd learned the facts, I was on that train before you could say Jack Robinson – whoever he was!'

'This is no joke,' Bobbie gasped.

'Oh, but it is.' Viv stood up and stretched, her bare arms clasped above her head, slim midriff exposed. 'I'm through with Giles Parseval. It's time to move on.'

'Giles is married' was the first thing that Bobbie said to Ray when he came to the Grange later that morning to pick her up in the cream MG. 'Why didn't you say so?'

Ray waited for Bobbie to get in and slam the door then executed a rapid three-point turn and roared out of the stable yard. 'Who told you that?' he asked carefully.

'That's beside the point.' Bobbie hadn't been able to squeeze any more information out of Viv, other than the basic fact. 'I'm asking you; why did you let us both think that Giles was fancy-free when all the time he has a wife?'

'*Had* a wife,' Ray said as he turned on to the main road. The car sped through a tunnel of trees just coming into green bud. 'Giles and Nora are about to divorce. She currently lives in the dower house at Abbot's Gate until the decree becomes absolute and the finances are sorted out, hopefully later this month.'

'So technically they're still married?' Bobbie insisted on being absolutely clear.

'Technically, yes, I suppose so. But Nora and Giles never got along, right from the start. It was more or less an arranged thing between the two families. Giles was only twenty at the time.'

Ray chose not to mention to Bobbie that he had warned Giles about misleading Viv. 'Come clean, old man,' he'd said. 'The mad wife in the attic is not a good look.' Not that Nora was mad, exactly – just extremely difficult to get along with. In any case, Giles had chosen to ignore Ray's advice. 'How's Viv taken it?' he asked Bobbie as they raced along the green lanes. 'I expect she's fuming.'

'She pretends not to care but yes, she's upset. Actually, I feel sorry for her.' Bobbie held on to the door strap as Ray took a bend at speed. With her free hand she jammed her hat down over her forehead. 'It's not nice being deceived in that way.'

'And you; are you angry with me?' Ray hoped not.

Bobbie stared at him from under the brim of her hat. He frowned and gripped the steering wheel as he waited for an answer. 'No,' she decided.

'Then stop looking at me like that.'

'Like what?'

'I don't know; just stop looking at me and let me concentrate on my driving.' Ray changed down through the gears for the next bend then up again for a straight stretch. 'All right, you can look at me again.'

Bobbie tapped his arm playfully with the back of her hand. 'I hope *you* don't have any such skeletons in your cupboard,' she warned.

'Apart from my inglorious career with the RAF, you mean?' As before, he mentioned the topic nonchalantly, as if his local football team had lost their latest match. 'No skeletons other than that one; unless you count a father who can't stay away from the booze and a horse-training business that's sliding into debt. In that case, you can practically hear the bones rattling to be let out.'

'But no wife?' Again Bobbie wanted to leave no room for doubt.

'Not even a fiancée,' he assured her flippantly. 'How about you? Have you ever been tangled up with any eligible chaps?'

'Not one.' All at once and for some reason that she couldn't fathom, it seemed possible to speak the dreaded name. 'Apart from Teddy Simpson.'

Ray drove on without comment, simply glancing sideways at her and waiting for her to go on.

'Flight Lieutenant in the RAF,' she explained. 'He's dead now. Killed in an accident.'

'I'm sorry.'

'Don't be. He wasn't . . . a decent sort.' Bobbie struggled to describe her attacker. Cad, bounder . . . The words belonged to the pages of cheap romances; they trivialized Teddy's premeditated assault and its dreadful aftermath – the missing, obliterated hours, the ongoing shame and confusion.

'Ah, I see.' Enough to understand something of what lay beneath Bobbie's nervous energy and her difficult-to-read attitude towards men. Ray remembered their one and only kiss – how he'd followed an impulse and she'd responded, only to draw back quickly and walk on, leaving him confused.

Teddy Simpson; finding the courage to name him had unlocked a door that had remained tight shut for many months. A chink of daylight entered the dark space inside Bobbie's head as she recognized the turn-off for Thresham and switched her thoughts towards visiting Ray's yard for the second time.

'About Giles and Nora; will you set Viv straight when you get back?' Ray wanted to know. He'd asked Ronnie Evans to saddle up Tudor Queen and Glasgow Girl again, and he wanted the Giles mix-up out of the way before he and Bobbie set out on their ride. 'Ask her to give the silly idiot a second chance?'

'I don't know about that.' Bobbie was aware that Viv would do exactly as she pleased, regardless.

'Tell her he deserves it,' Ray said as the car swished through the wide gates of the training yard. 'Giles

220

has had a difficult time lately and I think Viv Robertson could be just the tonic he needs.'

That afternoon Mary began her letter to Cameron by relating low-key, everyday events. She sat cross-legged in the window seat of her bedroom with a view of the woods to one side and the remnants of a formal garden to the other – a stone fountain in the centre of a circular pond with low box hedges radiating out to form flower beds that were now planted with vegetables and herbs. Ernest was out there with his hoe, working as she wrote.

'I mentioned when I saw you that Douglas and Jean have taken in a stray dog,' she wrote; 'he's a faithful Border collie that belonged to the old chap who lived in the cottage before them. They seem very happy there. Honestly, you would hardly know Douglas now that he's married. He goes everywhere with a smile, and whistles while he works in the garden with Patch the dog on the doorstep watching his new master's every move. I haven't seen much of Jean lately – we're both so busy.'

Mary paused to look down at Ernest hard at work. She found comfort in the sight of the handyman raking through the soil, stooping occasionally to pull up a tenacious, deep-rooted dandelion with a shaky hand. What else could she tell Cameron? 'I had a saucy seaside postcard from my brother Tom earlier this week. There was an English postmark so I presume he's home from Tunisia, at least for the time being. But typical Tom: he gave me no real news – only to say hello and tell me that he was safe and well, which is something, I suppose. Bobbie has heard from Angela in White Waltham – a long letter full of gossip about the new ATA recruits she must knock into shape. There's a girl who was a ski champion and one who was a hockey international, known as the Mayfair Minx – just Angela's cup of tea. We miss her at Rixley and Bobbie has written back to tell her so.'

Mary's pen ran out of ink so she paused to refill it from the bottle. Now she must stop skirting around the main issue and tackle it head on. 'Don't think that my life here goes on as normal,' she wrote when she resumed. 'I only describe these things in the hope that they will lift your spirits a little and give you fresh things to think about while you wait. Did the young sentry called Spud tell you that I cycled to Aireby first thing this morning but that I was prevented from seeing you?

'I suppose I should have expected it, but my dear, I yearned to talk to you face to face and see for myself how you are getting along.

'I think back to our last day together in Northgate and then to our ride out into the country – the wellington boots in the back of your car (very handy), the bench outside the fisherman's hut, the lambs in the field. Precious memories that must last me until the next time we're together.

'And of course there was our first night in Highcliff, six months ago now, but I can still relive every moment: how you told me that you would be happy even when I wasn't there by your side, knowing that we'd shared those moments, which made me cry even though I was happy.'

Mary stopped again, remembering how Cameron's

eyes used to come alive at the sight of her whenever their paths crossed on the stairs up to the ops room or in the noisy canteen, and how dull and blank they'd seemed across the table from her in the prison block at Aireby. She tried to imagine the silent, empty hours he spent locked up; too much time to brood over what had happened and what might be to come: a possible guilty verdict and an ignominious dismissal from the service that meant the world to him. What a blow to Cameron's pride and patriotism that would be.

'Please write to me,' she went on with renewed energy, scribbling down the words as they came into her head. 'Don't hold back – just tell me everything that is in your heart; your worst doubts and fears and your hopes as well. And remember that I will stand by you, whatever happens.

'I think of you every moment – how we first came together and how I could hardly believe that it had happened and had to pinch myself. And I never forget how you helped me to fulfil my dream of learning to fly. How you believed in me from the start. Write to me, dearest, and share your thoughts with me. Know that I believe in you. Please, please write.'

It was time to sign off, a wrench that brought tears to Mary's eyes. Time had certainly brought a fresh perspective to the mistaken close encounter with Stan. Mustering the courage to be frank with him had eased her guilt and she continued to see the kiss for what it was – a moment of madness that must never be repeated. And Stan, God bless him, seemed to have graciously accepted this.

Down below in the garden Viv had joined Ernest in unlikely gardening garb of sandals, shorts and halter-top, complete with white-rimmed sunglasses, her black hair tied back by a turquoise ribbon. The two worked together in quiet companionship.

'Dearest Cameron, I truly love you,' Mary wrote. 'I wait every day for a letter from you. Don't despair – the truth will come out and all will be well.' She signed her name with a row of kisses, blotted then folded the page, and slid it into an envelope with a trembling hand.

She paused again to gaze out over the woods. The truth was rarely set in stone; even she knew that. There would be Cameron's version against Bullen's and the impression they each made in court, the complications of what witnesses had or hadn't seen. And love too was a movable feast – L-O-V-E; four letters from the alphabet making up a simple word that held so many shades of meaning, including loyalty and steadfastness, desire, and tidal waves of longing and doubt that tossed Mary this way and that. *I truly love you.* Old insecurities fought their way to the surface from the dark depths of her mind. *I love you. But do you, Cameron, still love me?*

Glasgow Girl had pricked up her ears and swished her tail at Bobbie's approach. She stood next to Tudor Queen in the yard at Thresham; both horses were immaculately turned out, ready for action.

Ronnie was on hand to adjust Bobbie's stirrups after he'd given her a leg-up into the saddle.

'Let them down one hole, please,' she requested. 'I don't like to feel as if my knees are tucked right up under my chin.'

'Right you are, miss.' The groom moved calmly

and professionally around the handsome horses, running a hand down Glasgow Girl's neck after he'd lengthened Bobbie's stirrups before moving on to a fretful Tudor Queen.

Bobbie watched him stoop to tighten the grey's girth while Ray talked to one of the other grooms at the far side of the yard. 'How long have you worked here, Ronnie?' she asked.

'Nigh on twenty years, miss; since before you were born.'

She laughed. 'Not quite. I had my twenty-second birthday last October.'

He raised his eyebrows in disbelief. 'Never.'

'It's true, worse luck.'

'And how do you like Glasgow Girl?' Ronnie stood well clear of Tudor Queen, who had begun to kick out with her back legs.

'I like her very well indeed.' Bobbie leaned forward to pat her neck. 'Hurry up, Ray,' she called. 'Tudor Queen is champing at the bit.'

He came running and accepted a leg-up from Ronnie. Before long they had left the yard behind and were trotting smartly up the lane towards the gallops. 'We can relax,' Ray told her. 'Dad went to Ripon to see Mr Addyman.'

Bobbie allowed Ray and his excitable horse to move ahead. 'I thought your father didn't object to my coming over?'

'He doesn't. But it means we have the place to ourselves; I can show you the house later.' Tudor Queen pranced as the lane ended and the gallops began. Ray reined her back, inviting Bobbie and Glasgow Girl to take the lead.

At a squeeze from Bobbie's legs the chestnut mare was off, from trot to full-out gallop, taking away Bobbie's breath with her burst of speed. She sat tight in the saddle, urging her horse forward with slight shifts of her weight, looking straight ahead but aware that Ray and Tudor Queen were gaining on them. Then the horses were neck and neck at full stretch, their riders crouched low, thrilling to the power and rhythm of their mounts until they came to the copse of ash trees at the far end of the gallops.

'Dead heat,' Ray declared. 'Another photo finish.'

Every nerve in Bobbie's body tingled with energy as they turned for home. 'That was . . . splendid!'

'Stupendous, spiffing, smashing!' He ran through superlatives beginning with an 's'. '"Swell", as Viv would say.'

Ah yes, Viv. Bobbie wondered what her reaction would be to the news that Giles was practically divorced. She would seek her out as soon as she got back to the Grange and put her straight about the state of play; before tea if possible. Would Viv then be prepared to give Giles a second chance as Ray had hoped?

'A penny for them?' Ray asked as they trotted back easily, their horses snorting, their bridles jingling.

Bobbie shook her head. 'Tell me something: have you always wanted to work with your father, or did you plan to do something different when you were growing up?'

'Why do you ask?'

'No reason. I'm just curious.' The wind blew in their faces and made their eyes water as they made their way along the ridge.

'As a matter of fact, I only came to it after I left the RAF. Before that it was always going to be Frank working alongside Dad.'

Bobbie sensed a hesitation. 'Frank?' she prompted.

'My older brother. He was killed in the Far East, flying a Lancaster over Singapore in January nineteen forty-two. Tomorrow would've been his thirtieth birthday, as a matter of fact.'

'I'm sorry, I didn't realize.'

'Why should you?' Ray gave a shrug, as if ridding himself of an unwanted burden. 'Anyway, I said goodbye at that point to any hopes I might have had of becoming a vet. It's been the training yard for me ever since.'

'I see.' Bobbie wondered whether Frank's death had been an additional contributing factor in Ray's breakdown. But she didn't want to probe any deeper. When he quickly went back to discussing horses and training regimes, she fell in with that.

'Ronnie's the chap to go to with any problems,' Ray confided as they entered the lane. 'There's nothing he doesn't know about equine ailments and loss of form. We're darned lucky to have him, and to keep him, considering what he puts up with from Dad.'

Bobbie approached the yard with altered perceptions of the Moore family set-up. To lose a son or a brother was a common event during wartime, more's the pity, but it didn't make it any less painful. Perhaps that partly explained the older man's taking refuge in the bottle and Ray's tendency to shrug things off and make a joke whenever he could. She knew that everyone had their own way of coping.

Ronnie was there to greet them in his green

jumper and brown breeches. He stepped forward to take their horses.

'Can I brush her down for you?' Bobbie offered.

'No thanks, miss – you don't want to do me out of a job.'

So she dismounted and handed over her horse with a fond word in Glasgow Girl's ear. Then Ray led Bobbie out of the yard, up a side path towards the house, in through the front door into an oak-panelled hallway that rivalled Burton Grange in its magnificence.

Bobbie went straight up to a cabinet with a large display of silverware – engraved cups, bowls and shields that bore witness to the family's sporting successes. 'I'm impressed,' she murmured as she read the inscriptions. *Impressed and a little daunted.* Doors led off in all directions while a wide staircase split into two then curved upwards to right and left. Paintings on the walls were all of thoroughbreds, dating back many years.

Ray acknowledged the compliment then led her into a large room overlooking a well-tended lawn. The room was somewhat neglected, with scuffed green leather armchairs and low tables scattered with a week's worth of newspapers. A bronze statue of a horse took pride of place on a mantelpiece cluttered with tarnished silver candlesticks, a pipe rack and pewter plates – a man's room, without a doubt.

'Drink?' Ray suggested. He went to a cabinet to check its contents. 'I can offer you brandy or sweet sherry.'

'Neither,' Bobbie decided. 'How about tea?'

'Come this way, m'lady.' Out they went into the

hall and through another of the doors into an enormous kitchen with a solid-fuel stove, a scrubbed deal table running its entire length, and row upon row of mostly empty shelves lining the walls. There was a deep Belfast sink under a window overlooking a small apple orchard.

'Kettle.' Bobbie presented Ray with the one sitting on the stove.

He filled it at the tap then put it on to boil. 'What?' he demanded defensively when he found her following his every move.

'Nothing.' She went on studying him carefully. What was going on behind the m'ladies and the cheeky smiles?

'You're looking at me again.'

'Is it against the law?' In fact, Ray was extremely pleasant to look at – outdoorsy and dashing, with his dark, wavy hair dishevelled at this moment and with that suggestion of a lopsided smile offsetting his long, straight, otherwise symmetrical features.

'What are you seeing?' Ray moved closer.

'You,' she murmured.

'And do you like what you see?'

Bobbie cocked her head to one side. 'Yes.'

'Come here.' He took her by the hands and drew her to him, sliding his arms around her waist and studying her in return. 'Likewise,' he said softly, the kettle humming behind them and beginning to sing.

Bobbie braced her arms against his chest. 'I like what I see but I'm not sure what's going on inside your head.'

'I'm thinking how beautiful you are.' Quick as a flash.

'Oh, please!' Bobbie grimaced.

'Not that old chestnut, eh?' His hands stayed locked in the small of her back. 'But what if it happens to be true?'

'What else?' She searched for answers in his dark brown eyes, which she now saw were flecked with a lighter hazel colour close to the pupils. He had thick lashes and straight, almost black eyebrows.

'I'm thinking that you don't trust me and I'm beginning to understand why. It has to do with this Teddy Simpson chap.'

'Yes, but it's a long story.' That door was still open a tiny chink, light continued to filter through; but for now she didn't want to push it open any further.

'And would you mind if I kissed you again? I won't if you don't want me to.'

'I do want you to,' Bobbie whispered, tilting her head back and offering her lips. And this time she felt hopeful that she would discover how much it meant.

CHAPTER THIRTEEN

'I won't be long,' Jean called to Douglas from the foot of the stairs.

He was in their bedroom, re-laying a small section of creaking floorboards, sawing, hammering away, and doing his best to make the floor level.

He appeared in the doorway, shirtsleeves rolled up. 'Where are you off to?'

'To see Florrie and tell her we've decided to keep Patch.'

'Doesn't she already know?' Douglas was reluctant to forgo his wife's company.

'Not for definite. The last time we spoke I said we were still thinking about it. Anyway, it'll do me and Patch good to stretch our legs.' Promising to be back in half an hour, Jean donned her coat and hat then called for the dog to come. Soon they were both enjoying the dappled sunshine as they skirted the edge of Burton Wood and headed towards the village.

The dog didn't need to be shown the way – he trotted ahead, one ear pricked, the other flopping over his pale eye, tail wagging happily until they came within sight of St Wilfred's church and Jean

231

called him to heel. 'Just in case a car comes by,' she explained, stooping to put the obedient dog on the lead.

A west-bound goods train chugged to a halt in the station behind the main street. Jean heard the squeal of its brakes and saw a plume of steam rise into the still air. Close by, a trickle of evening worshippers strolled up the path and into church as Jean and the dog approached the Fox. The pub would be closed today, so they would have to make their way along the ginnel at the side into the backyard and knock on Florrie's private door. Before they rounded the corner, however, Jean heard the landlady's voice.

'You're not to come here again,' Florrie said sternly. 'Do you understand?'

There was a low, mumbled response, unintelligible to Jean.

'I'm under strict instructions not to speak to you. I'll get into trouble if they find out you've been here.'

Jean heard the word 'please' and then recognized Anna's stilted English. 'I come only one time . . . please tell me . . . I cry, I cannot sleep.'

In two minds whether or not to interrupt and unsettled by the anguish in Anna's voice, Jean stayed out of sight.

'Do you *want* to get me into trouble?' Florrie demanded. 'Because I will if people see me talking to you. You shouldn't have come.'

'Please,' Anna begged, her voice broken by a sob. 'I tell no one.'

But Florrie was adamant. 'I have nothing to say to you. Do you understand? You must go away and not come back.'

Jean heard the slam of a door and more sobs. Soon after, Anna appeared at the end of the ginnel, but when she saw Jean and the dog she stepped quickly back into the yard.

Jean rushed forward to find Anna backed up against a wall, roughly wiping tears from her eyes with the sleeve of her shabby grey mackintosh. She looked paler than ever and dreadfully distressed. 'Whatever is the matter?' Jean asked.

'Nothing. It is good. Sorry.' Anna darted forward, pushing past Jean in her haste to get away.

Not good, Jean thought. She went straight up to Florrie's door and knocked sharply. 'What's going on?' she demanded when the landlady appeared. 'I came across Anna in floods of tears.'

Florrie tutted and snapped the clasp of her hand-bag shut. She was wearing her best fawn coat and a green felt hat decorated with a small plume of speckled feathers. 'I'm on my way to church. I don't want to be late.'

'Why was Anna crying?' Jean refused to step out of the way.

'She was upset about something.'

'I could see that for myself. Look, Florrie, this may be none of my business—'

'That's right, it's not.' The landlady had shut up like a clam the moment she'd opened the door and she didn't try to hide her impatience.

Still Jean stood her ground. 'But I don't like to see Anna upset. Is there any way I can help?'

'Not you or the King's army, not with the mess she's got herself into.' That was it; Jean wouldn't get another word out of Florrie on the subject. The shrewish landlady pushed past her visitor, almost tripping over Patch, who sat half-hidden behind Jean. He yelped as she stepped on his paw. 'I hope you're not bringing that nuisance back here,' she said sourly once she'd righted herself.

'No. Douglas and I have decided to give him a permanent home.' Jean gave in gracefully over the subject of Anna – for the time being, at least.

'Fine. I don't have time to be messing about with stray dogs – or stray foreigners, for that matter.'

Jean bit her tongue and glared as Florrie flounced off to church.

Well, really! Jean thought. *I mean, really!* She would dash home and describe to Douglas the irony of it – of Florrie marching through the church gates for the evening service without having shown Anna Janicki one single ounce of Christian charity!

'If you're like me, you miss everyone back home,' Viv sympathized with Anna when she bumped into her in the stable yard at the Grange. Anna tried to avoid her by dashing up the stone steps into the grooms' quarters above the stables but Viv sought her out. 'Please don't cry; I can imagine what it's like for you.'

Her sympathy didn't have the hoped-for effect – instead, Anna sank to her knees and sobbed helplessly.

'There now.' Viv crouched beside her, put an arm around her shoulder and spoke softly. 'Sure, it's different for me; I can go home to Vancouver after we've cleaned up the mess that Herr Hitler's made, back into the arms of my loving family.' She ended abruptly without stating the obvious.

Anna's frail body shook. She crouched forward, covering her face with her work-worn hands. Gradually her sobs turned to low moans.

'It's tough. I feel for you, I really do.'

The two women stayed like this for a long time, among the dust and debris of the unused loft. There was a pile of broken furniture at the far end and an old wood-burning stove close to where Anna had collapsed. Rusty garden tools were stacked against the wall. Light came in through two small skylights and the open door.

'Hello?' Concerned by the sound of Viv's voice and a woman sobbing, Jean ran up the steps and appeared in the doorway. After the contretemps with Florrie she'd rushed home and left Patch with a bemused Douglas, then hurried as fast as she could to the Grange. 'Can I come in?'

Viv nodded. 'Here's Jean,' she told Anna with a sigh of relief.

Anna crouched lower, her head hanging and her arms crossed over her chest.

'Oh dear me.' Jean joined Anna and Viv in the middle of the room, stooping to rest her hand on Anna's back. 'We can't have this, can we?'

'No way.' Viv stroked Anna's hair. 'Whatever it is, you can tell Jean and me.'

'Do,' Jean urged. 'We promise not to tell a single soul.'

The hopeless, heartfelt sobs began again but there was no explanation from Anna.

'Help me lift her up,' Jean murmured to Viv. 'There's a mattress over there – she can lie on that.'

So they slid their hands under Anna's arms and

took her weight, helping her to stumble across the room. Then they lowered her gently on to the mattress where she curled into a ball, her back towards them.

'What shall we do?' Viv appealed to Jean.

'Wait quietly,' Jean decided. She glanced up at the small skylight above their heads and saw that the light was beginning to fade. It would soon be dusk.

So they sat beside the distraught woman, stroking her hair and reassuring her, exchanging looks and hoping that the sobs would ease.

Inside the loft the light grew dim until at last it was as Jean had hoped; Anna's body was no longer wracked and she fell silent. 'There, there,' she soothed.

Viv echoed Jean's soft reassurance. 'There, you see. There.'

Anna took a deep, shuddering breath. Slowly she raised herself until she sat, her thin arms hugging her knees to her chest as she rocked back and forth. Her face was a picture of misery – the corners of her mouth dragged down, her eyes swollen and red.

What now? Viv flashed Jean a panicky look.

Again Jean mouthed the word, *Wait*. Patience above all was what was needed.

'I am sorry,' Anna breathed, her shoulders sagging as she spoke at last. 'Leave me, please.'

'No way!' Viv was louder and more forceful than she'd intended and she watched Anna shrink away.

'Don't be sorry,' Jean told Anna. 'We want to help you. Please don't send us away.'

After an attempt to stand up, Anna sank back on to the mattress. 'My legs . . .'

'Rest a while; there's no rush.'

Viv retreated to the open door, letting Jean take the lead.

'Take some deep breaths.'

Anna obeyed Jean as if she were a small child.

'Better?'

'Yes. Thank you.'

Jean looked towards Viv. 'Could you fetch Anna a glass of water?'

'Sure.' Glad to be given something practical to do, Viv left quickly.

'Well?' Jean shifted position so that she sat beside Anna on the mattress. 'Florrie Loxley – what was all that about?'

Anna screwed her eyes shut and shook her head.

'I heard her telling you to go away and not to come back. What made her say that?'

'I make trouble.' The halting explanation emerged painfully slowly. 'Trouble for her. I do not mean to.'

'I'm sure you didn't.' *Patience, patience . . .*

'I want only name, nothing else.'

'Whose name?'

Anna turned her head away and there was a long pause. 'I have baby,' she whispered, turning back to Jean with a look of intense sorrow.

Jean hid her surprise and nodded slowly. 'When?'

'December. She is girl. I call her Dorota, my mother's name.' Anna seemed to drift into a faraway world and her words tailed off.

Jean grasped her hand. 'A little girl,' she breathed.

'Yes. She is beautiful. But I must not keep her.'

'Who said so?' *Too quick, too painful.* Jean watched Anna retreat into her own solitary suffering. 'No, it's

237

all right – there's no need to tell me if you don't want to.'

'I cannot keep baby. I love my Dorota and they take her from me. I do not know where.'

'But Florrie does?' Jean made sense of the landlady's cruel words and came slowly to the conclusion that Florrie Loxley had acted as a go-between.

Anna nodded. 'I want only name of people who have Dorota. Old woman does not tell.'

'I gathered as much.'

'She has name of family. I hear her talk.'

'Who with?'

'I do not see. It is outside this house in garden. They do not know I am near.'

So much now made sense to Jean, especially Anna's air of extreme reserve on arrival, which everyone had noted, and a sense that she'd experienced more than her fair share of deep sorrow. It turned out that not only had she lost her father, mother and sister in Poland's death camps, but recently she had also lost an infant daughter whom she had loved – surely that was enough to break the strongest of hearts.

'If I find name of family I can know Dorota is happy. I want good life for her. That is all.'

'I understand.' An unspoken question hung in the air but Jean couldn't bring herself to voice it: namely the identity of the man who had done this to Anna. She felt that probing for an answer might push her over the edge, back into black despair, so for now she listened and waited.

'I cannot be mother.' Anna faltered over the last word. 'I have nothing – no house, no money, no family. I cannot choose.' Once more she tried to stand up and with Jean's help she succeeded.

'Steady,' Jean murmured. 'Look, here comes Viv with a glass of water.'

Viv entered to find Anna on her feet, looking shaky and deathly pale but no longer sobbing and moaning, thank heavens. She wrapped Anna's fingers around the glass then let go.

'May I tell Viv?' Jean asked.

Anna's dark eyes flickered but then she nodded. 'Yes, she is kind person.'

Realizing that something big was coming, Viv held her breath and looked sharply from Jean to Anna then back again.

'Anna has had a baby daughter,' Jean explained in a quiet, calm voice. 'She can't bring up the little girl by herself so arrangements have had to be made.'

'Oh, Jeez!' Viv held back from spluttering out a set of urgent questions about the baby's father. *Who and where? What the hell is this guy playing at?*

'It's very hard for Anna, as you can imagine.' Jean held up a hand to warn Viv not to say too much. 'She would like to learn about the baby's foster parents but at the moment she's being prevented.'

'Surely we can help her to do that?' Viv saw immediately that she'd leapt two or three steps ahead so she turned from Jean to Anna. 'If you want us to?'

Anna swayed and wrung her hands. 'I cause trouble, I lose job,' she said faintly.

'Oh.' Viv's chest tightened as she worked out the implications. 'But surely not. Hilary would have to have a better reason than that to fire you. Even he would realize that a mother has a right to know what's happened to her own daughter.'

'Perhaps it's not Hilary's decision,' Jean said pointedly.

'No trouble, please.' Anna reached out to Jean, who grasped her hands. 'You do nothing, say nothing. I go on with work.'

'Yes, yes; we understand.' It was obvious that they needed to get Anna to her room where she could rest. 'We'll do as you say, won't we, Viv?'

Though her mind was working at a mile a minute, Viv nodded without saying anything. Together she and Jean guided Anna down the steps, across the stable yard and into the house through the side entrance. Luckily they managed to get her back to her room without meeting anyone then they put her to bed and made sure that she had what she needed – a fresh glass of water, an extra blanket for her bed, a fire newly laid and lit in the small grate. Meanwhile, Anna watched passively from her bed, as if drained of emotion.

'Sleep,' Jean told her once she was satisfied that they'd done all they could.

Viv and Jean backed towards the door. 'We'll leave you in peace now, but I'll come back and check on you in an hour,' Viv promised.

'Thank you, I am fine.'

'Goodnight,' Jean and Viv said softly.

'Je-sus!' Viv sighed as Jean clicked the door shut and they walked rapidly along the dark corridor.

Jean nodded.

'I mean—'

'You'll do as you promised – do nothing and say

'nothing?' Jean interrupted. Out in the entrance hall she looked at her watch. It was half past eight; Douglas would be wondering where she was.

'Of course.' The whirlwind inside Viv's brain made her step between Jean and the door. 'You want to know how I see things? I figure the father of that baby needs to be named. My guess is he forced himself on Anna and to hell with the consequences.'

'We don't know that,' Jean cautioned.

'No, but I'd put money on it. He gets her in the family way. But say the guy's married, what then? Then he has to hide both Anna and the baby – out of sight, out of mind.'

'Stop.' Didn't Viv see where this train of thought was leading? Think back – who had arranged for Anna to take the housekeeping job at the Grange? Who had brought her here and dropped her off?

'That's what these guys do,' Viv railed, eyes flashing as she beat the fleshy side of her fist against the door. 'They tidy up after themselves. The woman doesn't count, neither does the baby – the guy resumes normal service while the woman's life lies in ruins.'

Jean sighed and stared, waiting for the penny to drop.

'Don't look at me like that. I know what I'm saying.' Viv's heart raced along with her thoughts. 'I already figured it out.'

Neither noticed Bobbie and Mary on the first landing, drawn from their rooms by the sound of Viv's raised voice.

'It's as plain as the nose on my face,' she proclaimed. 'Who got Anna this job? Whose marriage just broke up? Yeah, Jean; you didn't know that part, did you? Well, it's true – according to Bobbie, Giles and his wife are getting a divorce.'

Bobbie broke away from Mary and rushed down the stairs to lay a restraining hand on Viv's arm. 'Good Lord, woman; keep your voice down. Do you want the whole house to hear?'

Viv paid no heed. 'I don't give a damn. We all know who this baby's father is.'

Mary ran to join them. 'Which baby? What on earth are you going on about?'

'Don't – you promised!' Jean pleaded.

But Viv broke free from Mary, Bobbie and Jean. 'Anna had a baby and they tried to hide it.'

'Who's "they"?' Mary turned to Jean for enlightenment. Jean frowned and shook her head.

'The Parsevals!' Viv threw back her head in exasperation and shouted the name up to the glittering chandeliers. To her, the identity of the father was crystal clear. 'To be precise, Giles Parseval. The idiot only got Anna pregnant and wrecked his marriage while he was at it. There, what do you both think of that?'

It was amazing to Mary and Bobbie that the world went on as normal. Anna's confession and Viv's rash accusation had changed nothing – the Atta girls woke up on Monday morning and dutifully went down for breakfast, passing the housekeeper on the stairs as she polished the brass stair rods. Anna didn't look up and not a word was exchanged about baby Dorota and the mysteriously absent father.

'We keep this under our hats,' Jean had insisted

242

before leaving for Fern Cottage the night before. 'Viv ought not to have said anything; Anna made it plain that she doesn't want anyone else to know.'

So the four women, including an abashed and by now subdued Viv, made a vow of silence and went about their business – checking met reports and receiving their chits, studying their Pilots' Notes before flying their Defiants, Beauforts and Hurricanes to far-flung RAF stations and ferry pools dotted along the south coast.

Everyone realized that the pressure to deliver was building and though the pilots mostly remained casual, even devil-may-care in their dealings with each other and with the ground crews who kept their planes in working order, the tension began to show in snappish remarks and frequent poor nights' sleep. On that first Monday in April Agnes reported sick with a bad headache while even Jean, the most modest yet the bravest and most skilful among them, confessed to Douglas that the stress of never putting a foot wrong was playing on her nerves.

On the Wednesday morning she stood with him on Runway 2, staring up at a wash of stratocumulus clouds against a pale blue sky. 'When will this be over?' she wondered aloud. 'When will Hitler finally admit defeat?'

'Soon, I hope.' Four and a half years of war had made death and destruction the norm so that he rarely thought about the overarching reasons for daily engagement with the enemy. He concentrated instead on the hazards of sending pilots out in questionable weather like today when a high dew point might easily combine with a small fall in temperature, quickly filling the sky with a blanket of condensation and cutting down visibility to almost zero. 'Keep a careful eye on your map today,' he advised Jean. 'Don't take any risks.'

She was bound for Andover in a Spit; not the latest type but still a pleasure to fly. 'I won't,' she promised. At the front of her mind was the report she'd seen pinned up on the noticeboard outside the ops room – a flight captain based at Hamble had recently been killed when he'd crashed his Percival Proctor into houses coming in to land over Southampton. Horrified witnesses on the ground had seen him hit a roof and had watched his tail unit break clean off before the rest of the fuselage had shattered into small pieces over a school playing field. The pilot plus four civilians were dead, five more injured, due to pilot error.

There were two planes lining up ahead of Jean's Spit: a Mitchell destined for Aston Down allocated to Bobbie and a somewhat battered Typhoon EK347 for Lancaster, which Douglas had assigned to Viv.

'One Landing Only,' he'd reminded her as Gillian handed over the chit. 'She has a snag sheet as long as my arm – Jerry scored a direct hit during her last mission over Normandy so her underside is full of holes. Luckily no damage to wings and tail.'

Jean saw Bobbie take off without a hitch then watched Viv approach her damaged crate with her usual bouncy enthusiasm, chatting for a while with Bob and Gordon before springing up on to the Typhoon's wing and sliding into her seat. 'Will she get to Lancaster in one piece?' she asked Douglas.

'I'm surprised you bother to ask.' Lately he'd

noticed a distinct coolness between Jean and the ebullient Canadian – something to do with an incident at the weekend that Jean had refused to talk to him about. 'I thought you two had fallen out.'

Jean frowned. 'Have I made it that obvious?'

'No, but I know you. What's got your back up?'

They watched Gordon signal chocks away and Viv power up the Sabre engine before taxiing into position. 'Sometimes she oversteps the mark, that's all.' *Too loud, too dramatic, too quick to jump to conclusions; too everything, for my taste.*

'You're chalk and cheese,' Douglas commented.

Jean didn't argue. He'd mentioned to her that one of the holes in Viv's Typhoon's fuselage was big enough to put your fist through, yet the Canadian girl's fixation on getting through, her apparently unshakeable belief that her name would never appear as a casualty on the ops-room noticeboard, had obviously not deserted her. Her take-off was perfect and now it was Jean's turn – her Spit carried a P.1.W. and was already blacked up ready for clandestine ops, yet another sign that the big push was imminent.

'Remember: no risks.' Douglas concealed the wrench he felt at watching his beloved wife turn and stride confidently along the runway to be greeted by Gordon and Bob.

Jean's mind clicked automatically into pilot mode – hydraulics, trimmers, throttle. Her smile was tight as she climbed into the cockpit and strapped herself in. Fuel mix, pitch, flaps, gills, gauges. Chocks away.

Back in the ops room, Hilary collared Mary and called her into his office. 'This won't take long,' he promised.

She gritted her teeth at the familiar phrase and prepared for more bad news. Sure enough, Hilary made her sit down and told her that he would come straight to the point.

'Cameron's court martial is set for Monday next week. I presumed you would want to know?'

'Yes, sir; thank you, sir.' Monday 10 April: red letter day.

'I'm informed that he intends to represent himself.' Hilary eyed Mary steadily. 'It's not something I would generally recommend but don't despair; Cameron is a clever chap and it's possible he can produce evidence or witnesses that we know nothing about.'

'Yes, sir.' A compression low in Mary's chest made it difficult to take a deep breath. 'Will that be all?'

Hilary continued to study her face for signs of emotion that might endanger her safety in the air. 'I take it you haven't heard from him?'

'No, sir, not a word.' Despite her own heartfelt letter sent two days earlier, time passed without a reply and the silence was tearing her apart – had Cameron cast her off for good or was he in such a poor mental state that he couldn't bear to put pen to paper? Mary veered wildly from one theory to the other, with half a dozen alternatives in between. Was he prevented from writing by a superior officer? Had letters been written then intercepted? Was he single-mindedly assembling a case in his defence and waiting for the court's verdict before he felt able to get in touch with her?

'Would you like me to arrange another visit?' Hilary noted that Mary's expression gave nothing away and meanwhile time was ticking on.

She shook her head. 'I'll wait for a letter, if you don't mind.'

'Probably best,' he agreed. Pushing his chair back from his desk, he stood up. 'Very well; that *will* be all, Third Officer Holland.'

'Thank you, sir.' Still short of breath, she mirrored his movement. The scrape of her chair across the smooth lino grated on her nerves and a flicker of distress crossed her features. She concealed it by quickly turning and leaving the room.

Should he have stopped her? Hilary was unsure. She seemed to have her feelings under control. Then again, Mary Holland was particularly difficult to read. He stood at the window watching her slight, determined figure leave the shadow of the control tower then cross the lawn, parachute pack slung over one shoulder, sheepskin jacket hanging open. How would it have been if Mary had been one of his male pilots? he wondered. Would he have had the same concerns over her fitness to fly?

They were living in strange times, with girls still in their teens in charge of thousands of pounds' worth of military hardware. Were they really up to it? The question would hover at the back of the ferry-pool commander's mind for the rest of the morning.

Monday the tenth. Five long days to get through and five mostly sleepless nights. The nights had been by far the worst. Mary had taken to leaving her bedside light on in an attempt to ward off the most dismal, darkest thoughts. When she did eventually fall asleep, she was plagued with a recurring nightmare in which she (or was it a stranger whom she merely observed?)

carried a swaddled baby in her arms as she walked at night beside what seemed to be the reservoir beyond the Warrens. The baby cried when she tried to give it away to a passer-by, and when in desperation the mother in her dream made as if to throw the infant into the black water, Mary would wake up in horror, her throat dry and her face cold with sweat.

Afterwards she would sleep fitfully until it was time to get up and face the day.

Monday the tenth. Wednesday, Thursday, Friday, Saturday, Sunday – as she counted the days she decided there and then to volunteer for weekend duty to avoid the empty desert of two free days. Flying would mean she would have to be constantly on her toes. Then it would be Monday and the waiting would be almost over.

'Ah, there you are.' Stan stepped out from under the wing of the Tempest 5 Mary was to take down to the Isle of Wight. He'd embarked on a second round of cleaning and polishing the already pristine fuselage. 'I was wondering where you'd got to.'

'Sorry, Stan; Squadron Leader Stevens wanted to have a word.' Already late, she decided to skip reading up about her unfamiliar aircraft in her Pilots' Notes. If need be she could check them mid-flight.

'What about?' Stan shoved his chamois leather into his overalls pocket then offered her a hand up into the cockpit. Mary didn't look as sharp as she usually did and she seemed agitated.

'It's private,' she answered shortly.

'All right, no need to bite my head off.' Thinking it best to let it lie, Stan ran through a few of the Tempest's quirks. 'This crate is brand new,' he reminded her. 'She's a follow-on from the Hawker Typhoon, but with thinner wings and better airflow. She's mighty fast, especially at low altitude. She can do over four hundred and sixty miles per hour if you push her.'

'Thanks, Stan.' Mary checked the instrument panel – nothing seemed too different from what she was used to.

'There's an extra tank in front of your cockpit,' he called up to her. 'You might need to switch tanks if you're low on fuel. How far are you going?'

'Isle of Wight.' Mary tested the throttle, at the same time noting the clever construction of the cockpit and the way that its narrow struts cut down on blind spots. A glance down at Stan on the runway told her that he was still shouting up instructions, though his voice was drowned out by the sound of the engine. Behind him she saw an Amazon truck towing another new Tempest to the end of the runway for Horace Jackson. He too was bound for the Isle of Wight. Time to be gone – she closed the cockpit and gave Stan a thumbs-up. He beckoned Bob from the neighbouring runway and between them they removed the chocks, then stood back to watch her move away.

'What type is she?' Bob asked his more experienced fellow mechanic.

'Tempest Mark One.' Stan kept a keen eye on Mary as she prepared for take-off.

Bob gave a nod of approval. 'She's a beaut; I've not seen one of them before.'

'She's new, that's why. They say she's streets ahead of the old Typhoons.' But Stan wasn't happy. In fact, he had a bad feeling in the pit of his stomach.

'Is she easy to work on – removable panels,

non-slip coatings and all that?' The apprentice was keen as ever to learn.

But Stan gave him short shrift. 'What're you asking me for?' he barked as he turned away abruptly and headed for Hangar 2. 'It's all written down in the manual. Read it for yourself, why don't you?'

Douglas had been right about a possible drop in temperature. Of all his pilots taking off from Rixley that day, none escaped hitting a sudden lump of cloud but all battled through. Jean climbed to a height of 10,000 feet in her Spit and sailed over the top. Bobbie, meanwhile, decided to stay low in her lumbering Mitchell, knowing that one lapse of concentration and she could well be a goner. Experience pulled her through, however, and she was able to climb again when the cloud cleared and carried on without further incident until she reached her destination.

Not so for Viv, who hit the cloud bank in her Typhoon as she approached the Pennines and felt the whole crate shudder. Her revs dropped perilously low and she was in danger of stalling, so she flew lower to give the engine time to recover but she encountered a strong headwind that slowed her down. Then suddenly, without warning, a whole section of damaged floor was ripped away by the wind and Viv was able to stare down in amazement at the streets of a mill town far below, through a hole that was twelve inches wide and over two feet long. A quick check told her that her undercarriage was intact. *Thank heavens!* Even so – she wasn't out of the woods; she felt freezing-cold air blast up through the gap and take hold of the map spread across her knees. Within a split second the wind had sucked it out of the cockpit. *Damn! Damn!* She opened the throttle to maximum and stamped on her rudder pedals in an attempt to stabilize the wretched crate. A glance upwards told her that the cloud was too thick and ominous-looking to attempt an ascent. There was nothing for it: Viv would have to drop low then go in for a forced landing.

But now she had no map and, of course, no means of communicating with the ground. By her crude calculation the nearest landing strip was at a small ferry pool thirty miles to the north so she kept low and altered course, flying on over bare hills, noting a viaduct and then a canal that helped her to get her bearings. She approached the Cumbrian Mountains and held her breath – where was that damned runway? And then yes, there it was: no more than three grass strips with a concrete control tower, a single hangar and a scattering of Nissen huts in the middle of nowhere.

Viv knew the drill – she circled the airfield a couple of times to alert the ground crew to a forced landing and prayed that the undercarriage would hold. A second strip of metal tore away from the fuselage and a fresh blast of air tore at her. After a third circuit she grasped the stick and prepared to land. As she approached the grass runway, she had a blurred view of fields and hedges beneath her feet, felt the jolt and then a drag as her wheels hit the soft ground then saw the crash team speeding towards her in a specially adapted Austin pick-up, complete with water tank and hose.

Viv slammed on the brakes and brought the Typhoon to a skidding halt. The truck drew up alongside and three men in overalls leapt out. Two unreeled the hose in case of fire and snaked it across the ground while the third scrambled up on to the wing to help the pilot out of the cockpit.

'No fire,' Viv reported, lifting the hood and calmly undoing her harness. 'No damned floor either.' She pointed to the gaping holes in the fuselage. 'I'd better call Mayfair 120 and report the incident to the Transit Officer – this crate is going nowhere fast.'

Mary too flew into bad weather in her brand-new Tempest. The cloud cut visibility dramatically to less than 100 feet, but the wind wasn't too bad so she made an instantaneous decision to use her aircraft's impressive power to fly over the top. Out of the corner of her eye she spotted fellow pilot Horace, whose own Tempest was tucked into her slipstream, taking identical action. They ascended effortlessly, emerging from the dense white mist into clear blue sky. Mary immediately eased off the throttle to allow Horace to fly alongside and they gave each other a cheerful thumbs-up signal – co-conspirators in the officially illegal manoeuvre that they'd just executed. They were at 6,000 feet and would maintain this altitude and a comfortable cruising speed of 250 mph until they flew clear of the cloud.

Mary settled back to enjoy the experience of flying a new type. The Tempest responded brilliantly – its engine was smooth, the kick when she opened the throttle immense. *A touch too much, perhaps?* She eased back but there was no response. Instead, the surge of power kept on increasing. Her speed shot up to 300 and then 350 and she left Horace and his Tempest trailing in her wake.

Again Mary tried to reduce her revs. The needle on her airspeed indicator tipped the 400 mark. Damn it: the throttle was stuck! *What to do?* She must at all costs keep her head. Try climbing to lose speed – no good; she hurtled on, holding her original course and fighting to control her valuable new crate. Try the throttle again. No change – well and truly jammed. *What to do? Think! Find an aerodrome – any aerodrome.* But that meant descending through the lump of cloud at immense speed. *Do it – there's nothing else for it.*

Down she dipped at a stomach-churning rate, back into the whirling white mist, praying that the sky below was clear of other aircraft and preparing herself for whatever she might come up against.

Which aerodrome? A swift calculation told Mary to head for Castle Bromwich with its familiar landmarks and choice of runways. There would be help on hand if she managed to land the damn thing.

The only way to do this, with the throttle refusing to shift, was to cut the engine as she approached the runway then glide in. *Completely mad!* she told herself. Who in their right mind would deliberately cut off all power before landing? But it seemed the only possible way out.

Mary descended until the mist cleared then flew at terrifying speed over clusters of houses that made up small villages, followed by a patchwork of fields and larger towns spreading in every direction.

Wait, there is another way! What if Mary were to ditch the plane and bail out? She could flip the crate upside down in a matter of seconds, release her harness, open the hood and let gravity take control – one pilot ejected from the cockpit into free fall. A sharp tug on the parachute ripcord would see her floating safely to earth.

No one would blame her – it was what her instructors at training school had drilled into them to do in just such an emergency. 'We pay you to be safe, not brave' was the motto tattooed on her brain.

But then the Tempest continuing without its pilot didn't bear thinking about – she pictured the brand-new crate hurtling out of control, hitting the ground, exploding in a ball of fire, killing who knew how many innocent people.

No, Mary decided not to abandon ship. She would go down with the plane if need be.

She continued to head south, searching desperately for the Castle Bromwich factory. *There it is!* Before she had time to react, she overshot the aerodrome at the same uncontrollable speed then turned back on herself and headed north, trying to judge the highly dangerous tactic that she'd decided upon. She passed over the landing strips a second time, turned again and flew in a wide circle. When was the optimum time to cut the engine and glide in? One second too soon and Mary ran the risk of falling short of the runway. Too late and her plane would overrun, crash into the enormous factory buildings and burst into flames. *Damn the factory that hadn't carried out the necessary checks. Damn the throttle. Damn the whole bloody situation!*

One more circuit – five runways to choose from, only two of them clear for landing. From a height of 500 feet Mary saw twenty new Spits lined up at the edge of the airfield and trucks beetling to and fro. She was able to make out several small figures standing outside the factory entrance gazing up in bewilderment at her wild antics.

This is it; I'm coming in to land! Mary cut the engine. There was a sudden, deathly silence.

Her plane slowed as it glided on horizontal air currents until, at what she judged to be exactly the right moment, she lowered the flaps and lost height – a slow, smooth descent with every nerve-ending in Mary's body buzzing out a danger warning as tons of streamlined metal dropped from the sky. Here came the airfield and there were the panicky faces of a dozen observers. Time slowed and practically stood still. She steered towards the chosen runway that was clear of planes. The tarmac rushed up to meet her. There was a bounce and a sudden squeal of tyres, the smell of burning rubber. Jaw tightly clenched, Mary stamped on the brakes with all her might but found she was almost out of runway and must swerve violently to starboard to avoid the factory buildings. As she did so, she burst through a tall wire fence and heard the tip of her port wing snap off before her plane ploughed into a copse of elm trees, tearing off branches and felling saplings until it wedged itself between two tall trunks.

Silence again. Mary's harness had cut into her shoulders and breastbone. A side window had caved in and shards of Plexiglas lay everywhere. A propeller had been torn clean off.

Then there were loud shouts and men came running. Hands reached in through the shattered canopy. Blurred faces appeared.

'It's a girl. Get her out, quick!' The order came and was obeyed.

Mary felt herself lifted and carried, dimly saw branches overhead.

'Careful – she might have broken something.'

It was hard to breathe, impossible to talk.

'What the hell did she think she was playing at?'

The whole world spun – green trees and white sky, black earth, blurred faces. There was no pain but no part of Mary's body seemed to want to move. Attempting to raise her head and speak, she only managed a few incoherent words.

'What did she say?'

'That she's sorry,' someone interpreted.

The rescuers carried the injured pilot clear of the trees then through the wide gap in the wire fence towards a first-aid centre next to the factory office.

'And so she bloody well should be,' a more cynical voice said. 'That's ten thousand quid's worth of fighter plane that the damn silly fool has just wrecked.'

CHAPTER FOURTEEN

'Yes, sir, that's right.' Horace gripped the receiver tightly and spoke down the line to Douglas. 'Yes, sir; Third Officer Holland has been taken to hospital. Her Tempest didn't come off too badly, thank heavens. The erks at Castle Bromwich have set to work on her right away. They reckon they can have the crate up and running again by the start of next week.'

'Never mind the plane, damn it.' In the ops room at Rixley, Douglas listened intently to Horace's breathless report. 'What more do we know about Mary's injuries?'

'Concussion, sir, and bruises. They don't know yet if there are any broken bones.' Most things were a blur to Horace – he did have one clear memory of coming alongside Mary in his own Tempest and exchanging signals with her about flying over the unexpected lump of cloud, but after that his under-standing of what had taken place was hazy. The routine (unofficial, of course) should have been to climb until visibility improved then level out and continue steadily on their original course. To Hor-ace's surprise, once level at around 6,000 feet, Mary had failed to ease off on the throttle and had shot ahead of him like a bat out of hell. He had tailed her for a while, wondering why on earth she was showing off like that – a complete and utter waste of fuel, in his opinion. She'd surged on then suddenly plunged into a wild descent, back down through the clouds.

Should he stay on her tail or fly straight on towards the Isle of Wight? Horace was of the opinion that it was always better to follow orders so on he went, cursing Mary for her recklessness until the weather improved at last and he had a clear run over London and all points south. On reaching his destination, he'd been greeted by the hot-off-the-press news that his fellow ATA pilot had made an as-yet-unexplained forced landing at Castle Bromwich.

'No rhyme or reason as far as anyone knows,' one of the ground crew at Ventnor had reported to Horace. 'Made a right bloody mess of the Tempest, by all accounts. That's what happens when you trust a woman with a powerful, brand-new crate – it either ends up in the drink or, as in this case, wedged between two trees at the edge of a bleeding wood.'

A shocked Horace had absorbed the information then got straight on the blower to Rixley and given his version of events to Douglas, including Mary's inexplicable burst of speed and probable failure to keep an eye on her fuel gauge.

'I see.' Douglas weighed his words carefully. 'You put this down to pilot error?'

'I don't know for certain, sir, but it seems the most likely explanation.'

'You didn't think to follow her and check that she was all right?'

Horace's hand began to shake. Damned if he would

accept any blame here! 'My orders were to deliver my crate to the Isle of Wight, sir, and that's what I did.' He spoke stiffly, with a tell-tale rising intonation that warned Douglas not to argue with plain fact.

Douglas shook his head in despair. Horace was a plodder who lacked the imagination to deviate from a clear order under any circumstances. 'Right you are,' he said curtly.

'I'm only telling you what I saw, sir.'

'Right, yes. We'll have to wait to get the full story from Mary herself. Which hospital did they take her to, do you know? Never mind; I'll telephone Castle Bromwich and find out.' Douglas clattered the receiver into its cradle then paced the floor.

'Is something the matter?' Gillian looked up from her typewriter, fingers poised over the keys. There was only one pilot named Mary at the ferry pool and Gillian feared the worst.

'Third Officer Holland – forced landing; no explanation as yet,' Douglas muttered as he strode from the office. 'Cuts and bruises; hopefully nothing serious. Hilary needs to know.'

'He's in the met room with Fred Richards,' Gillian called after him, logging the fact that Mary was injured. She'd been taken to hospital. Wait until Dotty Kirk in the met room got to hear about this; from there the news would spread like wildfire through the ferry pool – 'Mary Holland has crash-landed in Castle Bromwich in a brand-new Tempest; no one knows why.'

'I suspected as much.' Hilary's face was gloomy as he received the news – not in the met room but in his

259

ground-floor office, where he and Douglas had regrouped in order to avoid being overheard. 'I should have taken Mary off today's rota; ought never to have let her fly.'

'What makes you say that?' Douglas demanded an explanation.

'This morning I gave her the date for Cameron's court martial, which obviously upset her.'

'You think that might explain her erratic behaviour prior to crash-landing?' This was bad news indeed.

'She assured me she was fit to fly and I took her at her word.'

'And why wouldn't you? The thing is, with a more experienced pilot we wouldn't have had the same concerns.' Douglas's frown was deep. 'With Jean or Bobbie, for instance; they've both clocked up so many hours that they could do the job in their sleep.'

'After all, this is a brand-new crate we're talking about.' Hilary thought his way around the problem. 'It's bound to have been checked and double-checked at the factory and here before take-off. One possibility is that Mary temporarily blacked out – the G-force in a Tempest can easily build to that point. That would account for the sudden descent.'

'We won't know until we've had chance to talk to her.' Douglas didn't relish going home that evening to tell Jean all about it. She was bound to be upset and worried by what had happened to her friend.

'Yes; until then we'll sit on this.' Hilary feared the effect on Rixley morale that unsubstantiated rumour might have. 'Is that possible?'

Douglas nodded. 'I'll order Horace and Gillian to

keep schtum and I won't mention it at home. Meanwhile, I'll get on to the hospital – find out how long they intend to keep Mary for.'

It was agreed in a cut-and-dried fashion – two superior officers negotiating their way through a crisis in the ranks, determined to carry on as normal.

It was only when Hilary had finished his day's work and driven back to the Grange and to the privacy of his own second-floor room that he really let himself consider the knock-on effect. Say Mary had been more distressed than she'd let on, say the weeks of worry over Cameron had finally got to her and caused her to have a panicky, tearful breakdown in mid-flight? It would only have been a matter of seconds before she'd lost control of her aircraft – of her hand on the stick and her feet on the pedals, of her ability to judge speed, height and distance.

From time to time you heard of such things; there were top pilots whose nerve suddenly went in the midst of battle, who succumbed to weird hallucinations, seeing devils instead of bullets or else angels sitting on banks of golden clouds, directing them towards the pearly gates. How much more likely that a woman under stress would succumb to a deadly attack of the jitters?

Hilary loosened his tie with a heavy sigh then reached for a glass and the bottle of whisky he kept in his bedside cabinet. Tomorrow he would telephone Hubert Norris and ask him to pass on the news about Mary's injuries to Cameron (as if Cameron didn't have enough to worry about).

But not tonight. Tonight Hilary would blunt the day's sharp edges with alcohol – he would listen to the wireless and hear how the lads were getting on in Budapest and Bucharest then listen to a speech by General de Gaulle. He would put his trust in the fact that the Free French were now standing by, ready to assist the Allied invasion when, not if, it happened. It had to be soon, surely to God, for how much thinner could he, Hilary, stretch himself in the daily, relentless attempt to keep his ferry pool functioning as it ought – up at the crack of dawn, approving chits, sending youngsters with minimal training up in monstrously powerful aeroplanes, risking life and limb to give the RAF the support it so desperately needed.

Bloody impossible. The whisky hit the back of Hilary's throat and he slumped down in a chair by the window. Today Mary Holland had escaped by the skin of her teeth. Tomorrow Horace or Agnes, Bobbie or, God forbid, Douglas's Jean would face the same odds. As for Viv Robertson; who knew how long the Canadian girl's luck would last or how far her daredevil skills would take her in the insanely dangerous days ahead?

Nurses floated silently in and out of Mary's ward. Their soft-soled shoes made no noise on the polished floor and their expressionless faces gave nothing away. A doctor had come to examine her – testing her reflexes and shining a light into her eyes, seemingly satisfied by what he observed.

'We'll soon have you back on your feet,' he'd promised her as he'd scribbled on the chart at the end of her bed. 'You had a lucky escape, young lady, all things considered.'

The tightly tucked sheets felt like a straitjacket and the overhead lights glared mercilessly. Mary lay on her back, reluctant to move, trying to piece together the day's chain of events.

It was a terrible muddle. At first all she could remember were the faces and hands of the ground crew who had come to her rescue. 'It's a girl!' 'Careful, she might have broken something.' 'What the hell . . . ?' Her tongue had felt numb as she'd mumbled the word 'sorry'. Then nothing after that until she'd found herself here, trapped between starched sheets, her whole body aching and with a bandage round her left wrist and gauze dressings on her neck and shoulders.

A nurse came to take her temperature with a manner as stiff and starched as the sheets, scarcely looking at her patient as she slipped the thermometer into Mary's mouth. Her uniform was dark blue, her cap and apron a dazzling white. 'You're with the ATA, I hear?' she asked as she stood by, waiting the obligatory seconds before she withdrew the thermometer.

Mary managed to nod.

'My youngest sister filled in the forms last week. She's waiting to hear back. Our mother hopes she doesn't get in.' The nurse extracted the thermometer, took the reading then replaced the slim glass tube in the tumbler on top of the cabinet. She went on to take Mary's pulse. 'If they accept Babs, Ma hopes it'll all be over before she finishes her training – *auf Wiedersehen*, Herr Hitler, and good riddance.'

Mary pressed her lips together and said nothing.

'No offence,' the nurse said briskly. 'You girls do a grand job but . . . well, the risk . . .'

Weariness made Mary's body heavy as lead – she hadn't the strength to respond or even to think straight. Relieved when the nurse wrote down the results and went away, she drifted on through the night. She floated, eyes closed and on the verge of sleep, until she relived the heavy thud on landing and the screech of tyres, felt the jolt, smelt burning rubber as her Tempest whined to a juddering halt.

There in her hospital bed her eyes opened wide. 'It's a girl!' 'Careful!' The overhead lights glared. Mary had another sudden flash of memory – she'd been cruising comfortably with Horace close behind – nothing out of the ordinary; just a lump of cloud to get over. Increase revs to climb over it, level off, ease off on the throttle. *Ease off!* Nothing – no response! If anything, the revs had increased. The roar of the engine once more filled Mary's ears. *Ease off, ease off!* The roar and the panic, alone in the cockpit. She'd had only seconds to make a decision to climb and climb as high as she could in a desperate attempt to slow down the engine . . . but still no go.

Trapped under her sheets Mary experienced the sickening, stomach-clenching moment when she'd understood the scrape she was in. It made her bruised, exhausted body break out in a cold sweat – to be utterly alone, without help, thousands of feet above the ground, hurtling helplessly through the air. There had been no one to turn to, not a soul to save her.

Then she recalled how, out of nowhere, a sudden sense of calm had taken over. Is that what happened in the face of death: an inexplicable slowing down of the heartbeat, a strangely cool, detached awareness of what needed to be done to escape death's clutches, as if she, Mary Holland, were merely a spectator looking in?

Descend and land – don't bail, not over houses and factories – stay with the crate; find a safe place to land. Calm as anything. An aerodrome with five runways had appeared as if by magic. A row of new Spitfires were lined up outside factory doors. She'd flashed by in a rush and a roar then she'd circled twice, judging the exact moment to cut her engine . . .

It all came back, crystal clear – the silent drift to earth through white mist, the thud of tyres on tarmac, the screech of brakes.

'I did it!' Mary breathed into the quiet ward.

A woman in the bed opposite tossed and turned in her sleep; a nurse in the corridor paused at the open door to glance in.

'I did it,' Mary said again. She would sleep now. In a day or two they would discharge her, she would return to Rixley and all would be well.

'The whole damned floor dropped out from under me. There was a hole this big!' Viv stretched her arms wide for the benefit of her small but attentive audience in the lounge at Burton Grange. 'I could make out the sheep on the ground and practically every darned blade of grass.'

She was back from Lancashire soon after six and was entertaining Bobbie and Agnes in the relaxed atmosphere of the officers' mess. Jean had joined Douglas at the bar and there was a low buzz of conversation from their group, which included Fred and Ernest.

'How big?' Agnes challenged dubiously.

'This big, I swear. The crate had practically fallen apart by the time I landed. The damned thing was only held together by duct tape. Luckily I still had two wheels intact for landing.'

'And you made it back in one piece.' As usual Bobbie enjoyed listening to Viv's colourful stories and watching her blue eyes widen and sparkle. Who cared if she exaggerated? It was part and parcel of her new friend's personality and it brightened up whichever room she happened to enter.

'My poor tootsies and fingers were frozen solid,' Viv complained. 'Blocks of ice, I kid you not. And guess what: the crash team advised me that the best cure for hypothermia was for me to strip off and let them massage my circulation back into action.'

'And did you?' Agnes wouldn't have been surprised.

'Sure I did.' Viv winked at Bobbie. 'Those guys are medically trained – they know what they're doing.'

Bobbie shook her head. 'She didn't,' she informed a scandalized Agnes.

'I should hope not.' Agnes pursed her lips and tapped her fingers against the arm of the settee.

'Where does that girl hide her sense of humour?' Viv rested back in her armchair and grinned as a disgruntled Agnes went off to the bar for another drink. 'I was tempted by the offer of a rub-down, though,' she confessed to Bobbie with a wide grin. 'How about you? How did you get on in the old Mitchell?'

'Not too badly.' Bobbie was distracted by Ernest's sudden breakaway from the group at the bar. The handyman limped towards the door to speak with someone whom Bobbie couldn't quite see. 'The

Mitchell's not the nimblest of crates to handle,' she admitted to Viv.

'Who's Ernest talking to?' Viv had followed the direction of Bobbie's gaze and was in a better position to identify the newcomer. 'Oh, God; what now?'

'Why? What's the matter?' All was soon made clear when Giles entered the room. Bobbie put a restraining hand on Viv's shoulder. 'Stay where you are. We don't want a scene.'

Viv watched her current enemy number one engage in conversation with Ernest and George. He was in 'civvies' – slacks, pullover and an open-necked shirt, standing with his back to her and obviously dishing out orders. He seemed not to have noticed Viv and Bobbie on the far side of the room. 'Who says we don't?' she demanded. 'Giles deserves "a scene", as you call it – for squirrelling away a wife, if nothing else. Whatever happened to "Till death do us part"?'

'Granted.' Bobbie squirmed uncomfortably in her seat.

'Not to mention what he did to Anna.'

'Hush! We don't know that – not for certain.'

'He has a nerve.' Ignoring Bobbie's warning, Viv crossed her legs and jiggled her foot. 'Look at him – butter wouldn't melt.'

Giles pulled out a pocketbook to demonstrate the point he was making. George and Ernest bowed their heads submissively.

'If either of them had forelocks they'd be tugging them.' An exasperated Viv uncrossed her legs and made as if to stand.

'No,' Bobbie protested. 'Now is not the time.'

'Says who?' The anger that had simmered in Viv

since the day at the races came to the boil. Why did everyone kowtow to Giles Parseval? Well, of course she knew the answer to that – it was the rotten old British class system, stuck in a time warp where jobs and houses were on the line if you so much as sneezed. 'Just watch me,' she muttered to Bobbie as she strode towards the bar.

Giles sensed Viv's approach. Naturally he'd seen her when he came in – who could miss her? But he carried on with his pretext for coming to the Grange unannounced – pointing out to George a discrepancy between orders for beer from the local brewery set against last month's takings at the bar. It was a flimsy but adequate excuse to conceal his real intention of seeking out Viv to clear the air. After all, Ray had filled him in on the cause of Viv's vanishing act at the races and now he wanted to put things right.

'So!' she proclaimed from three paces away.

He turned and at the same time felt George and Ernest melt discreetly away. Gradually Douglas, Jean and everyone else in the room fell silent and fixed their attention on what promised to be an explosive encounter.

'What's up with Viv?' Douglas muttered to Jean.

'I have no idea,' she fibbed.

'Hello, Viv.' Giles's breezy tone didn't fool anyone.

'Hello, Giles. How's your wife?' She looked unflinchingly into his eyes, disregarding the gasp that ran through the room. 'You know, the one you neglected to mention to me.'

'I don't see that Nora is any of your business.' Instead of giving way to the force of Viv's attack, Giles held his ground. He stared straight back at her.

'Is that so? How about your not telling me you were married and leading me on? I'd say that was definitely my business.'

'I say; Viv . . .' Douglas stepped forward to intervene.

'Who was leading who on? That's what I'd like to know,' Agnes queried under her breath and to no one in particular. Viv really was the limit, washing her dirty linen in public.

'Can't we talk about this in private?' Giles protested.

'There's nothing to talk about,' Viv shot back. She glanced around the room, reading various expressions – from cynically knowing to quietly sympathetic – and coming to the shameful realization that she, Jean and Bobbie were perhaps the only ones present who hadn't known about the existence of Nora Parseval. 'Oh, Jesus!' she groaned then backed away. 'What an idiot!'

'Viv . . .' Giles reached out his hand.

'Don't!' She swung round, almost bumping into Douglas. 'Did you know he was married?'

Douglas was surprised by the genuinely wounded look in Viv's eye. 'I assumed everyone did.'

'Not me.' She'd been played for a fool – humiliated and made to feel two inches tall.

'Viv,' Giles said again. 'Please!'

She shook her head and rushed from the room, leaving a pin-dropping silence broken only by the swing of the door on its hinges and a quiet click as it shut.

'Shall we see if she's all right?' Bobbie whispered to Jean at last.

'Yes, I'll go up to her room. You try the library.'

Hearing their plan, Giles struck a worldly, conciliatory note. 'That's it, everyone; the show's over for tonight.' He went back to talking about the brewery bill with George, as if Viv's outburst hadn't happened. Then, after two or three minutes, he said his farewells and left quietly.

He met Jean and Bobbie as they reconvened in the entrance hall. Neither had seen any sign of Viv. 'Tell her I'm most awfully sorry,' he said to Bobbie. 'I ought to have followed Ray's advice and come clean.'

Bobbie nodded silently.

'Really; very sorry,' he repeated, going out on to the terrace. He walked briskly along its length to the stable yard where he'd parked his Austin. He'd been fully prepared for Viv's anger but had misjudged the outcome, expecting to placate her with some smooth words and details about his impending divorce. But, hothead that she was, she hadn't given him the chance.

How much did he mind? Well, Giles had been sufficiently intrigued by Viv's bubbly personality and attracted by her dazzling beauty to attempt a reconciliation after the fiasco at the races, but not enough to feel heartbroken by her rejection. After all, they scarcely knew each other. Descending the steps into the stable yard, he searched in his trouser pocket for his car key.

'So!' Viv sat on the bonnet of his car, ready to take up where she'd left off. She'd bolted from the lounge, straight outside where the night air had cooled her down. Then she'd planned her next move, which was to waylay Giles and launch another attack before he could drive off.

'Bloody hell, you made me jump.' Perched like a seductress of the silver screen, legs crossed, leaning backwards. The effect was helped by the tight black skirt and an off-the-shoulder scarlet sweater. A breeze played through her dark curls as if by design.

'You really think you're God's gift, don't you?' Viv continued, all guns blazing. 'Snap your fingers and the girls come running.'

'Do they?' Giles took out a silver cigarette case, opened it and approached warily. 'If you say so.'

'No thanks; filthy habit.' Viv rejected the offer of a cigarette.

'Quite agree.' He took one from the case then used a slim lighter to light up. 'About Nora,' he began, inhaling then aiming the jet of smoke straight up in the air.

'Ah yes; the wife tucked away in the dower house pending divorce – Ray told Bobbie all about it and she filled me in.'

'Guilty,' he said quietly as he leaned against the wheel arch, his back half-turned. 'Did Ray also say Nora was fifteen years older than me and has been married twice before?'

'What difference does that make?' It did, though, in a way that Viv didn't immediately understand. And it interested her. She slid down from the bonnet then made a slow circuit around the car.

'The previous husband died, leaving an enormous fortune built during the early eighteenth century on the importation of sugar from the West Indies.'

'Oh God; slavery.'

'Quite.' Giles inhaled again then flicked ash to the ground. 'It was too good an opportunity for my father to pass by: a wealthy woman of a certain age . . . I was the sacrificial lamb.'

'Worse and worse,' Viv muttered.

'I'm being honest – believe me, it wasn't a love match on either side. My family was strapped for cash, Nora was on the lookout for husband number three, and apparently I fitted the bill.'

'But why agree to marry her if you didn't love her? Why not sell Burton Grange or one of the other estates to free up some cash?'

'Back then it would have been seen as a come-down for the Parsevals; my father wouldn't hear of it. And I wasn't quite myself at the time – Veronica had recently died of scarlet fever.'

'Your sister?' The solemn girl in the pale blue dress in the painting; the owner of the pink tutu. The news left Viv speechless.

'The very one.' Damn it, he sounded flippant! Why did he do that, about Veronica of all people? 'Anyway, marrying Nora didn't seem the worst thing in the world. So I went ahead.'

Viv struggled to find the right words. 'I'm sorry about your sister.' Now she understood why the room with the childhood mementoes was kept locked. In a way there was blood on the floor after all.

'Not as sorry as I was a year into the marriage.' *Self-pitying now; damn, damn!* Giles shook his head as if to clear it. 'Best not to go into that.'

Viv's attack faltered. 'Look, you've told me some stuff I wasn't expecting, OK? I'm sure it was compli-cated.'

'You can say that again.' Complicated and miser-able, locked in a relationship to bolster family finances, married to an emotionally sterile woman who sprayed dissatisfaction like toxic weedkiller, shrivelling all who came into contact – the breakfast egg not boiled to Nora's liking, the seat at the opera not prestigious enough, the flaw in her diamond brooch not revealed by the jeweller, the crease in the table linen that had escaped the attention of the housekeeper; all formed an endless list of complaints.

'But it doesn't alter the fact that you made a fool of me.' Viv's mood was calmer now and she stepped away from Giles. She glanced up to see a large, bright moon rise above the roof of the stable block and the first pinprick glimmers of stars sprinkle the sky. 'As it happens, I wasn't about to fall in love with you anyway.'

Giles threw down his cigarette. 'Thanks. I suppose I deserve that.'

'You're good company, don't get me wrong. But I don't get the no-sir, yes-sir business; the way you expect the world to revolve around you. Plus the way your sort never really say what you mean. You don't ever feel the need to explain.'

'My sort?' He leaned back against the car and folded his arms, inviting Viv to say more.

'You think you're entitled – I don't know; to the best of everything, to respect when you haven't worked to deserve it. That's what sets my teeth on edge.'

'Because you weren't born into it,' he pointed out. 'You might feel differently if you had been.'

'Touché! And you're right – I wasn't born anywhere near a silver spoon.'

Giles shrugged. 'You happen to have got me all wrong. I work bloody hard at what I do. These

273

estates don't run themselves, you know. I'm responsible for helping dozens of tenant farms to pay their way and for meeting yields imposed by the War Office, not to mention mending Abbot's Gate's leaking roof and shoring up its crumbling walls.'

'Boo hoo; poor you.'

Giles grunted. 'I realize that we're never going to see eye to eye. But at least we're having this conversation and clearing the air. That's the real reason I came here – to say sorry and for us to part on better terms.'

Viv cocked her head to one side and considered the apology. *Not so fast; not so easy, buddy.* And yet Giles did sound sincere and he looked contrite; head bowed, arms folded, leaning against the gleaming grey car. If it weren't for the elephant in the room – Anna and the baby – she might at that moment have forgiven him. 'Aren't you forgetting something?' she warned with quiet insistence.

'Am I?' His mind flew back over their outings – lunch at the White Hart in Highcliff, the disastrous day at the races. 'What other heinous crimes have I committed?'

'Do I have to spell it out?' Viv kept her distance. There was no one around and she was determined to get her message across loud and clear. 'OK then: A-N-N-A.'

Giles stood up straight and let his arms fall to his sides. 'What are you talking about?'

'Come off it – you know full well! Anna, the baby, Florrie Loxley.' There; that had skewered him. The confident veneer vanished in an instant – Giles's chest caved and his shoulders slumped forward while his face was transformed by what Viv could only interpret as the dismay of discovery.

'What about them?' he gasped.

'Don't make it any worse than it already is.' Viv shook her head then mounted the first two steps up on to the terrace.

Giles ran after her and dragged her back down. He kept a strong grasp on her arm. 'Oh no you don't! Out with it: say what you have to say.'

She twisted free, rubbing the spot where his fingers had pressed into her flesh. 'The secret is out,' she hissed. 'Anna Janicki had your baby and you did what comes naturally – you covered it up.'

'Who says so?' Giles grabbed her again and pushed his face close to hers, his handsome features distorted.

'Ha, you don't deny it!' His silence was all the evidence she needed. 'There is a baby – your wife found out and that's why you brought Anna here: to keep her out of the way and hide what happened.'

'Who claims I'm the father? Does Anna say I am?' A desperate panic registered on Giles's features.

'The poor thing is too scared. She's terrified.'

Giles released Viv, turning away and muttering words that she didn't catch.

'Can't you at least tell Anna where the baby is?' She pursued him across the yard. 'For pity's sake, she needs to know!'

'What has it got to do with you?' He reached his car and wrenched open the door. 'I've seen to it that Anna has a job and a roof over her head; as far as I'm concerned that's the end of the matter.'

Viv watched him slide into the driver's seat and

turn on the engine. She held on to the door handle to prevent him from closing it. 'Can't you understand how cruel it is? Aren't you ashamed?'

'Please let go,' he said.

'Well, aren't you?' He was the stronger of the two and was able to pull the door shut so she hammered the side of her fist against the windscreen. She saw how Giles's features had now set in stubborn lines, jaw clenched and eyes narrowed.

He put the car into gear and released the hand-brake then put his foot on the accelerator.

Viv jumped back as the car jerked forward. 'That's right; run away, why don't you?'

The car gathered speed and swept under the arch out on to the lane, a pale ribbon in the moonlight, with trees forming a green tunnel and the tyres crunching and spitting up gravel as Giles swerved round the first bend.

Coward. The yard was silent. Viv watched the red tail lights disappear. *Dirty rotten, no-good coward.*

Up on the terrace a quiet, gaunt figure watched and listened.

CHAPTER FIFTEEN

'What's up?' It was Thursday evening and the end of another hectic day for Jean. A hop over to Aireby with an ageing Hurricane for the RAF mechanic recruits to disembowel and practise on had been followed by a longer run to Derby to deliver a spanking new B-17 Fortress: a Class 5 with four engines that could outstrip anything the *Luftwaffe* might throw at it. From Derby she caught a train home and found herself by coincidence in the same carriage as Horace. 'Why so down in the dumps?'

'I got held up,' he grumbled. 'Couldn't get off the Isle of Wight in time to catch the overnight train. Then this morning I got diverted out of King's Cross.' He was unshaven and bleary eyed, sitting with his shoelaces untied and his feet resting on his canvas overnight bag.

'That's right; you and Mary bagged the Tempests yesterday.' After placing her belongings on the over-head rack, Jean settled into the sway and rattle of the fast-moving train. 'Where is Mary, by the way? Why isn't she with you?'

Pretending not to hear, Horace stared out of the window at allotments clinging to the outskirts of the city, studying the various sheds and neat patches of tilled earth.

'Horace?' Jean queried. 'Did Mary get held up in Ventnor with you?'

He shook his head. 'I'm not allowed to say.'

'Why ever not?' She felt her heart skip a beat.

'I'm under strict orders; that's why.'

Seeing that Horace wanted to be left alone, Jean fell silent for a while. Rain began to spatter against the windows, streaking the glass and blurring their outlook. Allotments soon gave way to open country-side, to grazing sheep interspersed with fields of new green wheat. Had Mary got as far as the Isle of Wight, Jean wondered, or had she run into trouble of some sort? But in that case, surely Douglas would have passed on the information to her. It was no good; Jean had to press Horace further. 'Is Mary all right?'

Frowning, he leaned forward to rest his elbows on his thighs, hands clasped. 'You need to ask Douglas.'

'Douglas isn't here.' In some agitation she gestured around the empty carriage, 'Horace, you have to tell me or I'll imagine the worst. I promise I'll keep it to myself.'

'Hand on heart?' This was tricky; an order was an order but on the other hand Horace respected Jean and wanted to put her out of her misery.

'I swear.'

'All right then; no, Mary didn't make it to Ventnor. It looks like she ran out of fuel and was forced to land in Castle Bromwich.'

'Ran out of fuel?' Jean was incredulous. She gave a hostile stare to a woman with a suitcase who slid open the carriage door, convincing the fellow passenger to change her mind about entering. The woman slid the door closed then shuffled on down the corridor. 'Didn't the ground crew double-check the tanks before Mary took off?'

Horace stared down at his hands and didn't answer directly. 'We had to climb over a lump of cloud – that used up extra juice. Then Mary took it into her head to play a little game.'

'What kind of game?' This sounded more like Viv than Mary.

'She dared me to race her; shot ahead of me like I don't know what. I wasn't having it – let Mary play silly devils if she wanted to but don't expect me to join in.'

'I see.' But Jean didn't; not really. She grew ever more anxious on Mary's behalf. 'So you're saying that's why she ran out of petrol?'

'That would explain what happened. I told Douglas that he should get the Castle Bromwich erks to check the tanks and see.'

'Why not ask Mary herself?' Rain spattered and wind gusted while Jean's thoughts ran riot.

Horace mumbled his answer. 'She spent the night in hospital. She's not badly hurt but I'm not sure how much she'll remember.' There; he'd said enough.

The news shocked Jean into silence. Then a fresh thought struck her – Douglas must have known about this and chosen not to tell her. How could he have kept this from her? The repetitive click of the train's wheels became *how could he, how could he, how could he*? Last night they'd taken Patch for a twilit walk in the wood then slept in the same bed and Douglas hadn't said a word about Mary crash-landing and ending up in hospital. *How could he, how could he?* Jean leaned sideways and rested her flushed cheek against the cold window, fighting to hold back tears.

'Why didn't you tell me about Mary?' Jean flung her bag down on the kitchen table. The rain had drenched her from head to foot during the short walk home from the station. She'd arrived weary and still furious with Douglas.

He winced but quickly regained his composure. 'I'm afraid I was under orders not to.'

'Whose orders?' She kicked off her shoes then unzipped her flying jacket.

'Hilary's. The circumstances are unclear. He wants to wait until he hears Mary's version of events.'

'And meanwhile her friends are left in the dark.' Jean pictured Mary in a hospital bed, shocked, hurt and alone. 'Couldn't you have stretched a point for once?'

'I gave my word.' Douglas had been upstairs when he'd heard Patch bark at Jean's approach. His pleasure had immediately turned to dismay when he saw her pale, angry face. 'The main thing is, Mary's injuries aren't serious – cuts and bruises but no broken bones.'

'Thank heavens for that, but that's not what I'm upset about,' Jean interrupted. 'You should have ignored Hilary. Where would have been the harm in letting me and the other girls know that our friend had been hurt? Anyway, what do you mean "unclear"? Horace gave me a pretty straightforward account of what happened.'

'You learned about it from Horace?' It was Douglas's turn to interrupt.

'Damn!' Jean realized that she had broken her own promise. She grew more flustered than ever. 'The plain fact is Stan or Gordon or someone else in the ground crew must have failed to check that there was enough fuel in Mary's tanks to get her all the way to Ventnor.'

'Jean . . .' Douglas had never seen his wife so upset, with hectic red patches creeping up from her neck to her pale cheeks, her gestures clumsy and uncontrolled. He noticed that the dog, sensing trouble, had crept under the table with his tail between his legs.

Douglas ventured towards Jean and tried to put an arm on her shoulder.

'Don't!' She shrugged him off. 'How could you?'

'How could I what?' Helpless and confused, he realized he must wait for the anger to subside.

'Keep it a secret. We're meant to share everything now that we're married.' Once the tears started there was no stopping them. With a choked sob Jean sank into a chair, slumped forward and buried her face in her hands.

'Oh, love.' He crouched beside her and this time she didn't push him away. 'I'm sorry you feel this way. But I was under an obligation not to speak. And according to Hilary there may be a bit more to it than meets the eye.'

Jean spoke between sobs. 'Horace told me some nonsense about Mary wanting to get into a race with him but I didn't believe it. I know she wouldn't – she's not the type.'

Gently he prised her hands from her face. 'I'm not so sure. Apparently Mary wasn't herself when she took off in the Tempest yesterday morning. She was under a great deal of strain.'

Jean raised her tear-stained face and looked questioningly at him.

'About Cameron's court martial; Hilary gave her the date – it's this coming Monday. She was obviously very distressed but she insisted she was fit to fly.'

'And he let her?'

'It was Mary's decision. Hilary took her at her word.'

Jean accepted the handkerchief that Douglas offered her, allowing the implications to sink in. 'You're saying she may have acted out of character?'

'Perhaps. The evidence points in that direction. But as I say, Hilary wants to hear Mary's version of events before he makes any judgement.'

Jean let out a long sigh then dried her eyes. 'Yes,' she decided. 'But there's no need to worry; Mary will soon set the record straight. Have you any idea when the hospital plans to discharge her?'

'Tomorrow.' Giving her hand a reassuring squeeze, Douglas felt as if they had flown through a storm after this, their first row as a married couple. True, there might be a few more bumps ahead, depending on the outcome – if Mary's story didn't hang together, for instance, or if Stan or another member of the ground crew were proved to have failed in their duties.

'Good.' Jean was slowly getting back to normal, thinking straight and hoping for the best. It was high time to take off her wet clothes so she headed for the stairs. 'The sooner the better. Then this thing will blow over and we can all concentrate on what we're paid to do, which is to fly those dratted crates from A to B.'

An elderly porter at Snow Hill station in Birmingham carried Mary's bag on to the train and stowed it for her in the overhead rack. He wished her luck with her journey. 'Take it easy,' he advised as he surveyed Mary's bandaged wrist and the patches of gauze taped to her neck and forehead. 'You look as if you've been in the wars.'

She thanked him and smiled weakly at the platitude. If he only knew!

A broad-faced, middle-aged woman sitting opposite took out a bag of mints and offered them to Mary. 'Go on, love – help yourself,' she urged as doors slammed and the guard blew his whistle.

Mary took a sweet and popped it in her mouth, hoping that the kind-hearted mint-profferer didn't turn out to be a chatterbox who would engage in small talk for the length of their journey. To avoid it, she leaned back and closed her eyes.

'That's right, love; you rest.' The woman took out some knitting and began to work her needles with expert ease.

With a hiss of steam the train lurched forward, then it settled into a smooth rhythm that did indeed almost send Mary off to sleep. The rapid click of the woman's needles merged with the clickety-click of the train's wheels, and she let her mind drift back over her two long days in hospital then forward to her arrival at Burton Grange, picturing the smiles of welcome she would get from Viv and Bobbie. Then a frown flitted over Mary's face and she shifted in her seat as she envisaged an ominously quiet weekend in the uneasy build-up to Cameron's appearance at his court martial on Monday.

'Are you all right, love?' her fellow passenger enquired.

'Yes, ta,' she said without opening her eyes.

The clicking continued. 'Those bruises look nasty. Your uniform tells me you're one of those Atta girls. I'm right, aren't I?'

Mary sighed and opened her eyes. 'Yes; I'm a third officer with the ATA.'

'You don't look old enough. I bet everyone tells you that. I've always liked that uniform – it's a lovely shade of blue.' Clickety-click, chubby fingers looping wool, knit-purl, knit-purl. 'Very smart, I call it; especially the what-do-you-call-it – the forage cap. And everyone knows your lot do a grand job. My name's Ethel, by the way. What's yours?'

Olive was waiting at Rixley station to pick up Mary and drive her the short distance to the Grange. 'Squadron leader's orders,' she said with a swift, sharp-eyed glance at Mary's bandages and bruises.

'I could easily have walked,' Mary protested as she handed over her bag.

'Mine is not to reason why.' Olive had a feeling that all was not well at the Grange. Nobody had said anything directly but there was a rumour going round the ferry pool that Mary was in trouble and that Hilary was gunning for her. 'So what happened to you?' she asked as they got in the car.

'I wish I could be sure.' The familiar village sights

in patchy sunlight helped revive Mary's spirits. They saw Florrie sweeping her front step in readiness for her evening trade, then the church with its square tower and blue clock, and finally the post office at the end of a short row of terraced houses.

'You don't remember what happened?' Mary's answer surprised Olive as she turned down the back lane towards the Grange.

'Yes, but I can't explain *why* it happened.'

'No need to snap; I was only asking.'

Mary apologized. 'The damned throttle in the Tempest got stuck at full revs; that's what happened.'

'You don't say.' Driving into the stable yard under the clock tower, Olive's reaction was muted. She pulled up beside Hilary's car. 'The squadron leader wants to see you right away,' she informed Mary.

'Rightio.' She got stiffly out of the Ford then reached in the boot for her bag.

Olive got there first. 'I'll take this up to your room for you. He's in the library.'

'Right; better not keep him waiting.' Mary felt the first inkling that something unpleasant was in the offing. She straightened her tunic ('a lovely shade of blue') then her forage cap ('very smart') before she and Olive climbed the steps on to the terrace.

'Good luck,' Olive said as they entered the house by the main door then went their separate ways. *She'll need it if the rumours turn out to be true.* It was a pity because Olive had a soft spot for Mary, coming up through the ranks as she had. It was true that she could be prickly at times but she was a genuine sort and in for a shock, if she did but know.

*

'Surprise!' Ray made a beeline for Bobbie across the Fox's crowded snug.

Bobbie sat with Viv, enjoying a well-earned drink. The two girls were still in uniform, fresh off the train from Manchester Victoria. It was Friday evening and their time to relax.

'I hoped I'd find you here,' Ray told Bobbie as he drew up a chair. They'd made no firm arrangement after their last meeting at Thresham, which had seemed strange to Viv when Bobbie had mentioned it to her earlier in the week.

'You mean everything was going swimmingly between you until it came to parting company – you'd kissed, and so on?' Privately Viv had blamed Ray for not landing his catch; any guy with a grain of common sense would pin down a girl as gorgeous as Bobbie by making a follow-up date. 'Doesn't he know you could have your pick of any of the pilots here at Rixley?'

Bobbie had blushed and tried to make excuses. 'It's not like that.'

'Not like what?'

'It's not as if anything is settled between Ray and me. We're happy to take it one day at a time.' The second kiss in the house at Thresham had turned out not to be as conclusive as Bobbie had hoped. It had gone on for longer than the first and left her breathless. Her heart had fluttered but any hope that the embrace would lead to a declaration of feelings hadn't materialized. Instead, they'd held hands as Ray had walked her down to the stable yard and asked Ronnie to run Bobbie back to Rixley. 'Dad's due back any minute,' he'd explained. 'He'll want to go through the accounts with me.'

Viv had popped her lips at Bobbie's protestations. 'Pah! Who are you trying to kid? I have no clue what you two are playing at. He plainly likes you and vice versa. I've seen the way you look at each other. And you know what seals the deal for me?'

Bobbie had shaken her head.

'Horses!' Viv had been in full flow. 'I picture a future for you two perfumed not with roses but with fragrant liniment rub and mane detangler, hoof poultices and saddle soap. You'll arrive at the church for your wedding in a horse and carriage and you'll name the foals born on the Thresham yard Spitfire, Hurricane and Tempest, after the crates you flew as an Atta girl.'

'I think Ray's father might have something to say about that.' Bobbie had laughed and taken the ribbing in good part but had tried to think no more about it. She meant what she said: it was one day at a time with Ray Moore; two kisses and counting until she was more certain of where she stood.

So to have him casually dropping by at the Fox on a Friday evening was a nice surprise that made her heart skip a few beats.

'What can I get you to drink?' Ray asked Viv and Bobbie as he hovered by their table.

'Nothing for me, thanks.' Viv stood up. 'Three's a crowd. Anyway, Mary's due back at the Grange soon and I want to be there for her when she arrives – in case she needs moral support.'

She and Bobbie briefly discussed the rumours circulating about their friend – that she'd crashed her crate and ended up in hospital, that there was uncertainty surrounding the whys and wherefores.

'I won't be far behind you.' Bobbie's smile was nervous as Viv said she would leave the lovebirds to it then made a quick exit. 'Sorry about that,' she told Ray.

'Lovebirds,' he echoed with raised eyebrows. 'Is that what we are?'

'Take no notice of Viv.' Bobbie was sure that her cheeks had turned a bright, unbecoming red. 'I'll have a Dubonnet and lemonade, please.'

'Right you are.' Ray smiled as he went to the bar to wait his turn. Lovebirds was promising, even if Bobbie was embarrassed by it. Viv might be jumping the gun as usual but it was a definite nudge in the right direction. In Ray's quiet, reflective moments late at night or when he was out on the gallops, whenever his thoughts turned to Bobbie, he pictured her as a small, brightly coloured bird resting on a tree branch that was just out of reach. He knew he must stay very quiet and do nothing to alarm her and risk her flying off.

So he bought a pint for himself and Bobbie's Dubonnet then, with a spring in his step, carried them back to the table.

In her room at the Grange after her early exit from the Fox, Viv finished flicking through a magazine containing bright and breezy suggestions for housewives about how to spin out the week's food rations and then a piece on Bing Crosby, said in the article to be 'the person to have done most for the morale of overseas servicemen', ahead of Eisenhower, Roosevelt and Bob Hope. Viv remembered seeing the singer act the main role in *Holiday Inn* at an air-conditioned cinema in Los Angeles and recalled hearing his soothing, velvety voice crooning the words to 'White Christmas'. *This might help cheer Anna up a little*, she thought as she rolled up the magazine before slipping her bare feet into a pair of white tennis shoes. She was dressed in navy blue culottes and a white sweater with a red bandanna holding back her wayward curls.

We rattle around here like peas in a drum. The thought flitted into Viv's mind as she descended the wide stairs. All was quiet as she crossed the hall, walked quickly along the corridor leading below stairs then knocked on Anna's door.

There was no answer so Viv knocked a second time.

The same again – no answer and no sign of movement from within the room.

This was strange; Anna never went out. Viv felt the hairs on the back of her neck prickle as she knocked a third time then cautiously turned the knob and opened the door.

The room was orderly and spotlessly clean in the fading evening light. The bed was carefully made with the pristine sheets turned back. A pile of neatly folded clothes – Anna's black dress, cap and apron – sat on a bedside table, a towel hung from a peg behind the door, but what struck Viv was absence – she saw no personal items such as hairbrush or slippers under the bed. Three strides took her across the room to the small chest of drawers under the high window. She pulled out the drawers one at a time then slammed them shut – each one was empty. Then she flung open the door of the utility-style wardrobe and stood back in dismay as she took in a rail with three empty coat hangers and a naphthalene-saturated mothball hanging from a small hook.

Anna was gone without a trace.

Straight away Viv raised the alarm. She ran up the two flights of stairs to Hilary's room and reported that Anna had gone missing. Hilary took the news seriously and set about letting people know. He telephoned the emergency number at the ferry pool to organize an ad hoc search party, comprising Bob, Gordon and Olive. They were to concentrate on the aerodrome and its immediate surroundings. Meanwhile, Viv was to round up helpers to check outbuildings at the Grange, then she must spread the word in the village.

'Don't try knocking on Mary's door,' Hilary cautioned. 'She's back from Castle Bromwich but she's not in a fit state to help with the search.' *Far from it.* His interview with Mary in the library hadn't gone well. He'd begun by apologizing for not recognizing how upset she'd been on the morning in question.

'*Upset?*' Mary had objected fiercely to his use of the word. She'd refused to sit down, had insisted that a jammed throttle had been the cause of her crash-landing – in a brand-new Tempest, for God's sake! How did she expect him to believe that? Hilary had ventured to put it to her that emotional distress had played its part. Why else would she have misjudged her landing so badly? She'd vehemently denied it and had gone on insisting that both factory and ground crew had overlooked a serious mechanical fault. They'd soon reached an impasse. The further

Mary had gone down the jammed-throttle road, the less inclined Hilary had been to believe her (she'd displayed too much emotion and suffered from a serious lack of rationality; both cardinal sins in his book). Then, damn it, she'd started to cry.

'OK; I'll check in on Mary later,' Viv decided. Right now Anna was her top priority. She left Hilary preparing to call Newpark to inform Sir Thomas about the housekeeper's disappearance, then managed to collar Horace and Agnes to begin the search.

'How do you know for certain that Anna's gone missing?' Horace intended to get the facts straight before relinquishing his Friday evening for what could turn out to be a fool's errand. 'The rain's cleared up. Couldn't she have just gone for a walk?'

Viv soon put him right. 'Her wardrobe's empty, you idiot! She's packed up and taken everything with her.'

'When was she last seen?' Agnes followed whirlwind Viv out on to the damp terrace then down into the stable yard. 'Was she here at breakfast time?'

Viv didn't know the answer. She looked into every stable then ran up the stone steps to check the grooms' living quarters. Come to think of it, it was perfectly possible that Anna had made her getaway in the dead of the previous night, while everyone was asleep. Viv's nerves tightened another notch as she made a thorough search of the unused loft.

Agnes waited at the bottom of the steps. 'Where can she have gone?'

The pointless questions were slowing Viv down. 'Listen, Agnes, why not go and help Horace in the basement?' There was a warren of below-stairs corridors leading to boot rooms, walk-in larders and wine cellars for the two of them to search. Meanwhile, Viv decided to take a bike from one of the stables and set off towards Burton Wood. She left Agnes standing as she cycled at speed under the clock tower and along the lane.

Put yourself in Anna's shoes. Viv tried to focus as she rode the rough track through the wood. *You're sad as hell about giving up your baby. You're mad with Giles Parseval for covering things up. But you have no money; not one single cent to your name. No one in Rixley is on your side – in fact, they're part of the cover-up.*

What would I do? Viv's front tyre hit a tree root and threw her off-balance. She righted herself and kept on pedalling in the gloom. *If it were me I'd be hammering on Florrie Loxley's door and refusing to go away until she told me what I needed to know. But then Anna's different.*

Anna was the type to suffer in silence. How long had it taken her to open up to Viv and the others even just a little bit? She was like a thin, pale ghost, scarcely made of flesh at all. And now she'd vanished and left no trace.

Viv cycled on until she came to Fern Cottage. Luckily the downstairs light was on and the door stood open. 'Jean, Douglas; are you there?'

The dog barked then Jean appeared at the door. 'What's wrong? Is it Mary?'

'No; it's Anna.' Viv stayed astride her bike. 'She's disappeared.'

'Oh, good Lord!' Jean called for Douglas to join her. Quickly they gathered the bare facts from Viv. 'Right, I'll get my coat.'

'What do you want me to do?' Douglas asked.

'Come into the village with me and Jean. One of us should go to the train station and ask the station-master if Anna bought a ticket and if so, where to.'

'Good idea; I'll do that.' Douglas was calm as he fell in with Viv's suggestion, ordering Patch to stay in the house then closing the door on him. Jean and Viv were already twenty paces ahead so he hurried to catch up with them.

'Did Anna have enough money for a train ticket?' Jean wondered about the practicalities. 'Isn't it more likely that she set off on foot?'

'I'll try the station anyway.' Douglas split off from Jean and Viv as they emerged from the wood.

The two women hurried on through the village to the Fox and Hounds. The Friday-night swell of noise emerging through the open windows made them pause to discuss their tactics.

'What do we do? Do we go in and announce that Anna has vanished?' Jean asked.

Viv pictured the full-scale, public hue and cry. 'No; she would hate that.' Propping her bike against the lamp post and deciding to be more discreet, she followed Jean into the bar and picked out Ray and Bobbie among the crowd. Then they saw Florrie pulling pints in a bulky, plum-coloured dress that was thirty years out of fashion, serving a bunch of underage army apprentices and elderly local farmers, plus Ernest and a younger companion.

Spotting Viv and Jean, Bobbie beckoned them across with a smile. Ray looked less pleased to see them – it seemed the lovebird tag hadn't given him and Bobbie the whole evening to themselves after all.

Jean's explanation was quick and to the point. 'It's

urgent; Anna has vanished and we have to broaden the search as much as possible. Goodness knows what will happen to her if we don't find her soon.'

Ray was already on his feet. 'We can use my car – that'll speed things up.'

'Where shall we look?' Bobbie wanted to know.

'Anywhere, everywhere!' Viv called over her shoulder as she singled out Ernest and drew him away from his companion; a good-looking man in his twenties with neatly parted hair, dressed in a tweed jacket, collar and tie. 'When did you last see Anna?' Viv wasted no time in asking the Grange handyman the urgent question.

Ernest was taken aback. 'Steady on. Why do you want to know?'

'Her room's empty. She's packed up and left. Come on, Ernest; have you seen her today?'

'No, not today.' He seemed disgruntled and anxious to get back to his drinking companion, who viewed Viv suspiciously as he took a sip from his pint glass.

'Thanks, Ernest; you've been a great help!' Viv had practically heard his brain cogs whirring to arrive at his grudging answer. So she reached across the bar to tap Florrie on the shoulder.

'No,' Florrie said without waiting for Viv to speak. 'If it's the Polish woman you're after, I've not seen hide nor hair of her.'

Viv turned away with an exasperated sigh. She went back to Jean, Bobbie and Ray to discuss their next move.

'Perhaps we should involve the police,' Bobbie suggested. The nearest station was fifteen miles away in

Maltby Bay, manned by a desk sergeant and a solitary constable.

'Not yet.' Jean tried to keep a clear head. 'Not until we're sure that Anna's in trouble. Who's to say that she hasn't upped and left for a good reason?' There was perhaps someone Anna could have gone to if the work at the Grange had proved too much or if she'd been overwhelmed by grief over her lost baby; a friend they didn't know about with whom she could take refuge.

'No; she would have informed Hilary or at the very least left a note.' Instinct told Viv that Anna had no fall-back plan. 'Listen; Ray and Bobbie, you take the car and check everywhere you can think of, including farmers' barns and outhouses. Jean, you and I will find Douglas and do the same on foot – the bus shelters, sheds, outside privies, and so on. We'll all meet back here in an hour – OK?'

It was agreed. Jean and Viv then met up with Douglas, whose talk with the stationmaster had proved fruitless.

He produced a torch from his pocket as they ventured down a damp, dark ginnel at the back of the post office. 'This will come in handy.'

The yellow beam raked along the hedge bottom and across small yards attached to the row of terraced houses. A dog barked and brought a stout woman to her back door. The dog burst out of the kitchen and bounded towards Viv, Jean and Douglas, teeth bared. He reared up against the wall and his snarls were accompanied by some ripe advice from the householder not to skulk around in the dark. And no she hadn't seen the foreign woman, who was a German spy for all she knew and could therefore go to hell.

Viv glanced at Douglas and Jean with growing dismay.

'Let's go,' Douglas grunted. The alley ended in a dead end so it was necessary to retrace their footsteps until they came out on to the main street. 'Like a needle in a bloody haystack,' he complained.

There was more talk of the police and a decision was made that Douglas should at least make the telephone call. Meanwhile, Jean would run back through the wood to the Grange and collect Douglas's car.

'Ray and Bobbie headed off in the direction of Northgate. That means Douglas and I should follow the Highcliff road,' she decided.

Once more it was agreed.

'You'll be all right by yourself?' Jean asked Viv as Douglas limped towards the telephone box at the end of the street.

'I'll be fine.' Viv wanted to check the church porch. 'I just have this bad feeling that Anna might—'

'I know,' Jean interrupted. 'You don't have to spell it out.'

'We have to find her,' Viv said simply.

She ran off towards the church, approaching the graveyard with a mounting sense of dread. Anna might be desperate was what Viv had been about to say. She might have reached the point where the pain and suffering were too much and decided that she had nothing left to live for. And then what?

With a dry throat and pounding heart, Viv stepped into the shadow of the lichgate. She paused there and gazed across the ancient green mounds and

296

worn headstones then up at the square tower of St Wilfred's, her face dampened by a cold drizzle. A quiet church, a last refuge? Anna in her long grey coat, carrying her suitcase, might have walked this path, opened the oak door then stepped inside, intending never to come out. She would have seen a stone christening font to the left, a spiral staircase up into a belfry, light filtering into the apse through red-and-blue stained glass, rows of carved pews, a pulpit and an altar, and behind it the painted image of a crucified Christ.

CHAPTER SIXTEEN

'Douglas said that the police sergeant at Maltby Bay didn't seem interested.' Bobbie stood at Mary's window, looking down at the bomb craters encircled by barbed wire on the lawns of the Grange. She'd eaten breakfast then come upstairs to explain the events of the night before.

Mary sat on her unmade bed in her blue dressing-gown and slippers. The bruising under her eyes had darkened and stood out in stark contrast to the gauze dressings on her forehead and cheek. She cradled her bandaged wrist in her good right hand and listened in silence.

'He said Friday was his busiest night, what with men coming out of the pubs at closing time and getting into fights – local fishermen against Yanks based at Catterick Camp mostly. Said he couldn't spare his constable and we'd better carry on looking for Anna ourselves. Of course, we had no luck. At around one o'clock we were forced to abandon the search and come home to get some sleep.' Bobbie perched on the deep windowsill. 'I expect you were dead to the world through it all?'

'No, I was awake.'

'But shattered, I should think.' Bobbie had antici-pated more reaction from Mary. 'Shock does tire you out, I must say.' Herself, Jean and Viv; they'd all had more than their fair share of close shaves when flying their crates and knew how Mary must feel.

'Yes.'

'But the docs gave you the all-clear? How long before your wrist heals and you're fit to fly?'

'A couple of days, that's all.'

'That's terrific news.' Still no reaction: not a flicker of a smile or even a glance in Bobbie's direction. 'Doug-las will have you back on the rota before you know it.'

'Yes.'

A flat voice; eyes that didn't blink. Bobbie pushed herself up from the windowsill and went to sit beside Mary. 'Are you feeling really rotten?' she asked gently.

Mary closed her eyes. 'Yes.'

'Do you want me to leave you in peace?'

'Yes – please.'

Reluctantly Bobbie got up from the bed and made her way to the door.

'No, stay!' Suddenly changing her mind, Mary fol-lowed Bobbie across the room. 'I did hear what was going on last night. I'm really sorry I didn't help,' she said in a broken voice.

'Don't worry. Hilary has telephoned the police again this morning. Word has been sent around all the stations in the area; I feel sure it won't be long before Anna is found.'

'I wish I'd lent a hand. What will you all think of me?'

Bobbie led Mary to a chair by the window and sat her down. An early morning sun fell across her strained, anxious features. 'We won't think anything bad.'

'I should have joined in.' Self-recriminations crowded in and brought a flush of shame to Mary's cheeks. 'Do you want to know why I didn't?'

Bobbie drew up another chair. 'Yes, if you want to tell me.'

'I was thinking selfishly about myself, that's why.' Mary had heard voices and footsteps the evening before. She'd overheard Hilary ordering Viv to form a search party to look for Anna. Mary had even put on her coat, ready to join them, but at the last second her courage had failed her. 'I was afraid of what you would all say.'

'About what?' Bobbie patted Mary's arm. 'No one thinks any less of you for crash-landing your crate; you know that, don't you?'

'Hilary does,' Mary whispered haltingly before the floodgates opened. 'He thinks I'm to blame. Horace is backing him up and I don't know who else – probably the ground crew at Castle Bromwich, for a start. It'll be reported as pilot error.'

Bobbie sat back in her chair to consider this and set it alongside the rumours that had been flying around the ferry pool. 'But why? What does Hilary say you did wrong?'

'That I played the fool and dared Horace to race me.'

'That's ridiculous!'

'That I wasted petrol and that it was my fault I ran out.' Mary's voice almost failed her as she listed the charges against her. 'That I wasn't fit to fly in the first place.'

'Stop!' Bobbie urged. 'This is all rubbish.'

'But what if I can't prove it?' Mary couldn't forget Hilary's stern expression as he'd greeted her in the library and then the way he'd said the word 'upset', pausing to clear his throat and looking away as he'd spoken. He meant unfit to fly and the word was loaded with barely concealed scorn. 'It'll be like Cameron: one man's word against mine.'

Bobbie flashed Mary a questioning look.

'His court martial comes up the day after tomorrow. If Don Bullen refuses to change his version of events and he has witnesses to back him up, Cameron could lose.'

'Monday, you say?' Bobbie nodded slowly. 'No wonder you're upset.'

That word again! Mary sprang to her feet as if at an electric shock, almost knocking over her chair.

Bobbie gasped. 'What's wrong? What did I say?'

'Just because Hilary had given me bad news doesn't mean that I flew my crate like an idiot, if that's what you think!'

'It isn't. I don't,' Bobbie said hastily.

Mary rounded on her. 'You said I was upset.'

'But not incompetent.' If Bobbie wished to unravel this misunderstanding it was vital to stay calm. 'It would be typical of Hilary to mix up the two things, but he's a man – he doesn't understand.'

Mary took a deep, jagged breath. 'Really?'

'Yes, and you and I both know that it's something we women pilots regularly have to fight against. The hand that rocks the cradle outlook is . . . well, it's bloody nonsense!'

Another deep breath, a slight nod of Mary's head.

Bobbie made her case strongly. 'We're perfectly able to feel things deeply at the same time as keeping our brains in gear even if men aren't.'

That's right. Mary was astonished by the energy and confidence in Bobbie's voice. She was like a jumping-jack firework, hopping and fizzing around the room. 'That's what I did,' she said shakily. 'I kept my mind on the job and was calm as anything when Horace and I hit a lump of cloud. Even when the throttle jammed open I didn't panic.'

'The throttle jammed?'

'Yes, at full revs – that's what guzzled all my petrol. I said so to Hilary but he didn't believe me.'

'Thank you, Third Officer Holland.' He'd concluded yesterday's interview with a dismissive glance at the door. 'I'll take note of what you say.'

Her heart had sunk. 'Yes, sir; thank you, sir.'

'That'll be all.'

He doesn't like me. Mary had crossed the hall and climbed the stairs to her room with a sickening conviction that her squadron leader looked down on her. *I'm not Angela or Bobbie; he and I have nothing in common.*

She'd gone straight to bed to lick her wounds, growing more and more certain that her whole world was on the point of collapse. A phrase had lodged itself at the front of her brain: *All is lost!* Cameron would lose his case against Bullen and she, Mary, would be declared unfit to fly. They would both be cast adrift, unable to continue with the jobs they loved. *All is lost.* Forced to stand on the sidelines while the Allies made their final push, Cameron would be heartbroken. He would fall into a downwards spiral, drink heavily and cut himself off from all contact with her, the woman he'd sworn he loved. The hammer blows had fallen heavily; *all is lost*. They would take away Mary's uniform and her Pilots' Notes; she would never fly again.

'I believe you,' Bobbie said firmly. Forgetting about the injured wrist, she took hold of Mary by both arms.

Mary cried out in pain.

'Oh, I'm so sorry! But you're not to give in, you hear me?' Bobbie looked Mary straight in the eye. 'I believe you and together we'll prove it was a mechanical fault, not pilot error – without a shadow of a doubt.'

'Why is Ernest running around like a scalded cat?' Viv told Bobbie that she'd seen the handyman hurrying to sweep the yard and tidy away his wheelbarrow and gardening tools at the entrance to the walled garden. 'Are we expecting a royal visit?'

Bobbie had just come down from Mary's room and she stood at the main entrance wearing a distracted air. 'Let's ask him,' she decided as Ernest came up the steps on to the terrace.

Viv brushed past her. 'What's up, Ernest? Are the King and Queen coming to visit?'

He made it clear that he had no time to stand and chat. 'Sir Thomas is due here at ten o'clock, if that's what you mean. I'll have to ask the squadron leader to move his car.'

'And what about Anna – have you heard any news?'

'Not a dicky bird.' Head lowered, Ernest went determinedly on his way.

'A girl can't just vanish into thin air.' Viv paced the

terrace, recalling how she'd carried out a thorough search of St Wilfred's church, checking the vestry and the curtained alcove where the organist sat before becoming spooked by the eerie silence of the place. It had been too easy to imagine the voices of ghostly choirboys drifting up into the high rafters and the low incantation of prayers from the pulpit – *For ever and ever, Amen.* So Viv had escaped from the spooky crucified Christ and fled outside, slipping and sliding on the damp, greasy flagstones as she'd run towards the gate. Then she'd linked up outside the Fox with Bobbie and Ray, and Jean and Douglas. They'd had nothing to report.

'Poor Anna,' Bobbie sympathized. 'She has no one in the entire world. Imagine how lonely that must make you feel. What are we going to do next?'

'Carry on looking.' Viv had thought out a plan of action. 'Starting with Florrie Loxley – I swear to God she knows more than she's saying.'

'Good idea; I'll come with you.'

So Viv and Bobbie ran to fetch two bikes and reached the stable yard in time to see the tall, dark-suited figure of Sir Thomas Parseval step out of the back of a black Jaguar. Meanwhile the chauffeur, brass buttons gleaming and peaked cap jammed firmly over his forehead, stood to attention as he held open the door for a second passenger.

Sir Thomas glanced up and immediately recognized Viv. He acknowledged her with a curt, 'Good morning.'

'If that's Giles in the back of the car, I'll wring his neck,' Viv muttered, her temper flaring.

But it was a woman who joined Sir Thomas – slim

304

and dressed in the height of fashion: a pale green summer coat with wide lapels and blouson sleeves, a black patent-leather handbag hanging from the crook of her arm. A small pillbox hat in the same shade of green perched on the back of her head and her hair was swept clear of her carefully made-up face.

Viv saw straight away that it was the woman in the portrait – a little older, extremely pale.

As Viv and Bobbie hesitated at the top of the steps, Hilary hurried along the terrace, offering apologies and welcoming the visitors. 'My car is in the way – let me move it.'

'Butcher can do that.' Sir Thomas shook hands with Hilary, who handed over his car keys to the Parsevals' driver. He offered an arm to his wife then processed slowly up the steps, nodding once more in Viv's direction as they passed by.

Lady Jane gave the girls a stiff smile. 'No news of Anna, I assume?' she asked them.

The question put Viv and Bobbie on the back foot. 'None,' Bobbie confirmed.

'Come along, dear.' Sir Thomas pressed on with his wife and Hilary towards the main entrance. 'This is a nuisance for you, Squadron Leader. I'm sure you have better things to do with your time than to set up a search party for Anna Janicki.'

Bobbie held up a warning finger. 'No,' she breathed at Viv, who was showing signs of irritation.

'We're here for a powwow,' Sir Thomas explained to Hilary in his authoritative way. 'Please gather the troops.'

Hilary nodded then beckoned for Bobbie and Viv to follow. Inside the house they encountered Ernest, still flustered as he fell over himself to bow and scrape.

'Ah, Ernest; there you are,' Sir Thomas said. 'Let everyone know that we'll meet in the library as soon as possible, there's a good chap.'

'Yes, sir.'

The owner of the Grange motioned for Viv to join him and Lady Jane. 'Vivienne, isn't it? Jane, my dear, this is the Canadian girl pilot I may have mentioned to you.'

Lady Jane was gracious. 'Ah, yes; I believe we spoke on the telephone. It really is exceptionally plucky of you to have come all this way from your home country – and voluntarily, too.'

Viv smiled awkwardly.

'And you people do such an outstanding job, especially now that the invasion plans are well underway. We'll give Herr Hitler a good thrashing, just you wait and see.'

Does she expect me to curtsey? Viv considered a mock display of deference but, intrigued by the idea of a powwow, dutifully went ahead with Bobbie into the library.

Within minutes everyone was gathered, seated in a semicircle and waiting for Sir Thomas to speak. Lady Jane sat, ankles elegantly crossed, with her back to the long window overlooking the lawn, while Hilary stood beside Sir Thomas who began to speak.

'First of all, my apologies, everyone, for taking up your valuable free time, but as you may have heard, your housekeeper Anna Janicki has left Burton Grange without warning. My wife and I thought it advisable to come here and discuss with Squadron

Leader Stevens the best way forward.' He paused to scan the young faces of his audience, all dressed in weekend civvies and shifting uncomfortably on their hard wooden seats. 'As you may also know, the local police force is aware of Anna's disappearance and for that we're thankful. However . . .' Sir Thomas paused to clear his throat. 'Lady Jane and I feel that you should know a little more about the background to this situation.'

Viv frowned at Bobbie sitting to her left then at Mary on her right. *What now?*

Sir Thomas continued. 'Prior to coming to the Grange Anna worked for us at Newpark. However, she found it hard to settle, which is scarcely surprising given her tragic family circumstances. We were aware of these before she was offered the position and my wife was prepared to make many allowances.'

I see which way the wind blows. Sensitive to the pompous, self-righteous tone, Mary was the first to recognize that the Parsevals were here at least in part to shift the blame.

'All to no avail, I'm afraid,' Sir Thomas continued. 'Poor Anna frequently neglected her housekeeping duties at Newpark and no amount of encouragement from Lady Jane and other members of our staff seemed to bring about any improvement.'

Viv tapped her foot against the floor and glared straight ahead. *Snooty so-and-so; when are you going to admit Giles's part in all of this?*

Sir Thomas sighed. 'The point is, I feel it's my duty to inform you that this is by no means the first time that Anna has disappeared.'

In the background Lady Jane nodded quietly.

307

'It is possibly the fourth or the fifth.' Sir Thomas turned to his wife for confirmation. 'Following the last occasion a decision was made that Anna would be happier elsewhere – in a quieter location where there was less pressure.'

Never! Viv supplied the answer to her own question. Giles was deliberately left out of the equation; of course he was.

'We had high hopes that Burton Grange would be that place.' Sir Thomas rubbed the palms of his hands together, making a dry, grating sound. 'Unfortunately, we've been proved wrong.'

Hilary filled the pause that followed. 'Sir Thomas and Lady Jane are anxious to know whether or not Anna confided in any of you.' He looked expectantly around the semicircle of faces. 'Did she drop any hints?'

Bobbie checked with Mary and Viv, who quickly shook their heads along with everyone else.

'Very well; we do know that she kept very much to herself.' Hilary stepped aside with the air of a man who had done all he could.

'It really is most unfortunate,' Sir Thomas fretted. 'Our fear is that, not knowing this part of Yorkshire, Anna has become seriously lost. After all, we're in rather a remote area – open moorland, and so on.'

There was more shuffling and shifting and a general impatience with the fuss that was being made about one missing servant. Many of the officers billeted at the Grange had scarcely noticed Anna since her arrival and everyone was keen to get on with their day.

'So, in conclusion, I ask you all to keep your eyes

peeled as you go about your business.' Belatedly Sir Thomas picked up the mood in the room and quickly rounded off his speech. 'If you do see or hear anything, however insignificant, please be sure to report it to Squadron Leader Stevens or to the police.'

'Class dismissed,' Bobbie whispered, privately comparing ice-cold Sir Thomas with his more easygoing son. She stored up a couple of questions to ask Ray when they next got together – did Giles's father ever get off his high horse and had Giles confided in Ray when it had been decided to shunt Anna off to the Grange?

Whilst Hilary led the Parsevals out of the library, leaving his audience to mull over what they'd heard, Bobbie, Viv and Mary got into a huddle in a corner of the room.

'No need to say it.' One look at Viv's scowling face told Bobbie all she needed to know. 'You're convinced that those two don't really give a hoot about Anna.'

Viv gave free rein to her disgust. 'No, they just don't want to accept the blame. And there was no mention of Giles, you notice.'

'Or of baby Dorota, poor little mite.' Mary wore a blue sling fashioned from a rayon scarf around her neck. She thought that Viv might have a case. 'I suppose you can see why not – parents are bound to protect their own.'

'But it's a story as old as the hills – rich son gets housemaid pregnant.' Bobbie knew this from her own wealthy background and from the off-limits, racier novels in her father's study – *Tom Jones*, *Moll Flanders* and *Vanity Fair*. She was only surprised how keen Sir Thomas had been to suppress the facts. 'It's normally water off a duck's back.'

Viv pretended to be scandalized. 'And here's me thinking that you're little Miss Innocent.' Through the open door she caught sight of Sir Thomas and Hilary deep in conversation while Lady Jane hovered outside on the terrace. 'Watch this,' she hissed.

She made a quick exit before Mary or Bobbie could prevent her.

'She wouldn't!' Bobbie gasped when she saw in which direction Viv was headed. Viv and Lady Jane face to face didn't bear thinking about.

'She would,' Mary argued. When their Canadian friend set her mind on doing something, she was unstoppable.

Jane Parseval gazed up at the house that had once been her home. The German bombs had done a great deal of harm – many windows along the damaged side of the house were boarded up, and much of the masonry had been chipped and pockmarked by flying shrapnel. Part of the stone balustrade bordering the terrace was gone, as were the pillars supporting the portico over the main entrance. The mindless destruction of the Grange's symmetry and grace cut deep so Jane decided to hurry on and wait with Butcher in the car.

Where was the wisteria? Where were the party guests in floaty summer dresses, linen suits and panama hats who had peopled the smooth lawns? A memory of Veronica skipping on this very terrace took Jane's breath away – Veronica at the age of eight, dressed in a simple, white cotton slip, bare-armed and laughing as the rope whirred over her head. 'Lord Nelson lost one arm, Lord Nelson lost the other . . .' She could hear a faint echo of her daughter's happy voice chanting the rhyme. 'Lord Nelson lost one leg.' The rope had made a perfect arc.

'Lady Jane?' Viv came up quickly from behind then slipped ahead to block her way. 'Can we talk about Anna?'

'Of course.' She took a moment to gather herself. 'Do you have some new information?'

'No, but I was hoping you did.' Close to, Viv noticed faint lines and shadows on the older woman's face. It was heavily powdered, with patches of skilfully applied rouge to add warmth to her wan complexion. 'I know about Anna's baby,' she went on boldly.

Jane's grey eyes widened. 'I have no idea what—'

'Oh, come off it; of course you do.' This was no time for fake denials. 'Anna had Giles's baby and was forced to give her up. What I want to find out is what happened to that baby.'

The wide eyes flickered shut then open again. Once more there was no denial. 'If you don't mind, I'm feeling a little light-headed.' Jane made a polite attempt to get past, only to find that Viv wouldn't shift.

'Listen – Dorota is the key to this mystery.'

'Dorota?'

'That's the baby's name, as if you didn't know. I reckon that Anna is desperate to know where she is and it's the reason she's disappeared – to track down her own flesh and blood.'

'You have absolutely no evidence . . .' Unable to complete the sentence, Jane steadied herself against the balustrade.

Viv pressed on. 'She adores that baby. You're a mother; imagine the torture of having to part with your own child.'

Dark pain registered in Jane's eyes. 'You really must excuse me.'

'Oh!' Realizing the crassness of her last remark, Viv stepped aside. Jane was halfway down the steps before she went after her. 'I'm an idiot – I'm so, so sorry. But you understand what I'm saying: Anna must have been out of her mind with grief.'

Down in the stable yard, Butcher leaned against the side of the Jaguar, smoking a cigarette. Glancing up at the approach of the two women, he quickly tossed it to the ground.

'Yes and I agree.' A sudden weariness threatened to crush Jane. Her slight frame shook with the weight of it. 'It's true that there was a baby but quite untrue that Giles was the father.'

Viv paused to reflect. Who else might be in the picture? Another of the Newpark servants, perhaps, or else a man from the local village?

'Did Anna tell you that Giles was responsible?' Jane asked.

'No,' Viv admitted. 'She refused to say who the father was, but that was because she was afraid of losing her job.' Add to that the fact that Giles's marriage was in ruins and he still remained the most likely culprit.

'You don't know my son.' Jane battled the feeling of exhaustion. 'In fact, Giles was the one who was determined to help Anna once her condition became obvious. If it weren't for him, my husband would have dismissed her outright.'

'But I do know him,' Viv argued. 'As it happens, we got pretty well acquainted before I discovered that he was married – something that he'd neglected to tell me, by the way.'

'I see.' Jane raised her eyebrows and proceeded down the steps. 'So you bear my son a grudge. That's what lies behind your groundless accusation. Well, I'm afraid you're wrong. Anna repeatedly refused to give us the name of the baby's father. Giles felt sorry for her and did all he could to help her. And this is how she repays him: by running away and involving us all in a wild goose chase.'

'OK, OK; say you're right . . .' Viv ran after her.

'I am right.' Butcher held open the door and Jane stepped inside the car.

'Then why keep Anna in the dark about arrangements for the baby? What was the point of that? Who made those arrangements, by the way?'

'I have no idea; it was none of my concern.' Composing herself on the soft leather seat, Jane made it clear that this was her last word on the matter before motioning for the chauffeur to close the door.

'Excuse me, miss.' Butcher did as he was told, forcing Viv to step back from the car.

She glared at his impassive face then gave in. She'd got as far as she could with Lady Jane Parseval, which was nowhere at all. Viv's own reflection in the car window stared back at her, angry and frustrated. 'You Parsevals are the absolute limit,' she muttered as she walked swiftly away.

CHAPTER SEVENTEEN

Fern Cottage was a cool, calm oasis in Jean's hectic life. It was a place where she could slow down and give herself time to breathe in the scent of the bluebells that grew on the bank behind the house, and gaze up in wonder through the latticework branches outside her door. Gone were all concerns about rudder and throttle, altimeter and fuel gauge; gone, too, the natural fear all pilots experienced at every take-off, which with a strong effort of will Jean kept at bay until the moment of landing. Here at the cottage she was completely relaxed and happy.

'What are you up to today?' she asked Douglas when she came downstairs on Saturday morning after a long lie-in.

'I'm needed at the ferry pool, worse luck.' He was in uniform, sitting at the kitchen table and bending over to lace up his shoes. 'I was about to leave you a note.'

Jean stooped to kiss the back of his head. 'You should have woken me up.'

'What for?'

'Because!' She loved opening her eyes to see him beside her and luxuriate in those moments when their bodies lay entwined – the warmth and softness in the early morning light.

'You looked too peaceful.' Douglas stood up and embraced her. 'With a bit of luck I should be back by mid-morning. How about you – what will you do while I'm gone?'

'I'll take Patch for a walk, for a start.'

Hearing his name, the dog trotted to the door and looked up longingly at the lead hanging from its hook.

'There's an awfully clever dog,' Jean said with a laugh. 'But you'll have to wait for me to get dressed first.'

Douglas patted Patch on the way out. 'See you later,' he called to Jean as she ran back upstairs. Within five minutes she was down again, dressed in a cable-knit sweater and blue slacks, her fair hair pinned up in a French plait. Then it was on with a light jacket and a beret, ready for the walk.

She and the dog were deep in the bluebell wood when it occurred to Jean that there might yet be a way forward in the so-far fruitless search for Anna. It was a long shot but maybe, just maybe.

'Here, Patch!' she called him from his busy foraging through the undergrowth and he came obediently to heel, following her until they reached the edge of the wood where Jean put him on the lead.

Maybe Florrie will be in a better mood today, she thought as she approached the village. After all, the landlady had obviously been too busy to talk last night. Perhaps this morning she'd be more inclined to help.

There was no reply to Jean's knock on the front

door of the Fox, so she made her way down the gin-nel into the backyard where she found Florrie hanging out her washing.

'Now then.' Florrie eyed her visitor suspiciously from behind two pillowcases that she'd pegged on to the line. She was dressed in her wrap-over floral apron and carpet slippers and was frowning deeply. 'What can I do for you?'

'I hope I haven't caught you at a bad time.' Jean ordered Patch to sit then approached Florrie. 'Can you spare me five minutes?'

'What for?' Florrie took a third pillowcase from her washing basket and two wooden pegs from her pocket. 'If it's about the missing Polish woman, I've already made it clear I know nowt about it.'

'Yes, but I thought I might be able to jog your memory.' Jean spoke slowly, careful not to put too much pressure on the irascible landlady. 'There might be something that's slipped your mind.'

Florrie stepped out from behind the washing, care-fully wiping her hands dry on her overall. 'Such as?'

'I don't know – a chance remark from one of your customers or some village gossip that you've picked up.'

There was a dismissive sniff from Florrie. 'I've got better things to do than listen to tittle-tattle.'

'Of course, but the fact is we're all very worried about Anna. She's been through so much in her short life.'

Florrie shook her head. 'If that's meant to soft soap me, you're wasting your time. I've made it plain – I'm not interested in Anna what's-'er-name and neither is anyone else in Rixley.'

316

'Why ever not – what has she done wrong?'

'You ask me that!' The landlady turned back to her washing line and gave the pillowcases several sharp tugs. 'I should've thought it was obvious.'

Jean swallowed hard. 'Listen, I know that Anna had a baby, if that's what you mean.'

'That's exactly what I'm on about; these foreign girls, running around causing trouble – I have no truck with that. If they end up in a mess, it's up to them to get themselves out of it.'

'Wait a minute, Florrie – what if someone took advantage of Anna and it wasn't her fault?' Jean spoke earnestly. 'That does happen, you know. And you saw how heartbroken she was about having to give up her baby – that's why she came here and begged you to tell her what you knew. She admitted she was crying all the time and not sleeping.'

'How do you know that?'

'I overheard her that day she came to see you. That's why I dropped by this morning to ask you to think again.'

Florrie shook her head. 'I've got nowt to hide.'

'I'm not saying you have; not deliberately.' Jean struggled to make headway. 'But if you know anything – any scrap of information that might help us find Anna . . .'

'Keep your voice down,' Florrie hissed as she checked the yard and the alley for eavesdroppers. 'You'd better come inside.'

So Jean tied Patch to the gatepost then followed the landlady into her small, dark living room.

'This goes no further,' Florrie warned as she closed the door and told Jean to take a seat by the fire. She sat down opposite, her stiff, skinny body radiating a brittle defensiveness.

'Of course not.' Jean's hopes rose a fraction. She noticed a cheap and cheerful collection of china ornaments on Florrie's mantelpiece: two figurines of shepherdesses alongside three chipped Toby jugs. There was a worn rag rug on the flagged floor and a brass coal scuttle by the empty fireplace.

Florrie's face was grave. 'I've heard what you say but now you listen to me. For a start, I don't own this place – I'm only a tenant here.'

Jean absorbed more of her surroundings. The rose-patterned wallpaper was faded and there was a sense of make-do-and-mend about the outdated wooden furniture. 'So who do you pay your rent to?'

'I give you one guess.'

'The Parseval family.' A brief nod from Florrie told Jean that she was correct.

'If the Parsevals tell me to jump, I jump. If they order me to keep something to myself, that's what I do.'

'I see.' Jean thought desperately of a way to get past this obstacle. 'That must be hard if it goes against your conscience. After all, you're a regular churchgoer.'

Florrie gave a tight-lipped smile. 'I'm saying nowt; I pay my rent and I do as I'm told. If that includes summat I'm not happy with, what choice do I have?'

'But when it's urgent, surely . . .'

Florrie tapped the arm of her chair. 'Surely – what? If I dropped even the smallest hint about what Mr Giles might or might not have asked me to do as far as the Polish woman goes, word would get back to Newpark quick as a flash.'

'How would it?'

'Walls have ears' was all Florrie would say as she stood up. Her face was screwed into a tight frown and her eyes flicked nervously around the room. 'I'm well and truly stuck, conscience or no conscience – even you being here could count against me if I'm not careful.'

'I wouldn't do anything to get you into trouble.' Jean too got up from her chair. 'But if there's any way around the problem – an anonymous note dropped through the letter box at the Grange or a telephone call from the phone box on the corner . . .'

'There isn't.' Florrie was adamant as she gestured around the sparsely furnished room. 'Listen, love, this might not look much to you and your fancy pilot friends, but I'm a widow without any family to turn to and the pub is all I've got.'

'I understand.' Jean allowed herself to be shown out into the yard. 'I won't tell anyone I've been here,' she promised at the doorway.

'You won't have to.' Florrie's face darkened and she pointed towards the spot where Jean had left her dog. 'They already know.'

'Jean!' Viv left off patting Patch and darted through Florrie's flapping washing to grab her friend by the hand. 'Hey, great minds think alike.'

Bobbie followed more slowly, taking one look at the landlady's thunderous face before letting out a long sigh. 'Oh dear.'

'I'll "oh dear" the lot of you!' Florrie snapped before slamming the door in their faces.

'You beat us to it,' Bobbie murmured to Jean. 'No luck, I take it?'

'None,' Jean admitted. 'Florrie's not at liberty to talk. We'll have to think of something else.'

On the walk back through Burton Wood Patch ran ahead of Jean, Bobbie and Viv. They caught the occasional sight of the white tip of his tail in among the brown bracken and heard him rustle through the bushes ahead.

'He's after rabbits,' Bobbie decided.

Viv was unusually subdued after their latest set-back. 'I can't help thinking the worst as far as poor Anna is concerned,' she admitted as they reached Fern Cottage. 'What if she's starving in some ditch – or worse?'

'Please, don't . . .' Bobbie was also at her wits' end. 'Listen, I'll telephone Ray and ask him to drive over from Thresham as soon as he's free. He can help us with the search again.'

'Good thinking,' Viv agreed. 'And he knows Giles better than anyone. Maybe he'll give us some fresh ideas.'

'Get Ray to talk through what went on at Newpark – the baby and so on. There might be a fresh clue there somewhere.' Aware that they were clutching at straws, Jean stood by the cottage gate and called the dog to heel. She said a thoughtful goodbye to Bobbie and Viv.

'Tell Douglas we said hi.' Viv carried on through the wood, picking up a long stick that lay by the side of the path and using it to swish energetically through the bushes.

Bobbie had to hurry to keep up with her. 'You still think Giles is to blame?' she asked.

'He's my prime suspect. His mother denied it point-blank but what can you expect?' Viv quickly related to Bobbie her conversation with Lady Jane. '"You don't know my son. He was the one who stepped forward to help Anna . . ." Blah-blah.'

Bobbie listened uneasily. 'I'll ask Ray outright,' she decided. 'Is Giles the father of Anna's baby?'

Viv nodded and came to a halt. 'That woman is a mess,' she muttered to herself.

'Who – Giles's mother?'

'Yeah. She hides it pretty well behind the clothes and the make-up, but when I touched a raw nerve I saw how close to the edge she was. She lost a daughter to scarlet fever, you know – the one in the portrait.'

A shiver ran down Bobbie's spine as she listened to the details.

'It's OK; I apologized,' Viv added quickly. 'I guess that's why Giles and his father wrap Lady Jane in cotton wool, in case something tips her over the edge.'

'Do they?' Bobbie wondered.

'Yeah, they do – you can tell.' Viv was certain that Giles's mother led a life protected from harsh reality. She no doubt spent her time being chauffeured everywhere, having her hair done and her clothes especially designed and made. There would be tea parties and trips to the opera, the cool feel of silk underwear against her skin, a mink cape in winter and chiffon stoles in summer. 'My bet is they don't even let her read the newspapers in case the war upsets her.'

'Talking of which . . .' Bobbie looked ahead to see Horace cycling along the path towards them. He

321

wore a flat cap, sports jacket and bicycle clips around the bottoms of his green corduroy trousers and carried a rucksack on his back. '"Upset" is the word that sends Mary into a tailspin. She says Hilary has made up his mind that she wasn't fit to fly that morning. He maintains she was too *upset* about Cameron.'

Viv felt a twinge of guilt that events surrounding Anna's disappearance had pushed Mary's predicament into the background. 'Surely not; Mary is a cool customer. She's talented, too.'

'Horace isn't helping matters.' Bobbie saw him brake and swerve as a rabbit hopped across his path. Now was her chance to carry out her promise to Mary – to help prove that mechanical failure was to blame for her crash-landing. So she barred Horace's way and greeted him with false bonhomie. 'Hello, Horace; where are you rushing off to?'

He braked again and came to a reluctant halt. 'I'm playing in a football match – Rixley against Maltby Bay.' Damn it; these were the very girls he hadn't wanted to run into. Bobbie and Viv were bound to have a go at him over the Mary business, which he'd been doing his level best to avoid. 'I'm in a rush, as a matter of fact.'

'Good for you, Horace.' Bobbie stood her ground. 'What position do you play?'

'Right wing. Now, if you don't mind . . .'

Looking as if she were about to step to one side, Bobbie seemed to have second thoughts. 'Oh, by the way, have you talked to Mary lately?'

'No; why do you ask?' *Here we go; brace yourself!*

'She's in a spot of bother with Hilary, that's all. Surely she mentioned it to you?'

'No, I haven't seen her since she got back.' Horace looked warily from Bobbie to Viv then back again.

'Yes you have; she was at the meeting in the library earlier.' Viv's gaze was steely as she stood shoulder to shoulder with Bobbie. 'Her arm was in a sling. She's covered in cuts and bruises.'

'I meant I haven't had a chance to talk to her. Listen, I'm going to be late if I hang around here gabbing with you two.'

'Don't you want to know what kind of trouble she's in?' Bobbie said without moving a muscle.

'Oh, but you already know,' Viv cut in. 'It was you who fibbed to Hilary in the first place.'

'Fibbed? I don't know what you're talking about.' Horace tried to push past by thrusting his front wheel between Viv and Bobbie.

Viv place a hand on his handlebars. 'Oh no you don't.'

Damn and blast! He jabbed a finger towards Viv, who didn't flinch. 'You heard her, Bobbie – she accused me of lying! I only said what I saw, which was your precious friend messing around in a brand-new crate. What was I supposed to do – cover up for her?'

'No, but you could've waited until she got back to Rixley and listened to her version of events.' Bobbie stepped aside as Horace tried to wrest the bike from Viv's grasp. 'You should've known better; Mary of all people.'

'You do realize the best thing for you to do now?' Viv adopted what she considered a reasonable tone. 'I mean, the decent thing.'

'What's that?' *Bloody women – going on and on at a*

bloke. Horace glared at them, his face red with frustration.

'Talk to Mary about the jammed throttle,' Bobbie suggested.

'You what?' *How very convenient – a jammed throttle in a brand-new crate; I should cocoa!* Horace's gut reaction, like Hilary's, was to pour scorn on Mary's pathetic excuse.

'Jammed at full revs, no less.' Viv's arm was still braced against the handlebars. 'It gives you nightmares just to think about. Imagine it happening to any of us.'

'I'm only saying what I saw.' Horace grew more belligerent by the second. 'Let go of the bike, Viv.'

'Even though Mary faces disciplinary action?' Bobbie remained hopeful that Horace would soften once he'd thought it through. 'I mean it; if Hilary comes down on the side of pilot error, she could be forced out of the ATA. She'd have to leave Rixley, the Grange – everything.'

Finally managing to tug his bike free, Horace barged between them. 'That's her own bloody lookout,' he said with brutal force, starting to pedal furiously.

'It'll break her heart,' Viv called after him.

'The ATA is Mary's life,' Bobbie pleaded. 'Horace, please!'

He braked suddenly then waited for Bobbie and Viv to catch him up. 'I'd look a bloody fool if I change my mind now, wouldn't I?' he blurted out.

'That's not a good enough reason—' Bobbie began.

'Leave off, will you?' Horace broke in. 'Anyhow, what's your evidence? That was a new bloody crate, remember – straight out of Castle Bromwich. Not to mention our Rixley erks crawling all over the damned thing.'

'OK, but what if they all missed something?' Viv insisted.

He shook his head. 'No, forget it; it would never have got past Stan or Gordon.' Once more Horace set off along the rough track and this time he had no intention of stopping. 'Mary made her own bed,' he yelled over his shoulder, 'and now she damn well has to lie on it.'

Douglas's business at the ferry pool that morning included some work with the met boys on weather forecasts for the coming week followed by a quick meeting with Hilary in his office.

'I wanted to see you about this Mary Holland business.' Hilary gestured for Douglas to take a seat. He seemed on edge, shuffling papers around his desk and speaking rapidly, as if anxious to offload the problem.

'How is she?'

'On the mend; no serious damage. The thing is, old chap, I don't buy her story.'

'No?' Douglas leaned forward and looked quizzically at his commanding officer.

'It's too bloody convenient; a classic case of a bad workman blaming his tools. I want you to get on the blower to Castle Bromwich and get to the bottom of it – ask them to check the paperwork. Did their boys find a problem with the Tempest's throttle after they pulled her out?'

'Yes, that should settle it.' Douglas saw the sense of

what Hilary was asking him to do but he felt uneasy. 'I can't see it'll be top priority, though; not with the factory churning out crates as fast as they can in time for the big one – thirty-five thousand aircraft lined up along the south coast at the latest count, along with God knows how many pontoons and landing craft.'

'Agreed, but what more can we do? If Castle Bromwich comes back with a negative – no mechanical fault – then at least we'll know where we stand.'

'They might not,' Douglas cautioned. He for one was willing to give Mary the benefit of the doubt. 'Mary Holland is as straight as a die. I can't think she'd be making this up.'

Hilary looked up irritably from his paperwork. 'Normally I'd agree. But this Cameron business may be clouding her judgement. Has Jean said anything to you?'

'Nothing.' Getting a measure of how serious the situation was for Mary, Douglas gave a cautious response. 'Leave it with me,' he said, scraping back his chair and picking up his hat. 'I'll get on to it first thing Monday morning.'

A nod from Hilary closed the conversation and Douglas retreated to his own ground-floor office, where he stood by the window staring out across the small square of lawn, thinking of Mary's plight. He watched as personnel came and went – Dotty Kirk from the met room lugging a typewriter from A to B, Bob Cross in his too-big overalls sneaking a quick cigarette outside Hangar 1, Gillian Wharton cycling out of the base at the end of her night shift. It occurred to Douglas that a cup of tea would go down well and he was about to set off for the canteen when he suddenly changed his mind. Instead, he picked up the phone and quickly dialled the number for Aireby training camp.

He waited to be put through to the appropriate extension. 'Hello, Group Captain Norris?'

'Speaking.'

Was this the right thing to be doing? Douglas began to have second thoughts but ploughed on anyway. 'This is First Officer Douglas Thornton from Rixley ferry pool. You have a prisoner awaiting court martial – Flight Lieutenant Ainslie?'

'Correct.'

'We have his . . .' Douglas searched for the right word. 'His sweetheart stationed here.'

'Yes – what of it?' Norris implied that he had a thousand important things to do that morning and Ainslie's sweetheart wasn't high on the list.

'I'd like you to pull a few strings.'

'Yes, yes; get on with it, man.'

'Another visitor's pass for Third Officer Holland – for tomorrow morning, if that's at all possible.'

'Right; will do. Send her over for twelve o'clock.' With that Norris put down the phone.

Douglas clicked the receiver into its cradle. *Was* it the right thing? Would Mary actually want to see Cameron after what she'd been through? Women's minds often worked in mysterious ways, as far as he was concerned. He decided to skip the tea and go straight home. Jean would soon set him straight. And if Jean decided that, yes, Mary would benefit from visiting Cameron, then he, Douglas, would organize a driver to take her across to Aireby for noon tomorrow.

*

Viv hoped that weeding in the vegetable garden at the Grange would help her to work off some of the frustration she'd felt throughout the day. There was still no news of Anna and with every passing hour it became more obvious that she had planned her exit meticulously.

Take the state of her room, for a start, which had been cleared and cleaned so that it appeared as if she'd never been there. And it had proved impossible to pin down exactly when she'd left – most likely she'd stolen away during the night when everyone had been asleep but no one was able to narrow it down further. Had it been before or after midnight? Had she been able to catch a bus out of Rixley or had she walked? Above all, where had she been heading?

Viv stooped to pull out young shoots of dandelions that seemed to have appeared overnight. She tossed the weeds into a bucket then picked up her hoe once more.

At least the police had begun to take Anna's disappearance more seriously. A young, wet-behind-the-ears constable had called at the Grange that afternoon armed with notepad and pencil. He'd jotted down details of Anna's appearance – mid-twenties, though she looked older; very slight and pale, wearing a brown dress and grey coat – and promised to link up with neighbouring constabularies. 'Don't worry – she can't have got far without money,' he'd reassured Viv, who had been providing the details.

'That's true, but I am still worried; I'm afraid that Anna may plan to harm herself.' For the first time Viv had given voice to the fear lurking at the back of everyone's minds. It had come out cool and clinical – 'Anna may plan to harm herself' carried none of the emotional heft that Viv was feeling. 'She was the saddest, loneliest person you ever saw' was what she should have told the constable. 'Life dealt her a truly raw deal. She could be lying at the foot of a cliff, for all we know.'

'I see.' The constable had licked the end of his pencil and carefully written down two words – 'possible suicide?' – then flipped his notepad shut. 'I'll pass it on to the sarge,' he'd promised on leaving.

'What's up with you?' As Viv worked on in the garden, Ernest strolled in through the open gate.

'Nothing.' Viv jabbed at another weed with her hoe.

'Come off it – I've been standing watching you. You're treating them dandelions as if they've committed first-degree murder.'

She had the grace to smile and stop what she was doing to appraise the handyman's spruce appearance – thinning grey hair slicked back, sports jacket, collar and tie. 'Are you going somewhere nice?'

'Just over to the Fox. You can come with me if you like.' The invitation was accompanied by a cheeky grin. 'Then again, it's a Saturday night so you'll have better things to do.'

'Wrong.' Viv smiled to herself – Hollywood glamour was a fast-fading memory and these days her best offer came from a wounded Great War veteran nearly thirty years her senior. 'You never know, I might join you after I've finished here. By the way, Ernest, who was the young guy there with you last night? I'm guessing he's not from around here.'

'You guess right.' He chuckled as he pulled a pipe and tobacco pouch from his pocket. 'Arthur lives in

Maltby Bay. Trust you to pick out the best looking lad for miles around.'

'You know me!'

'Aye, but hands off – he's married.' Ernest struck a match and lit up.

Viv pulled a disappointed face.

'To my niece Betty, if you must know. She's a bright lass – that's why they put her in charge of finding homes for evacuees from Leeds and Bradford a while back. She did a grand job, by all accounts. Arthur works as a clerk for the Ministry of Agriculture and Fisheries.'

'Was his wife there last night?' Viv dabbed the blade of the hoe between rows of young broad bean plants.

'Aye. They rode over on Arthur's motorbike. Betty was keen to have a natter with Florrie.'

'Florrie was run off her feet – I'm surprised she had time to stop and chat.' By now Viv was only half-listening. She wafted away a cloud of acrid blue tobacco smoke then stooped to pull up a nettle.

'Plus, Florrie had some money to hand over to Betty – but that's another story.' Ernest stopped abruptly, frowning and tutting at himself for letting his tongue run away with him.

'You say she housed evacuees?' Viv left off working, her interest piqued by his sudden evasiveness.

Sucking at his pipe, Ernest's frown deepened.

This was intriguing, given the present circumstances. 'Good for her. I'd like to have a chat with Betty myself. Will she be there again tonight?'

'I doubt it.' Wanting to avoid Viv's gaze and eager to be on his way, Ernest bent down to knock the bowl of his pipe against the side of the nearby bucket. His fingers displayed their characteristic tremble as he stuffed the empty pipe back into his pocket.

'You say she and Arthur live in Maltby Bay?' Viv persisted. This could lead places – a woman whose job it had been to house evacuees was exactly the type of person Giles would have used in his attempt to offload his and Anna's baby, with all-knowing Florrie acting as go-between and paymaster.

'I'll be off now,' Ernest muttered between gritted teeth. He'd said too much and this Canadian girl was quick on the uptake.

Viv watched him hurry away. There couldn't be too many Bettys and Arthurs living together in the tiny fishing village of Maltby Bay – they'd be easy enough to find. *But I'd better talk with Bobbie before I launch into my bull-in-a-china-shop act,* she decided as she attacked the offending weeds with renewed gusto.

CHAPTER EIGHTEEN

'I wouldn't be doing this if it hadn't been for Douglas,' Mary confessed to Stan. 'Even now I'm in two minds.'

'Cameron will want to see you,' he assured her. He drove the back roads to Aireby in one of the ATA Austin pick-up trucks, taking care not to arrive before noon, which was when Mary's visitor pass came into force. It was an overcast, dispiriting sort of day, which somehow matched Stan's mood.

'Are you sure you want me to drive you?' he'd asked when he'd shown up at the Grange and noticed how on edge Mary had seemed. Though the two of them were back on a firm, friendly footing, he was still careful not to overstep the mark. 'Douglas sent me but I could easily fetch Bob if you'd rather.'

Her pained expression had told him that she didn't want to think about the dents and scrapes in their long-established friendship. She'd simply climbed into the truck in her best blue coat and hat, set her handbag on her knees and stared straight ahead.

'Cameron hasn't written to me for weeks,' she confided as Stan drove along the lane by the side of

Rixley reservoir. She took in the grey expanse of glassy water as ducks flew low and ruffled the surface upon landing. 'My last visit did seem to cheer him up, though.'

'That's the ticket.' Stan glanced sideways at her. She'd removed the sling, taken off the gauze patches that had covered her cuts and made an attempt to hide the bruises with make-up. But it was still obvious that she'd been in an accident. 'Cameron will want to know what happened to your face,' he warned.

'Don't worry, I'll tell him – after all, it's the risk we run.'

'You were lucky, though. You could've come off a lot worse.' Stan followed the shore of the large, man-made reservoir then turned left up a steep hill towards Longacre, a hamlet with little more than a pub and a chapel. After that they followed the road along a high ridge with moorland to either side. 'You gave me a sleepless night, I can tell you.'

'Why was that?' The truck swayed around a bend, pressing her against the door.

'When I heard you were in hospital – I thought, *What in the blazes has she been up to?*'

'I hadn't been up to anything,' Mary said stiffly. 'You don't believe those silly rumours?'

The truck dipped into a steep hollow, causing Mary's stomach to lurch.

'No, of course not.' Something about the situation – the road whizzing by, their close proximity in the small, steamed-up cab – threatened to loosen Stan's tongue.

'You don't sound very sure.'

'I am, honestly.' He blew out his cheeks and tapped

his finger against the steering wheel. 'In any case, you scared me stiff.'

'Why?'

As they came up out of the dip the first few spots of rain landed on the windscreen. Stan turned on the wipers. 'Because you mean a lot to me, Mary; that's why.'

She breathed in deeply, not trusting herself to reply.

He misread her silence as an invitation to carry on. 'That kiss wasn't easy for me to forget. I had hoped it was the same for you too.'

'Stan,' she protested softly. Her hands clasped the rim of her handbag as she swayed towards him. 'I've already explained.'

'You haven't changed your mind?'

She shook her head.

'I'm sorry to hear that.' As they reached the long, straight road leading to the RAF training camp, a downpour set in. Rain lashed the windscreen and reduced visibility to just a few yards. 'I hope you brought your brolly with you.'

'Stan,' she said again, urging herself to clear the air once and for all, 'you've definitely got hold of the wrong end of the stick. I made a mistake that day in the wood. It won't happen again.'

'So it meant nothing?' Stan imagined a door slamming shut in his face. So much for watching and waiting. And, boy, did the rejection hurt.

'That's not what I said.' She understood she ought to have gone more gently with him. She'd have been able to express herself better if she hadn't been so worked up about Cameron.

'As good as.' He slowed the truck and pulled into

the side of the road. 'And while we're at it, I might as well tell you what me and the rest of the boys think.'

'About what?'

'About them letting you fly last week.'

'"They" didn't let me fly,' Mary contradicted. 'That's a decision I made for myself.'

'All I'm saying is I knew you weren't yourself – Gordon said the same thing.'

'He did, did he? Who else has been gossiping about me? Olive, Bob, every Tom, Dick and Harry in the ferry pool, by the sound of things. Oh, and while we're at it, as you say, how come you missed a major fault with that Tempest?' There; it was out in the open and there was no taking it back.

'What fault?' Stan prepared to leap to his own defence.

'With the throttle setting, that's what. I opened up to get over a lump of cloud and, lo and behold, the damned thing stuck at max! Yes, that's news to you, isn't it?'

Stan sat open-mouthed, his cheeks suffused with red. 'It wasn't me – it was Bob who did the engine and instrument checks while I fetched the bowser for refuelling.'

'You're joking – you left the most important part of your job to an apprentice?' It was Mary's turn to stare in disbelief.

'Yes, because the crate was straight from the factory. The erks there had run all the checks in triplicate. Are you sure it stuck fast?'

'Yes, I was there, Stan! Up in that cockpit, jammed on full throttle – I could've been killed.'

He let out a long, low groan.

335

'And now I'm in deep trouble because of it. Hilary doesn't believe me and I don't have any witnesses.'

'What's he planning to do?' As the truth dawned and Stan realized that his own head might be on the block, he slumped forward over the steering wheel.

'I don't know yet. I want to get back to flying but I have to wait for Hilary to give me the go-ahead.' Mary's voice faltered and she had to compete against the swish of the wipers and the drumming of rain-drops on the roof of the cab. 'Don't worry – I won't land you and Bob in it.'

'No.' Coming to a resolution, Stan sat upright, his bare, muscular forearms braced against the wheel. 'You won't need to – I'll go to the top brass myself. I'll admit I didn't follow proper procedures.'

'You will?' Mary drew a jagged breath. Did Stan really mean what he said?

'First thing tomorrow,' he promised as he put the truck into gear. 'Come on; it's nearly twelve o'clock – best not keep Cameron waiting.'

'It's you again.' The young sentry recognized Mary the moment she stepped down from Stan's truck. He lifted the barrier without bothering to check her credentials. 'Remember me?'

She nodded. 'Spud, isn't it?'

'My real name's Arthur – Arthur Jenkins – but that's boring. I prefer Spud. You're here to see Flight Lieutenant Ainslie. What happened to your face, by the way?' The cheery cadet led Mary past thirty or more trainee airmen square-bashing in the rain. Their boots scrunched on the gravel; shoulders back, left-right, left-right, about turn. 'Did you have a prang in one of your crates?'

Mary raised her hand self-consciously to her forehead. 'A bit of one, yes.' Her heart raced as they approached the prison block backed by the shadowy stand of dripping pine trees.

The sentry continued to pass the time of day. 'Guess why they call me Spud. I come from Ormskirk, that's why. Ormskirk – potatoes,' he explained chattily as he went ahead and knocked on the door.

As they waited, Don Bullen strode towards them. 'Bang on time, I see,' he remarked in his lazy drawl.

Mary took a step back. As before, Bullen was obviously enjoying the situation, strutting across the square with his fists thrust deep into the pockets of his sheepskin flying jacket and grinning confidently. He was taller and heavier than she remembered.

'Wait by the door and escort Miss Mary back to the gate when she's finished here,' he ordered the sentry before swaggering off.

'Yes, sir!' Spud stood to attention in the pouring rain until Bullen had disappeared around the corner of the nearest Nissen hut. 'Not your cup of tea?' he muttered to Mary without moving his lips. 'Mine neither. Go right ahead. I'll be here when you come back out.'

She thanked him and went inside where she found Cameron sitting at the trestle table with the same burly, unsmiling guard standing behind him.

'Good Lord, Mary; your face!' were Cameron's first words. He attempted to stand up but the guard put a firm hand on his shoulder and he was forced back on to his chair.

'It's nothing.'

'They told me that you'd been in an accident.' Cameron studied the gash across her forehead and bruises on her cheeks. 'How bad was it?'

'Never mind – you go first. I've come here to find out how you're coping – you didn't write.'

'I tried to.' Cameron had to fight the same urge as during Mary's first visit to put his arms around her and hold her close. 'I tore up the letters – I'm sorry.'

'Why didn't you send them?' Mary couldn't control the tremor in her voice. His clothes were dishevelled, his chin unshaven, and deep misery was etched into his features. He seemed like a shell of the man she knew.

'They were no damned good. Anyway, they would only have made you miserable and you have an important job to do – you have to stay on top of things. Your poor face,' he added under his breath.

'Speak up!' the guard barked.

'Are you ready for tomorrow?' Mary asked.

Cameron nodded. 'I can't say much about it, though.'

'That's all right – I understand.' The straitjacket of the circumstances made her want to weep. She yearned to touch him and pour out her deepest feelings of love and fear. 'To tell the truth, it's not plain sailing for me either.'

'Choppy waters, eh?' He glanced over his shoulder at the sour-faced guard. 'Can you say more?'

'It's true, I was in an accident,' she admitted.

'When? Where?' Fresh jolts of concern ran through him.

She swallowed hard then gave him the bare bones.

Cameron was aghast. 'A Tempest? You cut the engine before landing?'

'I had no choice.'

'And you managed it?'

'I'm here, aren't I? And the crate wasn't wrecked. She'll be back up in the air tomorrow or the day after.'

He sat back in amazement. 'Mary, not one in ten pilots could have done what you did.'

She gave a long sigh of relief. Cameron didn't question her; he knew that what she said was true.

'And thank God you weren't badly hurt.'

'But about tomorrow.' She insisted on bringing them back round to the court martial. 'Who will be there besides you and . . . ?'

'Me and Bullen? There'll be Norris and four other high-ups deciding who to believe. Don't worry; I'll give it my best shot.'

'Make sure you do,' she urged. 'Promise not to let that . . . that man win.'

The guard cleared his throat in warning.

'I promise.' Cameron thought back through the long, tortured, self-sacrificing weeks of keeping his distance from Mary. He'd been deeply ashamed of the predicament he was in, had struggled with his feelings and in the end decided to leave her free to walk away if that's what she chose. It had left him in a terrible limbo, dragging through the days, sinking deeper into depression. But here she sat in this drab, bare room in the dull grey light with the sound of rain pouring from the gutter on to the gravel outside the door: the love of his life, boosting his fragile hopes. 'I've built up a pretty good case,' he assured her in a stronger voice.

'Yes.'

'I can't say any more.'

'No.' The light had come back into his eyes and a reassuring smile crept across his features. 'I love you,' she said loud and clear.

And so he, Flight Lieutenant Cameron Robert Ainslie, with thirty successful missions over the North Sea and Belgium under his belt, would fight tooth and nail to have his reputation restored and to be back by Mary's side. 'I love you too,' he replied.

Bobbie's voice over the telephone the day before had sounded determined – she needed to see Ray, he must come over to Rixley as soon as possible, if not today then the next.

'I'll be there as soon as I can,' he'd promised. 'There's a meeting at Ripon this afternoon that I can't get out of. How about tomorrow at two?'

And now as he drove the MG through a heavy April shower towards Burton Grange he was looking forward to seeing his lively Highland Girl again. Yesterday had been a washout – no winners had left his father in the foulest of tempers and the atmosphere on the yard had been even more fractious than usual. Luckily Ronnie and the other grooms had had the sense to keep well out of the way until a tot or two of whisky had quietened the old man down. By six o'clock Derek had taken to his room; he hadn't been seen since.

Ray saw Bobbie waiting for him as he pulled into the yard. She stood at the end of the terrace waving at him from under a green umbrella. Then, as he stepped out of the car she got rid of the umbrella and ran down the steps to meet him.

On impulse he put his hands around her waist to scoop her off her feet and spin her round, setting her down again with a broad smile. She was wearing a belted raincoat over trousers and a black beret set stylishly to one side over her tawny waves.

'Thank you.' Bobbie kissed him lightly on the cheek.

'What for?' The rain came down hard so he drew her into the shelter of the nearest stable.

'For coming.' She got out her handkerchief to wipe away the rain droplets that trickled down Ray's forehead then she kissed him again, this time on the lips.

With her arms still around his neck he leaned back and grinned at her. 'Wild horses wouldn't have kept me away – especially if I'd known this was the greeting I'd get.'

She blushed and smiled. 'You don't know why I asked you to come yet.'

'To help look for Anna,' he guessed. 'Still no news, I take it?'

'None.' Bobbie patted her own cheeks with the damp handkerchief. 'Jean went to Florrie to ask for her help but she came up against another brick wall. Oh, but Viv has a new bee in her bonnet about a couple living in Maltby Bay.'

'Why's that?' Ray found Bobbie's face as fascinating as ever. It was an open book, changing at lightning speed from bright gladness to shadowy worry and doubt.

'It was something Ernest Poulter said to her. To cut a long story short, Viv has come up with a theory

341

that Giles paid this couple in Maltby Bay to find a new home for Anna's baby girl.'

'Whoa!' Ray unclasped Bobbie's hands from around his neck and took a step back. 'No one mentioned anything to me about a baby.'

'You mean you didn't know?' Bobbie was taken aback. 'Poor Anna was desperate to find out who was fostering her daughter.'

'And what has Giles got to do with it?'

Bobbie bit her lip. She saw she must tread carefully. 'Perhaps you should ask him that yourself.'

'He's not— I mean, you don't think . . . ?' Ray was dumbfounded. It was true Giles could be an idiot at times, but getting a girl into trouble – well, that was serious.

'It looks that way. Giles was the one who installed Anna at the Grange – make of that what you will.'

Ray was still digesting this information and remembering the time he'd seen Giles deep in conversation with Florrie Loxley outside the Fox when he heard someone calling his name. Stepping out of the stable, he found Horace standing beside his MG, his hand around his mouth as he yelled Ray's name once more.

'Phone call for you,' Horace called when he spotted the visitor. 'Urgent!'

'For me?' Ray checked.

'That's right. A groom at your place is ringing every number he can think of.'

'I'll be right there.' No sooner said than Ray sprinted across the yard with Bobbie close on his heels; up the steps and along the terrace into the house. He snatched up the receiver from the hall table. 'Ray Moore here. Who's that?'

'It's me: Ronnie. Mr Derek's in a bad way. You should come.'

'Hang on – I'll be with you as soon as I can.' Ray's face turned deathly pale as he gave Bobbie a rapid explanation.

'I'll come too,' she decided on the spur of the moment.

'There's no need.' He gathered his scattered thoughts – was his father in one of his drunken stupors or was it worse than that? Had a doctor been called? Did a doctor even do house calls on a Sunday?

'I'll come anyway,' Bobbie insisted.

There was no time to argue. They jumped in the car and drove to Thresham mostly in silence, ignoring speed limits and both fearing the worst.

'I've warned Dad over and over,' Ray muttered as they rounded the last bend and the house and yard came into view. His jaw was clenched tight and a small muscle in his jaw jumped. 'I tell him: "Carry on drinking like that and you'll end up killing yourself." He never listens.'

'Perhaps it's not as bad as Ronnie made out.' Bobbie lurched forward as Ray drove into the yard and braked hard. At the squeal of brakes, horses' heads appeared at stable doors, all turned in the direction of the new arrivals, ears pricked with a sense of restless agitation. Some kicked at their doors to be let out while others whinnied.

A young groom whose name Bobbie didn't know rushed towards the car. 'Ronnie's in Tudor Queen's stable with Mr Derek,' he gabbled in the broadest of accents. 'He ordered me to turn 'oss out into t'field.'

Ray flung open his door and leapt out into the

rain. The lad stood, trembling and hanging his head. 'We called amberlance,' he mumbled at Bobbie, who hung back with a sense of dread. 'It'll be 'ere any time.'

Ronnie appeared in the open doorway, his long, lined face rigid with shock. 'Mr Derek's in here,' he informed Ray quietly.

At first Ray found it hard to make out anything in the dim light of the stable. Then he noticed that a water bucket had been kicked over and the straw bed disturbed. And then he saw his father.

Derek Moore lay sprawled on his back, still in the race-going clothes from the day before. His arms were flung wide and his face turned towards the door. Dark blood poured from his temple and stained the pale straw beneath his head. His eyes were open.

Ray dropped to his knees at his father's side. The sour reek of alcohol made him recoil at first then he leaned forward and spoke softly. 'It's all right, Dad – I'm here now.'

'Don't move him!' Ronnie warned as Ray attempted to slide an arm under his father's head. 'It's his neck.'

Derek stared helplessly at his son. He didn't seem distressed but when he tried to speak blood trickled from his mouth.

'How long's he been lying here?' Ray asked.

'A good forty-five minutes. I heard the racket from across the yard – the horse kicking out and stamping her hooves, your father cussing . . . The damned ambulance should be here by now.' Ronnie stayed by the door, gazing out helplessly as if by staring hard enough he could make it happen. 'When I got here

I found Tudor Queen standing over him. Mr Derek should never have barged in on her – he knows what she's like.'

'Dad?' Ray shuddered as he pictured the brief, violent scene that must have taken place in this confined space – his father taking out his bad mood on the horse, Tudor Queen rearing up, pawing the air, towering over the drunken trainer.

He bent over the prone figure and spoke in a whisper. 'Can you hear me?'

Derek's eyes signalled that he could.

'You're going to be all right – we'll get you to hospital.'

There was a groan but no movement of the head.

Ray glanced down at his own blood-stained fingers and quelled a rising panic. 'What the hell were you thinking, Dad? No one except Ronnie knows how to deal with that mare.'

His father's eyes flickered shut then open again.

Ray continued to piece together the build-up to what had happened – his father still half-cut, staggering out of the house and down to the yard, stumbling from stable to stable doing God knows what – swearing, banging into things, setting the horses on edge.

Tudor Queen had lost badly at Ripon. This fact lodged in Ray's brain and made the gorge rise in his throat. 'Dad?'

Derek's gaze was fixed on his son. His breathing grew shallow and ragged.

An ambulance appeared at the end of the drive. With a quick, despairing shake of his head Ronnie leaned heavily against the wall.

'It's all right. The ambulance is here. You're going to be fine.' Ray held his father's cold hand and watched his eyes flicker shut for the final time. There were no more breaths; only a slide into noth- ingness and the sound of men's footsteps running across the yard, too late.

CHAPTER NINETEEN

That night Jean walked through Burton Wood to join Bobbie, Mary and Viv in the lounge bar of the Grange. After what had happened at Thresham there was comfort to be drawn from the four women sitting together over a drink, looking out at the dramatic red and gold sunset, taking stock.

'Who knows what the day is going to bring?' Jean sipped from her glass and spoke softly. 'Something like this comes out of nowhere and turns the whole world upside down.'

'How is Ray taking it?' Viv was quieter and more reflective than usual. 'It throws a hell of a lot of responsibility on to his shoulders – funeral arrangements, horses and the business still to be looked after.'

'He's hardly taken it in yet.' Bobbie sat closest to the fire, cradling her glass and staring at its ruby red contents. 'I think he expected the ambulance men to perform a miracle but of course they couldn't.' She remembered Ray's frantic pleas, the two men ordering him to stand back while they tried to revive the patient and, in the stable next door, Glasgow Girl banging with her hooves and whinnying to be let out.

347

'Perhaps it's for the best.' Mary voiced what they were all thinking – who would want to go on living paralysed from the neck down?

'He was only fifty-six.' Wiry and active, restless, impatient, intemperate; in her mind Bobbie summed up what little she knew of Derek Moore. She'd stayed by Ray's side after the ambulance had taken away the body. There'd been no tears, just bewilderment. Ray had refused to leave the yard and go up to the house.

'Not very old,' Jean commented.

'What will happen to the horse?' Mary asked. 'I take it her owner will have to be told?'

'Ronnie's already done that. Mr Addyman has agreed to take Tudor Queen away from Thresham straight away.' The head groom had made the necessary phone call then done what needed to be done, turning all the horses out into the paddock to calm them down while the junior lads filled water troughs and mucked out stables. 'Ronnie's the dependable type,' Bobbie explained. 'It must have been awful for him, though – he was the one who found Ray's father and called for an ambulance.'

Sitting with Ray in the cart shed, she'd watched the head groom assume control. Ronnie had issued orders quietly and methodically, almost as if the tragedy hadn't occurred – gentle with the horses, abrupt with the lads, refusing to be drawn into conversation. Bobbie saw that this was how it would be in the days ahead: Ray lost in grief, Ronnie taciturn and carrying on as normal.

'Won't you come inside?' she'd asked Ray, laying a gentle hand on his shoulder and gesturing towards the house.

'I'd rather stay here,' he'd replied in a broken voice.

'You'll get wet.' The rain had formed large puddles and ran from the gutters in an endless stream.

'I don't care. If I go in the house I'll see Dad's things – his coat and hat, his newspaper.' Ray had feared a repeat attack of the heebie-jeebies, like the one he'd suffered two years previously after news of his brother Frank's death had broken on the day after Ray's plane had landed in the drink. Tears, the shakes, hallucinations – the lot. The doc's verdict: lacking in moral fibre – not once but twice over.

Bobbie had sat with him, watching the rain come down. Ronnie had brought an oilskin cape and wrapped it around Ray's shoulders. 'I've made up a bed in my quarters,' he'd said matter-of-factly. 'You can sleep there tonight.'

The light had begun to fade. Ronnie had asked one of the lads to drive Bobbie back to the Grange. She hadn't known whether or not to hug Ray before she left.

'You'll come back soon?' he'd asked, stepping out with her into the yard and catching hold of her hand.

'Yes.' The rain had soaked them both to the skin.

'When?'

'It depends on Douglas's rotas. I never know where I'm going to be sent from one day to the next.'

He'd let Bobbie go. She hadn't held him in her arms or found a way to comfort him.

'I'm glad Ray has someone to look after him,' Mary said, gently bringing Bobbie back into the present.

Firelight flickered across their sad faces as they sat in quiet contemplation. Viv felt far from home and vulnerable, while Jean was deeply moved by Ray's loss and Mary recalled the moment earlier in the day when she'd had to say goodbye to Cameron. Tears were close to the surface for all of them and words hard to find.

'Yes. Ronnie's known Ray for most of his life,' Bobbie agreed with Mary's well-meaning remark.

'She means you,' Viv pointed out patiently. 'Ray has you now, Bobbie. You're the one he's bound to turn to in the days to come.'

Next morning Viv was scheduled to fly first out of Rixley. 'A Wellington to an MU north of Derby,' she told Bobbie as she emerged on to the lawn pocketing her chit. 'They'll fit her with a new radio then send her on to Portsmouth ready for you know what.'

'Yes, it can't be long now.' Bobbie gave the stock response. 'Not long now'; a matter of weeks if not days before Churchill and Roosevelt gave the go-ahead for the invasion of occupied Europe. Everyone on the Allied side said it with eagerness and confidence – a mighty force soon to be unleashed against the weakened enemy, a joint attack by air, land and sea. 'I'm obliged to hang around here until Gordon unblocks a vent pipe on my Magister – it's a good job he picked up the fault, otherwise I'd have been in deep trouble.'

'Where are you headed when you eventually get off?' Viv checked her pockets for her map, compass and Pilots' Notes. She'd already fetched her other belongings from her locker.

'The back of beyond: a grass airfield in the depths of Kent.' Bobbie was frustrated by the delay. She'd slept badly, unable to get Ray out of her mind, knowing that the only way to clear her head would be to be up at 5,000 feet following landmarks and concentrating on her crate's climb and descent indicator, fuel pressure gauge and control column.

As Viv and Bobbie said their farewells, Agnes rushed across the grass towards the ops room, parachute pack slung over her shoulder and flying jacket tucked under her arm. 'I slept in, damn it,' she muttered.

Meanwhile, Jean emerged from the building armed with her chit for the day. 'A Spit to Leicestershire,' she reported to Bobbie. 'Ferry pool number six – not very exciting.'

'But in a Spit at least.' Bobbie was envious – the heavy Wellington bomber didn't provide the same thrill when airborne.

Jean and Bobbie set off together across the lawn – Bobbie towards Hangar 2 where Gordon worked on her crate and Jean about to follow Viv towards Runway 1. They glanced up at clouds to the north and exchanged remarks about the likelihood of rain, both setting their minds on the day's tasks.

Meanwhile, Mary stood by the canteen door and watched them come and go. She deliberately waited until the queue to the ops room dwindled to nothing before heading for Hilary's office where she knocked on the door.

'In!' Hilary abbreviated his answer to a terse one word. He glanced up from his desk to see Mary enter wearing her uniform and flying jacket. The bruises and cuts to her face were still plain to see but she'd removed her sling and walked in with a look of fierce determination. 'Yes?'

She approached his desk then stood to attention. 'A request to be put back on the rota, sir. I'm fit for duty.'

'Says who?' Hilary played for time. Douglas hadn't yet got back to him with the information he'd requested – until he did Hilary couldn't come to any decision about Mary's fitness to fly.

'I say so, sir.' She'd got up and put on her uniform in defiant mood, ready to challenge the world. Anything was better than sitting around doing nothing, today of all days. She'd combed her hair and put on her forage cap, straightened her tie in the mirror then cycled through the wood to the ferry pool.

'It's Monday the tenth,' Hilary pointed out unnecessarily. Mary earned full marks for sheer bloodymindedness, he'd give her that.

'Yes, sir.' She stared ahead at the typed sheets pinned to the noticeboard.

'The day of Cameron's court martial.'

'Yes, sir.'

'I'm afraid I can't risk sending you out, Third Officer Holland – given what happened last time.'

Mary flinched. 'That's not fair, sir; pilot error isn't proved.'

'It's not disproved either.'

'I stand by what I said.' She fought to keep her voice calm. 'I was in control at all times. The area was heavily populated so I didn't want to bail out and risk civilian casualties. I decided to stay put and bring my crate down as best I could.'

'Yes, yes. Agreed that would have been the right decision if . . .' Hilary hesitated under the force of Mary's argument and the fierceness of her gaze.

Then he responded to a second sharp knock on his door. 'In!' he barked.

'Sir.' Stan stepped into the room then stood to attention.

Mary jumped but didn't turn at the sound of his voice. Hilary's face wore a deep frown.

'Yes, what is it, Corporal Mechanic Green?'

Mary stared straight ahead. She held her breath until she was dizzy.

'I've come to report a procedural failure, sir.' Stan's shoulders were back, chest out and arms pinned to his sides. 'It concerns Third Officer Holland's Tempest Mark One, sir.'

Hilary slammed his pen down on his desk, looking quickly from Stan to Mary then back again. 'What procedural failure are we talking about?'

Still not daring to breathe, Mary closed her eyes.

'I didn't carry out proper checks on the Napier Sabre IV engine, sir. I left it to Apprentice Mechanic Cross. He's not qualified. The fault was all mine, sir.'

Cameron held his voice steady. 'I see. Carry on.'

'I'd already read up about engine development – there was a recognized problem with overheating and keeping revs under control. I was fully aware of that; I ought to have double-checked the crankshaft lubrication myself, sir.' Stan ended his confession then clenched his jaw, staring not at his superior officer but at Mary's back. She swayed slightly as he finished speaking.

Hilary picked up his pen and heaved a long sigh. 'Why didn't you report this sooner? No, don't answer that, Green – write everything down on a report sheet when you've had time to consider.'

353

'Will do, sir.'

'That's all.' Hilary dismissed Stan with a flick of his hand. He waited for the door to click shut before he spoke again, tapping the end of the pen against the desk. 'This will have to be taken into consideration.' *Damn fool Green – should've known better!* Hilary despised slip-ups of this sort and promised himself that the mechanic would get a rap over the knuckles at the very least, whatever the outcome for Mary.

Mary breathed at last. She hadn't really believed that Stan would carry out his promise. Now she resolved to take back the angry words that had passed between them and thank him from the bottom of her heart. 'What will happen to Corporal Mechanic Green now, sir?'

'Let's concentrate on the matter in hand, shall we?' Another dismissive wave was followed by the continuing tap-tap of Hilary's pen against the desk. 'The fact of the matter is, despite Green's somewhat tardy intervention on your behalf, I can't put you back on the rota until I receive a full report from Castle Bromwich.' Coming to a sudden decision, he stood up and told Mary to follow him, taking the stairs up to the ops room two at a time then bursting in on Douglas.

Telephone in hand, Douglas noted the irritation etched into Hilary's features. *What now?* He caught a glimpse of Mary hovering outside the door. *Ah, yes; Mary and the blasted Tempest!*

I'm on to them, he mouthed at Hilary, pointing to the phone.

'Is that Castle Bromwich on the other end?' Hilary demanded.

Douglas nodded then carried on with his conversation. 'I've already given you the plane's serial number and my pilot's name; Third Officer Holland is based here at the ATA ferry pool in Rixley, North Yorkshire. The date was the fifth of April; the Wednesday just gone . . . that's correct.'

From her typewriter station by the window Dotty Kirk spotted Mary, who looked to be on the point of collapse. She beckoned for her to come in then offered her a chair to sit on. 'Fingers crossed!' she murmured.

Mary clenched her fists in an attempt to control her emotions and sat stiffly. The cream-coloured walls of the cluttered room – piles of paper everywhere, typewriters without their covers, maps and met reports pinned to the wall – seemed to close in on her. She knew that her fate hung in the balance – what was it to be: a thumbs-up or a thumbs-down?

'What do they say?' Hilary demanded.

'Just a second.' Douglas calmly held up a warning hand then spoke again into the phone. 'You have the engineer's report in front of you? That's grand. Can you read it out to me, please?'

Mary heard the click of Dotty's typewriter keys resume in the background. Didn't they know that flying was more than a mere job? It meant everything to her, signifying how hard she'd worked and how high she'd aimed, having pulled herself up from nothing, from scratch, from a grim beginning as a girl who had gone to work in a woollen mill at the age of fourteen. It came to her now, the memory of the life-changing occasion at Highcliff fairground when she'd paid her sixpence for a ride in a rocket ship and first allowed herself to dream. She remembered soaring through the night sky to the churning beat of raucous music, to the dizzying flash of coloured lights – if only it could be real! 'Do it!' Stan had told her afterwards. 'Learn to fly. What's to stop you?' 'Here is the form, here is the pen,' Cameron had encouraged. Two good-hearted men had believed in her when she hadn't even believed in herself.

Hours, days, weeks of dreaming and applying her uneducated mind had followed. And then the moment of her first solo flight at the training camp in Hamble had arrived – 'She's all yours' – the hand-over by her trainer, the moment when she'd pulled down the canopy then taxied along the runway without her instructor, the jolt of the undercarriage as the plane had left the ground, the soaring sense of freedom as Mary had taken to the air.

Nothing in life came close to the triumph of knowing that she could fly.

'Faulty throttle.' With a glad glance in Mary's direction Douglas repeated word for word what he heard. 'Plus petrol leak in the port tank. Thanks a lot, that's good news. That's champion; thank you very much indeed.'

It wasn't in the rule book but it wasn't explicitly forbidden either. Viv reasoned things out as she stood in the corridor of the packed train back from Derby. As long as she reported for duty at eight o'clock the following morning, how she occupied her time between now and then was up to her.

She'd made good time in the Wellington, a reliable, twin-engined bomber that was now principally used as an anti-submarine aircraft. As she'd commented to

Bobbie first thing that morning, it wasn't a patch on the nippy little Spit and she'd been happy to hand it over to the boys at the Maintenance Unit. Liking the look of her raven hair and curves in all the right places, the men had been keen to keep her talking about the crate's Barnes Wallis-designed geodesic construction, which created space for three fuel tanks in each wing, would you believe. Yeah, yeah, Viv had said; tell that to the birds. Not interested in Duralumin W-beams and wooden battens, thanks a lot.

No; Viv had other things on her mind.

Now she stood in the corridor mulling over her options: should she head back to Rixley and find out from Mary how Cameron's court martial had gone, then liaise with whoever was back early about the next step in the increasingly urgent search for Anna? Alternatively she could do something completely different . . . 'Have you got a light, love?' the Tommy standing next to her asked. He carried a bulging kitbag over one shoulder and wore his beret at a rakish angle.

Viv thought that the clipped ginger moustache crouched above the over-friendly soldier's upper lip resembled a slug or a caterpillar. 'Sorry, I don't smoke,' she lied.

He shrugged and made no effort to prevent himself from swaying against her each time the train rounded a bend, until eventually a seat in the nearest carriage fell vacant and Viv swiftly took it. She looked out of the window to see that they had just passed through a small coal-mining town. She noticed the tall minehead workings and a grey slag heap rising higher than the row of terraced houses that it overlooked.

'Next stop Newton Bridge,' the ticket inspector informed each carriage in turn as he made his way down the corridor. 'Change here for Roebury district line.'

'It's fate,' Viv said to her puzzled neighbour, a cheerful young woman with a curly haired toddler perched on her knee. Without further ado she jumped up and collected her belongings from the overhead rack, before shoving her way along the crowded corridor towards the nearest door. 'Thank you . . . Excuse me, please . . . Thanks.'

What next? It was only when Viv was standing on the platform watching her train leave the station that she paused for thought. Newton Bridge was a name that Giles had mentioned in passing. Way back in the nineteenth century, one of his ancestors at Newpark had apparently sold land to the railway company to allow them to build the line, and a small village had since grown up around the station. Therefore, the ancestral home must be nearby. *Great thinking, Vivienne!* She looked around for the stationmaster.

'Hi!' She breezed towards an elderly, uniformed man brandishing a whistle and a flag. 'What's the quickest way to get to Newpark?'

'Shanks's pony' was the reply. 'It's only ten minutes up the road.'

'Up the road' meant that Viv should walk up a steep hill with rows of small houses and shops to either side. She passed a church then a school with children playing in the playground. A plaque on the wall of the building told her that a previous Sir Thomas Parseval had been the school's benefactor in Anno Domini 1874. Then, as she reached the brow of the hill, she was greeted by the sight of open, rolling valleys and green hills; trees, hedges, unfenced grassland spread before her as far as the eye could see. The vista was less dramatic than the Yorkshire moors and dales where she was stationed but beautiful nonetheless on this brisk, breezy day of windswept clouds and swaying branches. For a moment Viv took in the view and almost lost sight of her purpose.

'Can I help you?' a low voice asked. A black Jaguar had pulled up and the driver leaned out of the window. 'Oh, it's you.'

Viv recognized the Parsevals' chauffeur. 'Yes, Mr Butcher – it's me. I'm on my way to see Giles, if he happens to be at home.'

'Your luck's in.' From under his peaked cap the chauffeur's expression gave nothing away. His was not to reason why. 'Hop in,' he told her with a sideways nod towards the passenger seat.

So Viv arrived at the house in style, approaching up a short, curved drive and being deposited at the front entrance without a word from Butcher.

These Parsevals sure knew how to impress: stone lions sat to either side of broad steps that led to a shiny black door under an arched window designed like a fan. Before she could raise the gleaming brass knocker, a manservant opened the door on to a hallway as big as a baseball pitch. She had only a few seconds to take in the crossed swords mounted on the wall above the family crest and an array of portraits lining the stairway before Giles himself approached.

'Vivienne. How nice.' His polite greeting was accompanied by a guarded study of her appearance – in the full Atta girl outfit, complete with parachute pack and flying jacket. *What the hell is she up to, turning up out of the blue?*

'Yes, it's been ages.' As she'd expected, Giles was at ease on his home turf; dressed in slacks and a crisp white shirt, he studied her through narrowed, suspicious eyes.

'How have you been?' He walked her across the hall into a little used reception room at the front of the house – best to find out what she wanted in private and with the least possible fuss.

'Run off my feet,' she told him, removing her cap and dropping her parachute pack on to the floor. 'Nice room, by the way.'

'Thank you. What brings you here?'

'I've come to see you,' she said with her usual directness. A girl could easily be intimidated by these surroundings – big white fireplace, fancy plasterwork, brocade curtains, soft cushions, a bellpull to bring the servants running – just like the setting of a Leslie Howard movie. 'If you'd be so kind as to give us more information about Anna we'd be most grateful.' There; the bomb was primed!

'Indeed?' Giles relied on a lifetime's training to conceal his reaction. He kept his hands clasped behind his back and stood with his back to the fireplace, feet wide apart. 'What makes you suppose I can be of help?'

'Oh, come off it, Giles. This is me you're talking to – the girl who only found out you were married by accident.'

'Yes; I've already said I'm sorry. That was wrong of me.'

'So let's drop the play-acting, shall we?' Something

was happening that Viv hadn't expected – she'd forgotten how attractive she'd found Giles but now she was feeling it again – a fascination beyond the stiff-upper-lip, upper-class manner. 'I need you to come clean about why Anna ran off and where she might have run to.'

'How should I know?' He didn't drop his guard; in fact, the opposite – he grew more cautious still.

'OK, so for a start you're the one who organized her move to Burton Grange.'

'So?'

Viv sensed the mounting tension but didn't relent. 'So you were desperate to get her off your hands and cover up the baby issue. But it wasn't that easy – not when we found out that she'd had to give her daughter away.'

'Look here.' Giles shifted his position, taking a quick step forward and noticing that the door was ajar. He hurried to close it then came back. 'I know that you think badly of me but please don't jump to conclusions.'

'And don't you take me for a fool,' she retorted, eyes flashing. 'You're a guy who's hard to trust – you know that.'

'And you make accusations without the necessary evidence.' He shook his head, went to look out through the window then strode back. 'Viv, you have to take my word for it – I had nothing to do with Anna getting pregnant. There, I can't be clearer than that.'

'Your word?' she repeated scornfully. 'Oh, please . . . !'

'Viv—' He broke off with another shake of his head. 'Listen, can we just calm down? All I can say is: I'm genuinely sorry about what happened to Anna.'

'You can deny it all you like – it doesn't alter the facts.' The trick now was to shame him into helping with the search. 'After all, it was you who fixed up for Dorota to go to Arthur and Betty, the couple in Maltby Bay.'

How in Christ's name does she know about that? Giles exploded into fresh action, striding around the room until he reached the door. 'Please leave,' he muttered, with his head down and his hand resting on the handle.

No way! 'Maltby Bay is a small place – I can easily find them. But it would be quicker if you just came clean. You could drive me there right now if you wanted.'

'No, that wouldn't do any good.'

'It might,' she argued. 'Say, for instance, Anna worked it out the same way I have. Put yourself in her shoes – once you'd found out where little Dorota is being kept, wild horses wouldn't stop you.'

'From doing what?' Giles's palms were damp with sweat. This was too much – things were getting badly out of hand.

'From packing up and leaving Burton Grange then heading straight there to claim her.'

'You might take that course of action,' he countered, turning the handle ready to open the door, 'but Anna's not like you; she's different.'

'OK; I get it – you've already checked it out with Arthur and Betty?' Of course he had.

'Anna has not been to Maltby Bay,' he confirmed. 'And now, if you've quite finished—'

'No.' Viv slotted herself between Giles and the door. 'I'm not done yet. I'm looking at you and wondering what kind of man are you? You use a woman who isn't in any position to say no then throw her away as if she's not worth anything, just a piece of garbage. And then you lie about it.'

Giles gritted his teeth and took the sharp blows of Viv's anger without defending himself. Their faces were close enough for him to see her dilated pupils and to feel her breath on his half-turned cheek.

'You lie,' she repeated. 'You don't lift a finger to help Anna keep her baby. No, you send her to live among strangers in a room that's not fit for a dog. You don't give a damn about her or about the welfare of your own child!'

The door opened without warning, shoving Viv forward against Giles before Jane Parseval entered the room.

'Mother, there's no need.' Giles steadied Viv then placed a restraining hand on his mother's arm.

'Hush, dear.' Jane brushed past them both. 'There's every need.'

'Really, Mother . . .'

She turned to face them – Giles pale and tense, the strident ATA girl fired up, her lovely face flushed with anger. 'You're both so very young,' she said sadly before switching her attention back to the door through which she'd just entered. 'Come in, Thomas; do.'

Sir Thomas entered the room as if walking into a minefield, one slow step at a time. He wore a dark blue waistcoat over a crisply laundered white shirt and his grey hair was neatly combed back from his high forehead. 'What is she doing here?' he said about Viv with no trace of his usual urbanity.

'She's just leaving.' Giles took Viv's elbow and tried to steer her from the room.

'No; everybody, stay.' Jane was composed, her fair hair framing her pale face in neatly arranged waves. She wore a fitted dove-grey dress, a large amethyst brooch and earrings to match.

A classy act. Viv admired Jane's tailoring from coiffured top to elegantly shod kidskin toe. And surprisingly, she seemed to be the one in charge here.

'Giles, you have my permission to stop pretending.' Jane's voice rang out across the room. 'I understand that you did it for my sake and I appreciate your good intentions, but it's high time to face facts.'

Giles glanced uncertainly at his father, whose features had narrowed and frozen into a deep scowl. He had nothing to say, apparently.

'The fact is I know the truth,' Jane said as she turned to Viv. 'I always have. My son judged that I wasn't strong enough to endure it and sought to conceal it from me, but I've known from the start that Thomas, not Giles, is the father of Anna Janicki's baby.'

It was as if a mysterious hand had lifted a Christmas snow globe and turned it upside down. A whirl of white flakes obscured the miniature scene before slowly settling into new, smooth mounds.

Viv's eyes widened in disbelief. Was this it? Had Sir Thomas Parseval taken advantage of Anna then let the blame rest on his son's shoulders? Had Giles been obliged to uphold the lie under the illusion that he'd been protecting his mother? If so, Sir

Thomas, with his precious title and his coat of arms – the out-and-out snob who had married off his son for money and cheated on his wife – turned out to be the lowest of the low. Outrageous, despicable. It was a bolt from the blue.

'Well?' Viv asked Giles. The flakes whirled and settled.

Jane came between them. 'No more pretence, no more lies,' she murmured to her son.

'Yes, it's true.' Giles couldn't bear to look at his father, who stood ashen faced and silent in the doorway. 'But it doesn't go beyond this room,' he begged. 'For the sake of the family name, Viv, promise me that you won't say a word.'

CHAPTER TWENTY

Mary found Stan working on the engine of a Fairey Swordfish in Hangar 1. She'd come straight from the ops room to seek him out. 'Is there anyone up there with you?' she called, her voice echoing in the vast space. She stood among trucks and partly dismantled aircraft, next to a safety notice warning against smoking inside the hangar.

Stan put down a section of cowling then slid down from the aircraft's wing, wiping his hands on his overalls as he walked towards her. 'No; the others are taking a tea break. Well, what was the verdict?'

'Faulty throttle.' The relief on hearing Douglas relay those two words in the ops room had flooded through her and brought her close to tears. It had been a longed-for reprieve and the shock of it had made her gasp; Douglas on the phone to Castle Bromwich, Hilary standing close by as the information came through – not pilot error after all. Now that Mary was cleared of all suspicion her horizons instantly broadened; she was free to fly on and fulfil her destiny. 'It's official – I'm in the clear.'

'Back on the rota?'

She nodded. 'From tomorrow.'

'That's grand, Mary. Any news on Cameron?' Stan took out a packet of cigarettes and walked with her to the door of the hangar.

'Not yet.' The agony of waiting wasn't over and Mary wasn't sure how she would get through the long afternoon once she'd cleared the air with Stan.

'Fingers crossed.' He lit up then inhaled deeply.

'I came to say thank you for what you did for me.' Mary stood next to him, gazing up at banks of light cloud interspersed with patches of blue. There was a strong westerly wind but otherwise flying conditions had improved since early morning.

'I wish I'd done it earlier. I ought to have . . .'

'Stan,' Mary touched him lightly on the shoulder, 'there's no need.'

'I ought not to have doubted you, Mary. I'm sorry.'

'It doesn't matter.'

'Yes, it does.' Stan wasn't one for deep thinking – he was an ordinary, easy-going bloke who'd trained as a motor mechanic straight out of school, who had seen an RAF recruitment poster outside Highcliff town hall and answered the call to train to service fighter aircraft. But his doubts over Mary's accident had got under his skin and he'd had to ask himself why he hadn't believed her version of events. 'I reckon I was jealous,' he confessed through a cloud of blue smoke.

'Who of?'

'Of you and Cameron. No, don't say anything – let me explain. I kidded myself I was in with a chance – you and me. But once I saw how worked up you were over Cameron and his court martial and especially after you put me straight – not once

367

but twice over – that was it: I realized I never did stand a cat in hell's chance.'

Mary sighed. 'I'm sorry if I led you on.' Tears and a kiss followed by immediate regret.

'No; that was me grasping at straws.'

'You've been a good friend to me, Stan, ever since I arrived at Rixley. If it wasn't for you I'd never have signed up for the conversion course.'

'True.' She'd thought she wasn't good enough and Stan had convinced her of the opposite. And look at her now. 'They should award you a medal for bringing that Tempest down the way you did. I'm proud of you.'

'Thanks, Stan.' There'd be no medals but maybe a promotion to Second Officer if she was lucky. 'I want us to go back to how we were before – can we?'

'After what's happened?' He threw down his fag end. Gordon had just emerged from the canteen and was heading their way. 'It was my job to run the checks myself, don't forget.'

Mary nodded then smiled. 'None of us is perfect, not even you, Stan Green.'

'Especially not me,' he admitted.

Gordon strode towards them wearing a wide grin. 'Congratulations, Mary – First Officer Thornton says you're off the hook.'

'That's right, I am.' The quiet, confessional mood between Mary and Stan was broken. 'I'll see you tomorrow morning,' she told him breezily as she walked away.

'Bright and early,' he agreed. Friendship would have to do, failing anything more. Stan took out another cigarette then offered the pack to Gordon, who glanced at his watch. 'Time for a quick one before we get back to it – I won't tell anyone if you don't.'

Keeping moving was better than sitting twiddling her thumbs, so Mary left the ferry pool and strode briskly through Burton Wood. *Put one foot in front of another*, she told herself in an attempt not to think about what was happening at Aireby: Cameron against Bullen in front of five superior officers brought together especially for the court martial.

She soon passed Fern Cottage and carried on towards the rough, open slopes of the Warrens, up a steep hill then down into the neighbouring valley with a clear view of the reservoir. By the time she reached the water's edge the clouds had lifted and she found a rock on which to rest. Mary tilted her head to feel the warm sun on her face then closed her eyes and breathed in the fresh green smell of wild garlic. The wind sighed through the branches of a nearby beech tree. Taking off her cap, Mary ran her fingers through her hair then opened her eyes.

The water was beautiful – silver and sparkling in the sunlight. There was a stony beach strewn with driftwood that had been smoothed and twisted into fantastical shapes, and a narrow inlet where a bright stream trickled between rocks to feed the reservoir.

Mary went to the stream and cupped her hands to drink the cool, clear water. She patted her warm cheeks with her wet hands. It was when she stood up that she noticed what looked like a woman's coat and scarf on the opposite bank; not abandoned but carefully folded and placed on top of another object then anchored by a large stone. How curious that someone had purposely left such items in this remote spot. Mary glanced towards the rippling expanse of water then once more at the small pile of belongings. She crossed the stream and carefully removed the stone before lifting the damp coat and uncovering a brown suitcase underneath.

The discovery ran like an electric shock through Mary's body. She knew instantly what it meant – the coat, scarf and suitcase belonged to Anna, who must have sought out this lonely spot, far from help or interference.

They'd all been wrong – she, Jean, Viv and Bobbie had imagined Anna carefully planning to steal away from Burton Grange in order to take up the search for Dorota. She'd packed and left nothing behind except her uniform – otherwise no trace at all. But it turned out Anna had never nurtured any hope of finding her daughter. No; her purpose had been quite different. Mary's hand shook as she opened the suitcase. There were two clicks as the metal catches sprang open. Inside the case were a few clothes and a letter written in pencil on a piece of lined paper torn from a spiral-bound notebook.

'For my daughter, Dorota,' Mary read. Her legs gave way and she had to sit down on the nearest rock. 'When you can read this you will be grown into a beautiful girl. You will be strong. You will have the things I cannot give.'

Overwhelmed, Mary began to weep silently. Anna had walked here in the dark with her suitcase, in her flowered scarf and her grey coat. She had worn the brown dress that made her look like a nun. She had already written and folded the letter and placed it inside the case then walked to this, the furthest spot she could find, by the water's edge.

'My hope is in you, my Dorota. For me there is no future. I have lost all. You will grow and you will be strong, my daughter. You will be loved.'

These were her final words except for a signature at the bottom, written in a shaky hand. Nothing to live for and no other mark bearing witness to Anna's lonely existence.

Mary cried for a long time. At last she folded the letter and closed Anna's case. She picked it up with the coat and scarf then stared out across the deep reservoir at cold, clear water and an empty sky.

The rhythm of the moving train, homeward bound to Rixley, slowly calmed Viv's anger. She found it hard to understand some of Giles's reasoning and the unquestioning way he'd put family loyalty before Anna's welfare but she did have some sympathy with his desire to protect his mother.

'What would you have done in my place?' he'd asked her as he'd driven her from Newpark back to the station. 'When Anna's pregnancy came to light, everyone automatically assumed I was responsible.'

'Why was that, I wonder?' Viv had sat with him in the car until the train had arrived. 'It speaks volumes about your reputation that they blamed you.'

'Point taken,' he'd replied. 'But you're wrong about me – you always have been. I was married to Nora at the time, and in spite of everything my marriage vows were important. I kept to the straight and narrow.'

'Unlike your dad.'

'I repeat – what would you have done? I was well aware of the situation but when I confronted my father, he came out with the immortal line: "Don't tell your mother." No "please", no "thank you" – just "don't tell her".' Giles had stared straight ahead, scarcely moving his lips in that way he had, oblivious of his surroundings. 'It was an order, not a request.'

'And you saw it as your duty to protect the family and to hell with poor Anna?'

'To protect my mother, yes. I couldn't have cared less about him.' The bitterness had brought about a deep scowl.

'What about Nora?' Viv had pressed for answers. What a nest of vipers this was turning out to be.

'She couldn't have cared less about me. She had her own, shall we say, dalliances to keep her occupied.'

'And you were piggy in the middle. Since you don't deny it, I guess it's true.' Viv hadn't made up her mind what quality of Giles's character had made him toe the line. It could be cowardice but there again it could be a strength that she couldn't put her finger on. 'It can't have been easy, I'll give you that. And you did come up with a solution of sorts by finding Anna a new place to live and a possible home for the baby.'

'Damned with faint praise, eh?'

A sudden attack of conscience had brought Viv up short. 'Look, I'm sorry – OK? Genuinely, I am. I wish with all my heart that I hadn't been so hasty.'

Giles had managed a fleeting smile. 'Hasty is your middle name, isn't it?'

'Ouch, I guess I deserve that.'

Giles had drummed his fingers on the steering

wheel. 'I suppose you still want to know the exact whereabouts of the child?'

The train had steamed slowly into the station and passengers had begun to pour out on to the street. 'You bet I do.'

Giles had scribbled an address on a piece of paper then shoved it into Viv's hand. But he hadn't released it until he'd extracted a promise. 'Not a word about my father – understood?'

'OK, I swear.' She'd put a hand over her heart in reluctant agreement. 'Do you think Anna has any clue about this couple in Maltby Bay?'

He'd shaken his head. 'She hasn't been there; I do know that. You'll miss your train,' he'd warned her.

So Viv had gathered her possessions and scrambled from the car without a goodbye. *Coward or hero, playboy or wronged husband, weakling or dutiful son – or all of these rolled into one? With Anna as the hapless victim; don't forget that.* Viv had jumped on the train just in time and looked out of the window to see Giles still sitting in his car without moving, staring at nothing.

And so she mulled things over as the scenery outside the window went by in a blur. One good thing had come out of this damned mess and that was the scribbled address she now carried in her top pocket – *Mr and Mrs A. F. Raynard, 5 Harbour Cottages, Maltby Bay.* Viv could hardly wait to pass this information on to Bobbie, Jean and Mary.

The end of the journey couldn't come fast enough. As the brakes squealed and the train slowed to a halt, she was already on her feet, reaching for her parachute pack. She was out of the carriage and opening the door to jump down on to the platform where, to her surprise, Jean and Bobbie waited for her. One look at their drained, pale faces told Viv that something dreadful had happened.

'At last!' Bobbie cried. 'We'd no idea which train you'd be on . . .'

'It's Anna.' Jean interrupted. 'Mary found a note. By the reservoir. Along with her things. No sign of Anna.'

'Dead?' Viv whispered.

'We believe so.' Bobbie confirmed her fears. 'They'll have to search for a body – until then we can't be sure.'

Viv drew the address from her pocket with trembling fingers. 'Why couldn't she have waited?'

'Anna had already lost too much – that's what she wrote in her note.' Jean took the scrap of paper from Viv and guided her down the street towards the Grange. 'There wasn't any way we could have stopped her – I'm absolutely certain of that.'

There was a knock on Mary's door but in her exhaustion she didn't react. The best had happened and then the worst on what was already a momentous day.

There was a second knock. 'Mary, are you there?'

She recognized the rolling lilt of Bobbie's voice and dragged herself to the door.

'Cameron's here,' Bobbie informed her.

Mary gasped and clutched at the door handle for support. 'Has he said anything?'

'No. He's waiting for you in the library.' Bobbie's fingers were crossed for Mary as she stepped aside.

Mary's heart raced as she dashed along the landing and down the stairs. If the news was bad she would support Cameron through the worst of it, yet she hardly felt strong enough – not now, not after what had happened to Anna. *Please God, let it be good news!* Mary held her breath and opened the library door.

Cameron stood by the window where the low evening light cast deep shadows across his face. His tall, lean figure stooped slightly and he made no move towards Mary as she came in.

'Oh, love,' she murmured. He looked wrung out and wretched.

He reached out his hand.

She went to him and clasped him, holding him close until he was able to speak.

'I got through it.' He pressed his lips into her soft hair. 'Mary, I did it.'

She stepped back and looked up at him. 'Not guilty?'

Cameron nodded. He held her hands and sat her down in the window seat. 'When push came to shove, Bullen's story didn't hold up.'

'I knew it!' Relief made her sag forward and clutch his arm.

'It was touch and go for a while.' Two hours after the event Cameron was still coming to terms with what had taken place. He'd built his case around the fact that it was Bullen who had lost his nerve and gone berserk, pulling out a knife without warning. Taking into account the fact that Bullen was plausible and well liked by the men, Cameron had gone into the court martial armed with a few details about the Texan's past conduct – the recent incident concerning the Hurricane that he'd turned upside down to show off in front of the trainees and the much more serious suspicion that his accuser's gung-ho attitude had contributed to a mid-air collision with a Miles Magister.

'Bullen came to court and swore black was white and for a while they seemed to believe him.'

'What did he tell them?' Mary prompted.

Cameron's hands shook as he recounted events. 'He claimed I was drunk and incapable, that he had no idea why I'd turned on him and knocked him out – he'd done nothing to provoke me. He said there were witnesses who would back him up.'

'But they believed you over him?' Five RAF officers had stood in judgement and come down on Cameron's side – how could Mary ever have doubted it? The rapid beating of her heart eased and she smiled eagerly.

'Yes, thanks to a new witness I knew nothing about.' The drunk and incapable claim had been the hardest thing to deal with. Cameron remembered the cynical, world-weary looks that had passed between the highly decorated members of the panel as they'd jotted down notes from Bullen's account. 'A lad called Arthur Jenkins came forward and backed me up. He was the sentry on duty at the time. Without him it might have ended differently.'

'Arthur Jenkins?' *Nickname Spud; from Ormskirk in Lancashire!* Mary leapt to her feet and dragged Cameron up after her. She hugged him with all her strength. 'Bless him; what did he say?'

'That he saw Bullen pull out the knife. He swore on the Bible it was true.' It had been the turning point in a finely balanced case. Bullen, for all his swagger and self-belief, and despite some half-hearted support

376

from two other supposed witnesses, was declared the guilty party. The file was closed – all charges against Cameron dropped. 'So here I am – a bit the worse for wear, but nothing that a few good nights' sleep won't cure.'

'God bless Spud Jenkins!' His earnest account must have swayed the judges and sealed Bullen's fate. Delight showed in the deep flush that suffused Mary's cheeks. Now she had good news of her own to share. 'Well, Hilary came down on my side so we're both in the clear.'

It was Cameron's turn to hold her close. 'When are you back on the rota?'

'Tomorrow.'

'Are you sure you're well enough?' He pulled away to study the barely healed cuts on Mary's face. 'Oughtn't you to take a few more days off?'

She gave a decisive shake of her head. 'At a time like this – with the pressure on to ferry every available plane to the south coast?'

'Point taken. But you will be extra careful?' Reluctant to let her go, Cameron kept his arms wrapped around her waist. 'I can't lose you, Mary – not now.'

'You won't,' she promised. They'd come through a lot these past few weeks and she wouldn't let it be for nothing. 'Something else has happened and it's made me realize how lucky we are – no, don't say anything until after I tell you. It's about Anna.'

'The Polish girl?' Cameron had a vague memory – something about a housekeeper installed by the Parsevals. He saw that Mary had grown tearful and once more drew her close.

She rested her head against his chest. 'We think

she's drowned. There was a note inside a suitcase. I found it by the reservoir. Anna had no one – in this whole wide world there was not one single person she could turn to and trust. You see the difference?'

'We have each other and always will,' Cameron vowed. *Hold tight, don't let Mary go. Cherish her and be glad.* 'For as long as we both shall live.'

CHAPTER TWENTY-ONE

'Dear Giles,' Viv wrote. She'd had a couple of days in which to mull things over and she intended the letter as a kind of truce. 'Don't be scared when you open this; I have kept my promise not to reveal the family secret, though I was sorely tempted, don't you know . . .'

She sat cross-legged under an apple tree in the vegetable garden at the Grange, enjoying the spring sunshine. Ernest was at work in his greenhouse while Mary and Bobbie weeded a nearby plot. The passage of time had brought about a more reflective frame of mind; yes, Giles was married but on the point of being divorced. And yes, he'd kept from her the truth about the baby's father – but it turned out that it had been for the best of reasons: to protect his poor mother. So Viv was in a forgiving mood as she wrote on.

'I do see now why you were forced to keep schtum – believe me, I do. But mainly I'm putting pen to paper to tell you that I have decided not to follow up the address in Maltby Bay.

'You see, poor Anna is drowned. You may have heard this news already but if not I'm sorry to be the bearer of bad tidings. A body was found earlier today by the men who operate the pumping station at the reservoir. They found heavy stones in the pocket of Anna's dress, so make no mistake, she did intend to die.

'We are all terrifically sad here, as you can imagine. We liked and admired Anna very much. I don't say this to make you feel worse – it's simply the truth. In any case, the reason for tracing the whereabouts of Anna's baby no longer applies so I'm giving up the attempt.'

Viv paused to watch Mary and Bobbie work their way down a row of broad bean seedlings. Mary's return to flying duties had gone smoothly. Douglas had assigned her a Spit Mark 3 to ease her back in, sending her to Bristol then back from there in an equally lively Defiant. She'd been first off the Rixley runway and a gang of pilots including Jean, Bobbie and Viv had cheered her off, watching her skate smoothly along Runway 2 then rise effortlessly with just the right number of revs to a height of 800 feet before banking to port and soaring over their heads like a glorious bird of prey – oh, that streamlined, lean-bellied shape, those leaf-like wings, that azure camouflage and the sweet song of that Merlin engine!

'I have thought a lot about what you told me,' Viv continued in a free-flowing, forward-sloping hand. 'And one lesson to learn from this whole damned mess is: never underestimate a woman. No, don't shrug it off! Take your mother – beneath that fragrant exterior lies a core of steel. But you don't need me to point this out, not any more.'

Viv paused again, popping the end of the pen into her mouth as she shaped her next thought.

'A penny for them,' Ernest said as he wheeled his barrow along the path, sleeves rolled up and braces dangling from his waist.

'They're not worth it,' Viv replied with a light laugh, turning back to her letter.

'As for the bad feeling between us, I hope we can let it drop. Sure I was mad that you didn't do more to help Anna, but now that I have the full picture I can appreciate the complications of what you went through over the whole baby scenario. In other words, I'm sorry I came down so hard on you on Monday. Truly sorry.'

Her pen hovered over the paper. Where exactly did she want to go with this? Should she risk suggesting that they might meet again in happier circumstances or should she leave things in the air for now? Yes, it was probably best to break the habit of a lifetime and let the dust settle.

As Viv pondered, Mary put down her hoe and ran towards her, towing Bobbie in her wake. 'Listen to Bobbie's latest news: Hilary's granted her a day's compassionate leave to go to Thresham.'

Viv looked up from her letter. 'I didn't know she'd applied.'

'Me neither – she just told me,' Mary explained.

'Good – about time.' They'd all been urging Bobbie to bite that particular bullet.

'Ray might not be ready to see me yet.' Bobbie was nervous about going but had at last plucked up the courage to telephone the yard.

'He will be,' Mary and Viv chorused with total certainty.

'Who are you writing to?' Mary craned her neck to look at Viv's letter.

Viv blushed and turned over the paper so they couldn't see. 'None of your business.'

'I bet she's writing to Giles.' Bobbie was quick off the mark. 'Can you believe it – after everything he did, she's willing to give him a second chance.'

'Wrong!' Viv's hand kept the sheet clamped to the soil, waiting for Mary and Bobbie to go away. Was it true, though? Perhaps, perhaps . . .

Mary ignored her protests. 'Giles doesn't deserve it. His name is still mud, as far as I'm concerned.'

Viv cleared her throat. *Actually, Sir Thomas is the guilty party* . . . The words that would have put Giles in the clear were on the tip of her tongue but somehow she stopped herself from uttering them.

Bobbie cocked her head to one side and studied Viv's flustered expression. 'Is there something you're not telling us?'

'No; hand on heart!'

Bobbie glanced at Mary, who stood hands on hips and contradicted firmly: 'Yes, there is.'

'OK, then, but I made a promise.' Two pairs of eyes stared at her for what felt like for ever. 'Giles did his best – that's all.'

'Hmm.' Mary's brow wrinkled. How unlike Viv to have a change of heart.

'You've talked to him?' Bobbie probed.

Viv nodded. 'I called in at Newpark and had it out with him,' she confessed reluctantly. 'Don't look at me like that!'

'Now, that I do believe.' *Typical Viv*, Mary thought.

'And?' Bobbie demanded.

'And it turns out I was wrong all along – Giles wasn't the father.' *Thus far and no further* – Viv kept her word.

'Then who was?' Bobbie and Mary demanded as

one. They were by turns incredulous, dismayed and consumed by curiosity.

But however much her friends exclaimed and cajoled, sighed and swore that the secret would be safe with them, Viv's lips remained sealed.

'Sorry about the creases and the muddy marks,' she wrote after they'd given up pestering her and left her alone. 'I hope you can still read this. And I hope we can be friendly if ever we meet again, which is more than likely the way things are going between Bobbie and Ray. So friends it is, I trust?' How to sign off? *Wishing you well . . . With very best wishes . . . Fond regards . . . ?*

'Love, Viv,' she wrote in the end. Then she underscored her name and added a single kiss.

Jean sat at the kitchen table in her dressing-gown with Patch lying contentedly at her bare feet. It was past midnight but she couldn't sleep so she'd come downstairs and made herself a cup of tea, which had already gone cold by the time she heard Douglas's uneven footsteps on the stairs.

'What's wrong?' He appeared bleary-eyed in the doorway.

'Nothing.' A sigh escaped, nevertheless.

'Something's bothering you.' He'd woken up to an empty space beside him and had lain for a full ten minutes listening for sounds before coming downstairs. 'You usually sleep right through. It's Anna, isn't it?'

'Yes.' Jean waited for him to sit down opposite before she went on. 'I wish there was something we could have done. If we'd only known what a low state she was in.'

'Even then,' he told her gently.

'I know – even then.' There would have been no remedy. 'Unless we could have found Dorota for her – that might have helped.'

Douglas reached across the table to take his wife's hand. Jean was as beautiful in her sadness as she was when she was glad – her eyes spoke volumes, and she always had that graceful tilt of her head and a low, kind way of speaking. 'How?' he asked. 'Anna knew she couldn't care for the child herself, even if she had found out where she'd been taken. In a way that might have been even more painful.'

'Perhaps you're right.' Jean sighed again. 'But I can't help thinking of the sacrifice she made.'

They were quiet for a while, listening to the wind in the trees and the occasional distant hoot of an owl. The cottage was their haven, their safe place where the most intimate feelings were shared – everything in its place and in order, from the bluebells in their green vase on the windowsill to the trimmed wicks of the two oil lamps hanging from the beam above their heads.

'Right at the last Anna wrote down the love she felt for that child,' Jean murmured. 'She pictured Dorota as a strong, beautiful girl surrounded by love. I do so want that to be true.'

Douglas held Jean's hand and allowed her to work through her feelings. The dog shifted position to sit at his feet.

Jean took a scrap of paper from her pocket and pushed it towards him.

He read a name and an address – *Mr and Mrs A. F. Raynard, 5 Harbour Cottages, Maltby Bay.*

'Giles wrote it down for Viv. That's where the baby was taken by arrangement with Florrie and Ernest.'

'I see.' He waited again.

'It's the reason I couldn't sleep.' For thinking about the child and Anna's last, fervent hope that Dorota would be safe and cared for.

'You want to make sure?' Douglas asked.

'For Anna's sake – yes.'

'It would put your mind at rest?'

'Perhaps. And Maltby Bay isn't far away. We could go there together one evening.' Tentatively Jean worked towards what she felt she must do.

'We could, but would it be the right thing?' Concern about the fate of Anna's baby had obviously wormed its way deep under Jean's skin but Douglas doubted that the complicated problem could be solved by a simple visit.

'I can't settle until I know for certain. What if the Raynards aren't kind people – what then?' Jean's forehead creased and she grasped Douglas's hand more tightly. 'Don't we owe it to Anna to make sure?'

He nodded slowly. 'If it's what you want . . .'

'I don't know if it is.' She stood up and went to the dark window, resting her arms on the sill and staring at her own pale reflection, seeing him come up behind her.

'Things may look different in the morning,' he counselled as he wrapped his arms around her waist. He rested his chin on her shoulder. 'Sleep on it and see how you feel tomorrow.'

Douglas had loaned Bobbie his car for her visit to Thresham. 'Take it,' he'd said as he handed her the keys first thing on Thursday morning. 'There's plenty of petrol in the tank. Just make sure you bring it back in one piece – Jean and I might need it this evening.'

The drive over from Rixley had given Bobbie time to set her thoughts in order. In the four days since she'd last seen Ray he'd been constantly on her mind. Even the demands of flying in all weathers, in a variety of aircraft, hadn't banished him completely. She would be in the canteen studying her Pilots' Notes and Ray would suddenly spring to the forefront of her mind – his look of agony as he'd cradled his father's head, his desperate pleas to the ambulance men, his refusal to believe that they'd arrived too late to help. Or else Bobbie would be flying the famously difficult route up the narrow Dumfries Valley to Prestwick, with cliffs looming to either side and clouds gathering, when Ray's handsome face would flash before her: smiling cheerfully as he related a funny story, his brown eyes alight with laughter. She was sad now to think how completely Sunday's tragedy had extinguished that spark.

So Bobbie approached the training yard with mounting trepidation. There was a suggestion of rain in the air and deep puddles to either side of the narrowing lanes. The sound of her tyres splashing through them was an unhappy reminder of the overflowing gutters that had formed a background to Sunday's events. How would Ray be now – still in a state of shock or gradually coming round? She would soon find out the answer.

Driving into a seemingly deserted yard, she saw that the stable doors stood open and the horses and grooms were nowhere to be seen. A glance at her watch told

Bobbie that this was probably the time for the horses to be up on the gallops. But Ray had certainly been expecting her so perhaps he was at the house?

She set off up the path with doubt still fluttering in her heart.

'Bobbie!' Ray cupped his hands around his mouth and called from the top of the stone steps leading to Ronne's living quarters above the stables. He'd spotted an unfamiliar car in the yard and it wasn't until Bobbie had stepped out and set off towards the house that he'd emerged from the loft. 'Over here!'

She turned and saw him waiting expectantly. All doubt vanished; she ran towards him as he descended the steps two at a time. They met in the middle of the empty yard.

'You came?' Ray seemed surprised, as if he couldn't believe she was really there.

'Of course.' Bobbie took a deep breath. 'I said I would.'

'How did you get the time off?'

'Compassionate leave – twelve hours.' She sensed that he was holding back, not knowing what to do. There were dark circles under his eyes but he was freshly shaven and his hair was neatly combed. Slowly she put her arms around his neck.

Ray closed his eyes and bent his head at Bobbie's touch. He breathed in her perfume as she nestled against him – sweet, soft and silky, full of living warmth.

'How have you been?' she asked.

'Coping – just about. I'm glad I was there with him at the end,' he added quietly. He still hadn't wept over his father's death. He'd sent Ronnie up to the house to fetch clean clothes and his shaving gear but hadn't set foot in there himself. The funeral people and the vicar had visited and had things in hand – the coffin, the flowers, the order of service.

Bobbie stroked his cheek. 'Look at me. What can I do to help?'

'Just be here. Oh God, it's good to see you. Talk to me, tell me what to do.' Ray was living through a nightmare from which he hadn't been able to wake. Nothing had seemed real or made any sense until now, with Bobbie here in the flesh, fulfilling her promise, gazing into his eyes with deep tenderness.

'Have you been up there yet?' Stepping away, she glanced towards the main house. 'You haven't, have you?'

Ray shook his head. 'I couldn't face it.'

'Then let's do it now. The longer you leave it, the harder it will be.' She led the way up the path, making sure he followed. Then, when they came to the front door, she paused and turned. 'Do you feel strong enough?'

Ray nodded but didn't say anything. The house would spark acutely painful memories – his father's muddy boots kicked off in the hallway, his cap flung on to a bench, an empty whisky bottle in the waste-paper basket – but without the man himself swearing and blundering about, searching for his bloody reading glasses, stumbling into the kitchen in search of something to eat.

The door was unlocked so Bobbie opened it and stooped to pick up letters from the mat. An ornate grandfather clock ticked loudly from the far side of the hall.

Ray stepped inside. The clock had been there all his life – the round face was painted with a moon and stars; one of his earliest memories, along with a rocking-horse upstairs in the nursery, dappled grey and white with a long white mane and tail. 'I wish . . .' he began then stopped. He wished his father hadn't drunk, he wished with all his heart that his mother and brother Frank were still alive. But Ray didn't fall to the floor and wail, he didn't shake and tremble and fall apart. Instead, he picked up his father's cap and hung it carefully on the hallstand.

Bobbie watched him go systematically from room to room, putting things in order. He went into the lounge and folded a crumpled newspaper; he stacked empty glasses on a tray and tidied away Derek's pipe-smoking things. Then he picked up a pair of old brown brogues with knots in their laces and carried them to the foot of the stairs. Shoes took on the unique shape of their wearer's feet – Derek's were worn unevenly, one heel lower than the other. Bobbie sighed at the knowledge they would be worn no more.

'Kitchen,' Ray muttered then led the way. He sat down heavily at the table then stared at his hands clasped in front of him. 'Pretty grim, eh?'

Bobbie sat down next to him. 'Yes, but one step at a time.'

'I'm sorry I'm so pathetic.'

'Don't be; anyway, you're not.'

He acknowledged the truth of this with a brief nod. 'You know, I really didn't believe you'd come.' Why should she? After all, Bobbie had her own life and a set of firm friends to keep her company – rather alarming, death-defying, gung-ho women

389

like Viv Robertson, if the truth be told. 'I wouldn't have blamed you if you'd run a mile.'

'Then you don't know me very well.' Pulling at a person's heartstrings was a strange expression – not actual strings, surely? But that was how it felt; as if Ray's wounded spirit was tugging at Bobbie's heart, pleading for comfort and support. 'I'm here now and I won't run anywhere.'

'I was never sure how you felt about me.' He lifted his head and stared intently.

'Likewise.' A nothing-kiss or a something-kiss, a darting towards or swerving away from each other, the exchange of smiles, secret longing, a deep uncertainty.

'There always seemed to be the Teddy Simpson thing getting in the way.'

'There was. But there isn't any more.' Flooded with gratitude that Ray had never pressed her on the matter but instead had waited patiently and without judging her, she felt calm and strong. To hell with Teddy Simpson and everything that he'd symbolized – the threat, the menace and the dark ugliness of unchecked desire. She would sail clear of all that to be with Ray.

'Will you tell me about it?'

'Maybe sometime – not now.' The present and the future were what mattered, not the past. Smiling, she broke away to open cupboard doors and investigate their contents. 'Is there anything to eat around here? Where do you keep your supplies?'

'Here.' Ray opened the door to the pantry and watched Bobbie search the shelves.

She fetched eggs, flour, sugar and butter and put them on the table. 'Sultanas?'

'No sultanas,' he told her, finding a mixing bowl and egg beater.

'Then it'll have to be plain scones.'

Scones and tea with plenty of sugar would be the order of the day. There was the sound of soft, intermittent conversation as Bobbie found her way around the Aga, found a baking tray and a scone cutter and, soon after, there was the smell of baking. The sweet, warm scent brought memories of Ray's childhood and a happy time – Fridays during the school holidays when his mother had allowed him and Frank into the kitchen to help bake cakes and when his father, at the height of his powers and reputation, hadn't always carried a flask in his jacket pocket.

Ray noticed a speckled thrush perched on the wall outside the kitchen window, head cocked, a thin pink worm hanging from its beak, and the simple sight broke the dam that had held back his sadness. He bowed his head and wept without restraint.

Bobbie sat close to him, her arm around his heaving shoulders, listening to his sobs. She belonged here, by Ray's side – that's how it felt in this warm, sweet moment as his grief flowed.

Harbour Cottages was a row of six small stone houses with red pantile roofs overlooking a horseshoe bay. They sat at the bottom of a steep hill, tucked in beside a pub – The Anchor – that had served generations of fishermen, smugglers, excise men and sailors since the time of the Napoleonic Wars.

Douglas parked his car beside lobster pots stacked high on the harbour's edge. He and Jean stepped out at high tide to the sound of seagulls screeching and the sight of them wheeling over the choppy brown water, where fishing boats bobbed and crews clad in oilskins swabbed the decks in preparation for the next day's sailing. A salty, seaweedy, fishy smell filled the visitors' nostrils and waves slapped against the harbour wall, sending up a cold, salty spray that made their skin tingle as it drifted against their faces.

A stout woman wearing a plain calico apron over a brown woollen dress hailed them from the doorway of the pub. 'Are you lost?'

Jean and Douglas walked across the damp cobbles. 'No,' Jean said. 'Thank you anyway.'

'We don't see many strangers here,' the woman said sharply. Her jet-black hair was plaited and pinned like a coronet to the top of her head and provided a jarring contrast to her heavily lined face and sagging jowls.

Jean held back from stating their sensitive business. She looked nervously at Douglas, who, like her, wore his ATA uniform. He assumed an air of authority as he too expressed his thanks then turned away. 'All set?' he asked Jean as the disgruntled landlady disappeared into her pub.

With her heart in her mouth, Jean could only nod and silently steel herself for what was to come.

Number 5 Harbour Cottages was second to last in the row and the most neatly kept, with a polished lion's head knocker and white net curtains at the open window of the downstairs room. A wireless played a popular tune – 'Paper Doll' by the Mills Brothers – its faint strains reaching Jean and Douglas as they hesitated at the door.

The jaunty, modern words describing the truest

sweetheart in all the world jarred with the traditional harbourside scene and with the reason for their visit.

'Are you sure you want to go ahead?' Douglas checked.

Jean took another deep breath and raised the knocker, but before she could bring it down the door was flung open by a boy with short fair hair and large grey eyes. The song blared with increased volume out on to the narrow flagged path where Jean and Douglas stood.

'Hello, is your mother in?' Douglas remained composed even though the boy stared up at him with a truculent gaze.

'Ma!' the boy yelled before dodging back out of sight.

A blonde woman hurried to the door carrying a child on her hip. She was slim and well turned out in a green flowered dress with a white collar and matching belt.

'Mrs Raynard?' Douglas asked.

Jean stared at the toddler who bore a strong resemblance to the older boy – the same grey eyes and fair hair convinced her that they were brothers. She looked uncertainly at Douglas.

'Yes; who's asking?' A wary Betty Raynard blocked the doorway.

Douglas gave their names. 'We know your uncle, Ernest Poulter,' he explained.

'Do you now?' Betty's eyes narrowed and she stood her ground.

'Yes; we're stationed at Rixley ferry pool. We're sorry to barge in on you.' He and Jean ought to have planned this better – of course Betty Raynard would be on the defensive, given the secrecy behind the arrangements surrounding Anna's baby. 'We're not here to cause trouble,' he went on.

The tune on the wireless changed to Lena Horne's 'Stormy Weather'.

'We'd like to see Anna Janicki's little girl,' Jean blurted out.

A look of panic flashed across Betty's face and she made as if to close the door, but then a man in brown slacks and a checked shirt came up beside her. He was tall, with pleasant, handsome features, and wore a more open expression than his wife.

'Arthur Raynard,' he said as he offered to shake Douglas's hand. 'Betty and I come over to Rixley every so often but I don't think we've met.'

'Arthur!' his wife warned. She handed the toddler over to the older boy then stood guard at her husband's side. 'Mind what you say.'

'How did you find us?' Arthur asked Douglas in a more guarded tone.

The plaintive voice in the background sang about rain and storm.

'Giles Parseval gave your address to a friend of ours – Viv Robertson. She in turn gave it to my wife.' Douglas took the scribbled note from his pocket and showed it to the astonished pair.

Arthur raised his eyebrows. 'That's a turn-up for the books,' he muttered to his wife as they backed off from the door. 'You'd better come in.'

'Mr Giles wrote this himself?' Betty echoed. 'Are you sure?'

'It looks like his handwriting,' Arthur confirmed after he'd glanced at the paper.

Jean took in the cramped proportions of the

Raynards' living room. The rough plaster walls were freshly whitewashed and a model sailing ship in a bottle took pride of place on the tiled mantel-piece. A tapestry picture of a bouquet of roses hung on the chimney breast, next to a sepia photograph of bearded fishermen from a bygone era. The wide-eyed boy who had answered the door squatted on a stool in a niche by the fireplace nursing his toddler brother on his knee and listening keenly to the grown-ups' conversation.

Arthur went to the wireless and turned it off. 'Why do you want to see the baby?' he asked Jean. 'Are you checking up on Betty and me?'

'Not at all.' Jean denied that this was the case. 'I am . . . I was a friend of Anna's.'

'*Was*?' Betty raised her voice. 'Has something happened?'

With a glance at Jean's pale face and strained expression, Douglas stepped in to explain the pain-ful circumstances. 'We understand from what Viv has told us that Giles made arrangements for you to look after Anna's baby.'

'I only want to know that Dorota is safe and well – for Anna's sake.' Jean looked Betty in the eye and spoke plainly, one woman to another.

'We've changed her name to Dorothy.' Betty frowned as she corrected Jean.

'Yes; Dorothy. May I see her please?'

The frown remained. 'She's asleep upstairs.'

'I won't disturb her,' Jean promised, her heart still beating fast. One glimpse of the baby ought to be enough to satisfy her that all was well.

Betty glanced at her husband who nodded.

'I hope you're not judging us,' Arthur said to Douglas, picking up the whimpering toddler as the two women left the room. 'Just because we get paid to do this doesn't mean we don't care.'

'No, I quite see that.' The couple were to all appearances respectable, reasonable and honest, and their two boys were well cared for. Douglas saw no cause for concern.

'Betty's good with kids. We've fostered quite a few over the years – evacuees mostly, but some who've been put up for adoption too. A few of them still keep in touch.'

'That's champion.' Douglas hardly knew what to say. His mind was mostly on Jean as she quietly mounted the stairs behind Betty.

'My wife is the soft-hearted type.' Arthur turned to his oldest son. 'Jimmy, I'm telling First Officer Thornton that your mum sheds a few tears when the time comes to part with the littl'uns.'

'She does,' the boy agreed solemnly, with wisdom beyond his years. 'But Ma knows we don't have room to keep 'em. As soon as she finds 'em a good home we 'ave to say goodbye.'

At the top of the stairs was a small landing with two doors leading off.

'Dorothy sleeps in here with Jimmy and Tommy,' Betty told Jean as she opened the door to the right.

Dim evening light filtered into the children's bedroom through thin cotton curtains, allowing Jean to make out a narrow bed and two cots that almost filled the entire floor space. In the cot furthest from the door a baby was fast asleep.

'You can go in.' Betty whispered her permission.

So Jean tiptoed towards the cot. Anna's baby lay on her back with her arms curled around her head, the rest of her body tucked tightly beneath a knitted patchwork blanket. Her dark hair was a mass of curls, her eyelids fringed with thick lashes, her rose-bud lips shiny and partly opened. 'Beautiful,' Jean murmured. 'So peaceful.' One glance at the sleeping form; that was all it took.

Betty came up beside her. 'She's a good baby – hardly ever cries.'

'Beautiful,' Jean said again.

'You can hold her if you like.' Without waiting for a response, Betty untucked the covers and gently lifted Dorota from her cot.

The baby's eyelids fluttered but stayed shut as Jean took her and cradled her sleeping weight. She smelt of talcum powder and soap.

'I sometimes look at her and wonder, what mother could ever have given her up?' Betty's voice was soft in the background.

'Ah!' Jean breathed out as she held the warm baby and rocked her. Now she understood with every fibre of her being why letting go of Dorota had broken poor Anna's heart. 'Life can be cruel.'

Betty stood back and watched. 'It's decent of you to come all this way to check on the baby.'

'It's the least I could do. Anna loved her with all her heart,' Jean replied with absolute conviction.

The baby stirred. Her curled fingers brushed the cold metal of one of Jean's silver buttons and she opened her eyes. Dark and wide like Anna's, they gazed silently at Jean as she put her back in the cot and tucked her in.

'What will happen now?' Betty asked as she backed away then waited at the door. She meant: would the mother's sudden death make any difference to what the Parsevals proposed?

'I'm not sure.' Jean stayed by the cot, waiting for Dorota to fall asleep.

'Will you let Mr Giles know that you've been here?'

'Yes.' The baby's eyelids flickered then closed.

'Then you can tell him that I might have found a family for Dorothy in Highcliff – it's not certain yet but I expect to receive a definite yes or no by Monday.'

'You won't keep her yourself?' Fresh anxiety sent a shiver down Jean's spine.

'No, that wasn't the arrangement. It wouldn't be practical, not when my two grow bigger.' Betty gestured round the cramped bedroom. 'You'll pass on the message to Mr Giles – an older couple in Highcliff with no children of their own?'

Jean nodded slowly. 'I hadn't realized.' It pained her to think of Dorota being parcelled off to another new home with strange faces and spaces, colours and smells, and into strange arms.

'I'm sorry,' Betty said quietly. 'We simply don't have the room.'

'I see.' Jean gave a heavy sigh and gazed down at the sleeping baby, at her dark curls against the white pillow and at the slow rise and fall of her tiny chest.

CHAPTER TWENTY-TWO

Early on Friday morning Viv, Mary and Bobbie left the Grange to walk to the ferry pool through Burton Wood. All wore their sheepskin jackets over their thick canvas Sidcot suits on what was forecast to be a typically chilly April day.

'I wonder what Douglas has in store for us today.' Viv strode ahead along the narrow track. 'I fancy trying my hand at the B-17 Fortress that came in yesterday. I've never flown a Class Five.' Four powerful Boeing engines made the heavy bomber a challenge that she was eager to meet. 'They say she's a beast.'

'Her engine power is on a par with a Lancaster or a Stirling,' Bobbie advised. 'Bomber Command is keen on them because they can soak up any amount of enemy flak and still make it home in one piece. They say one even survived a mid-air collision with a Focke-Wulf.'

'That's good to know.' Viv's mind quickly wandered on to more personal matters. 'Say, girls, what would you think if I did call a truce with Giles?'

'I knew it!' Mary ran to catch up. 'You've finished that letter, haven't you?'

Viv winked and patted her jacket pocket where she'd stashed it. 'Maybe, baby.'

'You have!' With time to reflect, Bobbie had accepted that Viv had told them the truth about Giles not being the father after all – in which case, she wished him well. 'Tell me, Vivienne, what is it about the handsome, wealthy six-foot charmer that made you change your mind?'

'The same indefinable something that attracted Mary to her dashing flight lieutenant, I imagine.' Viv stopped in a small clearing to elaborate. 'Giles is not so wealthy, actually. He was forced into an arranged marriage because the Parsevals were running short of cash.'

'Oh, my heart bleeds!' Mary teased. She paused to enjoy the brisk breeze that swayed the branches overhead and flattened patches of fresh green grass all around.

'No, really – you've called a truce?' Bobbie was pleased to hear it. 'We should be happy for her, Mary.'

'Yes – be happy. Spread some of the sweetness and light you must be feeling about Cameron.' Viv had greeted Mary's good news over the breakfast table with exuberant congratulations – 'Oh boy, oh boy – that's terrific! That swine Bullen deserves a few months in chokey at the very least for what he did to your man.'

Bobbie had backed Viv up then shyly shared her own news about her visit to Thresham. 'Ray says he'll carry on at the yard with Ronnie Evans's help. They hope to rebuild their reputation as one of the best training yards in Yorkshire and get back on a proper footing once the war has ended.'

'That's an excellent plan.' Mary had been impatient for more information. 'But what about you and Ray?'

Bobbie's knife had hovered over her slice of toast and jam and a tell-tale blush had covered her fair features.

'Yes,' Viv had chimed. 'You and God's gift to women; what's the story?'

'There's nothing to tell.' Bobbie's cheeks had burned. She and Ray had baked scones, he'd wept and they'd talked away the whole morning. In the afternoon they'd ridden on the gallops.

'Pull the other one.' Mary had nudged her with her elbow.

They'd ridden out then handed the horses over to Ronnie. 'We'll be up at the house if you need me,' Ray had told him. And he and Bobbie had walked arm in arm up the path, still talking, touching, making plans.

'I've invited him to the Grange on Sunday,' she had finally admitted to Mary and Viv.

'Hooray!' Viv had raised her mug of tea in congratulations. 'I'll never know what took you so long.'

'But *I* know,' Mary had murmured. She'd stood by her friend through the dark days of Teddy Simpson and watched her slowly emerge into the sunlight of Ray's love. 'That's marvellous, Bobbie.'

'But no engagements?' Viv had seized Bobbie's and Mary's hands. 'No rings sparkling on anyone's fingers?'

They'd pushed her away with cries of indignation and Bobbie had wagered that Viv would be the first to fall.

'Giles would pop the question tomorrow if he was

in a position to,' she'd forecast playfully. 'He's aware that two like you don't come along in a hurry.'

'No, thank the Lord.' Viv had rocked back in her chair, grinning broadly. It had been at that light-hearted moment that she'd made up her mind to seal the letter, mud stains and all, then pop it in the postbox as soon as she got the chance.

So the start to their day had been full of laughter and hope and the mood continued as the jaunty trio approached Fern Cottage. At the sound of their voices Patch bounded down the path and jumped clean over the wooden gate. He raced towards them in a delirium of barks and frantic, frisky tail-wagging.

'Down!' Bobbie said sternly as Jean appeared at the cottage door.

She too was dressed for the weather. Calling the dog back, she asked the others to wait for her while she fetched her forage cap and sheepskin jacket.

Bobbie glanced at her watch. 'Get a move on,' she urged.

An out-of-breath Jean soon joined them and before they'd walked a few steps she made an announcement that far outdid Viv's, Bobbie's and Mary's news combined. 'Douglas and I went to see Anna's baby.'

There was a moment's startled silence then a cacophony.

'When?' 'Where?' 'What for?' 'Is the baby all right?' 'Is she pretty?' 'Does she look like her mother?'

Jean put her hands over her ears until the questions subsided. 'I did it for Anna. And yes, Dorota is being well cared for.'

Few words had passed between Jean and Douglas

as they'd driven back from Maltby Bay, each lost in their own thoughts.

One glance; one wonderful, life-changing glance. In that moment Jean's heart had opened to a world beyond Sidcot suits, maps and compasses.

Something important has happened; I'm not sure what. Douglas had said nothing as he'd parked the car at the Grange and they'd walked back hand in hand to Fern Cottage.

'Come inside. It's late.' Douglas had unlocked the door and waited.

Standing by the gate, Jean had broken her silence. 'Dorota can't stay with the Raynards.'

'I know – Arthur mentioned it.' The baby's future was uncertain due to practicalities of space and probably money too. The family wasn't well off and resources must be tightly stretched, living on the wages of a lowly clerk.

'They might send her to live in Highcliff.'

'Do come inside; it's cold,' he'd murmured.

'It's not fair for a baby to be handed from pillar to post. It's not right.'

Douglas had gone to her and held her in his arms. 'No, it's not.'

'You didn't see her, Douglas. I wish you had; then you'd know.'

'What would I know?'

Resting her cheek against the rough cloth of his overcoat and grasping his lapels, Jean had done her best to explain. So small, so helpless, so trusting and deserving of unconditional love. The words failed to do justice to the emotions she'd experienced when she'd stood with the baby in her arms.

'And what do you want to do?' Douglas had been sure of the answer. Jean would follow her heart.

They'd held each other at the entrance to their cottage, standing in the dark, finding a way forward.

'It's turned out to be more than a one-off visit?' Now in the early light, preparing for the day ahead, Bobbie listened and understood.

Viv frowned and glanced at Mary, who shrugged.

'I wish you'd all been there,' Jean murmured. 'Dorota has Anna's dark eyes. I didn't sleep for thinking about her. Neither did Douglas. We agreed.'

'On what?' Viv demanded an answer to the mystery.

'If it's possible, we want to adopt Dorota.' Jean spoke plainly, with a soaring feeling of serenity that felt like taking off in a Spit into a clear blue sky. Then she breathed deeply and looked from one to the other.

'I can hear a "but" in there.' Mary caught hold of the cuff of Jean's sleeve.

'Yes – if we succeed with the adoption I'll give up flying.' There; she'd said it and made it real. Jean would sign the papers and hand back the uniform. She would lose the title of Flight Captain and be plain Mrs Jean Thornton, no longer part of the mighty sisterhood, deprived of the thrill of taking to the air in the world's most powerful fighting machines.

'You can't do that – not now!' Bobbie gasped. There were still hundreds of crates waiting to be moved south; every day more pressure to make ready for the final push.

'The ATA needs you,' Mary pleaded.

'Dorota needs me more.' The words in Anna's letter resonated for Jean more strongly than ever – 'You will

404

grow and you will be strong, my daughter. You will be loved.' *By me and by Douglas*, she thought with a surge of pure joy.

'But you're the best we've got!' Bobbie struggled to grasp what Jean intended. 'And think of the sacrifice you'll be making. You've worked so hard to get where you are: an Atta girl, a flight captain no less.'

Jean looked towards Viv for her reaction.

'I get it.' Viv's three short words were almost inaudible. Forget the thrills and spills and the living in the moment; Jean had chosen love.

'But the war will soon be over; why not see it out?' Mary was desperate for her fellow pilot to change her mind.

'No; I get it.' Viv's voice grew stronger. 'Sorry, Mary, but the fighting could go on for ages yet – who knows? And every single time we take off in a Spit or a Mustang or any of those crazy crates – yes, it feels fabulous but we also have to recognize that we fly daily into the jaws of death; no question. Bad weather, Jerry, engine snags – they can all finish us off in the blink of an eye. Mary, you of all people know that.'

'I can't risk it,' Jean confirmed. 'Douglas and I have a long way to go before we're sure we can adopt Dorota but I daren't risk being blown to bits by Jerry in the meantime. So today will be my last chit, my last destination.'

'But what a waste.' Mary loosened her grasp and let her arms fall to her sides. The pilot she looked up to, the friend she admired the most, would no longer stand beside them in the morning queue or be there on the runway waiting for their safe return. 'Are you sure you're doing the right thing?'

'Never more sure in my life.' Jean knew that the war must be won without her.

'You're certain?' Douglas had asked, lying beside her as dawn had begun to break and Jean had made the hardest decision of her life. The cottage had been silent. The trees outside the window had creaked and sighed in the wind.

'Yes – if you are.'

He'd felt her gaze delve deep below the surface and read his heart.

Jean had kissed him. He'd promised to act swiftly – he would make phone calls as soon as he'd finished the day's rota and speak to the relevant authorities (fingers crossed there would be no objections). The adoption would have to be done properly.

'We're going to miss you more than we can say.' Bobbie linked arms with Jean and walked on towards the ferry pool. Viv and Mary followed close behind.

'We'll still be living in Fern Cottage. You can visit me and Douglas and the baby whenever you like.'

'Damn it; Rixley will fall apart without you.' Viv was determined to lighten the mood. 'Who'll keep me in line, for a start?'

Jean grinned and turned to the others.

'Don't look at me.' Bobbie threw up her hands in mock horror.

'Don't worry, I'll keep an eye on her,' Mary promised.

When they came to the edge of the wood the group paused again to take in the sight of the two vast hangars, the control tower and the collection of Nissen huts looking out over the three runways.

A morning mist shrouded the trees and hills beyond.

'I won't argue with you any more – I know you've made up your mind.' Unable to stop tears from welling up, Bobbie gave Jean's arm a final squeeze.

'So let's make this a day to remember.' Mary strode ahead of the others, past the formidable B-17 Fortress that Viv had mentioned, along the row of medium bombers and smaller, twin-engine aircraft all waiting to be ferried south. Across at the other edge of the pool were the Class 2s: a Corsair, two Mustangs and four Spits.

'Good morning, Gordon. Morning, Bob.' Bobbie waved at two of the ground crew working nearby.

Gordon stood, hands on hips, and watched admiringly as the four women walked purposefully towards the ops room. What he wouldn't give for a night at the flicks with any one of them . . .

'Morning, Stan.' Mary gave him a thumbs-up.

He winked back. 'Atta girl,' he breathed.

Viv was the first to join the queue for chits. Jean, Bobbie and Mary soon came up behind her.

'Mary's right; if this is to be Jean's swansong, let's make it count,' Viv said as the queue inched forward. She gathered them round and whispered a plan.

'Spit to Southampton, Priority One Wait.' When it came to Viv's turn, Gillian thrust a chit through the hatch. 'Spit to Ventnor, ditto,' she said to Jean. 'Spit to Portsmouth' to Mary and the same to Bobbie – all Priority Ones. Gillian grinned broadly. 'Your luck's in, girls – First Officer Thornton's orders.'

'We're the dream team!' Viv declared as they burst out of the building on to the lawn.

There was the usual scramble to the locker room for helmets and parachute packs then a race between the four of them towards Runway 3 to climb into their crates.

'"Eager for the air," eh?' Stan was there to greet Viv, who was scheduled to be first out.

'You betcha.' Helmet on, goggles down, strapped in and ready. Hydraulics – check; trimmers – check; throttle friction – check; and so on down the list. She glanced quickly at Jean now sitting in the Spit next to her – cool and professional as ever, waiting to taxi on to the runway for the very last time.

Fuel mixture – tick; pitch – tick; petrol – tick. Jean made her necessary checks.

Flaps – tick; gills – tick; gauges – tick. Inside the third Spit Mary was methodical as always.

Fuel booster, unlock controls – tick, tick. Superchargers – tick; tail-wheel lock – tick. Bobbie completed her list then gave the signal for chocks away.

Viv headed them up in the latest and greatest of all fighter planes. The concrete runway rumbled beneath her wheels and she felt that kick of fear and the inevitable dry mouth as she gathered speed.

'Watch for that G-force,' Stan reminded Jean as she closed the hood and increased her revs. She was second on the runway after Viv, with a full tank of petrol, already on the lookout for bad weather or marauding German bombers during the long flight ahead. Thumbs-up to Stan and Bob then she was off, in the air and at one with her glorious machine.

The thin mist swept across the runway as Mary watched Jean join Viv to circle over Burton Wood.

She would have to be careful to control any spin before take-off, not be too eager to be up there with them. Stay calm, wave away the chocks, fire up the engine, taxi to the take-off point – and off!

Wait for me! Bobbie was the last to strap herself in and lower her canopy. The seat wrapped around her like a glove. The control configuration had become second nature. *Let me at it!* At last Stan signalled chocks away.

Visibility wasn't perfect, thanks to the mist, but it was good enough for Bobbie to spot Viv, Jean and Mary circling overhead. As Bobbie joined them at 800 feet, Viv and Jean flew ahead, allowing Mary and Bobbie to come up close behind in a synchronized bank to starboard, just as Viv had suggested in the queue to the ops room. There was little turbulence and the four women flew in perfect formation over the ferry pool then off over the wood, skimming the ridge at the top of the Warrens – still according to plan. Four Mark 9s flew low and straight over the deserted reservoir.

'We'll do it for Anna,' Viv had told them, and Jean, Bobbie and Mary had agreed in a heartbeat.

'For Anna.' A turn of the head, a slight shift of weight and the wondrous machine practically flew itself. The mist cleared and Jean looked down on the clear water. With a touch on her rudder pedal she peeled away to port as Viv peeled to starboard.

Mary and Bobbie flew after them, wing tips only feet apart. They watched Viv and Jean split away then execute a quick half-roll of salute. Mary glanced up at a brightening sky then down at the sparkling water. She banked in pursuit of Viv and felt her crate shudder. 'You move; it moves' – that was the saying amongst Spit pilots. Adjust balance, foot on pedal, hands on stick – follow Viv and feel the power, hear the song.

Concentrate; one lapse and that would be it. Bobbie gave her own half-roll salute over the reservoir. The whole world was reduced to the cockpit of this miraculous contraption of light metal and Plexiglas – nothing else had significance beyond altitude and speed, the glint of sunlight on your wing as you gained height, the map spread out across your lap. Only the moment mattered. You gave it everything you'd got.

Bobbie left the reservoir behind, increased speed to come up alongside Jean, Viv and Mary. On the Atta girls flew, side by side, gaining altitude and speed, set fair for the south coast and for victory.

Read on for an exclusive extract of
Jenny Holmes's next novel

Christmas with the Spitfire Girls

available Autumn 2020

CHAPTER ONE

'Make hay while the sun shines – that's my motto.' Viv Robertson twirled in front of the long mirror in her bedroom at Burton Grange. She was dressed to impress in a red satin dress with a sweetheart neckline and a cinched-in waist. Her thick dark hair refused to conform to the current fashion for sleek, smooth tresses and instead tumbled down over her forehead to frame her delicate features with a mass of shiny curls.

Her fellow Atta girl, Bobbie Fraser, stood in her black lace petticoat, trying to decide between green silk and russet-brown crêpe de Chine.

'Definitely the green silk,' their friend Mary Holland advised from her position by the bay window. She was trying on a pair of black, high-heeled shoes belonging to Viv. 'It suits your colouring.'

Bobbie held the green dress against her pale skin. 'I wish my hair wasn't so ginger,' she said with a frown.

'Your hair's sandy, not ginger,' Viv soothed. 'And it does what it's told, which is more than mine does.' A second twirl and a flare of red skirt and white petticoat confirmed that she was almost ready to dance

413

the night away with the RAF boys at nearby Aireby training camp.

'You're sure you don't mind me borrowing these?' Mary was pleased with Viv's peep-toed evening shoes. They made her legs look more shapely and gave a sophisticated impression to match her dress in purple jersey knit.

'Feel free,' Viv assured her as she snatched the brown dress from Bobbie and threw it on the bed. 'Get a move on, Roberta McFlirta. 'At this rate all the decent dancers will be snapped up by the time we get there.'

Bobbie slid into the strapless green dress. 'Zip it up for me, then,' she told Viv in her soft Scottish brogue. The boned bodice gave her slight figure a more womanly outline, and she responded shyly to the whistle of approval from Viv and the smile and wink from Mary.

'Not bad,' Viv said with a grin. 'Now that only leaves make-up and hair.' She swept to one side her bottles of perfume, hairbrushes and powder puffs, making room at the dressing table for Mary and Bobbie to sit down and begin. 'Slap it on nice and thick, girls. The aim is to knock those RAF boys clean off their feet when we finally make our entrance.'

Mary and Bobbie knew from experience that Viv's exaggerations had to be taken with a pinch of salt. It was the Canadian girl's way of letting off steam after another strenuous week of ferrying fighter planes and heavy bombers from factory to RAF base, or from maintenance unit in the Midlands to secret airfield in the south. It would be the same with the jitterbugging when they got to Aireby: vivacious Viv would be first on the dance floor, loving the attention and making everyone smile.

But her pilot friends knew Viv's flipside: the gritty, determined, fearless flier who had grown up in Vancouver and made her way to this remote corner of Yorkshire to do her bit and help win the war.

'More lipstick,' Viv advised Mary. Then, 'Perhaps a touch more eyeshadow,' she recommended to Bobbie.

Bobbie hesitated. 'Are you sure? I don't want to look like a clown.'

'Honey, that's impossible.' Viv picked up a bottle of red polish and gave her nails a quick extra coat while she waited. 'You're the perfect English rose.'

'Except that I'm Scottish.' Bobbie gave a peal of laughter. She'd been born into money on a Highland estate north of Loch Lomond, complete with grouse moor and salmon fishing.

Mary put down the lipstick then studied the overall effect in the mottled mirror where Viv's room was reflected in all its faded glory. She took in floral wallpaper that curled at the edges, an old-fashioned iron bedstead in one corner, and a frayed rug placed in front of a small iron fireplace. It had to be admitted that Burton Grange was well past its best – built in the eighteenth century as a grand manor house with extensive grounds but now requisitioned by the War Office to house twenty or so civilian volunteers that made up the Air Transport Auxiliary at the North Riding village of Rixley. Turning her attention back to her newly made-up face, Mary grumbled quietly, 'I wish my nose wasn't so big.'

'It is not big, silly!' Bobbie declared then studied

her own reflection. 'You should have my ears. And on top of that, my toes are all squished.'

'Ears, noses-toeses-schmozes!' Viv blew on her fingernails to dry the varnish. 'Since we're in confessional mode – do you two want to hear my least favourite feature?'

'Yes, please!' Mary and Bobbie sang out.

Viv turned to present her back view. 'It's my derrière!'

More laughter filled the room and the other two girls sprang to their feet. 'Head, shoulders, knees and toes!' they chorused with accompanying actions. 'Head, shoulders, knees and toes, knees and toes!'

'And derrières!' Viv added as she led the charge out of the room, down the wide, bomb-damaged staircase and out into the dark, cold night.

A large green van was parked outside the RAF Aireby venue. Its sides were emblazoned with the words 'ENSA Road Show' and big-band music filtered out through an open door of the Nissen hut where the Saturday-evening dance was being held.

'See – we're late.' Viv got out from behind the wheel of the borrowed Ford. 'The fun has already begun.'

Bobbie and Mary slid gracefully from the back seat, turning up their coat collars against the blustery wind and clutching their handbags to their chests. As they rushed towards the door, ignoring posters inviting recruits to 'Make the RAF Supreme' and insisting that 'Every New Aircraft Needs a Crew', a gang of raucous cadets from the Initial Training Wing jumped out of the back of a Tilly wagon and made a beeline for the girls.

416

'Here's a sight for sore eyes,' one crowed in loose-jawed admiration.

'Blimey O'-Flippin'-Riley!' said another. 'Are you three girls real or am I dreaming?'

Viv, Mary and Bobbie found themselves surrounded by smiling, jostling suitors dressed in uniform with brutal short-back-and-sides haircuts and all smelling of shaving soap and Brilliantine.

Viv sailed on ahead of Bobbie and Mary. 'Make way there, guys. Let the dog see the rabbit.'

'Can I have the first dance?' a tall, gangly youth implored Bobbie. 'Say yes!'

'We'll see.' She followed Viv inside. 'Let me at least take off my coat.'

'I'll be waiting by the bar,' he promised as he was shouldered aside by two others eager to secure a similar promise from Mary.

'Hold your horses.' She fended them off with her handbag. 'Give a girl a chance.'

With the evening well under way, Viv, Mary and Bobbie were greeted by a swirl of dancers in close ballroom hold – the men in uniform and the girls in bright shiny dresses, bedecked with silk flowers, pearls and diamanté. From a temporary stage at the far end of the room a stout, middle-aged chanteuse with brightly rouged cheeks crooned 'I'll Be Seeing You' into a microphone, accompanied by a four-piece band.

'. . . in all the old familiar places.'

Mary turned to find her fiancé, Cameron Ainslie, murmuring the words from Bing Crosby's recent hit song. 'Cameron,' she breathed. There he was, in his flight lieutenant's uniform, waiting for her just inside the door – by far the most handsome man there. And by far the most distinguished – the most everything! 'You managed to get back from Liverpool in time.' She hadn't been sure that he would: as head of training command here at Aireby his duties often interfered with his weekends off.

'Wild horses wouldn't have stopped me.' Mary took Cameron's breath away, even after all these months of courtship. He thought she looked beautiful in her dark dress, the colour of ripe plums, with a silk spray of lily of the valley pinned to her shoulder strap. Her grey eyes shone as she looked up into his face and smiled.

'I'm glad.'

He smiled back and took her by the arm, leading her to the trestle table where drinks were being served. 'After I finished my meeting I was obliged to show some wireless operators around a Supermarine Walrus – they'd never seen the inside of one before.'

'Say no more.' Mary knew the difficult reputation of the amphibious biplane: hulking great things that flapped around all over the sky in cross-winds and were considered by many pilots to be almost uncontrollable. 'I just hope they don't put me in one of those lumbering crates now that we girls are finally allowed to cross the Channel.'

Permission to do so had been a long time coming and had only come into force since D-Day, thanks to the ATA's doughty commander, Pauline Gower, who had pushed hard for women pilots to fly beyond the south coast into foreign parts.

'No, you stick to your Spitfires.' Cameron ordered Mary's Dubonnet and lemonade without having to ask. 'And a pint of bitter for me, please,' he told the woman behind the bar. 'Anyway, from what I heard from the met boys in Liverpool we're facing a bad winter, so there'll be plenty of washout days where we all sit twiddling our thumbs.'

'Worse luck.' Mary preferred to be busy, liking nothing better than to collect a Wellington (no finesse needed, like flying around in an old railway carriage) from a maintenance unit and fly it up to Lossiemouth, where she would pick up a Dakota (tail-wheel lock positioned under throttle, not, as described in her Pilots' Notes, next to the oil controls) bound for Wolverhampton, then finally (joy of joys) back home to Rixley in a beloved Spitfire. All in one day, mind you, and so from the ferry pool straight back to the Grange and a hot-water bottle and bed.

Cameron and Mary took their drinks and found seats close to the stage. The blowsy ENSA singer had given way to a boy of sixteen or so with straw-blond hair, who began his stint with a lively tune on the piano. The dancers responded to the change of tempo by launching into a daring jitterbug, recently stolen from American GIs who had brought the craze across the Atlantic along with nylon stockings and a seemingly endless supply of chocolate.

'This lot make me feel old,' Cameron complained, though he was only twenty-four. With a grin Mary took his drink from him and pulled him to his feet.

'Come on, Granddad – let's dance.'

Soon they were rocking to and fro, tripping the light fantastic and twirling with the best of them. On the other side of the dance floor, Bobbie's gawky but persistent cadet had claimed her and was stumbling around, stamping on her feet and bumping into Agnes Wright and Horace Jackson, two ATA pilots from Rixley who Bobbie knew well. Poor Agnes was sent flying and had to be picked up off the floor.

'Sorry!' Bobbie gasped at Agnes as her clumsy partner whirled her away again.

'How about the next one?' he demanded as the piano player paused then went into a slow waltz. His hands were all over Bobbie as he tried to steer her into a space at the back of the room.

'No ta.' Escaping his clutches, she headed for the bar. 'Lime juice, please,' she ordered, only to find that she hadn't shaken off her dogged dance partner after all. 'Look,' she told him in a no-nonsense way. 'There really is no point.'

'How's that?' With a face as red as a turkey cock, the persistent cadet slid a long arm around Bobbie's waist.

She swallowed hard. 'Well, my . . . my young man's not here tonight but I'm afraid I'm already spoken for.' *What a ridiculous, schoolgirlish, Jane Austen phrase to come out with!* Bobbie immediately wished that the floor would swallow her up.

'She may be spoken for but I'm not!' Viv rushed in to save her incorrigibly demure friend's bacon. With a wink in Bobbie's direction she yanked the lanky air gunner into the centre of the dance floor and flashed him her most vivacious smile. 'Anyway, live for today – that's what I always say. My name's Vivienne, by the way. What's yours?'

If you loved The Spitfire Girls Fly for Victory *don't miss . . .*

The Spitfire Girls

'Anything to Anywhere!'

That's the motto of the Air
Transport Auxiliary, the brave
team of female pilots who fly
fighter planes between bases
at the height of the Second
World War.

Mary is a driver for the ATA
and although she yearns to fly
a Spitfire, she fears her humble
background will hold her back.
After all, glamorous **Angela** is
set to be the next 'Atta Girl' on
recruitment posters. **Bobbie**
learned to fly in her father's private plane and **Jean** was
taught the Queen's English at grammar school before
joining the squad. Dedicated and resilient, the three girls
rule the skies: weathering storms and dodging enemy
fire. Mary can only dream of joining them – until she
gets the push she needs to overcome her self-doubt.

Thrown together, the girls form a tight bond as they face
the perils of their job. But they soon find that affairs of the
heart can be just as dangerous as attacks from the skies.

**With all the fear and uncertainty ahead – can their
friendship see them through the tests of war?**

Available now

A Christmas Wish for Land Girls

Winter, 1942.

Land Girls Brenda and Una
have relocated higher up the
Yorkshire dales, to work on the
remote hillside farms. Despite
the bitter cold, there's warmth
to be found in old friends and
new faces – and plans for a
cosy Christmas are afoot.

But then a child evacuee goes
missing in the snow, and
everyone must rally round to
find the boy before it's too late.

**The Land Girls fervently hope for a happy outcome . . .
but will their wish come true this Christmas?**

Available now

Wedding Bells for Land Girls

Summer, 1942.

Britain is in the depths of war and the Women's Land Army is hard at work looking after the farms while the men are away fighting. While patriotism, duty and a wonderful spirit of camaraderie sustain the Land Girls through tough times, it's no surprise that love is also often on their minds.

For Yorkshire Land Girls and firm friends Grace, Brenda and Una, romance in wartime comes with a host of challenges. There's a wedding to plan, but married bliss is threatened when it's time for the groom to enlist. With lovers parted, anxious women have no idea whether they'll see their men again. And while single girls dance and flirt, will they be able to find true love among the men who've stayed behind?

With the uncertainty of the times hanging over them and danger ever closer to home – can love stand the test of war?

Available now

The Land Girls at Christmas

'Calling All Women!'

It's 1941 and as the Second
World War rages on, girls from
all over the country are
signing up to the Women's
Land Army. Renowned for
their camaraderie and spirit, it
is these brave women who step
in to take on the gruelling
farm work from the men
conscripted into the armed
forces.

When Yorkshire mill girl Una
joins the cause, she wonders
how she'll adapt to country life. Luckily she's quickly
befriended by more experienced Land Girls Brenda and
Grace. But as Christmas draws ever nearer, the girls'
resolve is tested as scandals and secrets are revealed,
lovers risk being torn apart, and even patriotic loyalties
are called into question . . .

**With only a week to go until the festivities, can the
strain of wartime still allow for the magic of Christmas?**

Available now

The Telephone Girls

1936. George Street, West
Yorkshire, houses a brand-
new telephone exchange
where a group of capable
girls work the complicated
electrical switchboards.
Among them are Cynthia,
Norma and Millicent, who
relish the busy, efficient
atmosphere and the
independence and friendship
their jobs have given them.

But when Millicent connects a
telephone call for an old friend, and listens in to the
conversation – breaking one of the telephonists' main
rules – she, and then Norma and Cynthia too, become
caught up in a story of scandal, corruption and murder.

Soon, the jobs of all three girls are on the line. Norma's
romance is in ruins. And Millicent has entered a world
of vice . . .

**In tough times, the telephone girls will need to call on
their friends more than ever.**

Available now

Great stories.
Vivid characters.
Unbeatable deals.